SHE WAS FAR TOO YOUNG AND DANGEROUSLY INTOXICATING. . . .

As he stared at Lizette, he felt an exciting warmth begin to flood through him. His eyes devoured her, and as she gazed up at him, her need was so strong she would have gladly begged him to take her.

He reached out and she surrendered to him with a wild abandon that took his breath away and filled them both with pleasure they had never dreamed existed.

When at last they lay silent, their passion spent, his voice, close to her ear, sent a shock through her. "Damn you, Lizette! Now there'll be hell to pay. God damn it, Lizette, you're only fifteen. You had no right . . ."

"I had no right? You're the one who raped me!" she cried out, hurt and angry.

He laughed, his laugh throaty and sensuous. "Rape? Nobody raped anybody, little girl," he said viciously. "You seduced me as surely as you're lying there . . ."

THUNDER IN THE WIND

THUNDER IN THE WIND

JUNE LUND SHIPLETT

A SIGNET BOOK
NEW AMERICAN LIBRARY
TIMES MIRROR

PUBLISHER'S NOTE

This novel is a work of fiction. Names, characters, places, and incidents are either the product of the author's imagination or are used fictitiously, and any resemblance to actual persons, living or dead, events, or locales is entirely coincidental.

SIGNET, SIGNET CLASSICS, MENTOR, PLUME, MERIDIAN AND NAL BOOKS are published by The New American Library, Inc., 1633 Broadway, New York, New York 10019

First Printing, January, 1983

1 2 3 4 5 6 7 8 9

PRINTED IN THE UNITED STATES OF AMERICA

To my dear friend Bobby

1

Columbia, South Carolina—February 1815

Sunlight streamed hotly through the open window, resting on the lonely figure sitting forlornly on the edge of the huge canopied bed. Heather had never felt so alone in all her life. Even when her mother had gone to Europe on vacations or gone to visit friends, she hadn't felt as alone as she did now. She paid little attention to the hot sun, even though she'd been wishing for weeks the weather would warm up. It caressed her mass of curly auburn hair, turning it to coppery flames, brought out the amethyst highlights in her angry violet eyes, and turned her pale cheeks to a rosy gold, yet she never felt its warmth.

Instead, she was cold. So cold the gooseflesh rose on her arms and she had to clench her teeth to keep them from chattering. Only it wasn't the weather that made her cold, because the weather had warmed beautifully, bringing the magnolias into full bloom as they always were this time of year. No, it wasn't the weather. It was her mother who had brought this cold, dead feeling to her insides. Who had changed her life so recklessly without even a thought to how she might feel about it.

Only moments before, she had stood downstairs in the parlor and heard her mother turning her life upside down. For seventeen years she'd been Heather McGill, the daughter of John McGill, a retired sea captain from Boston, who had died from a wasting disease a month before her birth, and of Darcy McLaren McGill, the daughter of the late Senator Victor McLaren. Her life was orderly. Her father had left her mother well provided for with businesses in Boston, and the late senator had also left his daughter a legacy, so Heather's life, although lacking ostentation, was filled with finishing schools, parties, and beaux.

Now suddenly she'd been wrenched from it viciously with no warning, no chance to prepare herself. A bastard! Oh, not in those words. Her mother would never have used those words, but she might as well have. She had stood in the parlor, her eyes glowing with a look Heather had never seen in them before, and informed her that she had been lying to her all these years. That she, Heather McGill, wasn't the daughter of John McGill. That in the fall of 1796 she had fallen in love with Heath Chapman, the man who was standing beside her now, tall and good-looking, and that something terrible had happened to separate them, and she'd later discovered she was to have a child. She had fled Columbia, planning to have the child in Boston and leave it there. But instead she had met John McGill, who'd known he was dying and offered her marriage to give the child a name. After his death, she had returned to Columbia and lived the lie.

She had never remarried until now. And that was a shock too. Heather knew her mother had been planning to marry an Englishman, Lord Teak Locksley, the Earl of Locksley, but now suddenly there she was, standing in the parlor, looking all starry-eyed and moonstruck, holding hands and gazing longingly into the dark eyes of this stranger she had introduced as her new husband, Heath Chapman, who was also, as she put it, "Your real father, Heather," and who, Heather learned, after a loud outburst, was the half-brother of the English nobleman her mother was supposed to have married.

Heather clenched her fists. She remembered Heath Chapman. He had come to the door several months ago looking for her mother. She'd thought he was so handsome then, with his dark curly hair and dark eyes.

Now she knew why Aunt Nell, who had lived with them all these years, had practically slammed the door in his face that day when he'd introduced himself. She had known. All these years she had known the truth.

Heather stood up slowly, walked to the window, and stood

quietly running her finger along the edge of the windowpane, trying to shake away the impact her mother's softly spoken words had brought to her life. But she couldn't. They kept running over and over through her head as if they'd never stop.

She shut her eyes and tears rimmed them as a knock sounded on the door behind her.

"Go away!" she yelled, but the knock was repeated.

"Heather, please," Darcy called from the hallway. "Please, let me talk to you." She didn't wait for an invitation and tried the knob. Finding it unlocked, she walked in.

Darcy McGill, now Darcy Chapman as of two weeks ago when she had married Heath in the chapel at his father's plantation, the Chateau in Port Royal, South Carolina, had given her daughter red hair like her own; however, Darcy's eyes were a cool green, like the green of the leaves on the trees in early spring, instead of violet like Heather's, and now Darcy's eyes sought her daughter's, frowning.

"Heather, it isn't right for you to carry on so," she said as she shut the door behind her.

Heather's face was still pale from the shock, and a lone tear rolled down her cheek. "Why?" she whispered, trying to keep from crying. "Why didn't you tell me before? Oh, Mother, why did you wait until now?"

Darcy pursed her lips, her full bosom heaving emotionally. She was a beautiful woman yet at thirty-six, and for the first time in years she didn't know what to say to her daughter.

"I thought I'd never have to tell you," she answered softly. "I wasn't going to. Even now, I was just going to marry Heath and let you go on being John's daughter, but I couldn't. It wouldn't have been fair to you, or to Heath. I love him so very much, Heather, I always have. That's why you have the name you have. I never stopped loving him."

"But if you loved him, why didn't you marry him?"

Darcy's eyes grew cold and distant for a moment, remembering the horrible scandal and the hurt that Heath had caused; then as quickly she brushed it aside. That was in the past. It had no right to intrude now on her newfound happiness. She stared again at her daughter, wanting so badly to draw her into her arms and comfort her, yet knowing that Heather's decision to accept Heath or reject him must be her own.

"Sometimes things happen and . . . whatever, Heather, it was impossible for your father and me to marry then. In fact, he never knew you existed until the moment you opened the door for him some months back. But when he saw you, he knew right away."

"How?"

"Your eyes," said Darcy, and moved closer to her daughter, reaching up under her chin, tilting her face to stare into her eyes. "There are very few people in the world with violet eyes, Heather," she went on. "Heath's mother, Loedicia, your grandmother, has violet eyes, as does his half-sister, your Aunt Rebel. Where else could they have come from?"

Heather stared back at her mother. Her eyes, although misty with tears, were still hostile, small flecks of blue glittering amid the violet.

"You shouldn't have run from the room like that, Heather," Darcy went on. "You didn't even wait to talk to Heath. He's so hurt."

She wrenched her chin from her mother's grasp. "He's hurt?" she cried, clenching her fists as she started toward the window, then stopped, looking back again. "What does he think I am? I suppose I'm not allowed to hurt!" She threw her head back angrily, her long coppery hair flying off the shoulders of her pale yellow dress. Her dress had a simple, high empire waist, accentuating her full young breasts, and a thin gold chain necklace framed her neck. "How would he like to suddenly find out at my age that he's a bastard? That the man he always thought was his father wasn't his father?"

"He did!" countered Darcy, and Heather stopped yelling, staring at her mother.

"What do you mean?"

Darcy's eyes faltered as she walked slowly over to stand beside her daughter, then pulled the ruffled curtain at the window aside and stared out into the yard. "I mean exactly what I said," she answered, her eyes intent on the yard below. "You see, Heath's mother, Loedicia, was married to a man named Quinn Locke before Heath's sister Rebel was born. Rebel's older than Heath. Loedicia thought her husband, Quinn, had been killed by Indians, and some months after Rebel's birth, she married Roth Chapman, an army major. Not quite three months after the marriage ceremony, her first husband, Quinn, turned up alive, and she went back to live with him on the frontier. Nine months later Heath was born. He was fifteen when Loedicia and Quinn finally told him about Major Chapman, that the major was his real father. So you see, he does know what you are going through. Only he didn't have his real father there to look at and get to know and accept. He went searching, and it took him three years before he finally found him. Can you imagine what those three years must have been like?"

Heather stared at her mother, watching the sun put shadows on her face. When she talked of Heath, there was a glow to her eyes, a warmth and a depth that had been missing before.

Heather swallowed hard and straightened, rubbing her arms to ward off the chill she had felt before her mother came into the room. "Does he mean so much to you, Mother?" she asked.

Darcy dropped the edge of the curtain, looking at her hopefully. "Yes, Heather," she said. "He means life to me, and I couldn't lose him again."

"What of the Englishman, Lord Locksley? You said he was Heath Chapman's half-brother?"

"Teak was born when Heath was three years old. He and Rebel are Loedicia Chapman's children by Quinn Locke. Teak's been in England since he was fifteen, when he inherited his father's title, but I don't have to worry about Teak," she explained. "He's married too by now."

"Oh?"

"I'm afraid it's all rather complicated, dear," Darcy continued, trying to explain. "You see, Quinn Locke was killed years ago while returning to America from England, and Loedicia married Roth Chapman again. They adopted a young girl they named Ann, who was part English and part Delaware Indian. When Teak and Ann met, they fell in love and by now should be married and safely on their way to England."

Heather stared at her mother, frowning, her eyes puzzled. "On their way to England? Was he in America?"

"Yes. It's such a long story, Heather," she said. "The important thing now is not Teak, but that you understand about Heath. I didn't plan for all this to happen when I left to go to Beaufort, I never expected to find Heath again after all these years. I do love him, Heather, and I know you can love him too if you'll only try. If you'll just give him a chance."

Heather's eyes narrowed and she turned from her mother, walking back toward the bed.

What was this going to do to their lives? What would her friends think? She had told them that when the war was over her mother was going to marry an English earl and become a countess. How could she ever face them? What was this Heath Chapman? Who was he? She knew absolutely nothing about him. Oh, yes, she did know he was her real father, that much was certain, but what kind of a man was he? There was something hard and forceful about him, yet he had a certain charm that was fascinating. Maybe because his dark eyes were so intense, although when they rested casually on her mother, a warmth crept into them that was alien to the hard facade he presented to the world. She wondered what he'd look like if he smiled, wondering if he ever did.

"Please, Heather," Darcy said from behind her. "Give Heath a chance. Come down and talk to him. He's been hurt so many times over the years. Don't give him another hurt. For my sake, please, just come and talk to him before you make any judgments one way or another."

Downstairs, Heath stood in front of the big bay window that overlooked the street and watched the carriages and people moving about. He sighed, shrugging his broad shoulders, his tall frame slumping in contemplation. They should have taken his mother's advice and sent for Heather first, explained everything that had happened, then been married, letting her be a part of the ceremony. But they had both been so eager to be together and had wanted it to be right this time. And now . . .

He turned, straightening to his full height as he heard a rustling noise behind him.

Darcy stood in the doorway, lovely in her dress of green silk that made her eyes shine even brighter, and beside her stood Heather.

Heather's chin tilted stubbornly, and her eyes, although rimmed slightly with red, were curiously alive, looking him over as if really seeing him for the first time.

He wondered what she must be thinking.

She was a beautiful girl. Well, not really a girl, a young lady and a daughter to be proud of. His dark eyes studied the youthful lines of her face. She was tense, still angry, her jaw held rigid, eyes appraising him hostilely. Her long tapered fingers fumbled with a lace-edged handkerchief and her young breasts moved almost imperceptibly beneath the bodice of her yellow muslin gown.

Heather felt her mother's hand at her waist, urging her farther into the room.

"Heather's feeling much better now," said Darcy, stopping in front of Heath, her arm still about her daughter's waist. "The worst of the shock, I believe, is over."

He looked from Darcy to Heather. "I'm sorry, Heather," he said, his deep voice vibrant with emotion. "We should have prepared you a little better for all this."

"I don't think there's really any way anyone can be prepared to learn she's a bastard, is there?" she asked flippantly.

Heath's eyes darkened.

Heather watched him intently. He was handsome, she had to admit, but a little frightening too. He reminded her of pictures she'd seen of pirates, with the dark clipped beard covering his chin, then merging with the black curly hair that touched the collar of his green velvet frock coat. He was a powerfully built man, ruggedly tanned, his clothes molded over a well-disciplined body.

"I deserve that," he suddenly said, and as she stared at him, his eyes slowly softened, relaxing his jawline, and crinkles appeared at the corners of his eyes. "I deserve anything you'd like to dish out, my dear," he said. "You have every right to be angry. What we did was unthinkable. We should have come to you first and explained. Perhaps it would have softened the blow."

She continued to stare at him, not quite sure of what to do; then, "You're really my father?" she asked reluctantly.

"I'm really your father, and I thank God for letting me find you after all these years."

"Why didn't you come before?" she asked. "Why did you wait so long?"

Heath glanced at Darcy, and once more Heather saw a change come to his eyes. They were filled with love and longing and something she couldn't put into words. His face was openly vulnerable as he stared passionately at her mother.

"I tried to come back so many times," he said softly. "But my search was always in vain. Your mother hid herself too well, so I'd go back to sailing ships and roaming the forests, losing myself in the world, trying to find something out there to take the place of the woman I loved and the family I wished she could have given me. It's a lonely life, and I'm glad I don't have to live it anymore."

"You were a sailor?" she asked.

Heath drew his eyes reluctantly from Darcy's lovely face. "For a number of years," he said. "Your uncle and I worked for the French."

"My uncle?" she asked, startled.

"My half-sister Rebel is married to Beau Dante. He's three-quarter Indian, one-quarter French, and currently regarded as one of the most respected plantation owners in Port Royal, South Carolina, but formerly he was captain of one of the fastest privateers on the high seas." Heath straightened, remembering for a moment a past filled with danger and adventure. "Oh, what we do when we're young and reckless," he said abruptly; then, "He was known as Captain Thunder and I was his first mate," he went on. "Later, I was in the Navy, but when the sea lost its savor after I spent two years in a dungeon in Tripoli, I gave it up for the life I was brought up in."

She frowned, puzzled.

"I was raised in a fort on the shores of Lake Erie," he explained. "My stepfather was a frontiersman, one of the best, and it's the only life I knew before I went to sea."

"You're a frontiersman?" she asked. "One of those mountain men?"

"I suppose you could call me that," he said, and she glanced at the fancy ruffled shirt, silk cravat, and gray satin vest he wore beneath his frock coat.

"You don't look like a mountain man," she said hesitantly.

He frowned. "What am I supposed to look like?"

She flushed, embarrassed. "Well, you're not supposed to look like a gentleman," she answered. "You're supposed to be wearing dirty old buckskins and have a scraggly beard. Everyone knows mountain men are crude and ill-mannered."

An amused smile played about the corners of Heath's mouth and his eyes glistened. "Would you rather I looked like that?" he asked.

"No!" She eyed him dubiously. "But how come you don't?"

"Because, as with everything else, people get the wrong impression. I concede some men who live on the frontier are there because they can't stand to live under the restrictions civilization puts on them. But there are a good many men like me, who just like the life and were born to it. You see, my mother was a lady, and even though we lived on the frontier, she made sure we were well acquainted with the finer things of life."

Her eyes darkened and for a brief moment Heath saw a resemblance to his mother in her eyes. He wished he could have watched this daughter of his grow up. "You'll like your grandmother," he said softly. "When I told her we were coming to Columbia to get you, she was so thrilled."

"To get me?" Heather panicked, glancing quickly at her mother. "What does he mean . . . to get me?" she asked.

"Why, Heather, dear, I thought you realized," Darcy said. "We're going to be living at the Chateau in Port Royal. We want you to go back with us."

"Go back with you? Oh, Mother, how could you ask such a thing?" she cried anxiously. "I can't, I can't leave here. I've always lived here, all my friends are here, and what about Aunt Nell?"

"Aunt Nell's going to stay here and keep the house. It's what she wants."

"Then why can't I stay with her?"

"Because I want you with me."

"But I don't want to go with you!"

Darcy stared at Heather, watching her eyes narrow stubbornly. "You'll meet new friends there, dear," she coaxed solicitously. "There's your cousin Lizette. She's almost your age . . ."

"I'll hate her!"

"Heather!" Darcy glared at her daughter. "Don't be so stubborn. You have to go with us. I've been counting on it, and so has your father."

Heather's stomach was full of butterflies. She didn't want to go to Port Royal. She didn't want her life to change like this, but it was changing, and there was nothing she could do to stop it. She stared back at her mother. "I suppose you'll make me go whether I want to or not, won't you?"

Darcy glanced quickly at Heath, then back to Heather. He had wanted so much for his daughter to like him. Maybe with time . . . "Yes," she said softly. "We'll start packing tomorrow and leave at the end of the week." And it was settled as simply as that.

The rest of the week was chaotic for Heather. Darcy had spoiled her over the years, and by the time they finished packing she had four large trunks stuffed full that they sent on ahead by freight wagon and two smaller trunks they planned to tie into the boot of the closed carriage they'd be traveling in. Heather had packed resentfully, still stubbornly insisting she didn't want to go and that she'd hate it in Port Royal. During every meal she silently gave both her parents the ultimate in woebegone faces, hoping they'd change their minds and leave her here with Aunt Nell. But they paid little attention to her antagonistic behavior; the only one it seemed to have any repercussions on was Aunt Nell, who proceeded to admonish her at some length for making her mother unhappy.

So it was with a dozen regrets that Heather apprehensively climbed into the closed carriage and sat rigidly across from her mother and the man she had so recently learned was her father. She had said good-bye to all her old friends, including the handsome young man she'd met only two weeks before at a party. Now, heartbroken, she watched out the window of the carriage, refusing to let the tears inside her reveal themselves, as they left Columbia behind.

The trip down to Port Royal was uneventful except for the usual dusty roads, inconvenient inns, and an occasional shower that turned the dust to mud. Heather closed her eyes and gritted her teeth as they hit another bump. She felt as if they were never going to stop riding. She prayed Heath had been right when he said they had only a few more miles to go to reach the Chateau.

She had been instructed to call him Father, but it wasn't that easy. He was still a stranger to her, although she had begun to know something of him during the trip south. Her first impression of him as an unsmiling, stern man had been replaced by the observation that he not only smiled, especially when her mother was the center of his attention, but that he was possessed of a rare sense of humor that more than once almost broke through her stubborn reserve. She had to admit he was not only handsome and charming but would probably even be likable if the necessity arose. However, she wasn't about to let him have his way without a battle, and she made up her mind long before arriving at the Chateau that she was going to hate it and everyone associated with it.

As the carriage ambled off the main road onto a long tree-swept drive, she leaned over, gazing out the window, her violet eyes catching a quick glimpse of a beautiful white mansion with a pillared veranda across the front. Red brick steps led to the veranda, with flower pots lining them, the bright pinks and reds of the azaleas in them contrasting against the green lawn and stark white of the house. Her eyes devoured the immaculate landscaping and well-kept lawns; then she sighed and pulled her head back, trying not to look too interested as the carriage began to slow down in front of the brick steps. She felt the carriage come to an abrupt halt and took a deep breath.

"Well, here we are," said Heath, straightening in his seat as he watched her.

She glanced quickly toward the window, then back toward him again, her jaw set stubbornly. "So I see."

Darcy glanced at Heath, shrugged, then turned to her daughter. "You'd better behave yourself, young lady," she said between pursed lips, "or believe me, you'll be sorry. We've put up with your nonsense on the way down here, but

I won't tolerate you being rude to your grandparents. They had nothing to do with bringing you into the world. Heath and I are to blame for that. I don't mind you taking your anger out on us, but you'll be decent to them. Do you understand?"

"I'm not a child, Mother," she said bitterly. "I'll be decent, but there's no law says I have to like them."

Darcy clenched her fists. "I could throttle you!" Suddenly she felt Heath's hand closing over hers.

"It's all right, darling," he said, understanding Heather's anger only too well.

The words had no sooner left his mouth than the carriage door opened. Heath stepped from the coach, then turned and helped Darcy out.

Heather sat rigidly on the seat. She didn't want to move, didn't want to meet these people who had suddenly become her grandparents. Holding her breath, she watched Heath's hand reach in, and tears came to her eyes. Then, summoning up all the courage she possessed, she reached out, grasped the long muscular fingers, letting them twine around her small hand, and moved from the seat, letting him help her from the carriage to the ground at the foot of the steps.

She trembled slightly, seeing only Heath's broad chest before her; then, as he stepped aside, she found herself looking into a pair of sparkling violet eyes so like her own that it startled her. She stared at the woman before her, her mind in a daze. The woman was small, well rounded, yet petite, and her lovely face put a lie to the gray that streaked her once raven hair. A delightful warmth emanated from her eyes and the healthy glow of her softly tanned flesh made her look far younger than her nearly sixty years.

She smiled, a smile that slightly dimpled her smooth cheeks and momentarily broadened her small nose, her mouth full and sensuously alive.

"So this is Heather," she exclaimed breathlessly. "My dear, how can I tell you what it means for me to have you here," and before Heather could even try to protest, she found herself wrapped in the woman's strong arms, being hugged with an enthusiasm that overwhelmed her.

"As you've probably guessed, Heather, this is your grandmother, my mother, Loedicia Chapman," Heath explained quickly as Loedicia finally released the girl.

"But most people call me Dicia," she said, holding the young girl at arm's length, realizing she was taller than she had expected. But then, most people were taller than she was, even her other granddaughter, Lizette, and she was only fifteen. "And this is Roth, your grandfather," Loedicia said warmly as she turned, her arm still about the young girl's waist.

Heather pulled her eyes from this remarkably vibrant woman and looked up into the dark eyes of a man who, although his face was lined with age and his hair pure white, looked so like the man who called himself her father that it was startling.

Roth Chapman was in his mid-sixties, but work on the plantation and his vibrant zest for living had kept him young in body as well as in spirit. He was dressed in casual work clothes, his cream-colored shirt, open low at the throat, revealing a muscular chest. His clothes fit him well, hinting strongly of the powerful muscles hidden beneath them. His shirt was tucked into dark green trousers with well-worn top boots completing his attire, and his tanned face lit up as he gazed at her. She was such a lovely young woman that suddenly he felt every bit his age.

Heather stared at this tall, good-looking man who, she was certain, sensed the anger and frustration she was going through, and for some reason she couldn't quite understand, she suddenly felt exposed. Roth Chapman was an exciting complement to the small, vital woman who still had her arm about Heather's waist.

"Well, come, let's not just stand here," said Loedicia pleasantly, sensing Heather's discomfiture. "Heavens, Heather's probably tired, and it's strange for her being thrown into such confusion." She smiled at her newly found granddaughter and started leading her up the brick steps.

Roth reached out and helped Darcy, who wound her arm through Heath's elbow and let both men escort her into the house, while her eyes rested apprehensively on her daughter. Would Heath's mother be able to bridge the years that turned the girl's life upside down? she wondered.

Roth ordered the servants to bring the luggage in from the carriage, then listened as Loedicia offered to show Heather her room.

"We're giving you the room your Aunt Rebel used when she was living with us," she said as she ushered Heather into the marble-floored foyer and on up the fancy staircase. "If it's too fussy for you, we can have it changed. Since it'll be yours from now on, we want you to enjoy it."

Heather stared apprehensively as her grandmother opened the first door on the left at the top of the stairs; then she held her breath as she stepped into a beautiful room all done up in white organdy with pink ruffles decorating the furniture and rose velvet draperies at the windows. Even the wallpaper was a delicate rose pattern. The room was soft and feminine, the kind any young woman would want. But because of the circumstances, and because Heather could be quite obstinate at times, she stared at it contemptuously.

"Do you like it?" asked Dicia, watching the girl's face.

Heather walked to the window and looked out, then turned, looking much older than her seventeen years. "I guess it'll do," she said caustically, and Dicia's eyes narrowed.

So she was going to fight them. Well, fine, let her. The fight wouldn't last long. When she began to realize it wasn't accomplishing anything, she'd quit. Loedicia ignored her sarcasm.

"Good, your trunks arrived before you did and your things are in the closet already," she said. "So if you want to freshen up before luncheon, I'll have one of the servants bring fresh water."

"If you want." Heather stood quietly, staring at her grandmother.

"Now, if you don't mind," Loedicia said, ignoring the girl's aloofness, "I have some things to attend to before we eat. When you're ready, come downstairs. The parlor's to the right of the stairs. We'll no doubt be in there." She started to leave. "Don't be too long," she said congenially. "We eat promptly at one, and it's almost that now." She smiled warmly at Heather and left the room, then stood outside, her hand on the knob, smile fading. This was going to be harder than she thought. She sighed. Oh, well, they had years to make up for; nothing was ever accomplished in one day. She hurried on downstairs.

Inside the room, Heather stood stock-still, staring at the closed door; then slowly she began to study the room. It was beautiful, she supposed, in a rather frivolous way. She walked over and glanced at the fancy bottles on the dresser, then looked up at her reflection in the mirror. But she still didn't like being here. So her grandmother wasn't what she had expected. So what? Nothing had changed. Nothing at all. She wanted her own room back with its comfortable feather bed, homemade quilt, canopy, dainty wallpaper, and everything she was used to. She bit her lip, trying to hold back the tears. Why did things have to change?

She picked up the hairbrush from the dresser, its tortoiseshell handle bent to fit her hand, and stared at it angrily.

She didn't want this hairbrush, and she didn't like this room and she wasn't going to be happy here either. She just knew it, and with an angry sob she turned, throwing the hairbrush across the room, where it bounced off the bed; then she walked to the window and pulled back the curtains, looking out. She wouldn't cry! Her mouth set in a grim line and she dropped the curtain, turning from the window, staring once more at the closed door. She'd show them! She headed toward the closet to change from her travel-worn dress.

The midday meal consisted of baked fish, steamed rice with lentil dressing, boiled greens with a choice of butter sauce or vinegar dressing, cornbread and honey, ham hocks, roast chicken, and hot bread served with various preserves. All of this was washed down with hot tea and cold cider. Heather had to admit to herself that the food was good, yet she stubbornly picked at it, eating sparingly, her temper overriding the hunger she'd felt shortly before arriving. She listened quietly to the conversation around her, spoke when spoken to, but other than that, refused to join in with the family.

"Do you ride, Heather?" asked Loedicia, suddenly addressing her granddaughter as one of the young black serving girls brought in a large bowl of sugared fruit for dessert and two others worked at clearing away the dishes from the main course.

Heather finished her last bite of rice, then set her fork down. "I did!" she answered belligerently, and glanced at her mother, eyes snapping. "In fact, Mother bought me a new mare last fall and I was just starting to get used to her when we had to leave."

Loedicia's eyes held a depth of sincerity. "Then why don't you have her brought down here?" she asked. "I'm sure we'd have room in the stables."

"Because Mother told Aunt Nell to sell her, that's why."

"I suggested it might be best to sell her," interrupted Darcy, trying to explain. She glanced at Heather. "You didn't seem to be concerned about it at the time, Heather," she said. "If you wanted the horse with you, why didn't you say so?"

"I did"—Heather's lips pursed—"but I don't think you even heard me." She glanced toward the man who called himself her father. "You were too wrapped up in other things," she said sarcastically.

Heath flushed. Heather was probably right. Things had moved so fast and there had been so much to do, the request had probably sailed right over both their heads. "Maybe we could rectify matters," he said, hoping to make amends. "I'll send one of the grooms to Columbia with a letter for your Aunt Nell. Perhaps she hasn't sold the horse yet."

Heather stared at him openly. He was trying to win her over. Well, it wasn't going to work. Oh, she'd relish having Jezebel with her again. The young mare was the most beautiful horse she'd ever seen, with a coal-black coat, shiny and smooth, with three white stockings. But Heather wasn't going to let his gesture influence her. "If you want," she said, as if she didn't care either way.

Darcy could have throttled her. "Heather, for heaven's sake," she said heatedly. "Your father's trying to please you. The least you could do is accept his offer graciously."

"Oh, I'm sorry," she retorted smartly, her eyes alive with anger, hands pulling the linen napkin off the skirt of her pale green afternoon dress. She wiped her mouth primly, making sure Heath was listening closely. "I didn't know I had to pretend to be liking this farce, Mother, because I'm sorry, I can't," she said, looking at her mother. "You didn't give me any choice when you told me who my father really was, and you didn't give me any choice about coming to live here, but I'm not a puppet in a marionette show. You can't force me to feel what I don't feel. I thank him for wanting to bring the horse here, yes, but if you expect me to do it graciously, I'm sorry, I just can't. Now, may I please be excused?"

Loedicia was sitting across from Darcy, and she looked at her new daughter-in-law knowingly. "Let her go, Darcy," she suggested, realizing that to keep the girl at the table would solve nothing. Maybe in time . . .

Heather tightened her mouth stubbornly. "Mother . . . ?"

"All right, go ahead," she gave in.

Heather glanced at Heath, politely excusing herself to him and her grandparents; then she left the dining room, sighing as she walked through the hall and out to the foyer. She stood in the foyer looking about, then saw the French doors in the back that led out to the terrace and the walk that went to the dock behind the house where the Broad River flowed. The doors seemed to draw her, and she walked over, gazing out at the lawn that stretched to the river. Flowerbeds graced it here and there, adding rich pinks, reds, yellows, and whites to the green, and large oaks, hung with Spanish moss, all but hid the paths on the left that led to the slave quarters.

Reaching down, she opened the door and slipped out onto the terrace, glancing behind her to make sure no one had followed her from the dining room. She closed the door behind her, then stepped away from the house, following slowly along the walk that led to the pier. To her right were the stables, carriage houses, storage barns, and beyond the barns was the cotton mill. Beyond the mill and beyond the slave quarters on both sides of the plantation house, fields of cotton and indigo, the two main crops that kept the Chateau going, stretched for acres, their monotony broken only by various stretches of wood and an occasional trickling stream.

There was no getting around the fact that Port Royal was every bit as lovely as Columbia, but it just wasn't the same. She strolled along, stopping now and then to finger a deep red azalea or watch a bee take nectar from a honeysuckle vine that climbed up an old pole where a wren's house hung. The air was warm, the sun actually hot, and she gazed up at a tuft of powdery cloud floating above the river down near the pier.

Halfway there she suddenly stopped, the sound of a horse's hooves turning her head toward the drive out front. Her hand moved to her face, and she shaded her eyes, focusing on the rider who had pulled up at one of the mounting blocks at the side, toward the back of the huge house. Squinting curiously, she watched as a young woman, perhaps in her mid-teens, not waiting for a groom to help her, jumped quickly from her sidesaddle, stepped down from the mounting block, patted her horse's nose, then tossed the reins to the young black groom who had run out from the stables to help her.

Lizette started to head for the house, then caught a glimpse of the afternoon sun on Heather's hair and stopped, staring toward the walk that led to the pier. So, they'd arrived. Good! She'd been waiting for days. She swung her arm up in a friendly wave, then lifted the skirt of her dark red riding habit so it wouldn't trail in the dust, and started across the lawn, a warm smile lighting her young features.

Heather watched closely as the young girl came toward her, realizing she wasn't as old as she'd thought at first, although she looked to be every bit as tall as Heather. This must be Rebel's daughter, Lizette. Heath had spoken of her now and then. She was fifteen, would be sixteen in June.

As Lizette neared, Heather's hand dropped from over her eyes and she stared openly. The crimson riding habit enhanced her coal-black hair that curled riotously beneath a matching plumed hat, and her green eyes were long-lashed in a face that resembled her grandmother Loedicia's. She was quite beautiful, and Heather felt a little intimidated.

"Hello," said Lizette confidently, ignoring the wary look on

Heather's face. "I'm your cousin Lizette, and I know you have to be Heather." She watched the hesitancy in Heather's violet eyes. "And I know you're probably upset because you had to leave your home and friends, but believe me," she went on, "you'll love it here, once you get used to it. I wouldn't want to live anywhere else."

Heather's eyes darkened. "I'll never get used to it," she said softly. "For one thing, Mother never owned any slaves," and she glanced toward the slave quarters beyond the moss-laden oak trees, their leaves opening with the coming of spring.

"Well, my father and grandfather don't really either," Lizette said. "You see, they buy the slaves, yes, but once they own them, they figure a fair wage for them and let them work off their price. When the price is paid off, they have a choice of going free or staying and working. They rent their own homes, grow their own food, and work a regular workday." She saw the skeptical look on Heather's face. "Naturally the other plantation owners don't like it, but there isn't much they can do about it. Grandfather has both freed slaves and darkies working in the fields and his mill. He's even helped some of them buy land north of here, up beyond our place."

"Where's your place?" asked Heather.

"Up the river the other side of River Oaks. Rachel Grantham owns River Oaks." Lizette rolled her eyes. "There's a mean one. I can't stand Rachel Grantham. She's had her eye on grandfather for years. That's why she bought River Oaks in the first place, you know, but that's a long story. I'll tell you about it sometime when we have nothing else to do, only first, tell me, were you surprised to learn about Uncle Heath being your real father and all?"

Heather nodded, a lump in her throat. "I hated it," she said softly.

Lizette frowned. "Hated it? Why? Uncle Heath's a charmer. A little frightening at times, perhaps, because he's sort of mysterious and so handsome and stern-looking. But he can be a lot of fun once you get to know him. You know, he actually danced with me at the New Year's Ball this year! It was my first one, and he made me feel so grown-up. But that's the way Uncle Heath is. He really loves your mother, too. You should have seen them dancing that night. I guessed right away that something was up when I saw them together, but no one else seemed to see it. Mother said it wasn't until the next day that everyone learned about you and that he was your father. It must have been so romantic for them, don't you think?"

Heather couldn't answer at first. "I suppose," she finally said, and Lizette stared at her, bewildered.

"I'm talking too much, aren't I?" she said. She pulled off her riding gloves. "I've been asking you questions, then not waiting for the answers." She glanced toward the river. "Want me to walk to the end of the pier with you?" she asked.

"If you'd like."

"Not if I'd like," said Lizette. "If *you'd* like."

Heather shrugged. "All right. You might as well."

"I don't have to," said Lizette testily. "I only thought you might like company. But if you're going to be a snob . . ." She flipped her head sharply and reached down, lifting her skirt, turning toward the house.

"No . . . wait," said Heather, stopping her. "Please, don't go. I'm sorry, Lizette. I shouldn't have taken my anger out on you. It's not your fault I'm what I am."

Lizette dropped her skirt and stared at her cousin. "What do you mean, what are you?" she asked.

"I was born out of wedlock. That means I'm a . . . a . . . well, you know what people call people like me."

Lizette sighed. "Oh, mercy, is that what's bothering you?" She rolled her eyes, shaking her head. Then her jaw set stubbornly, a twinkle reflecting in the depths of her green eyes. "You're in the wrong family to be worried about silly things like that," she said, amused. "Didn't your mother tell you about what happened when your father was born?"

"Yes."

"Well, he doesn't think it's so terrible. And my mother had my brother Cole when she was married to the Duke of Bourland, only my father's really his father too, not the Duke of Bourland. And Grandmother was expecting Mother long before she got married, and besides that, my grandfather on my father's side had four wives all at the same time. How would you like that one?"

Heather stared at her, frowning.

"My father's mostly Tuscarora Indian," Lizette explained quickly. "Some Indians can have as many wives as they want."

Heather inhaled sharply. "And that doesn't scare your mother?"

"Why should it? My father doesn't live with the Indians anymore. Besides"—she shrugged nonchalantly—"he's so in love with her, I don't think he even knows other women exist." She laughed. "I hope someday I can find somebody to love me like that." She went back to her former subject. "But anyway, as I was saying, I don't know why it should bother you so, just because your parents weren't married. They were very much in love at the time."

"But . . . I was always brought up to understand that it was disgraceful to do things that . . . Well, if Aunt Nell—or anyone else from back home, for that matter—knew the things you've just told me about your family . . . why, they'd be shocked."

Lizette blushed. "Well, I guess it's not really something we brag about, naturally, and I admit most of the people in Port Royal know nothing about any of it," she said sheepishly. "But honestly, it doesn't make any of us less human than anyone else. It's what you are that counts, not where or why you were born."

"You can say that easily," said Heather, watching her cousin closely. "You have a home and family you were born into. I bet your brother feels differently about it."

"Speaking of my brother," explained Lizette, "we got a letter that he's coming home soon. You'll like Cole. We always had fun together before he went off to the war."

"He's a soldier?"

"Fought with Jackson in New Orleans."

"I'm glad for your sake he wasn't hurt."

Lizette smiled. "Not Cole. He's inherited my father's Indian blood. He even looks a lot like our grandfather Telak, so my father says, except his eyes are green like mine and my father's. But he can track and shoot, and he's more at home in the woods than in a drawing room. I can hardly wait till he gets home."

Heather sighed as they reached the edge of the river and stood on the pier gazing into the deep water. There was a small ship tied up at the pier, with men moving about it, cleaning the deck, mending sail.

"That's Grandfather's private ship," said Lizette as she waved at the captain. "He calls it the *Interlude*, and Captain Casey's been with him for over twenty years. He and Grandmother still go sailing for weeks at a time. He just loves the sea."

Heather frowned. "But I thought . . . Isn't your father the one that used to be the privateer?" she asked.

"You mean Captain Thunder? That was before he and Mother were married. That's why our place is called Tonnerre, it means 'Thunder' in French." She glanced over at her cousin. "We have a ship too, called the *Duchess*. Have you ever been on a ship, Heather?"

Heather shook her head. "No. Mother went abroad a few times, but I always stayed home with Aunt Nell."

"Come on, then," said Lizette, and grabbed her hand quickly. "I'll show you around," and she pulled Heather with her up the gangplank, where she greeted Captain Casey, whose sandy hair had turned white over the years and whose freckled face had darkened and become leathery in the sun.

She introduced Heather, then strolled over the ship, acquainting her cousin with all the aspects of it, naming the different parts and showing her how the men handled the rigging and which sails were which.

When they were through on the *Interlude*, Lizette escorted Heather on a quick tour of the Chateau's outbuildings: the stables, where her mare would be kept when she was brought down from Columbia, if Aunt Nell hadn't sold her already; the carriage houses and barns; the warehouses where the crops were stored for shipment. Then they wandered off toward the cotton mill.

When they finally headed back toward the main house, strolling down a gravel lane lined with shade trees that separated the fields from the mill, Heather glanced over at her cousin curiously. "Did your grandmother tell you ahead of time to try to make friends with me?" she asked.

Lizette laughed, her laughter low and throaty. "Good heavens, no," she said. "In the first place, Grandma Dicia wouldn't do something like that, and if she did, I'm just stubborn enough I'd probably do the opposite. Don't worry, Heather, I came because I was curious. Except for my father's brothers and sisters, who are still living with his father somewhere along the shores of Lake Erie and probably have dozens of papooses filling their lodges by now, you're the only cousin I've got. Naturally I'd be anxious to meet you. I've been riding downriver every day hoping you'd be here." Lizette stopped, putting her hand on her cousin's arm, and Heather halted beside her. "I do want to be friends, Heather," she said anxiously. "Regardless of how you feel about Uncle Heath and the others, please may we be friends?"

Heather stared down at Lizette's hand on her arm, the fingers small and evenly tapered, the nails buffed to a shine. "I guess I can try," she said unhappily. "But I can't promise anything. I didn't want to come, Lizette. I had so many friends and all . . . but I'll try."

"Good." Lizette squeezed her arm, then let go, and they started again toward the house.

That evening Lizette stayed for dinner, and although Heather ignored everyone else, she and Lizette, as young people will, kept up a steady conversation. Then after dinner Roth ordered the carriage to be readied, Lizette's horse was tied to the back of it, and they all accompanied her back to Tonnerre, where Heather finally met her Aunt Rebel and Uncle Beau, the man who had once been the scourge of the English Navy, according to the tales Heather's father had told her.

After only a short time visiting with the Dantes, Heather agreed Lizette had been right. Lizette's father, Beau Dante, a man with dark good looks and piercing green eyes that warmed to emerald green when he looked at his wife, was exactly as Lizette had described him. And Lizette's mother was a remarkably beautiful woman.

At forty Rebel Dante's blond hair was devoid of any gray at all and her face was still youthful, the few lines in it barely noticeable. She was a fair-haired replica of her mother, but most important of all, her eyes, like her mother's and like Heather's, were the color of wood violets with the sun shining on them.

Later that evening, after returning once more to the Chateau, Heather sat in the upstairs bedroom they said was hers, propped up in the big frothy bed, staring into the darkened room, thinking over all that had happened since the day her mother had returned from Beaufort on the arm of the handsome dark-haired stranger.

She was no longer Heather McGill; that was for certain. From now on there was no more Heather McGill. She was Heather Chapman and her whole life was changing. She had cousins who were part Indian, a grandfather who had once been a British soldier, and a family with enough skeletons in its closet to start all the tongues in Columbia, South Carolina, wagging, and she wondered just what life was going to be like with all these strange people. From the sound of some of the stories she'd heard so far, it certainly wouldn't be dull.

She pursed her lips stubbornly. She wasn't going to be happy here. She couldn't be, ever. They had her body here, but they'd never break her spirit. She'd never consent to being Heather Chapman, and as she turned onto her stomach, snuggled down into the pillow, punching it up to make it more comfortable, she went to sleep trying to think of ways she could make life miserable for all of them so they'd give up the thought of keeping her here and send her back to Aunt Nell.

2

Late the next morning, Heather came downstairs to discover everyone else was already finished with breakfast. Heath had wanted to wake her, but Dicia had realized it would only add to the girl's hostility. Instead, when she did finally come down, her grandmother had Mattie, the cook, a big black woman who'd been with them for years, fix her whatever she wanted and serve her in the dining room as if she were an honored guest.

At first Heather felt guilty about giving the cook extra work to do, but eventually her obstinacy won out and she let her anger at having to stay at the Chateau override her sympathy for Mattie, and enjoyed every minute of the luxury. After breakfast she went back to her room, wrote some letters to friends in Columbia, making sure not to mention any of the scandalous tales she'd heard about her father's family, then, bored with nothing more to do, she roamed through the house, inspecting all the rooms, getting acquainted with the house she was going to have to call home from now on.

It was on this quiet, leisurely excursion through the rooms of the big house that she inadvertently eavesdropped on a conversation between her grandparents. She had wandered into the library, gazing at some of the paintings and fingering the titles on a number of books, pleased with what was available to read. Back home in Columbia they'd had a small library with only a few books, most of them dull philosophy books or boring histories. Here there was such a variety. Even some of those shocking new novels a few of the girls back at finishing school had been reading last year. What a surprise! She picked one off the shelf, started thumbing through it, then became interested, found a comfortable chair near the window, and made herself at home.

The chair she was sitting in had its back to the door, and she was so engrossed in the book that at first she hadn't heard them come in. The library was big, with a huge fireplace on the outside wall, shelves and shelves of books, two full-size sofas, a number of small tables and chairs, and a desk at one end where Roth headed, and it wasn't until she heard her grandfather speak that she realized anyone other than herself was in the room.

"I'm glad you told me Jacob was going into town for you," Roth said, taking some letters off the top of the desk. "I'll have him post these while he's there."

Heather stopped reading, surprised, then pulled the book hard to her breast and bent over, peeking around the back of the chair, only her grandparents didn't see her. She watched Loedicia put her hand on Roth's arm.

"Darling?"

Roth hesitated, shoving the letters in his pocket.

"What do you think of our new granddaughter?" she asked.

He stared at her for a few moments, then Heather saw his dark eyes crinkle warmly. "Except for the red hair, she reminds me a great deal of her grandmother at about the same age."

Her eyes warmed sheepishly. "Was I that high-spirited?"

"Dicia, my love, don't you remember what you were doing the first time I ever laid eyes on you?" he said softly. "You were berating a man for beating his horse with a whip, and there was fire in your eyes. For a minute I thought you were going to grab the whip from his hand and start flogging him with it."

"I guess I could get rather excited at times, couldn't I?"

He reached out and pulled her into his arms, holding her close, his hands caressing the curve of her back beneath the dark green cotton dress.

"I think I fell in love with you that very first day," he said huskily. "You were so vibrant, so full of life." One hand moved up, stroking her neck, and he bent his head, his lips pressing against the soft flesh beneath her ear on one side while the hand that was stroking her neck began to move down until he was cupping her breast.

Heather watched transfixed as her grandmother's head tilted back, her eyes closing and a low moan escaping her lips. A moan of sensual pleasure Heather had never heard before. The hair at the nape of Heather's neck began to prickle, and a strange sensation spread through her as she watched Roth's intimate caresses.

He continued to kiss the awakening pulses beneath Loedicia's ear, then nibbled at her earlobe, his words soft and passionate as his hand moved intimately over her breasts.

"You never cease to amaze me, love," he murmured, enjoying the feel of her beneath his hands. "After all these years, making love to you is still a pleasure I can never resist." He raised his head until he was looking deep into her eyes that were open now and filled with a burning desire that made Heather hold her breath in fascination. "Sometimes I'm still not sure this isn't a dream, darling," he went on lovingly. "When I think of all those lonely years I spent without you."

"Shhh . . ." She reached up, her fingers stopping his words; then those same fingers traced the outline of his jaw, caressing his face as she spoke. "We promised never to talk about those years, remember?" she whispered. "Those years belonged to Quinn. These years are ours."

"And I've loved every moment."

"You're still content?"

"Why shouldn't I be?"

Her eyes wavered momentarily as she gazed into his. "I'm not that young girl anymore, Roth," she said reluctantly. "I'm old and wrinkled and—"

"Hush!" His lips found hers and he kissed them lovingly. "Don't ever say you're old. You'll never be old." He cupped her face in his hand and his eyes devoured her. "You know yourself what you always do to me. If we were in bed right now, I'd show you." He kissed her again lightly on the lips, sipping at them fervently. "Dicia, Dicia! How else can I tell you I love you but with my body and my heart?"

"Oh, my darling." Loedicia pressed her body to his, feeling the arousal that was always there waiting to appease the hunger she had for him. A hunger only he could feed. Her eyes captured his, and as their lips met once more in a passionate kiss that left them both breathless, Heather swallowed hard, pulled her head back around, resting it on the back of the chair, and stared straight ahead.

She was so dazed she barely heard the kiss end and Roth playfully threaten to tumble Loedicia in the hay, and the soft laughter as they started to leave. Heather's head was filled with the strange new knowledge that there were things going on around her she knew absolutely nothing about. She had been brought up in a very sterile household. Living only with women around her, there had been no chance to even suspect the intimacy that was so much a part of marriage, and because for so many years her mother had denied herself the normal feelings of what it was like to be a woman, she had denied her daughter too, refusing to let Heather know what love was all about. The little Heather did know had been gleaned from school friends and whispered about as if it were wicked, but the whole truth was still a mystery to her, a vague something that happened between people who loved each other. From all the whisperings, Heather had a vague inkling that a woman's part in marriage was an unpleasant duty. But her grandmother had actually been enjoying the whole thing.

If they were young, it might not be so bad, but they were so old. She had never in her wildest imaginings suspected that old people kissed like that. Aunt Nell certainly didn't. And her mother—was that what Heath did to her? Was that why her mother had changed so since her marriage?

She shuddered, wondering if the girls at school had been right all along about what was meant by the marriage bed. The book she'd been reading was still clutched to her breast as Heather continued to stare toward the window, watching the shadows of afternoon creep onto the veranda outside. She felt warm all over, sort of a pulsing throb coursing through her veins at the remembrance of the look that had been on both her grandparents' faces.

Heather's face flushed crimson, her palms beginning to perspire, and she lowered the book from her breast, closing it, her fingers gently running over the title as she continued to stare out the window, her mind in a turmoil. If only she had someone to talk to. She couldn't ask her mother; it was just too embarrassing. A hundred questions surged forth inside her as she remembered some of the things Lizette had told her yesterday. She had complained to her newfound cousin that she didn't like being born out of wedlock. But now, as she thought of it, she had never really known why it was such a terrible thing, except that people said it was. But what made it terrible? And most of all, were her old schoolmates right? The thought was frightening. That a man should even want to touch her in such an intimate place, let alone do what they whispered about . . .

She frowned. Maybe Lizette knew. After all, she didn't seem to mind talking about such things. Heather's lip quivered nervously as she made up her mind that the next time she had the chance she was going to ask Lizette. She sighed, lifted herself slowly from the chair, then walked back to the shelf and replaced the book. This done, she smoothed the skirt of her gold taffeta afternoon dress and left the library, closing the door firmly behind her.

It was three days before she finally saw Lizette, and she didn't have the opportunity to talk to her alone. Lizette had ridden down from Tonnerre in a fancy carriage with a driver, and her chaperon, Hizzie, a black woman who'd taken care of Cole and Lizette when they were babies. Hizzie had never married and treated Lizette like her own child, sometimes to Lizette's consternation.

"She's stricter with me than my own mother," Lizette told Heather while she waited for her to change into a dress appropriate to wear into Beaufort. Lizette had coaxed Aunt Darcy and Uncle Heath into letting Heather go into town to help her pick out some new material for the dress she was going to wear for her grandmother's and mother's joint birthday party, which was only a few weeks away.

The two young women made a colorful picture side by side as the carriage pulled down the drive. Heather was dressed in a deep purple pelisse over a pale lavender muslin gown, her white straw bonnet decorated with lavender plumes and artificial violets. Beside her, Lizette's dark hair was made to seem even darker in contrast to her dusty-rose satin pelisse worn over a pale pink muslin, her rose velvet hat lined in pink satin with pink and rose plumes almost touching her cheek on one side. Hizzie, wearing her usual black linen and simple black cloak, sat opposite the two young ladies, watching them warily. There was a glint in Lizette's eyes she wasn't quite sure she liked. More than once she'd seen that look, and it usually meant trouble. Well, she'd just keep watch.

It was a two-hour ride to Beaufort, and the land they traveled through was quite swampy at times. The town of Port Royal and its surrounding plantations were built on land bordered on the west by the Broad River and on the east by Port Royal Sound, which came together at the town's southern tip. To the far north it was bordered by the Coosaw River that flowed in from St. Helena Sound. Actually Port Royal was an island in its own right, with Beaufort being one of the oldest cities at the northern tip of Port Royal Sound. As they rode into town, Lizette pointed out the landmarks to Heather: the old arsenal, the gardens at St. Helena's Church, and some of the homes that had been built before the Revolution. It was rich in history, but most of what Lizette told her fell on deaf ears.

Heather had so wanted to talk to Lizette, but with Hizzie along, her dark eyes watching so closely, and the driver sitting atop his seat where he could hear everything, she'd been unable to. Maybe later they could sneak a few minutes to themselves. As it was, the conversation on the ride to Beaufort was all about the ball they were having to celebrate the two birthdays on March 13, and of the people who were going to be there and the dress Lizette planned to have made. Lizette was excited because they'd received a letter from her brother saying he'd be home in time for the ball.

After taking the rest of the morning to select the material they would need for their ball gowns, Lizette talked Hizzie into letting them visit a friend of Lizette's who had attended her same finishing school in Charleston.

Lizette was supposed to have gone back to school after the Christmas holidays, but since she hated it, she had managed to convince her mother that she had learned all she was going to learn. "Of course, I had to do a little foot stamping and crying to get her to relent," she told Heather unashamedly. "But I couldn't stand that school with its rules and regulations."

"Then your friend quit too?" asked Heather as they pulled up in front of the young woman's house.

"Heavens no," said Lizette. "She was asked to leave for breaking curfew too many times."

Heather glanced hesitantly at Hizzie as the driver left his seat to help them down. "And your mother lets you visit her?"

Lizette smiled. "Felicia's mother and my mother are friends."

Hizzie frowned. "And they both don't know what to do with the two of you either," she said, grimly entering the conversation. "You never saw two young ladies who could get in so much trouble, Miss Heather," she said. "I'm hoping maybe your good influence will rub off on her highness here."

"Oh, Hizzie!" Lizette let the driver help her down, then stood by while Heather and Hizzie climbed down from the carriage. The house Lizette's friend lived in was a large brick with columns holding up a second-story balcony across the front and a huge lawn with a circular drive lined with magnolia trees.

Felicia Kolter was a pleasant surprise. She was less extraverted than Lizette, with huge amber-flecked brown eyes and hair the color of burned honey. She was pretty in a gentle way, her eyes large, her nose small and slightly snubbed, her mouth a little too generous. Her eyes shone with an impish delight, and she smiled easily.

"So this is your new cousin," she said as Lizette introduced them, and Heather saw the gleam in her eye.

Heather stared at her, a little awed. She was wearing an afternoon dress of pale green watered silk with a pleated top, squared at the neckline with a small ruffle of lace edging it, and long sleeves tipped with lace at the wrists, and her hair was pulled into a mass of curls at the back of her head, ribbons and combs holding it in place. She was staring at Heather curiously.

"I think it's excitingly wicked, don't you?" she exclaimed, grasping Heather's hands, squeezing them warmly. "I wish I could have been a love baby. Just to think that two people could love each other so much . . ." She rolled her eyes ecstatically. "But then, we can't all be so fortunate. My mother and father were married three years before my oldest brother came along." She glanced quickly at Lizette. "Sometimes I envy you, Lizette. You have such an exciting family!"

"Well, what about you?" Lizette countered as she and Heather let one of the servants help them off with their pelisses, then watched as Hizzie followed the servant, a young black girl, into another part of the house, while the three young ladies headed for the parlor. "Your brother Stuart's going to be a senator."

"If he's elected. But he lives the dullest life. He's been married to Julia for eight years and they have two children already. She caught him before he even got out of law school, and he's about as exciting as a snail. Oh, he's good-looking—at least he was the last time I saw him, which was four years ago when he was first running for Congress, but by now he's probably got a potbelly and takes snuff, like all the other politicians."

"Well, what about Bain? Cole said he ran into him down in New Orleans a while back, and he's traveled all over the country, just like Uncle Heath."

"But he didn't leave any love children behind."

"Now, how do you know that? Uncle Heath was only twenty when he met Aunt Darcy. Bain's older than that."

"He's twenty-three, but Bain isn't in love with anyone." She tilted her head proudly. "And guess what," she said excitedly. "He got home last night!"

"No! Did he say whether he saw Cole again? What was the fighting like? How long is he going to be home?"

"Hey, wait a minute." Felicia laughed as they entered the parlor. "Don't ask so many questions, Liz," she said, sitting opposite them in a green-and-gold brocade chair with carved wood arms. "But to answer, he did see Cole briefly, yes, but didn't get a chance to talk to him. He didn't talk about the fighting except to say it was 'hell.' " She smirked as she said it. "And I haven't the faintest idea how long he'll stay. He's already gone to the cockfights this afternoon."

"The cockfights!"

Heather watched Lizette's eyes light up.

"What are you thinking, Liz?" asked Felicia, and Lizette smiled mischievously as Heather continued to silently follow this conversation.

"Let's go to the cockfights," Lizette suggested in a whisper.

Heather's eyes widened as she saw Felicia contemplate the matter thoughtfully before asking, "What about Hizzie?"

"She'll stay in the servants' quarters as long as she thinks we're still on the grounds, you know that. We can do like we did the last time and tell her we're going for a walk through the gardens."

"You've been to the cockfights before?" asked Heather, finally joining in the conversation.

Lizette nodded. "Last fall. We told them we were going to take a walk out back. Felicia's father has beautiful gardens with lily ponds and all sorts of trails through them. The cockfights are only about a mile from here in an old barn, and we know the back way in. Of course, we had to watch from the hayloft, but it was really something."

Heather wasn't so sure. "What if Hizzie comes looking for you."

"She won't," said Felicia. "I'll have Susu fix her something to eat." She stood up. "By the way, you two haven't eaten either, I'll bet," she said. "How about if I have Susu fix us some sandwiches and tell Hizzie we'll stop in the summerhouse out in the gardens and eat them. That way we can take them with us and eat them up in the hayloft while we watch."

Lizette thought it was a great idea, but Heather still wasn't quite certain they were doing the right thing. However, not wanting to be a spoilsport, she tagged along with the two younger girls, eventually catching their air of excitement, and by the time they reached the old barn, approaching it from an overgrown field, she too was looking forward to the adventure. She'd never seen a cockfight.

As they stumbled through the high weeds, nearing the door in the back of the old barn, they could hear yelling and shouts from inside as the men who were gathered there tried to coax their birds on and others cursed when theirs were in trouble. For a second Heather hesitated; then the thrill of adventure began to fill her again, and as Felicia opened the door and they slipped inside, she held her breath expectantly. The door led to a small harness room, or granary, she wasn't certain which, since the room was empty except for some old straw on the floor. At one end was a ladder that ascended to the loft, and one at a time, with Lizette in the lead carrying the small picnic basket with the sandwiches in it, the girls began to climb.

It was cumbersome scaling the ladder in their long dresses, with petticoats and tight drawers, their thin-soled shoes giving little protection from the ladder rungs, and the scent of hay and horses was strong. As they reached the top, Heather swung her legs up onto the loft in imitation of Lizette and Felicia, then held her breath as she gazed back behind them to the empty room below.

"Oh, dear!" she gasped breathlessly, not having realized before they started climbing that it was so high. Lizette cautioned her to be quiet or someone might hear.

Heather pursed her lips and watched apprehensively as the other two pulled their dresses up so they could crawl on their knees. Lizette slipped the handle of the picnic basket onto her arm, and they began edging toward the other end of the loft, below which the men were gathered. Lizette reached the edge first, then turned back as Felicia reached her, and motioned for Heather to follow. Heather took a deep breath. Well, she had come this far. She pushed up on all fours, pulled the lavender dress up to free her stockinged knees, and crawled after them, then dropped to her stomach when she reached the edge of the loft.

Her eyes widened as she looked over the edge. Below them was a large group of men, and in the center of the barn floor was a circle marked with black paint. Around the circle the men were crowded close, watching the action, some leaning on cages, others sitting on crates. Inside the circle were two fighting cocks, their combs erect, spurred feet clawing the floor, strange gravelly noises coming from them as they eyed each other and squared off. Feathers littered the floor haphazardly and blood was spattered about, but Heather could see no blood on the two cocks who were in the circle. Evidently they had just been thrown into the ring.

"Five to one on the red!" someone yelled, and the challenge was picked up around the floor until all bets were in; then silence reigned momentarily as the spectators waited for the first strike.

"Which one's your brother?" Heather asked Felicia, who quickly put her hand over Heather's mouth to silence her so the men wouldn't hear. Then, as the cocks lunged for each other and the crowd erupted in a volley of shouts, she released Heather's mouth and answered, whispering, "Bain's standing over near that big cage to the right of the man wearing the purple frock coat and white hat. He's the one in the dark green frock coat, buff trousers, and shiny boots, holding his hat in his hand."

"The good-looking one with the dark brown hair and short clipped beard, like your father wears," added Lizette. "And that's DeWitt Palmer next to him."

Heather studied both men. Lizette was right, Bain Kolter was strikingly good-looking in a rugged way. He was quite tall. His hair, darker than his young sister's, held glints of gold in it as light filtering through the cracks in the side of the barn fell on it occasionally, and as was usually the case, his close-cropped beard was much darker than his hair. It was a deep russet brown. The man beside him was quite different. His fair hair lay in soft collar-length waves. Although he wasn't as muscular as Bain Kolter, there was nothing effeminate about him. He was nice-looking, but not extraordinary, his features a little too sharp to be considered handsome.

"Are your brother and DeWitt Palmer good friends?" Heather asked.

Felicia shook her head. "Not really, but they have been known to go places together on occasion, and DeWitt owns the fighting cock that's in that big cage beside them. That's his handler in the purple jacket and white hat."

Heather glanced quickly at the handler. His features were hawklike and hard. His eyes burned anxiously and never left the two roosters tangled together in the ring in a death struggle. Heather couldn't watch the birds; it seemed like such a brutal sport. Instead she gazed around at the men and listened attentively to Felicia and Lizette talking about the ones they knew, and for the first time in days Heather forgot about the scene in the library, letting the excitement of the afternoon hold her in its spell.

As the afternoon wore on, they ate their sandwiches. At least Lizette and Felicia did. Heather, after watching the blood being splattered about as each new bout began, had lost her desire for food shortly after their arrival and merely picked at her sandwich. The temperature outside was still cool, but inside the barn it was stuffy and hot and all three of them wiped perspiration from their foreheads as they lay watching.

They had no way of knowing what time it was when they finally decided to leave. Although the fights were still going on, some of the men just stood around talking and the crowd was beginning to thin out, so Lizette decided they'd probably better get back before Hizzie got suspicious. "After all, we have almost a mile to walk through the field, and that's going to take time," she reminded them.

Felicia and Heather both nodded as they took one last glance down at the dwindling crowd, then started to follow Lizette, who was scooting unceremoniously back toward the ladder, dragging the now empty picnic basket with her. Lizette swung her feet over easily onto the ladder, then motioned toward her friend and her cousin as she started to disappear into the room below. Both Heather and Felicia followed awkwardly.

The basket swinging from Lizette's arm hampered her somewhat as her feet moved slowly from rung to rung on the ladder. She went carefully so as not to catch the skirt of her dress, and was so engrossed in what she was doing that it was quite a shock to her, when she suddenly felt a hand clasp firmly over her mouth and an arm circle her waist, pulling her deftly off the ladder.

Her heart gave a turn and she started to struggle; then, as she turned her head slightly and caught a quick glimpse of the slate-gray eyes boring into hers, the fear left her, to be replaced by anger. Her captor set her firmly on the ground in front of him, then motioned for her to be quiet as his hand eased on her mouth and he let go of her waist. He quickly turned back to the ladder in time to catch Felicia.

But Lizette wasn't about to be quiet. She let out a quick shriek, warning Felicia, only it wasn't quick enough. As Bain Kolter grabbed his sister, hauling her fighting from the ladder, Heather, unused to acting the tomboy and frightened by Lizette's scream and Felicia's violent protests, turned to look back and lost her balance, her hands slipping from their hold.

She came crashing down the rest of the way on top of Felicia and Bain, knocking both of them over, landing on top of them.

Heather's heart was in her throat as she felt the tangle of bodies beneath her, and she gasped as Lizette reached out, helping her off them.

"Oh, I'm sorry!" she exclaimed, her voice breaking as she stood clear and grabbed Felicia's hand, helping her to her feet.

As both girls began brushing themselves off, Felicia stared at her brother angrily, her eyes blazing. "Just what did you think you were doing?" she yelled breathlessly.

"Me?" Bain was rising slowly to his feet, his hands cleaning the straw from his trousers and frock coat as he stared at his young sister and her friends. "What the hell did you think you were doing?"

"Isn't it obvious?" Felicia's lips pursed. "We were watching the cockfights!"

"And I'll wager Mother doesn't know it."

"Mother's at the Hamptons'."

"So you took it on yourself to decide it's all right to attend the cockfights?" His gray eyes darkened as he gestured toward Heather and Lizette. "Who are these two?"

Felicia glanced briskly toward her two friends. "This is Lizette Dante—you remember her, don't you? She's Cole's sister. And this is her cousin Heather Chapman." Her eyes caught Heather's. "Or is it McGill?"

Heather flushed. "Legally it's still McGill, but it's really Chapman."

Bain stared at Heather, his eyes still hard. "Well, which is it?"

"Either one," she answered, shrugging. "It doesn't really matter."

He studied her closely. She was quite pretty with her red hair and violet eyes, but there was a tenseness about her that distracted from her looks, as if she wasn't quite sure of herself, and her heart-shaped face seemed fragile and forlorn. He then glanced at the dark-haired young woman standing next to her, Lizette Dante, Cole's sister. His eyes caught hers and he stared into them, surprised for a moment at the vibrant sparkle that deepened their green color, filling them with warmth and life. They were the same color as her brother's eyes, but the black lashes surrounding them were long and curling, making them look larger than they were. He remembered momentarily that she was part Indian, although the only hint of it was the slightly dusky hue of her skin. She had been only about eight or nine when he'd left home. Now, nearing full bloom, she was strikingly beautiful, and he wondered what she'd be like in a few more years. As he stared into her eyes, a warmth spread through him that he quickly fought back.

He drew his eyes from her face and glanced over at his sister. "It's a good thing I caught you here, and not someone else," he said sternly. "You didn't do a very good job of keeping your heads down. It's a wonder everyone didn't spot you up there. Lying on your stomachs in the hay! Look at you," and he gestured to their clothes, where bits and pieces of straw still clung. "Where does Mother think you really are?" he asked.

"Like I said, Mother's at the Hamptons'."

He looked at Lizette, who was picking straw off her skirt. "What about your mother, Lizette?" he asked.

She glanced up, her green eyes stabbing him with pure malice. "My mother's at home," she said belligerently, "and so is Heather's."

"They let the two of you ride into Beaufort by yourselves?" he asked incredulously, then laughed sarcastically. "That I'll never believe!"

She tilted her head up stubbornly. "Why not? We're old enough."

His eyes sifted over her immature figure, the breasts pushing against the front of her dress but still not fully developed; then he glanced toward Heather, who was blushing outrageously, the pinkish tint of her fair skin blending in with her hair. Although both girls were of approximately the same height, Heather's frame had matured and ripened to full young womanhood and it was easy to see she had a few years on the other two girls.

"Your cousin here might possibly be old enough," he conceded as he drew his eyes from Heather's embarrassed face, "but I'll wager you're no older than Felicia here, and I happen to know she's only fifteen, so don't tell me you rode into Beaufort by yourselves."

"Oh, Bain, don't be a spoilsport," Felicia said, pouting. "Her servant is back at the house. I had Susu fix her some lunch. She thinks we're having a picnic in the summerhouse."

"But instead you came to the cockfights."

"Is that so terrible?"

"Felicia, ladies don't attend cockfights. Especially ladies who aren't even ladies yet."

"But, Bain—"

"Don't 'but Bain' me. It was bad enough you got kicked out of finishing school—"

"I didn't get kicked out."

"Mother said you had to leave."

"Well, there's a difference."

"The point is," Bain continued, "it's time you started behaving yourself." He glanced first at his sister, then Lizette, then hurriedly looked back to his sister again after feeling a slight shock run through him as his eyes clashed with Lizette's. Cole's sister, for all her tender age, was having a strange effect on him that he didn't quite know how to take. "DeWitt has his carriage out front waiting for me," he said firmly, staring at Felicia. "He picked me up earlier. I'm sure he won't mind giving the three of you a ride to the house."

Felicia's lower lip pushed out into a pout again. "We'll walk home, if you don't mind," she countered, but his eyes held on hers.

"You certainly will not," he stated. "I'm going to make sure that the three of you don't get into any more trouble this afternoon!"

Felicia stamped her foot. "I won't go home with you, Bain Kolter!" she cried, but his jaw tightened grimly.

"Don't tell me what you will or won't do," he said. "You'll go if I have to carry you . . . all three of you," and before she could protest further, he grabbed her arm, pulling her toward the door that led into the main part of the barn.

He stopped momentarily, his eyes on Heather and Lizette. "You'd better come too," he shot back angrily. "I'm stronger and I can run faster, and by God I'll get you all back to the house one way or another!"

Lizette saw the anger in his eyes and the firm set of his chin and glanced quickly at Heather. "Maybe we'd better," she said. She straightened her fancy dress, as did Heather, making certain there was no hay or straw sticking to it; then they followed Bain Kolter and his sister from the grain room into the main part of the barn. Much to both girls' surprise, there were few men left in the barn, and those that were, were so interested in what was going on inside the fighting ring that they didn't even see Bain drag Felicia toward the open barn door and through it, with the other two girls following reluctantly behind.

DeWitt's carriage was at the side of the barn and he was lounging against the tree it was under. He straightened as Bain turned the corner of the barn, and his hazel eyes held a faint amusement as he watched Bain pulling his sister along with him, two other girls hurrying along behind.

When the foursome reached the carriage, Bain yanked Felicia, whirling her to stand in front of him, then let go of her arm and pointed to the carriage. "In, young lady!" he demanded.

Felicia's eyes narrowed. "I'll pay you back someday, Bain," she said through clenched teeth, then glanced quickly at DeWitt. "Hello, Witt," she acknowledged, and proceeded to introduce her friends. "Witt, you know Lizette Dante . . . this is her cousin Heather."

DeWitt nodded toward Lizette, but his eyes hesitated as they sifted over Heather. "Heather what?" he asked intently.

"Chapman, I guess," she answered.

His eyebrows rose. "You guess? Well, is it or isn't it?"

Heather flushed.

"Legally it's McGill, but she's Uncle Heath's daughter," Lizette informed him.

It was hard to read DeWitt's thoughts, but one thing Heather did notice. He seemed to stare at her, and when he sat next to her in the carriage, she could feel the heat of his body pressing against her.

"Whatever possessed you to come watch the fights?" Bain asked as the carriage moved away from the barn.

"It was my idea," answered Lizette, and Bain reluctantly drew his eyes from his sister's face to look once more at her.

"And does my sister generally go along with all your rattle-brained ideas?" he asked.

Lizette's head tilted stubbornly as she stared at Bain Kolter. If only he wasn't so godawful good-looking. Felicia had no right to have a brother who looked like a Greek god. It had been at least six years since she had last seen Bain. He'd been home off and on during those years, but the opportunity to meet him again had never presented itself because she'd been spending most of her time at the finishing school in Charleston. Now she studied his arrogantly handsome face, wishing she were old enough to slap it for him, but knowing full well that he thought of her only as an insignificant child.

"I noticed you seemed to enjoy the cockfights," she said, bristling irritably. "So where is there a law that says I can't?"

He frowned. "You enjoyed it?"

"I didn't say I did. I only said there's no law that says I can't."

"There happens to be an unwritten law, Miss Dante, that

forbids women of the gentry from attending cockfights, and I'm certain you're aware of it."

"Oh, pooh!" said Lizette, scowling. "Men spoil everything for us women."

"Women?" Bain laughed. "Scarcely out of short dresses and you call yourself a woman?"

Her green eyes turned the color of dark waters and her full mouth tensed. "Age has nothing to do with being a woman, Mr. Kolter," she answered, emphasizing his name angrily.

For another brief moment as her eyes clashed with his, Bain felt a violent quickening deep inside, and for a few dangerous seconds he was almost inclined to believe her; then he took a deep breath. "I don't think your mother would agree," he said after a short pause. "I think if she were here right now she'd be inclined to turn you over her knee."

Lizette's eyes snapped furiously, and she turned away quickly.

Heather felt Lizette tense next to her, and she glanced over at the man who was causing her cousin so much discomfiture. Bain was still staring at Lizette, and his eyes held a strange gleam. If he considered her so much a child, why was he looking at her the way Heath looked at her mother? It was puzzling, and once more Heather remembered her reason for wanting to see Lizette alone. She frowned.

"Is something wrong?" asked DeWitt Palmer from beside Heather, and she cleared her thoughts abruptly, turning toward him as best she could in the crowded carriage.

"Not really," she said. "I was just thinking, what Lizette said . . . she was right, you know, it was rather exciting!"

Witt's eyes narrowed slightly. "But not very ladylike."

"No, I guess it wasn't, but then, I'm sure you've done things that haven't been considered gentlemanly, haven't you?"

"That's a man's privilege."

She watched the afternoon sun turning his hair to pale gold as they rode along. "I see," she said. "In other words, you don't necessarily have to act like a gentleman, but I'm expected to act like a lady?"

"Precisely."

"How interesting," she said thoughtfully. "And here I thought gentlemen were exactly that. I'm glad you enlightened me on the subject. You see, I've lived in a home devoid of men and never dreamed they were so deceitful, but lately I should have had my suspicions, shouldn't I?" she added caustically. "After all, look what my own father did."

"Your father? Oh, yes, the notorious Heath Chapman. I believe there was quite a scandal about him some years back, if I remember right," he said. "I don't really know what the whole thing was all about, but from some of the reactions when his name is mentioned, there are those who still do remember."

Bain wrenched his eyes from Lizette and glanced at Heather. It was very apparent from her violet eyes that she was Loedicia Chapman's granddaughter, but she more closely resembled her mother. His eyes moved to DeWitt, and he frowned at the interest Witt was showing in her. But then, why should he worry? It was obvious Heather was old enough to be courted. But he did worry, because although he'd known Witt a long time, he had never actually liked him. Not as a friend. He was too glib, too prone to anger, and too quick to sarcasm, and there was a hard streak in him that left little room for compassion. Bain was certain the man would make some woman a terrible husband, and he hated to think it might be Lizette's red-headed cousin. As he watched Witt trying to charm Heather, he had misgivings. But he soon forgot his misgivings as the carriage pulled off the main road, up the circular drive, and came to a stop in front of the majestic brick home.

Heather glanced past DeWitt Palmer as the front door flew open, and it was no surprise to see Hizzie come bounding down the steps, fire in her dark eyes, her dark face contorted with rage. "Miss Lizzie, where the devil have you been, child?" she yelled angrily.

Lizette took a deep breath. "You're out of place, Hizzie!" she said haughtily as she followed the others from the carriage.

Hizzie stopped at the foot of the steps, arms folded, waiting. "Your mama said I was to see you didn't get into no more trouble, and look at you," she said, unfolding her arms, gesturing at Lizette's rumpled dress. She glanced at Heather. "And dragging your cousin into it. Shame on you!"

"Oh, Hizzie," Lizette said, "all we did was go see a cockfight."

"A cockfight?" Hizzie's face went slack. "Oh, mercy, child. Why for did you go and do that?"

"Because we wanted to. But don't worry, I don't think anyone else knew we were even there, except Bain and Witt. Even if they did, it's none of their business."

Hizzie shook her head. "Your mama's gonna be furious!"

"She won't have to know."

"Oh, no you don't, young lady," Hizzie said, frowning at her. "Your mama's going to know all about your little escapade, you can count on that!"

Lizette made a face and started up the steps as Mrs. Kolter, who had come home early from the Hamptons', came out the front door. Madeline Kolter was an attractive woman in her early fifties with light brown hair and rich brown eyes that looked all of them over quickly. She confronted Felicia and Bain. "Is it true, Bain?" she asked as she stared indignantly at Felicia.

Bain watched the anger in his mother's eyes. "It's true."

"This is the last straw!" she snapped angrily. Then she turned to Hizzie. "If you'll come in the house while the girls get their pelisses, Hizzie, I'll give you a note for Rebel and Beau," she said. "I think it's time we did something to curb such behavior in the future." She turned once more to Felicia. "Now, get in the house, young lady, and up to your room. I'll settle with you in good time."

Lizette watched dejectedly as her friend entered the house; then she followed Felicia, with Heather close behind and the rest of them hurrying after.

Just before starting up the winding staircase that led to the second floor where her room was, Felicia turned, caught Lizette's eye, and winked. Then she picked up her skirt and hurried upstairs.

Later, on the way to the Chateau, Heather thought over the day's adventures. She had seen the wink between the two girls, and she also had to admit that Mrs. Kolter was right: her cousin and her young friend were decidedly bad influences on each other. She glanced over at Lizette. She was such a strange young girl. To look at her was to see a beautiful girl just becoming a young lady; to know her was to discover a bundle of energy—all of it channeled in the wrong directions. Sometimes it seemed like she purposely tried to think up ridiculous things to do. After all the upset over today's escapade, the first thing she did when they were seated in the carriage, while Hizzie was getting instructions from Mrs. Kolter on delivering the note she had written, was to lean close to Heather and tell her about the horse races that were being held on Saturday at one of the neighboring plantations. Now, as they rode along, Heather wondered if she should try to talk to Lizette as she had planned. Maybe she'd be no different from the girls at school with their giggling and half-truths. Yet, in spite of Lizette's apparent disregard for ladylike conduct, there was something captivatingly likable about her, and she always seemed to know what she was talking about. Yes, she'd talk to her as soon as she had the chance.

However, by the time they reached the Chateau, she knew her talk with Lizette would have to be postponed, especially after Hizzie made sure her mother and Heath learned of her part in the afternoon's escapade. As she stood at the window in her bedroom, where they had ordered her to stay for punishment, and watched the carriage with Lizette in it heading on upriver toward Tonnerre, she wondered how much longer she'd have to wait before she learned the answers to all the questions that were haunting her.

3

By the time Saturday morning rolled around, the household was no longer talking about the girls' escapade in town. Heather had recuperated fully from the scolding her mother had unleashed on her and was once more stubbornly resisting everyone's attempts at getting on her good side. Since the atmosphere at the Chateau was still so strained and tense, Loedicia and Roth talked it over with Heath and Darcy, and they all decided that maybe more exposure to Lizette's warm-hearted influence was just what Heather needed, and so shortly after breakfast Loedicia had a long talk with Heather and it was decided that she would ride up to Tonnerre with her and Roth to see if Lizette could come down and spend some time with them at the Chateau.

It was Heather's first time on a horse since arriving at the Chateau, so they picked a rather tame mare for her to ride, not knowing how good her horsemanship was. Heather didn't let it bother her however, and as she calmly rode along, sitting expertly on the sidesaddle, wearing a deep green riding habit, she glanced over to her grandparents, who were leading the way, and felt a twinge of regret. For a brief moment she wished that she had known them when they were younger, before age had begun to creep up on them. They seemed so much in love, even now. It was surprising. She had watched the intimate byplay between them while they were mounting their horses, and the way they laughed together, their eyes on each other as if each knew what the other was thinking. How wonderful it must have been for them when they were young. Once more the scene in the library held her thoughts as she stared at Loedicia.

Her grandmother was wearing a deep purple riding habit that enhanced her eyes and softened the gray that streaked her hair. It was unbelievable that Loedicia was preparing to celebrate her sixtieth birthday.

Remembering about the birthday ball brought back the remembrance of the trip into Beaufort earlier in the week to buy the material for their dresses, and she smiled to herself. As much as everyone made a fuss about it, she had to admit it had been fun. Except for the blood and gore at the cock-fight, everything had been rather exciting. Even though they had gotten into trouble, she had to agree with Lizette, it had been worth it. If she hadn't gone, she might never have learned what a cockfight was all about. It would have stayed one of those forbidden territories only men could know about.

Her smile deepened as she felt the horse beneath her. It had been a long time since she had been riding, and she wondered if Aunt Nell had sold Jezebel yet or if she was ever going to see her horse again. As they rode along, her smile slowly faded as she thought back to her years growing up in Columbia as Heather McGill.

It was shortly before noon when they finally reached Tonnerre, taking their time on the ride, stopping now and then for Loedicia or Roth to point out something to her, and stopping occasionally to converse with the occupants of a number of carriages that went past. As was the Chateau, the plantation at Tonnerre was built a short distance from the Broad River, the back terrace overlooking its bank, with formal gardens descending to the water's edge. A huge ballroom had been added to the back wing of the house some years before, and French doors at the far end of the ballroom opened onto the gardens. It was here at Tonnerre they were planning to have the birthday ball, since there was no ballroom at the Chateau.

They were greeted out front at the mounting block by Aaron, the head groom, who had been with Beau since he'd first built Tonnerre. He helped the ladies down, then headed toward the stables with their horses to have them rubbed down while they entered the house and greeted Rebel in the foyer, where one of the servants had ushered them.

"Mother, Roth, I'm surprised!" Rebel said candidly as she gave them each a hug and a kiss. "And, Heather, I'm so glad you came with them."

Heather pulled off her gloves, studying her aunt closely. Lizette's mother looked more than just a little surprised. "If it's all right with you, I thought I'd come say hello to Lizette," Heather said rather shyly.

Rebel's violet eyes deepened as she tucked a tuft of fair hair back into the chignon at the nape of her neck. "She's not in the house right now," she said quickly. "She's down near the slave quarters." She smiled warmly. "One of the young girls is in labor, and she wanted to help. You know Lizette." She glanced at her mother. "She has to be right in the middle of everything. I was down there earlier, but had to come back to the house. Beau will be coming in from the field for lunch soon, so I thought I'd better be here."

"How are the fields coming?" asked Roth as they made their way toward the parlor.

She smiled again happily. "They're almost ready to plant," she answered, then sighed, looking closely at Roth. "And I hope Beau isn't making a mistake. He decided to take your advice and put in that new Mexican variety of cotton in the upper field near the road this year. I sure hope you were right when you told him it'll double the yield per acre."

"I know it's risky to try something new," Roth said, assuring her, "but I'm glad he decided to try. I discovered a long time ago that it's the only way to progress. If we hadn't been willing to try new crops and new techniques, we'd have never started growing rice and would have just let the swamps keep claiming the land instead of making it pay. As it is now, we don't have to rely on just one crop, and the risk of loss isn't as great."

"Then you're planting the new variety too?" she asked.

"I am. In fact, Heath's clearing the stubble out of that twenty-five acres near River Oaks that I've been letting rest for the past two years," he said. "We should be ready to plant in another few weeks. In the meantime, we have a few dikes to repair in the rice fields, then we can go ahead with the planting there, and we've cut back on the indigo this year. I already told Beau the market's slack."

"He said as much," remarked Rebel. "But here . . ."—she glanced at Heather—"I imagine you're anxious to see Lizette. I'll send one of the servants for her. I'm sure the baby'll be born just as well without her assistance. Hizzie's there, and our servant Liza. Between the two of them they've helped bring every baby on Tonnerre into the world, including Lizette. But come. If you want, you can go along to fetch Lizette. I'm sure it'll be all right, won't it, Mother?" she asked.

Loedicia glanced over at Roth, who nodded lightly. "I guess it'll be all right," she answered.

Rebel motioned for Heather to follow her as she called for one of the servants, and before Heather could even attempt a protest, she was headed out the back door onto the terrace and across the lawn toward a gravel road that led to the small cluster of cabins that housed the slaves, a young black girl of about her same age leading the way.

Between the house servants and field hands, there were a little over fifty blacks at Tonnerre. Some twenty were freed slaves who had stayed on to make Tonnerre their home, including the big Watusi Aaron; Hizzie, who had been Cole's wet nurse when he was a baby and helped take care of Lizette when she was born; Liza, who did the cooking; and her husband, Job, who unofficially ran the place whenever Beau wasn't around. The rest would have the same choice eventually. Some would go, some stay, but in the meantime they were all a part of Tonnerre. The young woman leading Heather was one of the slaves. Her name was Pretty, and she'd been bought four years before and only had a short time more to work for her freedom.

As they neared some of the small white cabins, at the end of a field to the left of the house, Heather saw a few elderly women milling about, some small children playing, and a few young women in various stages of pregnancy lounging on the doorsteps. But near one cabin, more people than usual were assembled. Heather glanced at the young black woman who was leading the way. "Is that the cabin?" she asked, motioning toward the small cabin set back beneath a large oak tree.

"Yes, ma'am," the girl said, then stopped suddenly as the door opened and Lizette came out, wiping her hands on a stained towel. The front of her pink dress was spotted here and there and dark stains streaked it, but her face was wreathed in triumph, her eyes aglow. "I think we're too late to watch the birthing, though," the girl went on. "There's Miss Lizette now."

Lizette sighed as she stepped from the neat little cabin. The wonder of what they'd just accomplished was still with her, and for a moment the fact that Heather was standing staring at her didn't register. Then suddenly she smiled, pleased, and lifted a hand in greeting.

"Well, hello," she said exuberantly, striding briskly toward her cousin. "Were you looking for me?"

Heather, slightly shocked by Lizette's appearance, was hesitant. "Your mother said it'd be all right to come down."

"Why not?" she answered, smiling. "You should see the baby, Heather," she said affectionately. "He's so tiny, and he's got big brown eyes." She straightened proudly. "Hizzie and Liza let me help, and I even cut and tied the cord."

"Cut and tied the cord?" Heather frowned. "What cord?"

Lizette paused, standing motionless for a minute, staring at her cousin, then twisted the towel in her hands. "Heather," she asked, scowling, "don't you know what happens when a baby's born?"

Heather blushed, but couldn't answer.

"You don't, do you?" Lizette insisted, and Heather finally whispered:

"No."

Lizette rolled her eyes, "Oh, mercy, where's your mother been all these years?" she asked irritably. "Why, you're going to be eighteen in September. What was she going to do, wait until you got married and ended up pregnant before letting you know what it's all about?"

"Please, Lizette," said Heather self-consciously, not liking her ignorance to be known by the servants, who were standing around watching. "It was something we just never discussed. There just didn't seem to be any need."

Lizette sighed, exhaling. "No wonder you were so upset about your father and . . . Oh, dear, you and I do have to do some talking, Heather," she urged, and turned to Hizzie. "Go up to the house and tell Mother Carrie had a boy," she instructed her old nurse. "And tell her Heather and I took a short walk to the river. I want to show her the gardens."

Hizzie eyed Lizette skeptically, not quite certain she should leave the two girls alone.

"Go on, Hizzie," Lizette ordered stubbornly. "And take Pretty with you," she said, glancing at the young black girl who had escorted Heather out to the cabins.

Hizzie frowned irritably but motioned toward the young girl, and Heather and Lizette watched them disappear up the gravel drive toward the house.

"First of all," said Lizette, looking her cousin over carefully, "have you ever seen a newborn baby?"

"No."

"Then I think we'll start there." She grabbed Heather's arm, tucking her own through her cousin's elbow, and headed her for the small white cabin where the young slave girl lay cuddling her newborn baby.

Half an hour later the two girls sat on the bank overlooking the river, watching sunlight dapple the water with gold, both silent for a long time; then slowly Heather's head turned and she studied her young cousin.

Lizette's knees were drawn up and she was hugging them, her head resting on them as she stared back at Heather. "You don't believe me, do you?"

Heather licked her lips, then bit her upper lip nervously. "I don't know."

"It's true," Lizette answered her. "But it's not horrible and ugly, or to be laughed and giggled over like your friends have done. It's a beautiful time for both people, at least it should be."

"I don't understand," complained Heather, bewildered. "If it's so wonderful, then why do most people refuse to talk about it, and act like it's wicked and dirty?"

"Because for some people it is." Lizette straightened and gazed toward the river, trying to think of the best way to explain it. So far she'd been doing quite well; she didn't want to spoil it now. "How can I tell you?" she said, turning once more to Heather. "I guess the best way is by example. Let's face it, there are some men you'd find very repulsive to have to kiss, right?"

Heather nodded, "Yes."

"Well, it's the same way with making love. If a man tried to make love to you, and you didn't want him to, for any number of reasons, mostly because you didn't care a fig for him, or thought he was repulsive, then it'd be ugly and horrible. You'd hate every minute if it did happen. And if a man forces a woman to do it with him when she doesn't want to and threatens to hurt her if she doesn't, that's rape and that is ugly and wicked. And when people use it as an entertainment or cheapen it like the girls who sell themselves for men to use without doing it for love, then they make it dirty and degrading. But for a man and a woman who are truly in love and who want each other, it's as natural as eating or sleeping."

"Did your mother tell you about it?" asked Heather.

Lizette smiled wistfully. "In a way. She sort of let me learn little by little as I grew up, by watching the animals, then filling in the answers whenever I had a question. You see, I guess our family is different than most. I know if the other mothers in Port Royal or Beaufort knew I'd helped with Carrie's birthing, they'd be mortified. But Mother said it's good for me to know. When she was a girl she helped Grandmother Dicia when Indian babies were born, and she helped her father and mother both patching up the wounded after Indian attacks. She said a person can never learn too much about helping others, and my father's really a stickler about it. He said no daughter of his is going to grow up ignorant and useless for nothing else but having babies." She eyed her cousin firmly. "Now do you know why being born out of wedlock doesn't really have to be that tragic and why Grandma Dicia was enjoying herself when you happened to eavesdrop on her and Grandfather in the library?"

"Yes," Heather answered slowly.

Lizette frowned. "Then why are you looking so puzzled?"

Heather's face turned crimson and her eyes fell before Lizette's steady gaze. "It's probably silly, I know, and I probably don't even have any right to even ask it, but . . ."

"But what?"

Her blush deepened as she timidly asked, "Have you ever done it, Lizette?"

Lizette held her breath; then her eyes darkened. "Lord, no!" she exclaimed truthfully. "It's not just something to be taken lightly," she said, hoping she had not gone too far with her easy assessment of the whole thing. "Even though it's a wonderful thing between people who love each other, it's such an intense, intimate relationship that it should never be done lightly, without thinking of the consequences, because Mother said once done it can never be undone, and society frowns on doing it outside of marriage. Besides," she said, winking impishly, "I've never found anyone I'd like to do it with yet." She stood up. "Ready to go to the house now and get something to eat?" she asked. "I'm famished."

Heather stood up slowly and glanced over at her younger cousin. There were still a few things that puzzled her, but she decided it'd probably be best to sort out everything she had just learned before getting in any deeper. She nodded, and they headed back toward the house.

Lizette had to change her dress before lunch, and the conversation while she was changing was full of speculation about the forthcoming ball and about their escapade earlier in the week. Heather was surprised to learn that Lizette's punishment consisted of spending the day after their sojourn in town doing all the mending that was stacked up in the sewing room.

"I thought the servants did that," said Heather.

Lizette laughed. "They usually do, but Father always looks around to see what'll keep me busy the longest and punishes me by making me do it when I get in trouble." She giggled infectiously. "Once I had to scrub the ballroom floor on my hands and knees, and my knees were so sore when I was through that I couldn't even kneel in church that Sunday."

"And you don't mind at all doing the servants' work?"

"Mind? Certainly I mind, but Father thinks it's the greatest punishment in the world because he knows I hate work."

Heather watched her pull on a dress of pale blue watered silk with leg-o'-mutton sleeves, white lace edging them, and a big flounce of lace around the scooped neckline. What a strange punishment! Whenever she had done something wrong she was always just scolded and sent to her room. Her new relatives were certainly unorthodox.

They joined the rest of the family on the terrace, and it was during their brief luncheon that Lizette discovered that her parents had given their permission for her to spend a few days at the Chateau. So after lunch she changed again, this time donning her red velvet riding habit, then packed some clothes with her personal maid Pretty's help, and the small trunk was sent on ahead to the Chateau by buggy.

When the luncheon was over and Lizette was ready, Rebel and Beau stood on the veranda beneath the large white columns and watched the four riders moving down the drive, hoping all the while that Lizette wouldn't drag Heather with her into any more trouble.

Heather sat sedately on her horse, glancing over now and then to Lizette riding beside her and admired the contrast of her red riding habit against the soft gold beige of her mount. She had never seen a horse like it before. Not as sleek and shiny as her Jezebel, but perfect for her dark-haired cousin.

Lizette felt Heather's eyes on her and glanced over, reining her horse closer to her cousin. "Remember the horse race I was telling you about the other day?"

Heather nodded.

"Would you like to go?"

She frowned. "How?"

Lizette winked. "Watch this." She dug her horse in the ribs and pulled up close to her grandparents. "I thought you were going to go to the races at Palmerston Grove today, Grandfather."

"I was, but then decided a ride to Tonnerre would be more enjoyable," he answered.

She was undaunted. "But I thought you had horses running."

"I do. Heath and a couple of the boys from the stable were going to take them over this afternoon, after they quit in the field. They should be there by now."

"And you wouldn't like to go?"

Loedicia glanced over at Roth, then back to her granddaughter, and had a terrible time keeping a smile from forming. "I think Lizette's trying to tell us something, Roth," she said pertly, and Roth's eyes crinkled as he too tried to keep a straight face.

He looked at Lizette. "I suppose you want to go to the races."

Her eyes faltered innocently. "Well, I do think it's a shame you have to miss them . . . and since we're with you already, I don't see how it would hurt if we just happened to ride over with you."

"Even though you know it isn't exactly the thing for a lady to do?"

"Oh, pooh," said Lizette, her lower lip puffing into a pout. "I'm so tired of hearing what ladies are and aren't supposed to do. I know Grandmother's been to the races already, haven't you?" she asked abruptly, and Loedicia fought her smile even harder.

"She has you there, dear," Dicia pointed out to Roth. "I have been to the races. Of course, I've done a few other things the ladies in Port Royal have frowned on, too." She glanced back at Lizette. "But that's no reason for my granddaughter to follow in my footsteps."

"Oh, Grandmother, please," Lizette pleaded. "All they do is bet on horses and yell for one of them to win. What's so horrible about that? What do they do that's so awful a lady isn't supposed to see it?"

Loedicia eased her mount, slowing him so she was beside Lizette. "It isn't what they do, dear, it's just that it's always been just for the men."

"Why?"

Loedicia shrugged. "Who knows? Maybe because the language they use is a little coarse, or because it gives them a chance to get away from the women."

"But there are some women there. I know, I've heard talk."

"Yes, dear, but the women who accompany the men to the races are not usually considered ladies."

"But you went! And Mother goes too."

"We're married women, you're young girls."

"But if we were with our grandparents. How could Heather and I be any more respectable than that?"

Loedicia glanced ahead to where Roth was. She knew he was listening and she had a feeling from the lift of his shoulders what he was thinking. "Roth?" she asked, moving up next to him again. "What do you think?"

He glanced over at her knowingly. "I have a feeling that if we don't take them to see the races today they're going to make sure they get to see them one way or another before the season's over, and I hate to think what might happen if they go on their own."

Lizette looked over at Heather and winked again so her grandparents wouldn't see. Heather had to give her credit, she was certainly adept at getting her own way.

With the decision made, they turned onto the road to Beaufort at the next crossroad. The Palmer plantation, Palmerston Grove, was on the main road to town, and since Everett Palmer and his two sons, Carl and DeWitt, had a penchant for placing a bet, it had become the official gathering place of some of the fastest horses in the territory. The races were always held on the first Saturday of every month from March through October, and were attended by most of the local gentry.

There was an old exercise ring about a mile from the main plantation house; the Palmers had opened it up years before to their friends who wanted to settle arguments about whose horse was the fastest. The idea had slowly expanded, until now not only planters enjoyed the once-a-month affair, but men occasionally came from as far away as Charleston with the hopes of having a winning horse. Betting often ran heavy, and men had been known to lose near fortunes, yet they still came.

Sometime later, as the four riders pulled off the dusty road and cantered up the lane toward the clearing where the races were being held, Heather's stomach began to tighten nervously. Roth had said Heath was bringing a couple of horses over to race. What would he say when he saw her there? She'd just die of humiliation if he became angry and yelled at her in front of all these people.

Men were everywhere, scurrying about, tending to their

horses, placing bets. Occasionally she'd catch a glimpse of a woman in the crowd, but since she still hadn't met many ladies who lived in the area, she had no idea whether they were respectable ladies or the other kind. And now, since her long talk with Lizette, she finally had an insight to what being the other kind of woman meant. She blushed self-consciously at the thought.

Roth motioned for them to follow and stay close as he rode his gray stallion over to where all the horses and carriages were tethered. He reined up, dismounted, hitched his horse to the long wooden rail that had been erected for that purpose, and turned to the ladies, helping each of them to dismount.

Heather gazed around, taking in the overall scene. There was a buckboard close to the exercise ring, with kegs of beer, cider, and rum for them to quench their thirst, and off toward the woods, small narrow buildings had been erected, with footpaths leading discreetly to them. Everything for the men's convenience. But there was no way to keep down the dust, and as she glanced toward where the crowd was, a cloud of it spiraled into the air and shouts exploded from the crowd as the thunder of hooves mingled with it.

"They have elimination races all day," Roth said as they turned from the hitching rail and began moving toward the crowd. "Betting is usually light on most of them until the last few races."

Loedicia watched both girls closely. How curious, she thought. Lizette's eyes were taking everything in greedily, studying her surroundings intensely to make certain she didn't miss a thing, but Heather's eyes only skimmed the crowd, stopping hesitantly now and then on something that caught her interest. Yet both girls seemed to be excited. They probably shouldn't have brought them, but then, Loedicia never did think the tradition banning women from the Palmerston races was a fair one. She and Rebel had often broken it because of their love for horses. There were a few other women who had courageously joined their husbands over the years, but the majority, under direct orders from their domineering men, stayed away. Young men courting never brought their fiancées. It just wasn't the thing to do. Society! Loedicia almost smiled to herself as she gazed around. How easily most men broke its rules and still stayed gentlemen, and how quickly a woman was disgraced when she broke the same rules.

"Look, isn't that Mr. Kolter?" asked Lizette as she nodded toward a group of men at the edge of the crowd.

Roth glanced over and smiled. "It's Rand, all right. Since Bain's been home, I suppose he's talked his father into watching him ride that new horse he brought with him. I hear he has a black Morgan that's really fast."

They wandered toward the small group of men congregated around a sleek black stallion with not a white marking on him. Heather glanced ahead, catching a glimpse of Bain Kolter, who was flexing his strong hands across the mount's head, trying to keep him calm in the noise from the crowd. Next to Bain and at about the same height stood a solid man in his late fifties, and Heather could see where Bain got his looks. Randolph Kolter had dark brown hair with chestnut and gold highlights running through it, gray visible only at the temples, but his slate-gray eyes were softer and more welcoming than his son's, the smile lines about his generous mouth deep, the few extra pounds he carried distributed well. He was an attractive man for his age and readily grinned as he glanced up and saw the Chapmans.

"Roth, Loedicia, I thought Heath said you weren't coming," he exclaimed.

"Changed my mind," Roth said. Then he glanced around. "Where's Heath?"

Rand nodded with his head toward the rail that ran along the side of the track partway, to where Heath and some other men were standing. They were leaning halfway across the rail, and Heath, whose eyes were glued to a chestnut mare in the lead, was yelling for the black boy on the mare to keep his head down and give her rein.

"I suppose the betting's heavier than usual today, since it's the first time out this spring," said Roth as he watched Heath for a few minutes longer.

"Not just that," said Rand. "With the war over now, they feel like there's something to celebrate, and the drinking's a bit heavier too." He glanced at Loedicia. "You may have picked a poor day to come, Loedicia," he offered helpfully. "The men's spirits are running a bit high. There aren't too many other women here, either, and sometimes the men don't exactly conduct themselves like gentlemen, you know." He glanced behind her and suddenly realized Lizette and Heather were along. "My God, I didn't notice you brought them," he said, surprised.

Roth straightened solidly, his dark eyes steady on Rand

Kolter. "I figured since they were quite intent on discovering just what went on at the races, it'd be safer, after their excursion the other day with Felicia, that we bring them ourselves. That way they're not as apt to get into anything they can't get out of graciously."

Rand frowned. "I suppose you're right," he said thoughtfully, then shook his head. "But I certainly can't figure out young girls today. Madeline would never have thought of doing some of the things Felicia does when she was her age. Sometimes it's frightening."

"I think it's mostly just curiosity, Rand," said Loedicia. "I know I was forever asking questions and wanting to know about everything when I was their age." She glanced over at the girls. "We'll keep our eyes on them today, don't worry. I'm sure everything'll be fine. By the way," she said, looking back to Rand Kolter, "you and Madeline are coming to the ball and bringing the family, I hope," and they began discussing the impending birthday ball.

Heather glanced off toward her father, wondering what he was going to think when he realized she was here; then she was brought up short as a voice over her left shoulder interrupted her thoughts.

"When I saw the sun on that lovely red hair, I knew I couldn't be mistaken and that it definitely had to be you," said Witt Palmer, and Heather flushed as his hazel eyes caught hers, holding them intently. "Welcome to Palmerston, Miss . . . Have you decided which it's going to be—Chapman or McGill?"

Heather's blush deepened. "Chapman will do," she answered softly. "And thank you for the welcome, although I'm not quite certain what I'm doing here," she said.

Lizette, beside her, who had also turned at the sound of DeWitt's voice, laughed softly. "Don't take her seriously, Witt," she said, noting the blush on Heather's face. "She wanted to know what was going on just as much as I did."

Witt smiled but didn't take his eyes from Heather's face. "I don't blame her," he said softly. "And if she'll let me, I'd like to take her to an advantageous spot where she can see exactly what's going on," and he pointed to one end of the area where a small stand was built, and two men, one with reddish-blond hair, the other quite gray, seemed to be looking over the heads of the crowd. They were sitting on a bench on top the platform, and above them a roof had been built to ward off the sun. The platform was just high enough so they could see everything that was going on, and as she watched, a stocky black slave brought them each a mug of ale, then stood aside waiting in case either man required anything further.

Heather stared at both men. The family resemblance was unmistakable; it had to be DeWitt's brother and his father.

"I think I'd rather stay with my grandparents," she answered quickly. For some reason, the thought of sitting up above the crowd with the Palmers didn't appeal to her.

"Then do you mind if I join you?" he asked.

"You'll have to ask my grandparents," she answered, and at that moment Loedicia turned, realizing DeWitt was there.

"Ask us what, dear?" she asked, ending her conversation with Rand Kolter.

"I've asked your granddaughter if I might join her and the rest of you while you're here," DeWitt said quickly. "You and Mr. Chapman don't mind, do you?"

Loedicia glanced at Heather but was unable to read in her eyes whether she wanted the young man to join them or not. "It's up to Heather," she said congenially.

Heather wasn't really sure. DeWitt seemed nice enough from the little she'd talked to him, but it was hard to get to know a person in so short a time. Maybe letting him spend the afternoon with them was a good idea. She looked up at DeWitt, her violet eyes curious. "If he really wants to, it's all right with me," she said, and her decision brought a smile to his face, softening his rather sharp features.

Lizette, who had lost interest in DeWitt's arrival rather quickly, reached a hand out to stroke the soft velvety nose of the coal-black horse Bain was rubbing down very gently. "He's beautiful, Bain, what's his name?" she asked.

Bain's hand stroked his flank, and she saw the horse's withers vibrate, muscles rippling beneath the sleek hide. "I call him Amigo."

She eyed him skeptically. "A Morgan horse with a Spanish name?" she questioned.

He stared at her, unsmiling. "I bought him from a Spaniard in the Florida territories. The name seemed to fit."

"That's strange," she said, watching him closely. "Father had my horse shipped here special from Spain—an old friend of his raises them. He has a Spanish name too, Diablo."

Bain's eyes were steady on hers as he continued to stroke his mount. "I saw you ride up," he said. "He's a beautiful horse, but then, we see few like him around here, so I imagine when you ride him, all heads turn."

For once Lizette blushed. "That's not why I ride him," she snapped defensively. "He was a Christmas gift from my father because he knows how I love horses. I ride him because he's the fastest horse in South Carolina and I love to ride a fast horse."

This time a slight smile began to play about the corners of Bain's mouth, and his eyes challenged her. "He *was* the fastest horse in South Carolina," he drawled lazily. "Until I arrived with Amigo."

"This?" she asked, feigning surprise. "You're trying to tell me that this horse will beat my Diablo?"

"Hands down."

Her eyes sparked, picking up his challenge. "Not on your life! Why, Diablo would leave him at the gate."

"Prove it!"

She stared at him hard, then lowered her voice. "I can't race him here," she said irritably. "You know very well they wouldn't let me."

"Then find someone else to ride him."

She shook her head. "No, if he races, I ride him."

"Then I guess we'll never know, will we?" he said smugly, but she had an idea.

"Wait," she half-whispered, and moved closer, pretending to inspect the horse's sleek black coat and the fancy tooled-leather Spanish saddle on his back. "I have an idea," she said. "Do you know where that small pond is on the southern tip of the Chateau? The one near the swamp where they built the wooden bridge?"

"I haven't been there for some time, but I think I could find it. Why?" he asked.

She took a deep breath, making sure her voice was barely a whisper. "I go riding there a lot when I stay with my grandparents. At one end of the pond there's an old road that leads all the way to the river. Weeds have grown up a little, but it's smooth and well over a mile long. I'm going riding tomorrow afternoon, and I'll meet you there between two and three o'clock and I'll prove Diablo's faster than your stallion."

His eyes studied her hard for a minute before he answered. "You're crazy," he said softly.

"I am not." She pursed her lips and dared him. "You're afraid!" she said.

His jaw set hard. What was it about this willful young girl that seemed to provoke him so? From the moment he'd seen her ride in on that fancy horse, he'd had a tight feeling that made him testy. "All right," he said, whispering back, knowing neither grandparent would approve of their escapade if they found out. "But why don't we make the challenge interesting? Shall we say a five-dollar wager?"

"Five?" she asked. "You don't have much faith in Amigo, do you? Let's make it ten."

"Ten it is," he said softly, and his eyes caught hers, holding them in a silent prison as he stared at her.

Lizette felt a warm glow as she looked deeply into Bain Kolter's dark gray eyes, suddenly realizing what she had done. But instead of fighting the feeling that was filling her, she let it spread through her, and with it came a warm tingle that flowed to her loins and made her knees weak. She wanted to cry out, but instead grabbed the cantle and horn on his fancy saddle and hung on to keep her knees from buckling, unaware that Bain too was feeling the effects of their encounter and trying to convince himself she was still only a child.

She recovered quickly and wrenched her eyes from his, turning toward the others, joining in the conversation, trying to act nonchalant and forget part of what had just passed between her and Bain. It was silliness, really. After all, he was only Felicia's brother. The way she had felt couldn't have had anything to do with him. It was probably just coincidence that she'd been looking into his eyes at the time. It had probably only been something she had eaten, or maybe it was nearer that time of the month than she had realized. It couldn't have had anything to do with Bain, she just knew it couldn't, and with that thought in mind she dismissed the whole affair from her mind and concentrated harder on other things going on around her.

The afternoon went well, although there were a few people who showed their shock at the girls' presence. But Loedicia and Roth's close supervision of them saved any talk of scandal, and before long they were all enthusiastically enthralled by the proceedings. As the elimination races went on and on, and Bain won every race he entered, Lizette began to wonder if maybe he had been right after all about his horse's superior abilities. When the day's racing was over, with Bain's small black stallion Amigo copping all honors as the fastest horse, she began to have second thoughts. But then, none of them had seen Diablo run yet. That's why he was named Diablo, because he ran like the devil. No, she wouldn't worry. When the races were over and she rode away from the race grounds on her flaxen-maned palomino, looking back toward where the men were all still gathered around Amigo and congratulating his owner, she knew that tomorrow afternoon Bain Kolter was going to be in for a big surprise.

4

"But you have to come with me," Lizette begged Heather early the next afternoon. "I can't go out there all by myself."

"Why not? You do any other time. You even said so."

"But that's different," Lizette insisted. "Bain Kolter was never waiting out there before."

Heather frowned. "But we're only going to get in trouble again," she said, worried. "And your mother said if you got in any more trouble you wouldn't be able to go to the birthday ball."

"Oh, pooh! She was only threatening. She didn't really mean it. Besides, she won't even know about this. No one will. And even if she did find out later, she wouldn't make me stay away from the ball, she'd find some other way to punish me." Lizette stood in front of Heather, who was sitting on the bed in her room, dressed in a pale green flowered muslin, refusing to put on her riding habit. "Now, come on," Lizette pleaded. "Don't let me down, please, Heather. It'll be fun and it's far enough away from the house." She straightened stubbornly, looking elegant in her crimson riding habit. "And if we should get caught, I'll take all the blame, telling them you had no idea what I had in mind. If you don't go, they won't let me go, and I have to go, I've got a ten-dollar wager."

"And I bet you don't even have the ten dollars, do you?"

"No, but then, I won't lose. And even if I did, I have some money up at Tonnerre. I just didn't bring it with me."

Heather sighed. "I wish I could understand you, Lizette," she said. "You don't seem to care if you get into trouble."

"It all depends on what you want to call trouble," said Lizette. "I'm only having fun, I'm not doing anything destructive or hurting anyone." Her green eyes glistened as she stared at her cousin. "Please, Heather?"

"All right!" Heather sighed again, defeated. "But we'd better not get in any trouble." She got up and walked to her closet, pulling out her dark green velvet riding habit.

It took her not quite half an hour to get out of her dainty green muslin and slip into the riding habit, pulling on her small black leather riding boots to complete the outfit, then fixing her hair back with a ribbon and putting the hat on with its plumed feather, a big hat pin holding it tight to her head.

"You're a dear, Heather," Lizette cooed appreciatively as they started down the stairs. Within minutes, Lizette on Diablo and Heather on the same tame mare she'd ridden the day before were headed down the drive that led to the slave quarters beneath the big moss-laden oak trees and on beyond it to the fields.

Lizette glanced over at her cousin as they rode along the narrow trail, scaring up an occasional small animal or frightened bird. There were times her new cousin tried her patience. Of course, she had to be understanding; after all, Heather had been raised to be a lady in every sense of the word. She might be as spirited as the rest of the clan and just as stubborn at times, but she hadn't been raised with the same outlook on life that had been handed down to Lizette from her grandparents and parents. She'd been raised like most young ladies of the day, to suppress her instincts and remember that there were certain things nice ladies didn't do. Oh, well, it'd take time, but Lizette was certain that eventually she'd pull Heather out of her reluctant attitude when it came to the unconventional.

It was almost three o'clock when they finally reached the small pond, and as Lizette expected, Bain was there waiting. Much to her surprise, DeWitt was with him.

"I hope you don't mind," Bain said as they rode up slowly and reined their horses in close, looking down at him. "I felt it only fair I have someone with me who's on my side, since I knew your cousin would be with you."

"I don't mind at all," said Lizette confidently. "It's all right with me if he watches you lose."

"Oh ho, aren't you cocky," said Bain, and glanced at DeWitt. "In case of a nose-to-nose, I expect your eyes to give the right decision," he said.

DeWitt nodded, then glanced up at Heather. "Here, let me help you down." He reached up.

Heather was a little reluctant at first, then let his hands circle her waist, lifting her from the sidesaddle, setting her on the ground. He stared down at her and she felt uneasy.

"We'll stand by that tree where we'll be in line with the road," he said, taking the reins of her horse and fastening them to a nearby bush where his own was tethered.

Lizette was still in the saddle and watched Bain start to mount his horse. Her voice stopped him. "What are you doing?" she asked, frowning.

He turned, one foot headed for the stirrup, and glanced back at her, putting his foot back on the ground as he did so. "What does it look like I'm doing?" he said. "You challenged me to a race. I was only getting ready to oblige."

She pursed her lips. "Well, I'm not ready yet," she said quickly.

He held the reins tight, staring at her. "You're on your horse, aren't you?"

"In the first place, I just got here and I'd like to give Diablo a few minutes' rest." She looked over at his horse. "After all, Amigo looks like he's had a good breather, and besides, I can't ride him like this."

"You can't . . . ? How do you intend to ride him?"

"If you'll help me down, I'll show you," she said.

Bain eyed her skeptically. What the hell was she up to? He ground-reined Amigo and walked over, lifting her easily from the sidesaddle.

"Thank you," she said as her feet hit the ground. His hands left her small waist and she straightened the skirt of her riding habit, then reached up under the crimson jacket and began to fumble with the hooks that held the skirt about her waist. With a deft twist she unhooked the last one, let go of the skirt, and it dropped to the ground as Bain stared, dumbfounded. Beneath her skirt she had on a pair of boy's pants tied at the waist with a narrow sash from one of her dresses, the legs tucked into her black riding boots. Without another thought, she stepped deftly away from the skirt, picked it up, and handed it to Bain, who stared at it in wonder.

Then, while he watched in awe, she reached up and began

unbuttoning the waistcoat to her habit, and as he shook his head in disbelief, she slipped it off to reveal a lightweight thin silk shirt that undoubtedly had belonged to her brother at one time.

"You intend to ride in those?" he asked incredulously, unaware that both Heather and Witt were also astounded by her attire.

She frowned at him, apparently unconcerned. "Why not?" she asked, glancing at his clothes as she snatched her skirt back from his hands and began folding it together neatly at the waist. "You certainly are dressed comfortably for riding."

He glanced down at his own clothes. She was right. He was wearing soft doeskin pants tucked into black top boots and had discarded his frock coat, hanging it in the crotch of a small tree at the side of the road, and the cotton shirt he had on was full-sleeved, open low at the throat, his cravat tossed atop his frock coat, with his hat resting neatly on top of the pile.

She looked him up and down knowingly, then walked over to the same tree, picked up his hat, deposited her crimson habit over his things, took off her plumed hat, balanced it on top of his, and set them back down gently in the crotch of the tree. Then she turned back toward her horse.

"Now what?" Bain asked as she started unfastening the saddle.

"You don't expect me to race you sidesaddle, I hope."

"But what'll you use for a saddle?"

"I don't need one."

"You intend to ride him bareback?"

"That's right."

He exhaled in surprise, then turned toward Heather and Witt, shrugging his shoulders. "Did you hear that one, Witt?" he asked.

"Should be interesting," Witt called over; then his eyes rested on Lizette. "Are you sure you know what you're doing?" he asked as she slipped the saddle from Diablo, grateful for Bain's sudden assistance as he helped her set it in the grass beside the road.

She straightened, ignoring Witt's remark, then walked back to Diablo and began smoothing the sleek golden horse, talking to him softly, nuzzling his nose as she stroked him. Turning, she once more faced Bain. "All right, now we'll start here. See that big willow?" she asked pointing about a quarter of a mile down the road to where it started to bend.

He nodded.

"We'll ride around the willow and head back. The first one past this point . . ." She picked up a stick, dragging it across the road, making a furrow in the dirt. "First one wins. Agreed?"

He glanced down the road, then eyed her warily. "You sure your fancy horse can make it?"

"Diablo's a palomino, and, yes, he can make it," she said. "You'll be eating my dust all the way."

He laughed. "Obnoxious child, aren't you?"

"I'm not a child!"

"Aren't you?" His eyes sifted over her attire, noticing the hard nipples pressed against the silk shirt. She was naked beneath it. Child? He began to wonder, then shoved the thought from his mind as she asked him to help her mount.

Reaching down, he put both hands together forming a pocket for her to put her foot in. She grabbed the reins and reached her foot up, letting him boost her onto the back of her horse; then he walked over to his own horse, flipped up the stirrups, and began to take off the saddle.

She squeezed her legs, putting pressure on her horse's sides, and nudged him forward, reining him around, moving over to where Bain was just setting his saddle aside.

"You're not," she said, surprised, but he smiled triumphantly.

"The lighter the horse, the faster it goes, so you know," he said. "I'm not that dumb. Bad enough I was suckered into riding against you. Already my horse is carrying more weight. If you think I'm going to make it worse by using a saddle, while you ride bareback, you're sadly mistaken."

She watched him walk over to his horse, grab the reins, give a hard leap, and land on his back. He straightened, smiling. "Ready?" he asked.

She nodded. "Ready."

Heather and DeWitt watched the pair line up their horses even with the furrow she'd marked in the dirt road. DeWitt stepped forward, took a handkerchief from his pocket, and held his arm up. "Ready, set, go!" he yelled, and as his arm dropped, waving the handkerchief, both horses broke their stance, leaping forward, heading down the road. Before they were even ten feet, Witt quickly grabbed another stick from the side of the road, reworked the furrow so that it was neat again, then eased back where he could watch their progress.

He was amazed. As he stared down the road, he saw both horses still side by side. He strolled over to where Heather was watching, still in shock over Lizette's bizarre change of clothing. "I think Bain's met his match," Witt said as they watched the horses racing down the old dirt road. "That girl not only can ride, she's got a hell of a horse to boot!" He leaned out away from her a little, watching down the road where the horses were just starting around the willow tree. They were still neck and neck.

He straightened again to make sure he was in a good spot to see them when they passed over the mark in the road.

Heather watched the riders come into view again and saw the determined look on Lizette's face. She was bent over, leaning close to her horse's mane, as if she were talking to him, her feet hugging his sides, and beside her Bain was just as determined. His body hugged his horse, mouth grim, jaws clenched beneath the clipped beard.

Heather held her breath as the deafening noise of the horses' hooves grew louder and the air seemed to vibrate with emotion.

Witt stood rooted to the spot he'd picked, eyes tensing as the pair drew near; then, as they careened over the finish line at full gallop, he felt a triumphant surge as Bain's Morgan nosed out the palomino by barely a few inches. He let out a shout as Bain pulled back, easing on the reins, letting his horse slow to a loping gait, Lizette, beside him, doing the same.

Lizette glanced over, anger filling her. She knew he'd taken those last few feet, and cursed her stupidity for underestimating the Morgan. The worst part of it was, she knew Diablo was capable of more speed. Her eyes were burning as she watched Bain rein his horse around, heading back to where DeWitt and Heather waited.

"Did I or did I not nose her out?" Bain asked Witt, and Lizette pursed her lips stubbornly as Witt answered:

"You did, friend. You certainly did."

"It was pure luck," said Lizette breathlessly, reining up abruptly beside Bain. "Another five feet and I'd have had you."

"But you didn't." Bain, breathing heavily, relaxed on the back of his horse. "I believe you owe me ten dollars," he said.

She grimaced. "You'll get your ten dollars."

"When?"

"I don't have it with me. It's up at Tonnerre."

His eyes pored over her. Her hair was damp with perspiration and curled tightly where it hit her forehead. He realized her body was also damp from sweat, as was his, and the thin silk shirt she had on was clinging outrageously to her skin. He glanced at DeWitt and saw his friend's eyes settle on the dark nipples plastered against the inside of Lizette's shirt, and anger began to well up inside him. His jaw tightened. "Let's take a slow ride this time to the willow and back to cool down," he said quickly. "All right with you?"

She nodded. "All right."

They moved off, and DeWitt smirked, then turned back to Heather. "They're going to cool the horses," he said.

She shook her head. "I don't know why Lizette does these things," she said.

His smirk had warmed to an engaging smile. "Because she's still a child," he said, then decided to make his play. "But you're not. The fact is, I was talking to your father yesterday. He said you'll be eighteen in September and he also said it wouldn't be out of place for me to invite you to go for a buggy ride some evening—that is, if you'd be willing."

She drew her eyes from the road where the couple on horseback were growing smaller as they rode farther away, and suddenly she realized she was being left alone with Witt. Her violet eyes lowered self-consciously; then she gazed up into his face. It wasn't that she didn't like him, it was just that she felt nothing when she looked at him. She just wasn't attracted to him. Not the way she'd been attracted to that new young man she'd met just before having to leave Columbia. He had made her feel warm and strange inside whenever he looked at her, and she wondered what might have happened between them if she could have stayed. Oh, well, maybe . . . Until someone else came along, she could try to be nice to DeWitt Palmer.

She smiled up at him. "If you'd really like," she said.

"I would definitely like," he replied. "I was going to ride over today and ask you, but when Bain told me about his bet with your cousin, I figured you'd probably come along."

"I almost didn't," she answered. "But I couldn't disappoint Lizette."

"I'm glad you didn't, because I've have been disappointed too," he said. He reached out and took her hand, caressing it affectionately between his. "Will tomorrow afternoon be all right?" he asked. "I could pick you up about two. We'll ride into Port Royal, I'll show you some of the sights, then bring you back in time for dinner."

"You're sure my father said it's all right?"

"I wouldn't have asked if he hadn't."

She sighed, trying to show a little enthusiasm. "All right,

then, two o'clock tomorrow." She drew her hand from his and wandered away from the old cypress tree, moving closer to the road, glancing in the direction Bain and Lizette had gone, wondering what Lizette was up to now. They had been gone quite some time.

Lizette jogged along silently, head up, feeling the cool breeze that blew in from the woods cooling her face; then she reached down and caught the front of her shirt, near the neck, fanning it to let in air. It had been sticking to her, and as she glanced down toward the front of her, a deep flush suddenly swept through her, turning her face to crimson.

Bain had a hard time holding back a smile as he watched her. "I see you finally realized why I got you away from there so fast," he drawled, half-amused.

"Why didn't you say something?"

"And bring more attention to it? As it was, DeWitt was enjoying the display far more than he should."

She tried to keep her torso turned from him. "My God, what you both must think!"

"I think you're a delightful child," Bain said, not really believing a word of what he was saying. He admitted to himself she wasn't full grown, but dammit, she wasn't really a child, either. She was somewhere in between, and it was embarrassing. "Still, I thought perhaps you'd appreciate getting away from Witt's prying eyes for a few minutes."

"You're terrible," she said, perturbed at the thought that he felt it was all right for him to see, his only concern being that Witt had seen it too.

"I know," he agreed.

She glanced over at him, making sure she kept on an angle as they moved slowly along, so she was almost having to look over her right shoulder. "Why did you agree to race Amigo today?" she asked suddenly.

His eyes darkened. "Hell, I don't know! Maybe because I never could refuse a challenge."

"Then it had nothing to do with me?"

"What do you mean?"

She flushed, turning away as his eyes seemed to devour her. "Never mind," she said softly, but he reached out and grabbed her horse's bridle, stopping him, bringing his own mount to a halt beside hers.

"Never mind? You asked me a question and I answered it. Now I'm asking you: what did you mean by what you said?"

Her blush deepened. Her back was still to him, yet she could feel his eyes on her. Why did they always do this to her? She felt so vulnerable. Ever since he'd come home from his wanderings she had been so unnaturally aware of him. She swallowed hard, took a deep breath, and slowly looked back at him, her eyes wavering, hesitant. "I . . . thought maybe . . ." She just couldn't say it. For the first time in her life Lizette was unable to put into words what she felt inside, especially in front of the man who was causing the distress she was in.

Bain suddenly felt sorry for Lizette. For all her brash willfulness, she was having a hard time coping with her emerging womanhood. As he stared at her, watching her emerald-green eyes staring back at him, aware of the way her hair tightened into ringlets about her face, and the sensuous curve of her back as she tensed, her full lips parting hesitantly, he felt a tingling sensation shoot through him.

"Don't say it!" he suddenly said, his voice harsh, interrupting her. "I had no right to ask for an answer."

Relief shone in her eyes, and he sighed.

"We'd better ride back," he added more coolly. "I don't want Witt to get the wrong idea."

Tears welled up in her eyes, but he didn't see them as he let go of her horse's bridle. She straightened, making sure the warm afternoon air had dried her shirt enough so it was no longer transparent. "Yes, we'd better get back," she agreed. "I wouldn't want to get Heather in trouble. I promised her nobody would find out about this afternoon."

"They won't," he said as they turned their horses back the way they had come. "At least not from me."

"What about Witt?"

"I'll handle Witt."

"Thank you," she said self-consciously, and as they rode back to where Heather and DeWitt were waiting, Lizette had a feeling that this was an afternoon she was going to be a long time forgetting.

Lizette's ride back to the house with Heather was a rather quiet one, and Heather was surprised to see Lizette so subdued. "What happened between you and Bain Kolter?" she asked after a while.

Lizette shook her head. "Nothing," she answered softly. "I lost, that's all."

Heather stared at her for a minute, then shrugged. Well, she couldn't force Lizette to confide in her, so until she did, there wasn't much to do except to try to make her forget what was bothering her, so she confided in Lizette instead, telling her about DeWitt's offer to go buggy riding Monday afternoon.

For the rest of the week Lizette stayed rather reticent and to Heather's surprise didn't once think up something that could possibly get them into trouble. They played games together, went riding again, to the pond more often than not, where Lizette would stand for a long time staring into the water before deciding to go home. The exuberant joy of youth that had been there only a few days before had suddenly been replaced by a pensive melancholy attitude that everyone at the Chateau began to notice, until Loedicia finally asked her if she was homesick, since DeWitt was now coming over most afternoons and some evenings and Heather didn't need her to keep her company as much as she had before.

But Lizette assured them she was all right, so she stayed the full week, finally going home on Sunday afternoon as planned.

The next week went quickly and Rebel was so caught up in preparations for the forthcoming ball that she didn't notice the subtle change in Lizette. Once home, Lizette swung back into being much her old self, helping out with the slaves when needed, going over the preparations with her mother, trying to keep herself busy so she didn't have time to think. It was only when she went riding that the melancholy mood would come back. Puzzled herself by her reaction, suspecting the reason, yet trying to ignore it, she was in a constant turmoil.

The ball was to be on Monday, March 13, when spring was at its most beautiful. The Saturday before, Lizette woke up restless. It was extremely hot by early afternoon, and when she left the house she walked through the formal gardens, then left them behind, moving off away from the house toward a small branch of the river that flowed inland, where Cole and his friends had built a log dam to make the water deep enough for swimming. She suddenly felt her old self again. The lethargic melancholy she had felt so often the past two weeks had all but disappeared.

The air smelled sweet and clean, the fields earthy, and birds sang from every tree along the way. She hummed to herself, gazing at everything around her with a new vigor, as if seeing it all again for the first time. The wild honeysuckle along the fences, Spanish moss hanging from the trees, wildflowers close enough to pick and smell, squirrels and rabbits running at her approach. The whole world seemed to be in tune this morning.

She sighed, reaching the old swimming hole, and dropped to the soft grass on its banks and just sat there for a long time feeling the heat of the sun on her face. It was hot, really too hot, and the longer she sat there, the more uncomfortable she became. Perspiration trickled beneath her clothes, making them stick to her, and she stared at the water. Cole had taught her how to swim, but it had been a long time since she had gone in, because he'd always cautioned her never to swim alone. Since he was gone there'd been no one else to swim with, so she hadn't. But now? She wondered. What would it hurt?

She took a deep breath, stood up, and within minutes had shed her outer clothes, leaving on only her chemise and lace-trimmed drawers.

The grass felt good beneath her bare feet. A smile brightened her face and she moved slowly, expectantly toward the water. Should she wade in or just stand on the bank and dive as she'd seen Cole do so many times?

For some reason, the past two weeks had made her a little more cautious, so instead of diving in off the bank, she moved to the upper end of the glistening pool of water, where she could see the gravelly bottom, and stepped in. It was cold, brisk, and invigorating, and she inhaled sharply as the water lapped at her ankles, then moved up her legs as she walked farther out away from the bank toward the deeper end.

When the water reached her waist, she stood for a minute, getting more used to it; then, the heat of the sun on her face and shoulders scorching, she leaned over, gliding into the water on her stomach, and took long even strokes, coming to a stop on the other side of the small body of water, where, as she stood up, putting her feet on the bottom, the water reached to her shoulders.

She shivered slightly and took a deep breath. When summer truly came, the water would be warmer, but now it still held the chill of winter. She ducked down until her shoulders were covered again, away from the heat of the sun, and luxuriated in the coolness, her body feeling light and unrestricted beneath the surface. The pool of water was some fifty feet wide, and she glanced across to where her pile of clothes lay on the bank. No wonder Cole had always loved to come here. It was so peaceful and isolated, only the gentle sound of the birds to break the quiet, or the occasional chatter of a squirrel mixing with the splash of the water as it cascaded over the small dam.

She was just beginning to ease forward to start swimming toward the bank where her clothes lay when she saw a slight movement in the grass near the edge of the water. She froze, senses alert, and stared for a long hard moment. Then her eyes widened, transfixed, as a huge snake, some five or six feet long, slithered through the low grass and weeds and slipped into the water so easily it barely made a ripple.

She held her breath as she watched its flat head ascend slightly above the surface of the water, and it began to circle, swimming leisurely, as if looking for something.

Slowly, every movement deliberate, every gesture carefully timed, Lizette backed away from the cottonmouth, hoping he hadn't seen her and praying he wouldn't. She was far enough away, and there was every chance he hadn't, but with each forward thrust he made in the water he seemed to be coming closer. Fear coursed through her and she continued to back up slowly, the water deepening as she neared the far end of the pool near the dam, where some brier bushes hung down at the edge of the water, thick and green. They were so heavy with leaves the tips sank below its surface. With a swift gliding motion, her toes barely touching bottom to keep her head above water, she pushed herself back into the bushes, hoping to blend in with the leaves, and stood motionless, barely breathing, as the snake loomed nearer.

He moved gracefully through the water, circling, moving in straight lines, changing course now and then as if he had all the time in the world, while Lizette watched helplessly, afraid to move, afraid to breathe for fear he'd detect her and come to investigate. Her heart was in her throat, her insides shaking, as he just swam slowly through the water, hesitating occasionally with his head high and alert, as if he sensed something was amiss.

Then finally, just when she was certain she couldn't bear standing on tiptoe in the water any longer without moving, the poisonous cottonmouth gave one last wide sweep of the place and moved upriver, swimming along the edge of the bank in the shallow water, until he was lost from sight.

Lizette watched him disappear, and an agonized sigh escaped her lips as she began to breathe normally again. She'd been holding her hands pressed against her chest, and now she flexed her fingers, lifting her hands from beneath the water as her legs began to move and she started to leave her hiding place. Her only thought now was to reach the bank again and pull herself from the water before another snake might appear. But as she started to move forward, she was jerked back unexpectedly, her head snapping, and she realized her hair was caught in the briers she had backed into.

Quickly pulling her body back to balance herself once more on the tip of the river bottom, she reached up and began trying to untangle it. Her hair was long, thick, and very curly, and her fingers worked with it deftly, pulling, tugging, unwinding. But the more she tried to free it, the worse it seemed to get. Her fingers began to fumble nervously. My lord, what was the matter? Why couldn't she get loose? The briers were part of an old blackberry patch, the branches thick, covered with thorns, and they bit into her flesh cruelly as she tried to pull her hair from their grasp.

She was getting nowhere. The briers were holding her fast, with thick curling strands of hair wound about them, and the longer she fought them, the more desperate she became. As she tugged and pulled, she kept remembering the snake, and the way his sleek body slithered silently through the water, knowing full well he could come back at any moment.

Tears filled her eyes, and she swallowed hard. Her legs were beginning to ache, the toes rigid as they barely touched the soft, muddy bottom, and her neck was getting a kink in it from its awkward position. She couldn't even move her head from side to side anymore, the hair was so tightly held. The more she had tried to free it, the more the thorns had captured it, until now the brier branches were like a dozen strong fingers holding her in their viselike grip.

Panic seized her and she began to struggle harder, fighting the briers and the water. She had to get out of here. The scratches and cuts on her fingers didn't matter anymore. Her scalp hurt, smarting where the hair pulled, yet it held fast.

She stopped struggling against it for a minute and swallowed hard, then breathed heavily, trying to regain strength for another try. Her mouth tightened grimly, and once more she began her battle, grappling with the curly black hair, trying to wrest it free. But it was hopelessly entangled in the brier bushes and there was no way she was going to free it by herself. Oh, God!

Her eyes closed and she pursed her lips, toes digging into the soft river bottom. She tried to collect her thoughts and stay calm, but her heart was pounding frantically. What was she to do?

For over an hour she hung in the water, suspended by her hair, her toes barely touching the bottom to relieve the pull on her scalp, and over and over again she tried to tear her hair loose. It was no use. At any moment she knew that same snake or even another could invade the water again and she'd be lost. She prayed and cried and yelled and cursed, until, now, exhausted, sobbing softly, she was certain she was going to die here in this watery grave where she wouldn't even be found for months.

Suddenly, as she was trying to get up the strength to make one last effort to free herself, she froze, listening, fists clenched as a new sound caught her ears. It wasn't the birds, or an animal running through the underbrush, or even the trickle of the water as it leaped over the rocks upstream or crashed unhampered over the top of the dam close beside her. It was a soft, low whistle accompanied by the slow, walking gait of a horse on the path that led from the woods.

She wrenched her head around, almost tearing the hair from her scalp to get into a position where she could see who it was. The path wasn't far from the bank where her clothes were, and as she watched anxiously, her stomach tightened, her heart beginning to pound again as Bain Kolter rode out of the woods, reining Amigo to a halt, and she saw him gaze about, frowning.

The small clearing was deadly quiet and for some reason it made Bain uneasy. He held the rein on Amigo tight as his eyes flickered first over the pile of clothes a few feet from the water, then moved into the water itself, yet there was no sign of Lizette or anyone else. For a second or two he was hesitant; then suddenly a deep smile tilted the corners of his mouth. He relaxed in the saddle, resting his hands nonchalantly in front of him, and called out, "You can't hide forever, you know, Lizette. You ought to know better than to swim in the altogether."

Lizette, staring at him from her brier prison, was aghast. He thought she was hiding from him because she'd been swimming in the nude. If she wasn't so upset, she'd give him a thing or two to think about, but common sense told her he might be the only human being who'd venture this far for a while, and she'd better take advantage of it, so she swallowed the angry pride that was gnawing at her, and, relieved at the thought of being rescued, answered, her voice breaking tremulously.

"Help! Help me! Oh, Bain, please," she pleaded, half-crying. "Help!"

Bain straightened, cocking his head, trying to ascertain where her voice was coming from. Unable to see her because she was in the shade from the trees on the opposite bank, he thought at first she was trying to play some sort of trick on him. But when her voice, sounding even more pathetic, begged him again, he slid from his horse, ground-reined him, raised a hand over his eyes to shade them from the sun, and began to scan the pool of water. "Where are you?" he shouted, frowning anxiously.

"Here!" Lizette raised her hands and splashed the water.

As Bain's eyes focused on her, he cursed. "My God!" He began tearing off his clothes, stripping hurriedly until he had on only his pants, then he plunged into the water without a second thought, long strokes bringing him quickly to her side.

He stood up next to her, the water barely to the middle of his bare chest, and grimaced as he took a closer look at her hair. From the far bank he had realized it was caught, but he hadn't imagined it was quite this bad. Lines creased his forehead as he drew his eyes from the scrutiny of her hair and gazed into her face. She was scared to death.

"How long have you been here?"

"It seems like hours," she gasped breathlessly. "A cottonmouth frightened me and I backed into the briers without thinking."

His scowl deepened. "You realize I'm going to have to cut it, don't you?"

Her eyes widened. "My hair? Oh, God no, don't cut my hair!" she begged frantically. "You can't cut my hair, Bain!"

"I have to. It's too big a mess." He reached up with his fingers and tried to work her hair free, to untangle and separate the thorns and snarled branches, but it was impossible. His hands dropped and he reached down into the water, to the back of the waistband of his pants, where he carried a bone-handled knife in a small sheath.

Lizette saw the knife and her heart fell to her stomach. "No, you can't, please," she begged. "There has to be some other way. Please, Bain, not my hair! Not my hair!"

He shook his head. "There is no other way, you little fool," he exclaimed grimly. "You've got yourself in one hell of a mess this time." He started to reach out for her hair, and she grabbed his arm, trying to hold him back. Tears were streaming down her face.

He wrenched his arm away from her hands and grabbed a handful of her thick curly hair, trying to keep the thorns from his own hands, and as she let out an agonized cry, he began to cut through the first strands. His jaw tightened as he slashed away and pulled the wad of tangled hair and branches free, tossing them aside; then he began to hack at the rest of it. It wasn't easy. He wanted to leave her as much hair as possible, but the blackberry bushes were old ones, the thorns tough, and even though his knife was sharp, there was no way he could avoid multilating her beautiful tresses.

As he cut the last few strands free, for a brief moment he stared at the dark curls in his hand, remembering how they had once framed her face; then abruptly, as her body began to sink, he threw it away and gathered her to him holding her close.

"Can you stand?" he asked huskily as he held her limp body against his chest while he slipped the knife back in its sheath.

She shook her head, sniffing in unhappily. "I don't think so."

He reached down and picked her up, cradling her against him, and made his way around the brier patch to where the water became shallower. He walked with her cradled in his arms, moving upstream to where it was shallow enough to see the bottom, where he could wade across to where their clothes were.

Lizette was trying to keep from crying, but not very successfully, and as he carried her, her head resting against his shoulder while she stared tearfully at his stern face, the melancholy mood of the past two weeks began to grip her again, and she became unreasonable. He had had no right to cut her hair, in fact he had no right to be here at all. He had probably cut it on purpose, just to be mean. She began to squirm in his arms.

"Put me down," she gasped breathlessly.

"Not until I'm sure you can stand."

"I can!"

"Don't be a little fool, the current's swifter here."

"I'm not a fool."

"No," he said, feeling the warmth of her body clad only in wet chemise and underdrawers pressing against him. "No, you're not a fool. You're a spoiled brat."

She inhaled sharply. His face was only inches from hers, mouth grim, eyes staring straight ahead. He wasn't even aware she was anything more than a wet soggy mess, and once more she started feeling sorry for herself and began to cry, passionate heartrending sobs that seemed to well up from deep within her.

"Now what's wrong?" he asked briskly.

"My hair," she murmured, burying her face against his shoulder. "You cut it off! You cut off all my hair, and now I'll never be able to face anyone again!"

He looked down at her. In spite of the childish way she always baited him, he felt sorry for her. Her hair had been beautiful, exceptionally so. "I'm sorry, Lizette," he said gruffly, not knowing quite what to do with her. "But it couldn't be helped."

Her face was still pressed hard against his tanned skin as he carefully moved through the waist-deep water, fording the stream, hoping to reach the other side without losing his balance on the slippery rocks, and suddenly his nearness bothered her. The feel of his skin against her face and warmth of his body next to her made her swallow hard as a frightening, tingling sensation flowed through her. She shifted uneasily in his arms.

"Hold still," he ordered.

She raised her head. "Why?"

"Because I . . ."

His warning was too late. Her slight movement had come at a bad time, just as his foot came down on a slippery rock, dislodging it, and before he could catch himself, the rock slid from beneath him and he began to fall.

Lizette screamed as they both hit the water. Her head went under and she swallowed a mouthful before Bain's arms finally circled her waist, pulling her to the surface. Then he began dragging her against the current, pulling her with him toward the bank, slipping and sliding as he struggled with her. Her head was out of the water now, but the shock coupled with the ordeal earlier had left her weak, and as he pulled her limp body onto the bank, she fell exhausted, landing on her back in the grass, eyes shut, gasping for air. "I want to die!" she wailed, her voice breaking. "Oh, God, my hair! Why didn't you let me die?"

Bain stared at her curiously as he tried to catch his breath. He lay on his stomach beside her, his lungs filling quickly with air, then raised his head. Water dripped from his hair onto her face as he leaned over her to make sure she was all right, and he brushed it from her cheek as she opened her eyes.

He frowned. "No, you don't want to die."

She sniffed in, staring up at him. "How do you know what I want?"

His eyes locked with hers, and he suddenly trembled. "Because I think I know you better than that."

"You don't know me at all!"

"Don't I?" He pulled his gray eyes from hers and they caressed her face. His hand followed his eyes, touching first her hair, where he let one of the tight curls wrap itself around his index finger for a moment before pulling it free, then tracing her jawline, fingers softly stroking her flesh from temple to chin, then moving up to her lips. As he stared at her mouth, he suddenly became aware, as on the day they raced their horses, that although he chided her about being a child, she was frighteningly close to being a woman.

An exciting warmth began to flood his loins, and his breathing quickened. How strange that she should make him feel like this, and how lovely she was. Even short and chopped unevenly her dark hair was sensuously alive like the iridescent feathers of a bird, and it brought a brilliance to her emerald eyes that made them glisten, and her skin was soft, the flesh like cool velvet. His finger drew a line across her full lips, then dropped from the middle of them to her chin and on down, drawing an imaginary line from them down her throat, to the edge of her wet chemise that was plastered against her firm young breasts.

Lizette tensed as she stared up into Bain's face, suddenly realizing that he wasn't looking at her with his usual disgusted grown-up look. He was looking at her in an unnerving way that made her shiver. She lay still, holding her breath, letting his eyes slowly sift over her.

Bain's eyes found his finger at the edge of the chemise. So smooth . . . so firm, her small breasts rose in stiff peaks, not large and voluptuous, but small firm mounds of flesh, aroused and waiting, clearly outlined beneath the wet cloth. Not fully ripe as those of an older woman would be, but enough to make the heat rise in his blood. Once more he trembled. What the hell was the matter with him?

He drew his eyes reluctantly from her bosom, but his finger still rested in the valley between her breasts at the edge of the chemise. He just couldn't seem to relinquish the intimacy of its touch, and as he gazed down into her face once more, hoping to find an answer for the savage pangs of desire that were beginning to flow through him, he suddenly found himself drawn to her as he'd never been drawn to any woman before. She was intoxicating. There was something about her . . . But she wasn't a woman, not yet, she was only a girl. If only his common sense would start remembering it.

Lizette's green eyes locked with his, and something vibrant and intense passed between them. She'd never felt quite like this before. Her heart fluttered wildly, then began to pound, and the weird desire to touch him that had filled her that day they had raced once more possessed her. But this time, instead of being puzzled or frightened by it, she sighed and reached up, exploring his face with a gentle touch.

Tiny droplets of water still clung to his clipped beard, and as her fingers moved over it, a wild thrill swept through her. Her fingers hesitated, then moved again slowly, touching his mustache, brushing lightly across his lips, and his eyes darkened to a stormy gray. He kissed her fingertips lightly and felt the fire shoot through him.

"Lizette!" he cried harshly. "My God, don't do that!"

She frowned. "Why not?"

"Because . . . because you're just a child . . ."

Her hand dropped. "A child? A child? You're always telling me that!" she whispered breathlessly, then ran her hand through the dark russet hair on his chest, to the tip of his ear, her fingers toying with his ear, circling it, then dipping down to his clipped beard again, tracing his jawline. "If I'm such a child, then why do I feel the way I feel right now and why are you looking at me that way?" she asked.

He flushed while her fingers dropped to his shoulder. "I'm not looking at you any differently than I always do," he said. His voice was deep with emotion, and she knew he was lying.

"Aren't you?"

Their eyes locked once more, and again the stirrings inside him deepened into such a strong desire he wanted to cry out. "Damn you!" he muttered helplessly. His insides were tied in knots, and yet he knew that to take her would be sheer folly.

His eyes devoured her, and she gazed up at him with longing, the strange, weird frightening sensations that had tormented her the past two weeks exploding inside her with a violence that shattered all her illusions of love being gentle and tender. She was being torn apart, the need for him to hold her so strong she would have begged him gladly.

Bain read the hunger in her eyes and groaned agonizingly from deep in his throat as his lips came down on hers. His mouth moved with a sensuous rhythm that brought heat flooding through every nerve in her body. He kissed her lips, her eyes, her neck, the pulse throbbing at the base of her throat. Then his mouth captured hers once more, his tongue parting her lips to explore the passion that lay within. His hands caressed the soft mounds of flesh beneath the wet chemise and then groped their way to the hooks of her lace-trimmed underdrawers. As his mouth moved over hers, he peeled them from her, caressing her nakedness lovingly.

Bain's every nerve ending filled with excitement as his lips thrilled her until she writhed beneath his hands. There was no way he could stop now.

His mouth eased on hers, and in seconds he was naked beside her, pulling her closer against him. He moved over her, his eyes gazing into hers with a passion that fired her to a fever pitch. She welcomed him lovingly, her cry at his entry muffled against his lips. Then as the pain of his entry began to subside, it was replaced by a passionate longing that urged her on, and her strong young limbs moved around him, holding her to him, and he began to move slowly inside her.

She moaned. This was heaven, they were gods, drifting, and feeling, her whole body alive and vibrating from head to toe. Bain moved, gently at first, thrusting with loving caresses, letting the magic wonder of her young body soothe and appease the heat of his loins, and the only time his eyes left her was when they closed in rapture, the feel of her filling him with pleasures he never knew existed. He had had women dozens of times before, but none had ever made him feel like this, none had ever awakened the surge of passion within him this lovely young girl was arousing. Her lips answered him with a teasing warmth that made him weak, and her body was surrendering to him with a wild abandon that took his breath away.

Lizette lay beneath Bain, her body filled with longings she had never dreamed it possessed, and sighed as Bain tried to fulfill them. She was racked with a throbbing need to become a part of him, and arched upward, searching, desperately demanding, until suddenly a shock went through her, tearing her insides with its sweet savage wonder and she was carried to heights beyond comprehension. Over and over again the joy of that moment rushed through her, taking her breath away. Then seconds later she felt Bain tremble above her, his body shaking violently, and he buried his face in her neck, his lips against her ear, and grew still.

For a long time he lay spent, breathing heavily, the sun hot on his bare back while Lizette lay beneath him marveling at the violent passion that had consumed her only moments before. Only it was gone now. Not really completely gone, but the burning flame within her seemed to be quenched, and the intense longing to be a part of him was replaced by a satisfied lethargy that had sapped all of her strength. She felt the heat of Bain's breath on her neck and now suddenly she knew the tortured longing that had filled her off and on for the past two weeks had been there for a reason. She was in love, in love with Bain Kolter. Had been from the moment she had looked into his gray eyes that day when he'd pulled her off the ladder at the cockfights.

She reached up now and buried her hand in his dark brown wavy hair, opening her eyes to see the sun glinting off its russet highlights. Her heart was warm and full and she was just about to whisper her feelings to him, when his voice, close to her, sent a shock through her that took away all the joy of what he'd just given her and left her empty and hollow.

"Damn you, Lizette!" Bain cried breathlessly. "Now there'll be hell to pay. Why did you have to do that? Why couldn't you leave well enough alone?"

She froze, motionless, her hand still in his hair. "Bain . . . ?"

He raised his head slowly, her hand falling from his hair, and he looked down into her eyes; only this time, his passion appeased, he was able to fight the strong feelings her nearness aroused.

"You had to do that, didn't you?" he said harshly. "You just had to prove you were right that day we raced!"

"I didn't—"

"Don't say you didn't know! You knew very well what you were doing to me. Jesus Christ, Lizette," he cried huskily. "You're only fifteen. My God!" He could feel the sun hot on his bare skin and felt sick inside, because even now, even knowing he was courting trouble, he also knew he'd never enjoyed any woman this way. The thought angered him. He reached over beside them for her damp chemise and underdrawers, shoving them against her firm young breasts, trying to still his heart from racing. "Here, put these back on," he ordered, and slid from her quickly, grabbing his own clothes.

He stood over her as he put his clothes on and stared down as she sat up and began to pull her chemise over her head. "Don't look at me like that," she said, her voice breaking.

"How am I supposed to look at you?" His eyes flashed. "Goddammit, Lizette, you had no right."

"I had no right?" She pulled her lacy underdrawers up, standing to fasten them, then stared at him belligerently. "I had no right? You're the one who raped me," she said angrily. "I didn't rape you!"

He laughed, the sound throaty and sensuous. "Rape? Nobody raped anybody, little girl," he said viciously. "You seduced me as surely as you're standing there, and you know it."

Lizette's legs were still weak from the onslaught of Bain's

lovemaking, her body still primed in the aftermath, but as his words sank in, chilling her to the core, anger began to replace the warmth. "Don't worry, I don't intend to go crying rape," she said angrily. "If you think I want anyone to know what happened, you're sadly mistaken." Her hands began to shake and her lips twitched nervously. "I . . . I don't really know what happened myself." She sniffed in as tears flooded her eyes. "I . . . I only know you made love to me, Bain Kolter," she said bitterly. "And you can't deny it, can you?"

He shuddered, remembering, and the memory was agonizingly sweet, but he'd never let her know. "That's right, I made love to you because you asked for it," he said. "But it'll never happen again. I'm not interested in making love to young girls who aren't even dry behind the ears yet."

He didn't care! It had meant nothing to him, the soft caresses and passionate kisses. The thrills he'd invoked in her had been no more than what he'd give any woman who happened to be beneath him. Could it be? She had seen love and tender yearning in his eyes. Was it only make-believe? If Bain Kolter was capable of deceiving her so completely, then how would she ever know when love really came along? And she had given herself to him willingly, wanting it as much as he. Oh, God, how ashamed she was. Her heart froze inside her and she wanted to die. He didn't care, not about her hair, or her body, or her love, or anything else. All he cared about was himself.

She walked toward him, running her hand through her hair as she walked, feeling the short ends. Suddenly tears flooded her eyes and ran down her cheeks. She stooped, slowly picking up her dress, putting it on, and the tears built to aching sobs. By the time she fastened the last hook at the back of her delicately embroidered white muslin dress, she was crying so hard her whole body shook.

"What's the matter with you now?" Bain asked guiltily.

She shivered and sniffed in, turning angrily. "I hate you!"

He winced. "Fine, then I won't have to worry about any repeat performances of today, will I?"

"You're despicable."

"Good, keep hating me, Liz," he said roughly. "And go right on hating any man who'd do what I did to you today without the promise of marriage. We're not worth it, any of us, believe me."

He reached in his pocket and pulled out a handkerchief, handing it to her.

She took it from him reluctantly and wiped her nose, but it didn't do much good; the tears were still coming. "Why?" she asked, gulping back sobs. "Why, Bain?"

He stared at her hard, then walked over, picked up her shoes and stockings, and handed them to her, waiting for her to put them on.

She sat down, and he watched her slip her feet in the stockings and pull them up over her shapely young limbs.

"I don't know why," he said miserably as he watched her. "Except that for a while I forgot that you're just a child and I guess I saw a glimpse of the woman you will be someday. Part of me is sorry for what I did, Liz, and yet . . ."

"Yet, what?"

He saw the expectant look in her eyes and knew that just one tender word, one acknowledgment that what happened had meant something to him, and they'd both be sunk, and he couldn't let it happen, not again.

"Nothing," he said, taking a deep breath. "Now, put your shoes on and we'll ride back to the house on Amigo," and he turned from her, walking to his horse where it had stood grazing the whole while.

She began putting on her shoes as the tears once more reached her eyes. So sweet, yet so bitter, she thought miserably, and vowed that sometime, someday when she grew up, when she was really an honest-to-goodness woman and he couldn't call her a child anymore, she'd make Bain Kolter love her, if it was the last thing she ever did.

5

Their ride back to the main house was anything but pleasant. Bain knew Lizette was crying off and on even though she tried not to show it, and every time her head came near his chest, her dark curly hair brushing his beard or playing softly across his lips, he flinched as if he'd been stung. He knew what he'd done was unforgivable and that if her father knew he'd kill him, yet for some strange reason he was having the hardest time erasing from his memory those glorious moments when she'd given herself to him.

He had to, though. Regardless of how he felt, there was no way he'd admit to himself or anyone else that he had made love to a fifteen-year-old child.

They were nearing the slave quarters, and he glanced down once more at her slim shoulders in front of him on the horse, at the tilt of her head, and he could feel the warmth from her buttocks where she sat in front of him on the saddle.

He should never have come to Tonnerre today; he should have told his father he was busy and couldn't bring those papers for Beau Dante to sign. If he hadn't come, he wouldn't have decided to take a ride down to the old swimming hole and none of this would have happened. Damn! He swore to himself as they began riding up to the main house.

Lizette was still crying, and Rebel met her daughter at the

side door with a puzzled look on her face, surprised to see Bain bringing her home.

"What on earth?" she exclaimed.

Bain slid from the horse's back, then helped Lizette down, and suddenly Rebel got a good look at her hair.

"What happened?" she asked, dismayed, but Lizette couldn't answer. Her heart was in her throat, and with a loud wail she reached out, grabbing her mother, crying into her shoulder as if her heart was breaking.

Bain flushed crimson. He knew she wasn't crying just because of her hair. "She decided to go for a swim," he explained quickly. "Saw a cottonmouth and backed into a brier bush trying to get away from it. I had to cut her loose. I'm sorry, Mrs. Dante," he apologized. "There wasn't anything else to do."

Rebel stared over Lizette's shoulder at this good-looking young man who suddenly seemed so ill-at-ease. Her violet eyes were curiously alive and she wondered why he was so nervous. She had known Bain for years and he'd never been uncomfortable before when he was around them. She glanced at Lizette's hair, then reached out, gently stroking the short chopped-up mess. But then, Bain Kolter had never shorn her daughter's beautiful tresses before, either, she thought.

"She was caught fast, really tangled in the briers, ma'am," he continued explaining. "If there'd been any other way . . ."

Rebel shook her head, hugging Lizette to her. "It's all right, Bain. I'm only glad you were there to help. I don't know what I'm going to do with this child, though," she said. "She's always insisting on doing things she shouldn't. She's been told not to swim alone. Sometimes I wish Cole had never taught her how."

Bain's eyes lowered to the back of Lizette's head, where Rebel's hands were testing the length of the curls left, as she comforted her daughter. He straightened, trying to ignore the warm feelings that were flooding him as he stared at her. "I'm just glad I happened to decide to take a ride to the swimming hole," he said. "As it is, she was in the water for quite some time. I hope she'll be all right."

Rebel sighed, "I'm sure she will."

"Then I think I'll be going," he said, and turned, mounting his horse.

"Thank you again, Bain," Rebel said thoughtfully. She gazed up at him while she held Lizette close to her bosom, letting her cry. "We will see you Monday evening, won't we?"

He nodded. "If I'm still around," he said, then took one last look at Lizette, dug his horse in the ribs, and started down the drive toward the main road.

"Oh, Mother!" wailed Lizette as Rebel hurried her into the house.

"I know, I know," soothed Rebel. "But your hair'll grow in again, darling," she assured her. "In the meantime, we'll just trim it a bit, it's curly enough, it'll look fine."

"Oh, Mother, it's not just my hair," she cried helplessly, then suddenly stopped. She couldn't tell her mother. She just couldn't. Her father'd kill Bain if he knew. "It's . . . it's just everything," she said finally.

"What do you mean, everything?" Rebel asked, bewildered.

Lizette only shook her head. "You wouldn't understand. Oh, please, Mother, just leave me alone," she cried, and pulled away.

As Rebel watched her young daughter scurry up the stairs, she stood motionless, wondering. Was there something she had missed? Her frown deepened as she remembered Bain's nervousness, and she began to wonder if maybe Lizette had become infatuated with him. It certainly would be embarrassing, to say the least, especially as sensitive as she seemed to be lately.

Rebel turned from her contemplation of her daughter and left the foyer to search for Pretty, and ordered her to see that Lizette had a warm bath.

Lizette reached her bedroom, flung open the door, and ducked inside, leaning back against it, a deep sob wrenching from her throat. "I hate him!" she whispered savagely. "I hate him!" Then she staggered helplessly to her big bed, fell across the gold floral satin bedspread, and moaned agonizingly, "No . . . no . . . I don't really. Oh, God that I could hate him . . . I *should* hate him, but . . ." She gulped back the sobs. "Oh, God, I love him . . . I love him!" she whispered, and the realization was almost more than she could bear.

Monday evening, the night of the birthday ball, Lizette stepped from the tub of sudsy water, wrapped the towel around her, and stood beside the tub, letting the towel beneath her feet absorb the water that dripped down her legs. This was the second day. Would she ever get over it? Would she ever forget? Everything was still so vivid in her memory. She began to towel herself dry, then walked slowly toward the vanity with its huge oval mirror. When she reached it, she stopped and stood motionless for a long time, staring into the mirror, gazing curiously at her naked young body.

It didn't look different, but oh, it felt so different. It was as if the glorious deed was branded onto her body with a hot iron so everyone could see. And yet she knew no one knew except her and Bain. No one else must ever know. It was a secret only they could share, and something she'd never forget as long as she lived. Bain had called her a child, but she wasn't, not anymore. Perhaps in years, but not in her heart.

Slowly she moved to the bed, tossed the towel aside, and began to dress for the ball.

Heather wasn't sure she was going to like this. Her dress had turned out beautifully—its soft white gossamer sheer was like wearing a cloud—and the amethysts at her ears and throat made her feel like a princess. But she couldn't help remembering the last ball she had attended, back in Columbia, where she'd met the young man she'd been so reluctant to leave. Tonight as the carriage pulled up in front of the beautiful white-columned mansion at Tonnerre and deposited her, her parents, and grandparents at the doorstep, an empty ache gripped her.

She glanced over at her mother, but Darcy was so engrossed in what Heath was telling her that Heather might as well have been invisible. But then, it had been like that ever since her arrival at the Chateau, so why should tonight be any different?

"Come along, Heather, dear," Loedicia said, smiling. She saw the hurt look in her granddaughter's eyes and knew what was the matter. "You'll have to forgive your parents, dear," she said quickly. "After all, they do have a lot of years to catch up on. I'm sure they don't mean to ignore you."

Heather's eyes grew hostile, sullen. "Don't worry, I'm getting used to it," she said, and lifted her skirts, accompanying her grandmother and grandfather up the front steps, where they were greeted by Rebel and Beau.

They had arrived for the ball early, since Loedicia and Roth would also play host. The other guests would be greeted at the entrance to the ballroom in the back wing of the house, but they weren't due for almost an hour yet, and there were still some preparations to be made.

"Why don't you go up and visit with Lizette while she gets ready," suggested Rebel as she saw Heather's lower lip pucker into a pout every time she glanced toward her parents.

Heather watched Heath and Darcy leave the parlor, heading toward the gardens at the back of the house, gazing at each other rapturously. She might as well, she guessed, and excused herself, heading back to the foyer and the broad curving stairs that led to the second floor of the magnificent house.

She reached Lizette's bedroom door as Pretty opened it to leave, her face flushed with the excitement of the evening.

"Oh, Miss Heather, you surely scared me!" Pretty exclaimed, wide mouth warming into a big smile as she stood in the doorway. "Miss Lizzie isn't quite ready. She don't know what to do with her hair, and neither do I. Land sakes, of all the times for somethin' like this to happen . . ."

Heather frowned. "Like what?" she asked, bewildered. No one at the Chateau had as yet learned of Lizette's Saturday escapade, and now, as Heather's frown deepened and she stepped into Lizette's room, she let out a gasp.

"Oh, my God!" she cried, shocked. "Lizette, your hair!"

Lizette stood in front of the mirror in her new dress, a dazzling array of delicate white lace with small diamonds sewn intermittently about the skirt, satin ribbon adorning the high waist and low neck and small short puff sleeves of the delicate lace, slashed to show her tawny suntanned arms. About her throat was a delicate chain of diamonds with matching earrings in her pierced ears. Framing her lovely face, beautiful, yet out of place with the feminine mood of her lace dress, were short stubby ringlets of dark hair, falling onto her forehead and curling about her ears.

Lizette's green eyes darkened as Heather stared at her. "Well, don't just stand there gawking," she yelled angrily. "Come in and shut the door!"

Heather stepped into the room and moved gingerly toward Lizette, her eyes glued to her head. "What happened?" she asked breathlessly, staring at her.

Lizette cringed. "Bain Kolter's what happened," she answered. "That's what!"

"Bain Kolter? You mean he did that?" Heather's eyes widened.

"Well, I guess it wasn't really his fault," Lizette began, and told her cousin of her swimming expedition on Saturday, but only up to the point of her rescue. She finished her story and turned, looking again in the mirror. "What do I do with it, Heather?" she asked, pleading. "It's too short for anything. Mother evened the ends out, but I can't even put a ribbon around it, the curls just keep pulling out."

Heather studied her thoughtfully. "I really think it's pretty," she said after a few minutes of pondering the situation. "The only thing is to pull it back up from your ears." She moved to the dresser. "Where are your hairpins?"

Lizette showed her, then Heather made her sit on the vanity while she worked on her hair, smoothing the curls back away from the sides of her face so they didn't look quite so unruly, sticking hairpins in to hold them in place.

"That's fine," Lizette said, watching her reflection in the mirror. "But the hairpins show."

Heather gazed about the room, then frowned. "Did you have any lace left over from the dress?" she asked.

Lizette shook her head. "No."

Heather's eyes fell on a fresh bouquet by the back window. She walked over and touched the large white blooms, then inhaled their sweet scent. "These ought to do," she said briskly, and broke off four or five blooms, leaving the stems long enough to handle; then she came back and began working on Lizette's hair again, tucking the fragrant cape jasmine against the curls, securing them with more hairpins.

"How come you were swimming alone?" she asked as she fastened down another creamy bloom in Lizette's hair. "I thought you said your brother was coming home in time for the ball."

"He was," she answered. "At least he was supposed to, but we haven't heard a word from him since that last letter. I suppose he's gotten delayed somewhere. Mother's terribly disappointed and a little worried. Of course Father said she's worrying needlessly and that he probably got distracted somewhere by a pretty face. I sure hope he's wrong," she said thoughtfully as she watched Heather putting the flowers in her hair. "Cole's too young to settle down yet."

"You never did say, how old is he?"

"He turned twenty last month," said Lizette. "And I hope he hasn't changed. It's been two years since we've seen him." Lizette frowned. "I'd hate to think of what the war might have done to him. He was just barely seventeen when he talked Father into letting him go."

Heather glanced quickly into the mirror at Lizette's face, pleased with her handiwork. "There," she said triumphantly, forgetting she had asked the question about Cole. "Now folks won't really know whether your hair's short or just tucked up on top of your head, will they?"

Lizette straightened, examining herself in the mirror. Heather was right. She had used the jasmine, framing her face on each side, letting the flowers hold the curls back. In the very front she had brushed the curls back, then let some fall onto her forehead in wispy strands. The effect was very feminine and even made Lizette look older than her fifteen years. She looked up at Heather and smiled. "It looks beautiful," she said. "I was frantic." She took one last look in the mirror, then stood up. "Now I guess we'd better go on downstairs. The guests will be arriving soon, and we don't want to miss anything."

Heather caught a little of Lizette's excitement as they left her bedroom and headed downstairs, but a little later, her shyness surfaced once again as more and more people came and eligible young men began clamoring around her hoping to lead her in a quadrille, a lively reel, or one of the new slower dances that were gaining popularity with the younger set. But trying to get along, she took Lizette's advice and welcomed their attentions, somewhat shyly, but honestly.

Lizette too had her share of dancing partners; however, whereas the young men eyeing Heather were in their early twenties, the young men who flirted discreetly with Lizette were much younger. After all, this was her first year for long dresses and she was still considered a child by everyone, albeit a lovely child, and Heather's camouflaging of her hair led to more than one curious head turned her way, yet no one was bold enough to comment.

No one except Bain, that is. Even Felicia, when she strolled into the crowded, noisy ballroom, wearing a gown of blue silk with heavy satin embroidery on the skirt and trimming the bodice, made no reference to Lizette's hair, except to wink at her conspiratorially, to let her know she knew, but would keep her mouth shut. Lizette had frowned slightly, wondering how much Bain had told them, but then reassured herself that he wouldn't be stupid enough to admit to his family that he had seduced the daughter of their best friends.

Rand and Madeline Kolter were quick to join the couples wishing a happy birthday to Rebel and Loedicia, who were at the opposite end of the ballroom near the table of food, and it was then, with Felicia excusing herself momentarily to run after her mother to ask her something, that Bain spoke.

"It looks lovely," he said, nodding toward her hair. "Who fixed it?"

"Heather came to the rescue."

His eyes studied her curiously, their slate gray picking up blue reflections from his frock coat. "Are you all right?" he said suddenly.

Her jaw tightened. "Yes."

"You didn't say anything to anyone?"

"I'm not a fool, Bain. No," she said angrily. "Much as I hate you, I wouldn't want to see you dead."

He sneered. "Thanks."

"No thanks called for," she said hostilely. "I didn't tell for my own sake, not yours. I have a reputation to live up to too, you know."

His jaw twitched nervously and she knew he was about to retaliate, when Felicia came back, interrupting them. She glanced at her brother, then to Lizette, then back to Bain.

"Oh, for heaven's sake, Lizette," she said disgustedly. "Are you still mad at him for cutting your hair? Gracious, if he hadn't, you might still be out there. I'm only glad he was around to rescue you. Just think, if it weren't for Bain, you might be dead."

Lizette's eyes locked with Bain's and regret shot through her. If only he had told her he loved her. But then, how could he? To him she was only a child. But she hadn't felt like a child when he'd made love to her, and he hadn't treated her like one, either. She flushed crimson at the remembrance, and Bain, seeing the blush on her cheeks and sensing the passionate feelings hidden in the depths of her eyes, excused himself quickly and walked farther into the ballroom, trying to lose himself in the crowd. Lizette watched him go, the tall, straight, muscular frame beneath the deep blue frock coat moving gracefully across the floor, buff trousers hugging the strong legs she knew they encased. He was so sure of himself she wanted to scream, but instead she turned to Felicia and forced a smile.

"How about some punch?" she said, pretending a merriment she didn't feel.

Felicia smiled back at her, and as they moved through the crowd, smiling graciously at all the young men, no one was aware of the turmoil that was warring inside Lizette.

The party had been going on for some time now. Heather had danced every dance so far, and although the young men had been nice, she had found them as uninteresting as DeWitt Palmer. He was there too, and was at her elbow now, trying to be amusing and failing miserably, although she didn't let him know it. She didn't want to hurt his feelings, so she laughed at his jokes and pretended an interest when he talked about his father's plans for Palmerston Grove, and his winnings at the races, and raising game cocks. But she wished with all her heart that life held something more for her than this.

She gazed about the huge ballroom, then turned to Witt, frowning. "Have you seen Lizette lately?"

He stared at her, then took a quick glance around, shaking his head. "Not for some time."

Her frown deepened. "That's what I thought." She looked at him apologetically. "If you don't mind, Witt," she said hesitantly, "I'm going to take a quick look around to see if I can find her. I know she wasn't exactly in the best mood tonight, and I'd hate to think she wasn't enjoying herself."

"I'll help you," he offered, but she wouldn't let him.

"No, please. Lizette wouldn't appreciate it." She put her hand on his arm, making him promise to wait for her, then turned hurriedly and walked away, her eyes scanning the room as she made her way along the perimeter of the dancers, and it was moments later, as she headed for the main part of the house, suspecting that perhaps Lizette had sneaked off to her bedroom, that she ran into a very upset Felicia.

"Oh, Heather," Felicia exclaimed breathlessly as she grabbed Heather's hands and pulled her to a quiet corner of the ballroom. "Am I glad to see you!"

"What's wrong?"

Felicia shook her head. "You'll never believe it."

"What?"

"It's Lizette."

"Where is she?"

Felicia exhaled, exasperated. "She's out past the flower gardens, down near the river, sitting on the bank with a snoot full!"

"A what?"

"She's drunk!"

"Drunk? How did she get drunk?"

Felicia kept her voice to a whisper and nodded toward the banquet table where most of the grown-ups were congregated. "There's brandy in the punch bowl."

"But she wasn't supposed to drink any out of the big punch bowl. That's for the grown-ups."

"You didn't think that would stop her, did you?" Felicia wrung her hands. "I don't dare tell her mother."

Heather sighed. "Take me to her," she whispered calmly. "Maybe I can help."

Felicia nodded and glanced about to make sure they weren't being followed, then grabbed Heather's hand and dragged her out the French doors, into the garden and beyond, across the drive and on down to a grove of trees along the riverbank not far from the slave quarters.

Heather glanced back toward the house, listening to the faint strains of music filtering into the night air. A thousand candles in the chandeliers of the ballroom lit the windows like gold, sending shafts of light out into the night, which was warm with the fragrance of spring blossoms. But now, away from the house, it was so dark she could hardly see.

"There she is," said Felicia, and stopped, pointing toward a vague outline of white beneath a moss-laden oak tree.

Heather stopped beside her, adjusting her eyes before going on. "I thought you said she was crying."

Felicia nodded. "She was."

"Well, she's laughing now."

And Lizette was, at least part of the time. Heather moved toward her slowly, then stooped down near her. "Lizette? Lizette?"

Lizette turned toward her and squinted, trying to see in the dark, but everything was a blur. "Heather?" she asked.

"What have you done?" exclaimed Heather, scolding, but Lizette only laughed.

"Oh, don't be an old prude, Heather," she said, giggling. "I just took a few drinks, that's all."

"That's all? You're drunk, Lizette. If your mother finds out . . ."

"She won't—that is, she won't, if you don't tell her." Her words were slow, slurred.

"But how are you going to get back in the house?"

Lizette's jaw tightened stubbornly. "I'm not going back in the house. I'm going to run away. I'm going to be like Cole, I'm going to go wherever I want and do whatever I want, and to hell with being a lady!" She pointed off toward the river, where a large two-masted ship was docked at her father's pier. "Do you see that ship?" she asked thoughtfully, continuing to point. "That's my father's ship, the *Duchess,* and as soon as everyone down there's asleep, I'm going to sneak on board and stow away, and when it leaves in the morning I'm never going to have to worry again about ever growing up or being a lady and falling in love, and I'll never hurt again."

Heather turned to Felicia and scowled. "How long has she been like this?"

"She's been talking crazy for the past half-hour, but that's the first she's talked of running away." Felicia was quite upset. "What'll we do?" she asked anxiously.

"You'll let me take care of her," said a deep voice from behind them, and both girls whirled around, startled, as a man stepped toward them, his broad shoulders silhouetted in the lights from the house in the distance.

"Bain?" asked Felicia, recognizing his voice.

Bain stepped closer, his face still shadowed, but his eyes were on the vague white outline of the young girl lying in the grass. "I saw her earlier at the punch bowl and saw the two of you talking and put two and two together," he said huskily. "Now, if you'll both go back to the house and not say a word to anyone, I think I can sober her up. If not, I know the way to her room. I'll see she gets inside and have Pretty take care of her so none of the guests will have to know."

"Do you think you can?" asked Heather.

His eyes darkened. "I can't promise."

"Don't worry," Felicia told Heather, "I'm sure Bain can handle her. What we've got to do is make sure she's not missed at the party and cover for her." She stood up. "Come on, Heather."

Heather wasn't certain they were doing the right thing, but then she looked down at Lizette who was lying all the way down in the grass now with her eyes shut, singing softly to herself. Perhaps it was worth a try. At least if Bain could sober her up, maybe she wouldn't get punished too severely. She stood up and relinquished her spot near her cousin. "Well, I wish you luck," she said softly. "And please, let us know one way or the other how you make out, will you, so we know whether to keep covering for her or not."

He nodded, then watched as his sister and Lizette's cousin picked their way cautiously back across the field, over the drive to the gardens, and disappeared toward the house. When they were out of sight, he turned back to face the young girl who was still on her back in the grass. She was quiet now. The song she'd been singing had faded to nothing, and all he could hear was her deep breathing.

He moved closer and knelt down on one knee, leaning toward her in the dark. "Lizette?" he whispered softly. He heard her inhale, but she didn't answer. "I know you can hear me," he went on. "This isn't going to help, you know."

"Who said it won't?" she replied. "Already it's making me forget."

"For how long?"

"For a while . . ." He heard the catch in her voice and knew she was starting to cry. "I don't remember anything anymore," she continued, verging on tears. "Not your kisses, or the way you held me . . ." She laughed heartbreakingly. "Funny, but I can't even remember the way it felt when you did it to me. Isn't that crazy?" she said, her voice ending on a sob. "You'd think I'd remember something as wonderful as that, wouldn't you?" she said. She was really crying now, the tears flooding her eyes. "But I can't remember any of it, not any of it, not the wonderful warmth of your arms, or how sweet your lips were . . ." She turned to him. "And if I drink some more, maybe I won't even remember that it happened at all, do you think, maybe?"

"Lizette, you're not forgetting," he said, trying to show a calm he didn't feel. "You're only dulling the pain, but the memories are still there."

"No. No, they're not! I don't want them," she cried.

"We can't always have what we want."

She stared up at him, her green eyes glistening with tears. "You seem to get what you want."

"For God's sake," he said. "You wanted it too, so don't deny it."

She turned from him and moved onto her elbow, pushing herself into a sitting position, then glanced back over her shoulder at him. Her head was still cloudy and she felt strangely disoriented. "Bain? That is you, isn't it, Bain?" she asked.

"Yes."

"Was I just talking to you?" she asked.

"Were you?"

"I think I was." She shook her head. "Bain? Please, Bain . . ." Her voice was soft, a shaking sob. "Put my hair back, Bain," she whispered.

He swore. "Damn!"

She reached up and pulled the flowers from her hair, holding them out to him, and their sweet fragrance filled his nostrils, making him wince. "Here, take these away and put my hair back, Bain!" she pleaded pathetically.

Bain inhaled. "I can't, Liz," he said softly. "I wish I could."

"But you took it off. Why can't you put it back on?" She moved closer to him and grabbed his hand, holding it up, plunging it into the curls that had fallen free when she'd taken the flowers out. "Here, see," she said, whispering softly. "Here, why can't you put it back?"

He wanted to pull his hand away, but the silky curls enticed him and instead he let his fingers linger on her hair;

then his hand cupped her head and he tried to see her face in the dark. "Lizette, you've had too much to drink," he said softly. "I want you to stand up, and I want you to walk."

She stared at him, puzzled, trying to sort out his words and make sense of them. His face was shadowed beneath the tree, but she knew what he looked like so well. She reached up and touched his face, running her hand over his beard as she had before, the day he'd made love to her.

"I don't want to walk," she said playfully. "I want to make love."

He swallowed hard. "Don't be ridiculous!" He pulled his hand back from her hair and reached down, grabbing her by the shoulders, and pulled her to her feet with him. "We're going to walk," he said stubbornly.

She laughed. "But I don't want to walk. I want you to kiss me." She giggled frivolously, and he swore under his breath as he turned her so he could hold her about the waist and keep her on her feet, and he began to walk with her, letting her protest all the way as he forced her to move her feet, one in front of the other, until she began to cry.

"I can't go anymore," she said a short while later as they stood some hundred feet farther down the riverbank, where he'd been pacing her back and forth. "I'm too tired."

He stopped, staring down at her. "How does your head feel?"

"It hurts!"

"Still fuzzy?"

She shook it. "No . . . not really, I guess . . . Oh, I don't know." While he had forced her to walk, she had slowly begun to feel the effects of the brandy wearing off, and although her head wasn't completely clear, it was clear enough that she suspected she had once more made a fool of herself in front of him. She tried to push him away now, her head still slightly disoriented, but her senses keen enough that his nearness was arousing strange feelings within her. "Please," she said hastily, "I'm all right now."

He held her by the shoulders, looking down into her face. "Are you sure?" he asked.

She frowned. "What do you care?"

"Don't say that," he said. "I do care, that's just the trouble." His hand moved up, cupping her head, his fingers caressing her hair. "You're beautiful, Liz," he went on huskily. "Too beautiful for your own good, and you're so vibrant and alive, but you're only fifteen, and I'm almost twenty-four. I can't deny that there's something about you . . . but it can't be, don't you see?"

"I'll be sixteen in June."

"You know damn well that doesn't change things. You're still not old enough."

She bit her lip, trying to hold back the tears. "I won't be too young forever, Bain," she said softly.

He nodded. "I know, and someday the right man will come along, and when he does, you'll wish to hell Saturday hadn't happened. I can't give you back your virginity, Liz, but I can try to give you back your pride," he said. "Be proud, you have a right to be." His voice was deep with emotion. "Because if you were a woman I wouldn't hesitate to make you mine."

Lizette felt her knees weaken, and her throat went dry. "But I love you," she whispered softly.

"No"—he shook his head—"you don't love me. You're judging your feelings by what happened Saturday."

"I am not." Her heart was in a turmoil. "I know how I feel. I'm tired of being treated like a child. I'm not a child, Bain. If I were a child, Saturday wouldn't have happened."

"Saturday was a mistake."

This couldn't be happening. He had to love her. Waves of light-headedness swept over her off and on, but one thing was certain. She was with Bain and he cared, he'd even said so, and she did love him, she did. "Bain, make love to me again," she pleaded breathlessly. "Please, you want to, you know you do, and no one has to know."

Her words were still a little slurred, and although he knew she meant every word, he was also certain that if she were sober, she'd never utter them. He swore under his breath.

"Jesus Christ, will you stop that." He reached out and grabbed her hand, pulling her with him toward the house. "Come on. Since I can't seem to sober you up, maybe I'd better take you in the house so you can sleep it off."

She tried to pull back, fighting him. "I won't go."

"You'll go, or else!"

"Or else what?" Her lip pushed into a pout.

"Or I'll carry you in."

"You wouldn't dare!"

"Don't tempt me!" He stared at her hard, his eyes cold, unfeeling. "Now, come on!"

She moved with him slowly, reluctantly, forcing him to pull her every inch of the way. Bain muttered curses under his breath all the way to the house as she tripped on tree roots, slipped on the grass, and slid on the gravel, turning her ankle, sitting down in the middle of the drive halfway to the house.

"Get up," he ordered quickly, but she was crying now.

"I can't!"

"Why not?"

"I hurt my ankle!"

"Oh, Lord!" He knelt and began to feel around in the dark. She lifted the skirt of her dress and he grasped her right ankle, his fingers pressing into her flesh.

"Ow!"

"All right, put your arms around my neck. I guess I'll have to carry you," he said, and reached out, pulling her into his arms, then straightened and got a firmer grip on her before continuing toward the house again.

Since everyone else was at the back wing of the house in the ballroom, Bain hurried to the front of the house, trying to keep in the shadows, hoping no one would see them. He managed to reach the front door unobserved and held his breath as he opened it awkwardly, still holding her in his arms. There were only dim lights in the huge foyer, and he was grateful, because all the rest of the way to the house, while he had carried her, Lizette had quit crying and begun tormenting him unmercifully, kissing his neck, rubbing her nose around his ear, the warm soft breath hot and sensuous. And while she plied him with these endearing little gestures, she kept taunting him recklessly, murmuring love words.

He glanced around quickly, then hurried to the stairs, avoiding looking at her, his face livid, jaw clenched as he fought the desire she was coaxing from deep inside him. She was light in his arms, and he took the stairs two at a time, eager to deposit her where he hoped she wouldn't be able to do any more harm.

"Do you still have the same bedroom you had when you were younger?" he asked huskily as he reached the top of the carpeted stairs.

She muffled a lilting laugh. "Guess."

"Damn you!" He started down the hall toward where he knew her room used to be. "All right, then, if you don't want to tell me, that's your problem," he said, and stopped in front of her bedroom door. He leaned down, turned the knob with his right hand, tilting her backward as he did so, and she squealed, her arms tightening about his neck. He kicked the door open and ducked inside quickly, thankful he still hadn't been seen. Then he lifted his foot unceremoniously and kicked the door shut again behind them.

The room was dark, the only light in it coming from outside, and he swore again. "The least you could have done was had a light on so you could see," he said. "Weren't you expecting to come to bed tonight?"

"Pretty would have made sure the light was on before I returned," she whispered. She moved her head closer to his, burying her face in his neck, his bristly beard scratching lightly against her cheek as her lips wreaked havoc on his senses.

He wanted to turn her over his knee and paddle her until she couldn't sit down, yet in the same breath he felt the warmth of her lips on his neck and remembered what it had been like to make love to her, and his body warred with his reason, wanting only to crush her against him and make her a part of him once more. He broke out in a cold sweat, his stomach tightening as he felt the sweet surge of passion building in his loins.

"Lock the door, Bain," she whispered softly in his ear, her lips teasing him. "It'll be so easy."

He took a deep breath.

"You want to, you know you do," she went on.

"Lizette!"

His protest was too late. Her lips found his in the dark, and with the first light touch he was lost. His mouth clung to hers until he couldn't bear the agony; then he murmured a curse against her lips and reached back, turning the lock. With quick strides they were at the bed and he fell onto it with her, gently, so as not to hurt her, all thoughts of leaving her gone.

"Lizette! Lizette!" he cried plaintively. "Why do you always do this to me?" He took her face in his hands and looked down into it. The pale light streaming in at the window next to the bed fell across it. She was so lovely. The faint smell of brandy filled his nostrils as he bent down, his mouth covering hers, but he didn't care. All he cared about was the thrill of touching her again, feeling her lithe body beneath him, and the satisfied look in her emerald eyes as he looked into them.

His hands left her face and moved down her body and he turned her onto her side, fumbling with the hooks on her dress. He was holding her close, his arms around her, his lips teasing hers, brushing them lightly, then possessing them hungrily as if he just couldn't get enough. As her dress eased off her shoulders, baring her breasts, she moaned ecstatically and moved closer against him, her body trembling fervently, waiting for his hands to begin their exploration.

But her room was at the back of the house, and as he kissed her, his mouth hungering for her with a need that was twisting him up inside, the strains of music from the ballroom came floating in the open window. The musicians were playing a lively quadrille, and as the strains of the song began to penetrate the quiet of the room, reminding him of where he was, and why he was here, a bitter pang of conscience skewered Bain's insides into a white-hot fury, and he tensed, pulling away from her, gasping for breath. My God, what was he doing?

"No! Jesus, no! Not again, Liz," he protested angrily, the music suddenly bringing him back to his senses again. He closed his eyes, breathing deeply, clearing his head, and reluctantly but deftly freed his hands from her hot flesh. He began moving to the edge of the bed.

"Bain!"

"No!" he said forcefully, and stood up, straightening his clothes.

She tried to reach for him, but he grabbed her wrist, holding it tightly as he gazed down at her. Her young breasts were heaving and her face had gone pale.

"You did it once, you little vixen," he said, his fingers digging into her skin. "But you're not going to do it again, do you hear me, you're not!"

"Please, Bain," she pleaded, tears welling up in her eyes. "Please, don't leave me like this."

He stared at her, his slate-gray eyes darkening. "I should turn you over my knee and slap the hell out of you," he said roughly. "That's what I should do!" His jaw tightened and he brought his face down close to hers. "And if I don't get out of here right now, that's just what I'm liable to do, too." His eyes were blazing and he forced himself to ignore her tears and the trembling sobs that were making her shake. "So help me, if you weren't still half-drunk, I'd slap you silly for what you just tried to do."

She stared up at him, her eyes filled with torment. Her body was aching for his touch, for the feel of his arms, and the tantalizing warmth of his lips. She didn't want him to stop. Oh, God, he couldn't stop, not now, not when it was so close. Why was he saying these things to her, why was he doing this?

She opened her mouth to call his name again, only he stopped her.

"No, Lizette!" He pushed her down hard on the bed and stared at her long and hard for a brief moment, the pain of having to deny her twisting him up inside. Then, abruptly, in a brief moment of rationality he forced himself to listen to, he turned and headed for the door.

"Bain, come back, please come back," she cried breathlessly.

He kept on going, flipped the lock, and flung the door open.

"I hate you!" she yelled from the bed. "Do you hear me, Bain Kolter? I hate you for doing this to me, and I'll hate you for the rest of my life." Tears were streaming down her face. "You can't, Bain, you can't leave me like this," she screamed agonizingly. "What'll I do?"

He straightened, his hand tightening on the doorknob as he paused for a moment, hardening himself to her pleas. Taking a deep breath, not daring to look at her, afraid the self-discipline that had carried him this far would crumble altogether if he looked at her again, he said, "Don't worry, I'll send your little maid up—what's her name, Pretty—to take care of you, and you'll live. Maybe you can sleep it off." And with that he stepped out the door and closed it firmly behind him. But instead of stepping away from it, he stood for a moment, leaning back against it, breathing heavily.

What was it about the little minx that made his blood turn to molten fire and set up such a raging hunger within him every time he saw her? She was only a child. A sensuous, spoiled child at that, and he had to remember it. If he didn't, there'd be hell to pay. With sheer determination, his jaw clenched, he straightened, tugging at the ends of his blue frock coat. Then he lifted his head stubbornly and started walking toward the stairs.

Lizette watched the door shut behind Bain, and an empty feeling swept over her, followed by intense pangs of yearning that filled her with despair. The room was still one big blur, except for the closed door, and it looked a hundred feet tall and so far away. Why had he gone through it? Why had he left her?

Tears ran down her cheeks, and she began to tremble. He shouldn't have left her. Not like this. She was leaning on her right elbow and reached up with the other hand to pull her dress up over her breasts, and in doing so, her hand brushed against the hard nipple and she wanted to cry out. She wanted his hands on them again, his mouth on them. Instead there was only the night air to caress them and make them ache with longing.

She shuddered and fell onto her stomach, burying her face in the bedclothes, the room tilting around her like a ship tossed on a stormy sea, and she had to face it alone. Deep sobs were heaving her stomach now, and nausea began to make her start gulping back as the room spun around and around.

She was still lying with her head on the pillow, crying bitterly, some ten minutes later when the door suddenly opened again and Pretty stepped into the room.

The young slave girl stood staring toward the bed for a few minutes, listening to Lizette cry, then shook her head and went to the dresser. She used a flint and lit the lamp, carrying it to the bed. Her mistress's dress was unhooked, her hair disheveled. But then, that was to be expected. She leaned over and shook her gently. "Come on, Miss Liz, honey, come on, turn over, please," she said coaxing her. "Let me see how bad the drink took you."

Lizette heard Pretty's voice as if in a fog, and she tried to put a person to it. "Pretty?" she asked unhappily.

"Yes, Miss Lizzie, it's me."

"Oh, Pretty!" Lizette raised a hand to her face and wiped her eyes and nose with it, then wiped her hand off on the beautiful brocade bedspread.

"You're going to mess your bed up somethin' terrible doin' that, Miss Lizzie," Pretty said quickly, and she went to the dresser, took out a dainty handkerchief, and brought it back to the bed. "Here, use this," she said, and put it in Lizette's hand.

"I'm sick, Pretty," she groaned. "I feel awful."

"I don't doubt it," Pretty said. "Mr. Kolter said you drank a whole lot of the punch that was made for the grown-ups."

"Well, I am grown up."

Pretty shook her head. "Not quite, Miss Lizzie," she disagreed. "Not quite, but you will be soon." She straightened and moved to the dresser again, pulling out one of Lizette's cotton nightgowns. "Now, if you'll sit up a bit, I'll help you get your dress off so's we can put you in bed right."

"But I don't want to go to bed!" She shoved Pretty's hand away when she tried to help pull her into a sitting position. "I want Bain to come back. I want Bain. He has to come back, Pretty. He just has to," she cried helplessly.

Pretty's eyebrows raised as she stared down at Lizette; then, as suddenly as they showed surprise, they narrowed thoughtfully. She glanced quickly at the back of Lizette's dress, then up to her hair, remembering the hysterical frenzy Lizette had been in back on Saturday. She bit her lip. Was that what Mr. Kolter had meant when he said the girl was saying crazy things? What had happened between them? And why was it Mr. Bain Kolter who had brought Lizette to her room? She wouldn't say anything to anyone, at least not now, but as she bent over and took Lizette by the shoulders, turning the unhappy girl over onto her back after unhooking her dress the rest of the way, then helped her into the palc yellow nightgown, Pretty listened closely to her mistress's intermittent mumblings, trying to make some sense out of them and hoping for Lizette's sake that the little she could understand didn't mean what she was beginning to think it meant.

When the young girl's nightgown was on, Pretty pulled back the covers on the bed and tucked her in, then stood staring down at her suspiciously. "Are you sure all you did was drink too much punch, Miss Lizzie?"

Lizette's eyes were shut because her stomach was heaving inside her and her head was beginning to hurt like a thousand demons were hammering at it. "Oh, go away, Pretty," she said. "I just want to be alone!"

Pretty sighed. "All right, I'll go." She walked over and blew the candle out on the lamp. "But I thought you ought to know," she went on as she watched Lizette curiously, "Mr. Kolter said he'd go tell your mama you was stealin' the grown-ups' punch and got sick and I put you to bed. He said he'd try not to make her worry too much, but you know how your mama is."

Lizette's mouth was dry and she felt as if nothing belonged to her, not even her toes, and now Mama was going to find out. Well, so what? The way she felt now she'd probably be dead by morning anyway, so what did it matter?

"Oh, go to bed, Pretty," she said angrily, keeping her eyes shut so the world would quit moving. "Go to bed and leave me alone in my misery," and she turned over, burying her head in the pillow again, trying to forget the feel of Bain's hands on her and the warmth of his lovemaking as Pretty, shaking her head, went out the door.

6

Lizette stirred ever so slightly, then winced. Oh, Lord! Her head felt like it was being squeezed into the size of a pea. Her eyes were still shut and she took a deep breath, burying her face against the pillow, trying to stop the pain. After a few minutes she realized it wasn't working, so she flipped over onto her back and exhaled, then opened her eyes, looking up into Pretty's dark face as she finished opening the rest of the curtains, letting more sunshine in.

"What time is it, Pretty?" she asked hesitantly.

Pretty smiled. "Breakfast time." She turned from the curtains. "But your mother wants to see you before you go down," she said. "She's still in her room getting dressed."

Lizette moved slowly into a sitting position, cushioning her head the best she could, favoring it so it wouldn't hurt any more than it already was. She started to bring her knees up to ease some of the discomfort in her stomach, but as she moved her right leg, pain shot through the ankle and she let out a sharp cry.

"What is it?" asked Pretty.

Lizette reached down beneath the covers and touched her ankle. It was swollen to twice its normal size.

"I'm afraid Mother will have to come see me," she said. "I

vaguely remember turning my ankle last night. At first I thought it was a dream. I guess not."

Pretty reached out and grabbed the covers, pulling them back so she could get a good look. She bent down, her hands gently pressing the swollen flesh. "If I had known this last night, I could have tried to keep it from swelling," she said, then shook her head. "You'll be lucky if you're standing on that by the end of the week."

Lizette leaned back against her pillow, pulling it up higher to cushion her head better. "I guess I really made a fool of myself last night, didn't I, Pretty?"

Pretty glanced at her. "You was drunker than a lord," she said. "And rattlin' off about all kinds of things."

Lizette frowned. "Like what?"

Pretty stood up, tossing the covers back over Lizette. "Nothing to make any sense of," she said. "But you sure were mad at Mr. Kolter."

"Bain?" Lizette's face turned crimson. "My God, what did I say?"

"Couldn't make much sense out of it," said Pretty discreetly. "But I'll tell you, Miss Lizzie, it sure didn't sound like anything a girl your age should be spoutin', and if your mother knew about it, she'd probably have your father skin Bain Kolter alive and tack his hide to a tree."

"Oh, Pretty, I didn't!" she exclaimed.

"You did." Her eyes narrowed. "He didn't force himself on you or nothin', did he, Miss Lizzie?" she asked. "After all, he was up here alone with you, and you were so upset when I came in."

Lizette shook her head, and tears began to gather in the corners of her eyes. "Good heavens, no, Pretty," she said indignantly, holding the tears in check. "You surely ought to know better than that. Bain wouldn't do anything like that."

Pretty shrugged. "Well, you never can tell. Some folks do change, you know."

"Not Bain Kolter," Lizette said, and tried to remember everything that had happened last night, but couldn't. All she could remember, and that wasn't even too clear, was kissing Bain. She let the memory of those kisses bring a wistful look to her eyes, then realized Pretty was staring at her rather intently. She straightened quickly, pulling herself back to this morning. "Bain Kolter is still an egotistical, insufferable male, just as he's always been." She had to make sure Pretty wouldn't say anything to her mother or Hizzie, because if Pretty just so much as happened to hint anything in front of

Hizzie, her mother would find out in Hizzie's next breath. "I suppose the party lasted until late last night," she said, changing the subject.

Pretty nodded as she walked about the room fussing with the clothes she'd helped Lizette remove last night, readying them to take downstairs to be cleaned. "Most everyone got to bed about three in the morning."

"Who stayed over?"

"Your grandma and grandpa, aunt and uncle, and cousin, the Tollivers, Sinclairs, Epworths, and Costigens from Charleston, Governor Williams, and the Kolters."

"Did Bain stay too?" she asked.

"As far as I know."

"I see." She glanced at the dress in Pretty's arms, trying to remember more of what she'd said to him last night and why she'd been kissing him, then frowned as a little of it came back to her. She looked up into Pretty's face, her own face flushed. "Tell Mother why I can't come to her room," she said quickly. "And bring my breakfast up, will you, Pretty? Maybe if I eat something I'll be able to get this horrible taste out of my mouth."

Pretty nodded and left, leaving Lizette alone at last with her thoughts, which were a little frightening. She stared across the room to where Pretty had just closed the door, and her eyes fell on the lock. She kept staring at it, trying to remember. There had been something about the lock last night. She rubbed her temples, but it just wouldn't come, and she was still staring at the lock when the door opened and her mother came in.

Rebel was wearing a bright blue silk morning dress, with a high waist, squared neckline laced with satin ribbons, and short puffed sleeves. She stifled a yawn, still tired as she closed the door behind her, then walked slowly toward where Lizette was propped up in the big bed. She straightened, forcing the tiredness from her body, and stared hard at her young daughter.

"Pretty said you hurt your ankle last night," she said, frowning as she stopped beside the bed. "Really, Lizette, what on earth got into you? You knew you weren't supposed to drink the punch with the liquor in it. That's why we made sure you young folks had your own punch bowl."

Lizette's eyes snapped as she stared at her mother. "That's just the trouble," she said, pouting. "You're always putting me with the young folks! I'm not twelve anymore, Mother."

"No, but you're not eighteen yet either, young lady," her

mother countered. "So I wish you'd quit trying to act it. I only thank God no one else found out about your little escapade last night. As it is, Bain knows, and that's bad enough. I made him promise not to tell anyone else. But he said Felicia and Heather are the ones who got him to help, so that's three people who know. I guess we'll just have to hope no one tells."

"So what if they do?" said Lizette. "I'm sure I'm not the only one who had too much to drink."

"You're the only fifteen-year-old girl who had too much to drink. Good God, Liz, what were you thinking of?"

Lizette flushed. "I didn't really mean to drink that much, Mother," she said, showing a hint of penitence. "I only wanted to prove that I wasn't still a child like I'm always being treated. I didn't think one or two glasses would hurt."

"Felicia said you had at least six that she counted." She eyed her sternly. "Now, Liz, you know better than that."

Lizette stared into her mother's violet eyes, then studied her face curiously. "Mother, didn't you ever do anything you weren't supposed to when you were my age?"

Rebel felt warmth flood into her face. "That's beside the point," she said, flushing self-consciously.

"No it isn't," insisted Lizette. "I hate being fifteen, Mother. I'm too old for toys and not old enough for anything else."

"Like what?"

"Like last night. I had to dance with Robert and Horace. They're both fifteen. Not one man asked me to dance except Father, Uncle Heath, and Grandpa, and it's the same with Felicia. Heather doesn't have to worry, she's almost eighteen, she was dancing with everybody, but I get treated like I'm still in short dresses."

Rebel stared at Lizette. "But, honey, you're only fifteen," she said. "Whom did you want to dance with?"

"Never mind," said Lizette angrily. "It wasn't just that. It's everything. I'm not old enough for this, not old enough for that. I hate being fifteen!"

"You'll be sixteen in June."

"And I still won't be old enough."

"Old enough for what?" asked Rebel, puzzled by her attitude.

"For everything," Lizette said, then sighed. "Oh, forget it, Mother," she said disgustedly. "You wouldn't understand. You probably don't even remember what it was like when you were fifteen."

Rebel frowned. "That's just the trouble, dear," she said

hesitantly. "I do remember what it was like, and that's why I'm concerned."

Lizette tried to change the subject. "How did the party go?" she asked abruptly.

Rebel walked over and glanced out the window that overlooked the gardens at the back of the house. "Except for the fact that you were missing at the big finale, it went beautifully," she said. "Everyone seemed to enjoy it, although Rachel Grantham was quite put out again when your grandfather refused to succumb to her charms."

"Why did you invite her anyway?"

Rebel sighed. "It was your grandmother's idea, not mine," she said. "Sometimes I think she does it on purpose just to get even with Rachel. Mother knows she's secure with Roth's love and it's a way of getting even with the duchess for the shameful things she's done to her over the years. Mother enjoys seeing Rachel's attempts at seducing Roth frustrated, because it upsets Rachel so. But as far as I'm concerned, I couldn't care less if I never set eyes on her again. There are too many painful memories to haunt me whenever I see her. But Mother enjoys seeing her squirm, and in a way, it is funny when you think of it. Rachel thinks she's being very subtle and that no one knows what she's up to, when in reality she's become a laughingstock." She stopped and suddenly turned back to Lizette. "But we were talking about *your* ridiculous behavior, young lady, not Rachel Grantham's!"

Lizette made a face, and Rebel's eyes darkened as the sun shining in the window caught the highlights in her pale hair, turning it to burnished gold.

"Lizette, please promise me you'll stop doing this," she pleaded seriously. "It's getting to the point where I'm afraid one of these days you'll do something that will really hurt you. In a way, you already have. If you hadn't disobeyed us and gone swimming alone, you'd still have all your hair."

Lizette reached up, tugging the end of a short curl. "It'll grow back."

"Yes, your hair will," she said thoughtfully. "But there are some things that won't, Lizette, and you're getting old enough now to realize that." She stopped for a minute, trying to gauge her daughter's mood, then, when she couldn't, went on anyway. "Liz, how well have you gotten to know Bain since he's been home?" she asked abruptly.

Lizette could feel her face turning crimson. "I've seen him a few times. At Felicia's, then the day of the races, and you know about last Saturday." She tried to be nonchalant. "What are you getting at, Mother?" she asked.

"Well . . ." Rebel had always been able to talk freely to Lizette, but suddenly she felt hesitant. "I know it's quite common for a young girl to become infatuated with an older man, and, well, dear, I just don't want you to be hurt. Bain's rather good-looking, and I imagine it'd be very easy for a young girl to get carried away by his charm. And you're such a precocious child, but you are still a child, dear. I'd hate to see you embarrassed by thinking perhaps you were in love with him or something."

"Me? In love with Bain Kolter?" Lizette laughed, but it was hard to disguise the brittle mockery in her voice. "I hate him," she said defiantly. "He's always spoiling all my fun, and especially I hate him for cutting my hair," she said. "He could have cut the briers instead, and maybe we could have untangled it when I got home. Love him?" She sneered. "Don't be ridiculous, Mother."

Rebel's eyes lingered on Lizette's face. Was Lizette protesting too much, or did she really mean what she was saying? It was so hard to tell. She tried to remember back to when she was her daughter's age, but it didn't help. She would have lied too under the same circumstances. But was Lizette lying? First loves could be so terrifying, especially if they weren't reciprocated, and to fall in love with an older man was heartbreaking. She hoped to God she was wrong, yet instinct told her she was right, especially when she thought back to the melancholy mood Lizette had been in ever since the day Bain had caught the girls at the cockfight. Rebel's heart went out to her, because she knew the torment her daughter must be in.

"I'm glad," she said, pretending to believe Lizette. "Because I'd hate to think you were making a pest of yourself or bothering him. You haven't been, have you?"

Lizette exhaled disgustedly. "I told you, Mother, I'm not a child," she said. "I didn't ask him to rescue me the other day or to carry me up here last night. Last night was Felicia's doing. If you want to blame someone for pestering Bain Kolter, blame his sister. I don't know why she had to call him anyway. I wasn't that drunk, and I could have easily walked up here myself if I hadn't twisted my ankle."

"Well, then, let's just forget it, all right?" Rebel said, anxious to relieve some of Lizette's misery. "But please, dear, let this be your last escapade, will you?"

"All right." Lizette sighed, then gazed at her mother sheepishly. "How did father take it?"

"I think you can expect your father to be a little less understanding," she answered. "After all, he was never a fifteen-year-old girl."

Lizette's bottom lip pushed out. "Can't you explain to him?" she asked.

"I'll try, but I can't promise. So for now I suggest you try to be as little trouble as possible, and maybe with the excitement of having so many people in the house, he might even overlook what's happened. At least I hope so."

Lizette's eyes softened. "Thank you, Mother," she said.

"For what?"

"For being understanding. I didn't mean to drink too much. I only wanted to prove I was grown up."

"I know," said Rebel. "It's hard growing up." She reached out and took Lizette's hand, squeezing it as she bent and kissed her on the cheek. "But for now I think we'd better try to forget what happened. The important thing is that no one else learns about it. I'll just tell them you hurt your ankle and had to leave the party. They don't have to know how it happened." She looked at Lizette hopefully. "And I'm holding you to your promise, young lady," she said. "No more foolishness."

Lizette made a face. "Life is going to be so dull."

Rebel smiled. "Do you think you can stand it?"

"I'll try." She let go of her mother's hand and frowned. "Mother, how long does it take to get over a hangover?"

This time Rebel couldn't help laughing, and a smile was still on her face later in the hall when she ran into Loedicia.

"My, you look happy," said Loedicia as she stared apprehensively at Rebel. "I assume you found out what was wrong with Lizette and everything's all right."

"I did find out, and I hope it's all right," she said. "But I'm afraid Lizette's in the throes of her first big infatuation."

"Oh, dear, who?" Loedicia asked.

Rebel glanced over at her mother as they walked down the hall. "If I tell you, will you promise not to let Lizette know?"

Loedicia nodded.

Rebel's mouth tightened. "Bain Kolter," she answered grimly.

Loedicia stopped.

"What's the matter, Mother?" Rebel asked.

"Are you sure?"

"Naturally, I can't be positive," answered Rebel. "But she's been acting so strangely ever since he returned home, and when I asked her about him just now, she became quite hostile."

Loedicia sighed. "But he's so much older than she is."

"Let's face it, Mother," said Rebel. "When a young girl loses her heart for the first time, age doesn't have much to do with it. It's the man that counts. After all, Father was ten years older than you, and it didn't seem to make any difference."

"But Lizette's still a child."

"I know, that's what I don't like."

"Bain hasn't been encouraging it, has he?"

"I doubt it. If I know Lizette, she's probably an embarrassment to him. I didn't tell you last night, and if I tell you now, you've got to promise not to tell anyone else except Roth," she said quietly.

Loedicia frowned. "Tell me what?"

"You promise?"

"Of course," she answered, and her violet eyes caught her daughter's, concern showing in them.

"Lizette drank the grown-ups' punch and got drunk last night," she said. "Felicia couldn't handle her and called Bain to help."

"Oh, no."

"Oh, yes, and I don't think it helped Lizette's emotional state any knowing the man she thinks she's in love with saw her making a fool of herself. He came to me last night and told me what happened, and he seemed quite uncomfortable."

"Poor Lizette," said Loedicia, shaking her head. "I can imagine how humiliated she feels."

"I didn't have the heart to scold her too much," said Rebel. "I only hope Beau will understand."

"I'm sure he will, dear," Loedicia said, and they continued on downstairs.

But Beau wasn't quite as understanding as Rebel. It was only the fact that Lizette's ankle would confine her to spending the rest of the week sitting down, forcing her to give up all the pleasures she had heretofore enjoyed, that made him decline any set punishment for her. He felt that not being able to do all the things she loved to do, including riding Diablo, was punishment enough.

Later that same morning, Heather and Felicia came to console Lizette before leaving, as did a few other guests, and Lizette put on a show of being unconcerned, but in reality, the idea of having to spend the rest of the week nursing a sore ankle, and not being able to see Bain again before he left with his parents, made her moody. Even after everyone was gone, nothing seemed to cheer her up. Unlike her usual self, she moped around and made herself miserable for the rest of the week.

It was the following Saturday when she was finally able to walk without limping, and the first place she decided to go was into Beaufort to see Felicia. At least that's what she kept telling herself when she got up that morning. The fact that she was secretly hoping she might run into Bain, she wouldn't admit even to herself. They still hadn't heard from Cole, and Rebel decided to go to the Kolters' with Lizette, hoping perhaps Bain might know of a way they could reach him, since he had been in and out of New Orleans near the end of the war.

The day was cool as Lizette got ready to go. She sighed as she finished her bath, dried herself briskly with a towel, then let Pretty slip the camisole down over her curly head. She inhaled tugging it down over her breasts, then looked hurriedly into the mirror.

"Is this my new camisole, Pretty?" she asked, frowning.

Pretty nodded. "I took it out of the top drawer where you said to put it last week after you tried it on. See, it's got the flowered lace design across the front and the little blue ribbon."

Lizette looked down at the front of her camisole. Pretty was right. There was the blue ribbon. It had to be the new camisole, but it was pulling across her breasts and fit her almost skintight farther down. She tugged at the ends, sucking her breath in, then smoothing the material down against her rib cage. It barely fit.

"Too much food and not enough exercise the past few days," said Pretty as she watched the worried look on Lizette's face. "Don't worry, Miss Lizzie, you'll lose it as soon as you start riding again and can do all the things you're used to doing."

"I hope so," said Lizette, exhaling breathlessly, and her eyes sifted over the camisole disgustedly.

Pretty handed her underdrawers to her and they too were tight when she pulled them up and tried to hook the waist.

She inhaled, pulling her stomach in as far as she could, but it still wouldn't hook.

"Hand me another pair," she told Pretty quickly as she

peeled the lace-trimmed drawers from her body. But the next pair was just as tight.

"Oh, Pretty," she wailed miserably. "What am I going to do?"

"You're going to let me move the hook over for you, that's what you're going to do, Miss Lizzie," she said.

Lizette stared at her, exasperated. "Now?"

"Now."

Pretty hurried from the room and was back quickly with a needle, thread, and scissors, and it took her only a few minutes to move the hook over closer to the end of the waistband.

"It isn't much," she said. "But you'll be able to breathe and we'll put it back later."

Lizette took the drawers from Pretty and tugged them on again. This time they fastened, but were still tight. While Lizette studied herself in the mirror, bemoaning the extra pounds she'd acquired during her convalescence, Pretty moved the hooks on her petticoat too, just as a precaution. It was a good thing she did, because as it was, the petticoat was tight at the waist too.

By the time Lizette slipped into her green silk, tugging it down over her breasts, inhaling while Pretty struggled to fasten it, she was in tears. "This never happened before, Pretty," she complained breathlessly.

"You never hurt your ankle before," said the maid, hoping to make her feel better.

"No, but I've been in bed sick."

"And couldn't eat."

She made a face. "You're right, I suppose."

"I know I am, Miss Lizzie. You've done nothing all week except enjoy Liza's cooking. All those pastries. I know if I eat too many my clothes get tighter too, and you've done nothing but munch on them all week."

Lizette exhaled, glancing at herself in the mirror. Well, one thing, at least it wasn't too noticeable, but when she bent over to put on her shoes and stockings, she could hardly breathe.

"Phew!" she exclaimed as she finished tying on her green kid shoes with their soft soles and sat up straight on the bed. "I swear to goodness I'm not going to eat another bit of food today," she said testily, and she meant it.

But by the time they reached the Kolters', after stopping to see if Heather wanted to join them, not only was Lizette hungry, she was starved, as was Heather, and their arrival was too close to luncheon for Madeline not to ask them.

"Good heavens, you have to stay," Madeline said as she greeted them out front, taking Rebel's arm, ushering her inside while Felicia welcomed Heather and Lizette.

"Don't go so fast," said Lizette as they headed up the steps and into the foyer. "I can walk, but the ankle's still sore." She had her cashmere shawl pulled tightly around her, hoping Felicia and Heather wouldn't notice how snug her dress was. "This is my first outing since it was hurt," she went on as she limped into the house, hanging on to her cousin and her friend.

Felicia hugged Lizette's arm, then glanced at Heather. "I hear you've really been getting out, Heather," she said smugly, and glanced around Lizette to where Heather was holding on to her young cousin's other arm.

Heather was dressed in a deep shade of gold that contrasted with her red hair and violet eyes. A flush reddened her cheeks and she leaned forward a little so she could see Felicia as she answered. "I presume you're referring to DeWitt."

Felicia smiled. "Who else? Rumor has it that he's been at the Chateau lately more than he's been at Palmerston Grove. And everyone said he danced with you more than anyone else at the ball."

"I guess he did at that," said Heather, and her jaw tightened stubbornly. "But don't assume it means anything. I find him amusing at times and he is attentive, but as far as liking him, he's just someone to spend time with until I can talk my parents into moving back up to Columbia."

"You're joking," said Lizette. "What makes you think you can talk them into going to Columbia?"

"Well, I'm not positive," said Heather. "But it seems to me Father's bound to get restless sooner or later. He's not used to being in one place any too long, and when he does, I intend to take advantage of it."

"And if he doesn't?" Lizette watched her cousin closely as they reached Madeline and Rebel, who were waiting at the bottom of the stairs.

Heather didn't have a chance to answer without her aunt and Mrs. Kolter hearing, so instead she only smiled self-consciously and shrugged at Lizette as the two older women bade the girls join them for a light lunch in the back garden.

The Kolters' gardens were lovely. There was a flagstone terrace with wrought-iron furniture on it directly outside the door of the sun room in the back, and Madeline, dressed in a dress of pink cambric with lace and ribbon adorning the skirt and bodice above the high empire waist, escorted them through the house, stopping one of the servants on the way to have three more places set at the table.

"I hate dropping in like this right at lunchtime," apologized Rebel. They had left their shawls and bonnets at the front door, and she tucked her sky-blue silk neatly beneath her as they all sat down at the table. "But Lizette was so set on coming in." She glanced at her daughter, then back to Madeline. "And I did want to see you, Madeline," she said. "We haven't heard a word from Cole yet since that last letter saying he'd be home, and I'm worried." She glanced about as if looking for someone, then again looked to her hostess. "I was hoping Bain was around so I could ask him if he had any idea what might have happened," she said anxiously. "Or if perhaps he thought it might be possible that Cole couldn't get away. After all, Bain was in New Orleans too for a while."

Madeline was sympathetic. "Oh, Rebel, dear, I'm so sorry," she said, and her eyes were troubled. "I thought almost everyone knew by now."

"Knew what?" asked Rebel curiously, suddenly noting out of the corner of her eye that Lizette had begun listening to her mother's conversation at the mention of Bain's name.

Madeline's brown eyes were sad. "He's gone again, Rebel," she said, a catch in her voice. "Bain's gone. I don't know why, but then, I never have known why he liked to wander so. I guess he just can't seem to stay in one place long enough to take root anymore. But we came home from your place on Tuesday and he seemed rather moody, and irritable, and distant all day, then Tuesday evening he told Rand and me that he was leaving first thing in the morning." She frowned. "We tried to talk him out of it, only he wouldn't listen."

"And he didn't say why he was leaving?" asked Rebel.

Madeline shook her head. "He never does. All he said was that it was impossible for him to stay any longer."

"But he's only been home a few weeks."

"That's what I told him. It didn't do any good."

Rebel glanced quickly toward Lizette, trying not to show concern. Her daughter was staring at Madeline with a look Rebel couldn't interpret.

Lizette sat motionless. She was stunned, and kept staring straight ahead, trying to let it sink in, only for some reason it just didn't seem real. Bain gone? He couldn't be. Why? It didn't make sense, he had just come home. He couldn't be gone! Blankly she gazed across at Madeline.

The conversation continued to go on around Lizette, but

she wasn't a part of it. She nodded, mumbling answers when spoken to, but had no idea what she was hearing or saying. All she could think of was that Bain was gone. She stared, mesmerized, remembering the day he'd caught them at the cockfights, when she'd looked into those stormy gray eyes of his. Then there was that day at the races when she'd challenged him to a race and the afternoon he'd won it. But most of all she was remembering Bain's lips, his arms, his body covering hers as they lay in the grass making love. And it was love. Oh, God, he couldn't be gone, but he was. She fought back the tears.

Then suddenly, as she tried to keep the tears from flooding her eyes, a sickening feeling began to grip her. She moved for the first time since hearing the news, feeling the tight pull of her dress across her bosom, remembering her petticoat and drawers that wouldn't fasten. It had never occurred to her before, but now abruptly she thought back to that precious moment when she had given herself to Bain and the world had been so rich and full. What if she were pregnant? Oh, Lord! Could she be having symptoms already? Or was Pretty right? Had she merely put on a little weight from sitting around eating all week, or was her body trying to tell her something? What should she do?

The hair at the back of her neck prickled and a chill ran down her spine, and for the rest of the afternoon she hardly knew what was going on around her, although her preoccupation with her own uneasy thoughts wasn't apparent to the others.

The rest of the afternoon was lost to her, as was the ride back to the Chateau and Tonnerre, and even after arriving back home, the turmoil inside her never ceased until the middle of the next week, when her menses suddenly began and she flowed heavily, relieving her mind of the burden it had been carrying. A burden no one else had even remotely guessed at. But nothing could relieve the pain in her heart at the thought of perhaps never seeing Bain again, and more than one night was spent dampening her pillow with tears as she tried to soothe her aching heart.

In the meantime, a shadow of anxiety was hanging over Tonnerre as each new day dawned and Cole still hadn't returned.

It was the middle of May. Heather had given up hope of ever returning to Columbia, especially since Aunt Nell had arrived at the Chateau the third week in April with Heather's horse, Jezebel, which she had refused to sell, and she was determined to stay if they'd let her, because she simply was tired of living alone.

Naturally Loedicia and Roth had greeted her with warmth and concern, as had Darcy and Heath, but Aunt Nell wasn't the easiest person to live with, and although she was absorbed into the household, she never really seemed to become a part of it. It was hard for her to accept the fact that the house didn't belong to her, and wasn't hers to run as she saw fit. She was also used to living in a female-oriented world, and the change was trying at times.

The whole world had changed for Heather too, and she had begun to change with it. At least Aunt Nell accused her of changing, although Heather couldn't see it. It had become obvious, shortly after the birthday ball in March, that DeWitt was courting her, but then, so were several other young men. At least for a while. But eventually they stopped coming around and she was seeing more and more of DeWitt, although her feelings for him hadn't changed. She was nice to him, treated him fairly, but that's as far as it went.

Although Tonnerre was some distance from the Chateau, Heather and Lizette became more than just cousins. By summer the girls were very close, and Heather often spent weekends at Tonnerre, where more than once she was instrumental in keeping Lizette out of trouble, reminding her of her promise to her mother every time her thoughts became dangerously liberal.

It was May. Lizette's birthday was a month away, and since Heather had come to stay for a few days, the girls had spent most of their time trying to guess what Lizette would be getting for her birthday from her parents. She wanted a new riding habit, or perhaps a new dress.

"Let's face it," said Heather as the two young women walked along the edge of the river in the late-afternoon sun, watching it reflect off the water. "You're going to need some new clothes." She glanced at her cousin apprehensively. "I think Pretty has let yours out as far as they'll go, hasn't she?"

"I know," complained Lizette bitterly. "I put on that weight back in March when I hurt my ankle, and I can't seem to take it off. Instead, I seem to be putting on more." She reached down, running her hands over her waistline that was no longer as slim as it had been only a few short months ago. She glanced over at Heather. "What am I going to do, Heather?" she asked helplessly. "You saw at breakfast, I hardly ate a thing, but I'm hungry already. And I know by lunchtime I'm going to be so starved I'm going to end up eating too much. I'll never lose weight this way."

"Well, it's not too bad yet, Liz," Heather said, trying to make her feel better. "But you are somewhat rounder than you were when we first met."

"Rounder?" said Lizette, disgusted. "I feel like I'm poured into my clothes. Pretty told me to get more exercise, but that doesn't seem to keep me from eating."

"Oh, I wouldn't worry too much if I were you, Liz," she said. "You'll probably lose it if you just give yourself time."

The conversation changed as they neared the house, and by the time they reached the terrace, both girls were laughing about something that had nothing to do with the loss of Lizette's slim figure.

It was early the next day that Lizette was forced to spend the morning in the house being fitted for some new clothes her mother insisted she have because she was splitting the seams on her old ones, so Heather tried to find something to while away the time until her cousin was through. Earlier in the spring Lizette had taken Heather for a walk to the old swimming hole to show her where Bain had cut her hair, and now, as the warmth of the day began to fill even the shadows with heat, she decided to see if the place was as cool and shady as she remembered it.

It was a long walk, but peaceful, the overgrown path easy to follow as it wound its way through the woods. Birds flew back and forth in front of her and squirrels chattered from the trees. She probably should have told someone at the house where she was going, but the decision had been a sudden one and she hadn't felt like walking all the way back up to the house from the garden.

She reached the clearing and stopped, gazing around. It was just as she remembered it, only the water didn't look quite as high as it had earlier in the year after the cool rains of the winter months, and the leaves were heavy on the trees now, giving more shade than what she had remembered.

She breathed in deeply, the heat of the day making her clothes stick to her. No wonder Lizette decided to go swimming that day, she thought as she walked through the grass toward the water. It was terribly hot, and the water did look inviting. But Heather didn't know how to swim, so instead, she sat on the bank, as close as she could without taking a chance on falling in, and occasionally dipped her hand in the water, running its cool wetness across her forehead and splashing it over her arms. At first she had almost succumbed to the temptation of taking her shoes and stockings off and dangling her feet in, but the thought of the snake that had frightened Lizette made her change her mind.

The cool water felt good and she was enjoying herself immensely, when suddenly she stopped with her hand still in the water and gazed off toward the path that led to the house. How strange. For some reason she had the weird feeling she was being watched, yet no one was there. She stared toward the path for some time, then shrugged and looked back down at the water, running her hand through it. Even though she hadn't seen anything, she still had the feeling someone was close by.

Her eyes shifted from the water to the opposite bank, scanning the bushes closely, moving along the bank slowly. Then suddenly her hand froze in the water. There was someone. She knew it, and her heart fell to her stomach. A man was standing a short way down river, below the dam. The sun was behind him, and his silhouette was ominous among the trees and bushes. He was tall, lean, and muscular, at least six feet, and as she watched closely, he stepped away from the trees and moved closer to the edge of the river, beginning to move to where he was directly across from her.

His coat was slung over his arm, and he carried a battered hat in one hand, a long-barreled rifle in the other. He looked tired and dirty, but she could tell he was wearing the remnants of what had once been an army uniform. The sun was on his face now and she could see his features clearly. At first she thought his face was only tanned; now she could see the high cheekbones and prominent jawline, almond-shaped eyes slanting above them, and suddenly she knew who it had to be and that those sloe eyes staring across at her had to be as beautiful a shade of green as those of his sister, Lizette.

She straightened, tensing, and took a deep breath. "Cole?" she challenged across the water.

He frowned. "You have me at a disadvantage, ma'am," he yelled back.

"I'm Heather," she called over. "Heath Chapman's daughter!"

His eyebrows rose, then lowered to a scowl. "Uncle Heath doesn't have a daughter!" he shot back.

"You've been away too long!"

"Two years?" He laughed. "I'd say it took longer than two years to come up with the likes of you!"

She smiled demurely. "I'll be eighteen in September!"

His laughter faded, to be replaced by a look of appreciation. "Wait there and I'll come across," he called quickly, and moved farther upstream to where the water was shallow and he could see the bottom. Sitting down, he began to take off his boots and stockings, then rolled up the legs of his brown linen fatigue pantaloons.

Heather watched curiously as he made his way across the river. As he reached her side of the pool of water she stood up, brushing the bits of leaves and grass off her pale lavender cotton. The dress had delicate embroidery decorating the bodice and deep violet ribbons trimming the high empire waist that emphasized her well-rounded bosom, and she felt very feminine.

Cole's eyes watched her furtively as he pretended to be absorbed in putting on his stockings and boots. He had lost his shoes and garters weeks ago, replacing them with a pair of used top boots, and he was wearing a nonregulation ruffled shirt that had seen better days.

He stood up, rifle in one hand, tall shako hat in the other, and now took a closer look at this young woman who claimed to be his first cousin.

Heather was standing directly in the sunlight, and it caught her hair effectively, turning it to flame. Her delicate coloring and small features gave the impression of softness, like a delicate flower or a painting that was almost, but not quite, finished. As if the artist were afraid to capture all of her for fear of imprisoning her soul in his work.

He blinked once, squinting in the sunlight, then walked toward her, hoping the ethereal quality that seemed to surround her would disappear. It did, but in its place stood a young woman so lovely that for a moment he'd forgotten who she was.

"What did you say your name was?" he asked hesitantly as he reached her.

Heather stared into his eyes and swallowed hard. She had been right. His eyes were every bit as green as Lizette's, a vibrant warmth turning them into fiery emerald. "It's Heather," she said softly.

He smiled, and for the first time she was aware of his even teeth and the faint hint of a dimple that dented his right cheek. His nose was classic, yet had the broad bridge of his Indian heritage, and the combination, along with his other features, made him ruggedly handsome.

They stood in the clearing only a few feet apart, staring at each other for a long time, not knowing quite what to say.

Then suddenly Cole laughed. "Hello, Cousin Heather," he said softly.

Her mouth tilted up at the corners. "Hello, Cousin Cole." She drew her eyes from his and glanced at his dirty clothes. His pantaloons had gotten wet during the river crossing and water was dripping from them onto his boots, making rivulets in the dust that covered them, and he looked like he'd come a long way on foot. "They expected you home weeks ago," she said. "Your family's quite worried."

"We had a little cleaning up to do around New Orleans. Then I came cross-country, never did like the water," he said. "Would have been here two to three weeks ago if I hadn't had some trouble near the Chattahoochee."

"The Chattahoo—what?" she asked.

"It's a river that flows down to the Florida territories. Some of the tribes along there aren't any too friendly."

She eyed him curiously. "Oh?"

He saw the puzzled look on her face, then understood, and his eyes darkened perceptively. "All Indians aren't friends with each other, dear cousin," he said caustically. "Being part Indian isn't always an advantage. I'm afraid my welcome wasn't any too cordial."

"But they let you go?"

"After I proved to them that I'm truly the son of the son of a chief."

Her forehead creased into a deep frown. "How?" she asked.

"If you don't mind, I'd rather not go into it right now," he said quickly, and delicately changed the subject. "But tell me, what are you doing out here alone?"

"I've been visiting with Lizette for a few days. She had to have some fittings for some new clothes and I didn't want to sit in the sewing room and watch."

He glanced off toward the path. "How about walking to the house with me, then? Maybe you can bring me up-to-date on how you happened to become a part of the family."

She nodded as he flung the rifle over his shoulder and they turned toward the path through the woods.

Lizette was in agony. She had purposely tried to control her appetite the past few days, and still the dress was so tight she could hardly breathe. It was one of her favorites too—a pink muslin with delicate flowered embroidery bordering the skirt and satin ribbon gracing the high empire waist. But at the moment she felt like a stuffed turkey in it, and the face she was making in the sewing-room mirror reflected her frustration.

"It isn't fair, Mother," she said unhappily as she turned to Rebel, who was staring out across the back lawn while Hizzie finished putting away the sewing things.

Rebel turned around to face her daughter. "What isn't fair?"

Lizette's eyes flashed angrily. "I don't eat any more than anyone else," she said bitterly. "At least I try not to, but I get so terribly hungry sometimes, and it seems like the more I try to keep from thinking about food, the more I end up eating, even when I don't really want to."

"Maybe you're not meant to be thin, dear," Rebel said, trying to ease her daughter's unhappiness.

Lizette didn't agree. "All the rest of you are thin."

"Your one grandmother was quite plump, dear," Rebel answered. "She was never thin in all the years I knew her. And your father's sister, Little Fawn, had gained considerable weight by the time she was your age. So it undoubtedly comes naturally."

"Well, I don't want it!" Tears forced their way into Lizette's eyes. "Oh, Mother, I don't want to be fat!" she wailed pitifully. Her eyes narrowed as she turned once more and stared at her figure in the mirror, watching miserably the way her hips brushed the sides of her full-skirted dress as it hung to the floor, and the way her breasts pushed up at the neckline. "I'll starve myself!" she vowed furiously, and tugged at the bodice of her dress, then tucked a hairpin back into her hair from where it had fallen. Her hair was almost grown out again, and although it wasn't as long as it had been before, it was well past her shoulders.

She finished primping her hair, then walked over to the window to join her mother. "Did Heather say where she was going?"

Rebel shook her head. "No, but she's outside somewhere." Her eyes scanned the landscape and suddenly she caught a glimpse of bright crimson through the trees.

The sewing room was at the back of the house, in the right wing to the north, and beyond the long expanse of lawn, broken only by the dusty lane between, were the fields, stretched out in the open sun. Trees lined the lane like sentinels, and as Rebel watched, two dark figures entered the end of the lane from a narrow path at the edge of the woods. She frowned. "Was someone with Heather?" she asked, squinting, hoping to see better, but the sun was casting shadows from the trees.

Lizette leaned closer to her mother, her own eyes studying the distant lane. "There *is* someone with Heather, Mother," she said anxiously. "It looks like a soldier." She scowled, her eyes narrowing. "It's a man, that's for sure . . . Oh, my God! Mother!" she shrieked suddenly. "It's Cole! Mother, it's Cole!" she yelled excitedly, and without waiting for her mother to recuperate from the sudden shock of seeing her son so unexpectedly, Lizette ran recklessly from the room, through the house, then out the French doors to the terrace and gardens. She slowed momentarily as she rounded the corner of the ballroom, then picked up momentum again until she reached the lane. Her eyes were glued to the tall figure walking beside Heather. Then, with her heart singing and her skirts flying, Lizette reached her brother in the middle of the lane and threw herself into his arms.

7

Lizette's uninhibited welcome surprised Cole, and now, after twirling her happily while she hugged him for all she was worth, he set her on the ground and straightened, staring at her, amused. "It is Lizzie, isn't it?" he asked looking her over carefully, his eyes sparkling.

Lizette's eyes were shining too. "You know very well it is, Cole."

He frowned, gazing down at her. "Well, now, I don't know," he said. "The sister I left behind was about yea tall," and he gestured with his hand somewhere between his waist and chest. "And she was as skinny as a string bean." His hand shot out and tilted her chin up so he could look directly into her eyes. "You've grown up into a beautiful lady, little sister," he said, and there were tears in his eyes.

Lizette's heart was warm and weak as she gazed up at her big brother. But as he looked down into her eyes, he was suddenly distracted by a movement closer to the house.

A woman was standing, holding on to the side of the house as if to support herself, and he inhaled sharply. There was only one woman he knew with pale hair that turned to gold in the summer sun like hers did, and behind her, hands pressed against her face to keep from crying, so that only her eyes shone dark and glistening, was Hizzie.

"Go to her, Cole," Lizette whispered breathlessly, still looking up at him. "She's been so worried."

He moved off hurriedly, eating up the space between himself and his mother. But when he finally reached her, he stopped dead, directly in front of her, and could only stare. He had waited so long for this. Just to come home and be a part of a family again. And she looked so beautiful. As he stared at her, he remembered all the love and warmth she'd given him over the years. How he'd snuggled on her lap as a little boy, letting her arms console him. She wasn't just a beautiful woman, she was his mother, and he loved her so very much.

Rebel was overwhelmed as she stared up into Cole's face; then suddenly she sighed, her lips trembling. "My heavens, you've gotten so tall," she whispered in amazement, and with the silence broken between them, she was suddenly engulfed in his arms.

After a few minutes, Cole's arms eased from around her and he set her on the ground, stepping back to look at her. "Sorry I couldn't make it for your birthday like I'd planned, Mother," he said, his voice breaking. "But a few unforeseen things came up."

"It's all right, Cole. It's all right," she said quickly, and sniffed in, smiling happily at the sight of him. "You're here now, and that's all that really counts." Her hands kneaded his arms and she was amazed at the strength in them. He was no longer the young boy she'd said good-bye to two years ago. He was a man, a tall, serious, handsome young man, and except for the green eyes, he looked so like his Grandfather Telak had looked when he was in his prime.

She caught the sound of Hizzie's sniffing behind her and looked over her shoulder, then back to Cole. "You'd better give her a welcome too, dear," she said. "Or we're going to have one unhappy lady on our hands."

Cole looked over the top of his mother's head, his eyes settling on his old nurse's face. She had been around for as long as he could remember, her broad warm smile soothing him more times than he could count. She was more to him than just a servant who had watched over him and been his wet nurse when he was a baby. She was more like a second mother.

Rebel released his arms and he grabbed Hizzie, hugging her close, laughing away her joyous tears.

"Land's sake, child," she cried happily. "You nearly gave us all the vapors, sneakin' up on us like that." She relished the feel of him in her arms again for a few minutes, then pushed herself back, her short frizzy hair framing her dark face like a silvery halo. "Don't tell me you walked all the way home?" she asked.

His smile was strained. "I rode most of the way, but lost my horse back at the Chattahoochee. I left New Orleans with two other men and moved north, where we picked up the Natchez Trace. But I left them and headed east toward Horseshoe Bend, where we fought the Creeks a year ago. I ran into a few disgruntled Creeks near the Chattahoochee." He ran his hand through his ebony hair, the sun on it giving it a blue cast. "I managed to keep my head, though, and that's more than I can say for most men who venture into that territory."

Rebel shuddered at the thought of Cole making his way through desolate and hostile territory. But as Beau had said so many times, Cole had inherited a natural instinct for living in the wild. She gazed at her son thoughtfully as Lizette and Heather joined them. He had grown so over the past two years. The last time they had seen him was the day he'd left to become a member of General Jackson's army and during the years he was gone he had become one of Jackson's best scouts, working his way up to lieutenant. Now he was no longer a soldier, but the strict discipline had left its mark on him. He stood tall and erect, his muscles tense, alert, as if coiled ready to spring at a moment's notice, and his eyes surveyed everything with an intensity that made them brilliantly alive. He was still her son, yet he was a son she wasn't sure she really knew anymore.

They all began to talk again enthusiastically until Cole suggested they go into the house, so as Hizzie wiped her eyes, he put an arm around his mother's shoulder and one about Lizette after first plopping his hat back on his head, and Heather stepped back so they could lead the way. She studied him carefully as he turned his mother and sister toward the French doors. Neither Beau Dante nor Lizette gave any hint of their Indian heritage, except perhaps for the dusky hue of their skin. But there was no way anyone could deny Cole's heritage. Heather had never dreamed he would look so much like an Indian. Lizette had spoken of him so often that Heather almost felt she should know him, yet this tall, good-looking man walking briskly between Lizette and Aunt Rebel was nothing like she had imagined him to be, except for those intense green eyes.

A strange warmth gripped her as she remembered the way

those eyes had looked at her back at the swimming pool. It had been a look she wouldn't soon forget.

They all entered the parlor, Cole letting his mother and sister follow Hizzie in first; then he turned to Heather, gesturing for her to enter next, as any gentleman would. "After you," he said pleasantly.

Heather nodded, her eyes answering him shyly and she stepped in behind her cousin and aunt.

Cole watched Heather move gracefully into the room, realizing once more how lovely she was. Her hair, away from the brilliance of the sun, was a deeper auburn, the highlights like warm mahogany, and he had noticed back at the swimming hole that her eyes were the same violet as his mother's and grandmother's. He frowned. Too bad she was such a close cousin.

He drew his eyes from her as she turned around, then glanced quickly at Lizette, trying not to look too obvious in his appraisal of his new cousin. Lizette had not only grown four or five inches during his absence, but had widened considerably. He was about to mention the fact when, instead, he looked up into her face and suddenly realized that she was probably all too conscious of the fact herself. To mention it might hurt her feelings, so he shoved the thought aside and turned to his mother. "Do you suppose I could clean up some before we talk?" he asked, gesturing toward his clothes.

She nodded, then looked at Hizzie. "Have Liza heat some water, Hizzie," she said quickly. "And you'd better get some of Beau's clothes from our room for him," she said. She glanced at her son and smiled. "I don't think any of the clothes you left behind are going to fit anymore, do you?"

She was right. He was going to need all new ones, but in the meantime, after excusing himself, going upstairs, and soaking in a hot tub, he fit perfectly into a pair of his father's pants with one of his father's shirts tucked in at the waist. And by the time his father returned from Beaufort, Cole looked far different from the straggly soldier Heather had first glimpsed by the old swimming hole. He was sitting on the terrace, his once dusty top boots glistening with a new shine, wearing a clean set of his father's work clothes, telling his mother, sister, and cousin all about his adventures.

Beau couldn't get over the change in Cole and was as proud as a father could be. He hugged him, exclaimed over his height, which now equaled his own, and let him know how glad he was to have him home again to help run things. Beau sent one of the servants to the Chateau with a message announcing Cole's return, and that very evening his grandparents, accompanied by his Uncle Heath and Heath's new wife, the former Darcy McGill, arrived, and he began to understand a little easier how Heather had come into existence, for she looked very like her beautiful mother, who had become his new Aunt Darcy.

They stayed all that night, the next day, and the next night, finally leaving on Wednesday, the seventeenth of May, to return to the Chateau. Heather didn't return with them, however. Instead she talked them into letting her finish out the week, which had been her original plan.

Although his father managed to keep him quite busy learning how to run a plantation, Cole still found time to spend with his sister and his new cousin, who seemed to fascinate him, and both girls were enjoying themselves immensely.

Two days after their grandparents' departure, the day dawned hot and muggy. A light rain had fallen the night before, and when morning came, steam came with it, swirling off the river and swamps, gilding the sun in a shroudy mist. But by late afternoon the mists were gone, replaced by heat that seemed to penetrate everything.

Cole had gone with his father early that morning to help split logs and clear away some land up north along the river. Lizette and Heather had wandered around the house most of the morning trying to find things to keep them busy. Now, shortly after luncheon with Rebel on the terrace, the two girls decided to take a walk to the old swimming hole.

On the way they discussed preparations for Lizette's birthday a month away, Cole's unexpected return, and the hot weather. As they neared the swimming hole, Lizette sighed. "I wish Cole hadn't had to go with Father this morning," she complained. "I'd love to go swimming, but after what happened the last time, I certainly don't want to go in alone. You don't swim, do you?"

Her cousin shook her head. "Heavens, no!"

"Well, you don't have to make it sound like something wicked," Lizette retorted. "There's nothing wrong with swimming."

Heather eyed her skeptically. "If it's so proper, then how come more women don't do it?"

Lizette shrugged. "Who knows? They're probably afraid to try," and as she finished the sentence she stepped into the clearing and stopped abruptly, a startled look on her face. "Wait," she whispered cautiously to Heather, who was close at her elbow.

"What is it?" Heather asked, keeping her voice low.

Lizette put a finger to her lips, then motioned toward the water some distance ahead of them.

Heather stared, trying to see into the shadows made by the branches overhead. Her eyes suddenly stopped their searching and she gasped as Cole's head, then his shoulders, emerged from the water and he flung his wet hair back with a quick gesture.

Cole didn't see them at first. They had finished the job upriver early, and since the day was hot, his father had told him he could have the rest of the day off. It was logical he'd head here. He had tethered his mare at the edge of the woods a little upriver where she could graze and was now enjoying a relaxing swim. The cool water was invigorating, but as he started to lean back, pushing with his feet to float onto his back, a movement caught the corner of his eye and he forced his muscles to reverse their backward thrust. He raised a dripping hand to shade his eyes. "Hey!" he called, when he had determined the identity of his intruders. "Come on in, the water's fine."

Lizette giggled when she realized they'd finally been seen, and quickly moved forward toward the water. "Do you really mean it?" she asked as they neared the edge.

Cole smiled. "Why not?"

"You're not in the altogether, are you?"

"Not yet."

"Cole!" Lizette's eyes brightened and she laughed as she reached up, starting to unfasten the back of her dress.

"What are you doing?" asked Heather.

Lizette looked at her, startled. "Why, I'm going swimming."

"You're not!"

"Oh, Heather, don't be such a dunderhead. Why don't you come in too?"

Heather's eyes widened. "Me? I can't swim. Besides"—her face turned beet red—"what are you going to swim in?"

"My underthings."

Now Heather knew she was crazy. "But that's indecent!"

"What did you think I swam in?" Lizette asked as she finished unfastening her dress and began to slip it off her shoulders.

Heather shook her head. "I don't know . . . I never thought about it, I suppose."

Lizette stepped out of her dress and laid it aside, the petticoat following it hurriedly, then sat down and started taking off her shoes and stockings.

Cole watched from the water, studying Heather. "Aren't you coming in too?" he asked.

Her head jerked toward the water. She didn't know what to say and could only stare at him.

"Well?" he asked again.

"Oh, come on," said Lizette as she set her shoes and stockings aside and stood up. "Don't be such a ninny, Heather. It's fun, and Cole doesn't care, really he doesn't. I ought to know, he's seen me in my drawers and camisole dozens of times."

Heather blushed. "But he's your brother."

"And he's your cousin. Come on, please," she begged, but Heather still shook her head. "Oh, pooh! You're no fun at all," Lizette said, exasperated, and turned toward the water. "Is it cold?" she asked her brother.

"No colder than usual. Come on, jump," he yelled. "It's deep enough."

Lizette checked the pins in her hair, tugged at her underclothes to make sure nothing was loose or awry, then, as Heather watched in horror, she ran to the deep end, put her hand to her nose, holding it tight between finger and thumb, gave a leap high into the air, and plunged in feetfirst.

Heather held her breath, waiting; then, as Lizette's head finally broke the surface, she exhaled, relieved.

Lizette looked so funny with her hair soaked, yet she was smiling, her eyes aglow. She wiped the hair from her eyes, then gazed at her brother standing just a few feet away. Cole was staring at Heather. Probably trying to figure out why she was such a prude, Lizette thought. She ducked down in the water, letting it caress her chin, its coolness embracing her body. What a wonderful feeling. Her eyes studied Cole's face. He looked so serious.

With a flick of her wrist she splayed her hand quickly, shooting a spray of water at him, and abruptly the serious look changed to one of surprise.

He smiled, then his head disappeared beneath the water, and seconds later she felt his hand clamp about her ankle. With a shriek that was half laughter and half pretended fright, she struggled against his hand, then took a deep gulp of air just before her head disappeared beneath the surface.

Heather watched Cole and Lizette for a while, laughing and splashing playfully in the water. Finally she sat down near the edge, dipping her hand in the water as she had done the day Cole returned. The water did feel good; it was cool compared to the heat of the day. She watched her fingers play across the surface, then glanced up as Cole approached, walking toward her, only his head and the tip of his shoulders visible above the water.

"Why don't you come in?" he coaxed again, his voice was husky with warmth. "It wouldn't hurt, and the water's deliciously cool."

"I don't know how to swim."

"I'll teach you."

For a long time she stared at him, wanting to say yes, yet afraid to. It looked like such fun, and what they were doing didn't seem to be wrong. Yet she was still apprehensive. She had never done anything so outrageously unladylike in her life. To be so exposed in her underclothes. It was actually scandalous, or would be if anyone found out. She bit her lip, and Cole sensed her indecision. He began to coax again, a little more forcefully this time, and Lizette joined him, and between the two of them Heather had finally met her match.

She felt the sticky heat of her clothes against her skin, then watched the beads of cool water rolling off Lizette's face. Why not? she suddenly asked herself. If Lizette could, why couldn't she? After all, as Lizette pointed out earlier, there was really nothing for Cole to see except the material of her underdrawers and camisole. The essential parts of her body would be completely covered.

She stood up gingerly and reached around, slowly unfastening the back of her dress, and within a few minutes she was standing barefoot on the bank, lips trembling at the sudden realization of what she was doing. She almost turned back. But in those few unsure seconds she looked down into Cole's eyes, saw his hand stretched out for her, and knew she couldn't change her mind.

She sat on the grass at the very edge of the water, put her feet in, then let Cole take both her hands and pull her in the rest of the way, and as the water engulfed her body, a feeling of exhilaration seized her. The water moved quickly up her body, and for a second she thought her head was going to go under, but instead, strong arms circled her and she felt herself pulled against Cole's muscular frame. He smiled at her, and for the first time in her life Heather felt a rush of heat flood through her that left her breathless and all quivery inside. His arms were exceptionally strong, holding her fast and firm, and for a moment she felt weak all over. Then a rush of air once more filled her lungs, bringing with it a few strangled words: "I almost went under!"

"Never," he said firmly. "Now, we're going to teach you how to swim or die trying," and still holding her in his arms, he began to move into deeper water as she clung to him desperately.

But it took only a short time to teach her that the water was there to enjoy, and before long she was more at ease, feeling the water's soft caress as it flowed about her. The hot sun had parched her skin, and the cool water soothed it, and although she was still unskilled and unable to keep up with her cousins as they cavorted in the water, she began to enjoy it more and more with each passing minute and soon forgot all about the impropriety of the whole thing.

She moved her hands beneath the surface, watching the water run over her arms, then tried to remember what Cole had told her to do. He was standing a short distance away, trying to fend off Lizette's attempts at dunking him, and his back was to her as he splashed water into his sister's face. Heather bent her knees slightly as her arms moved out, and with a slight leap her body floated to the surface, arms moving alternately as they knifed the water, and with a feeling of pride she swam to him, reaching to touch his shoulder just as he turned.

Cole laughed, catching her hand, and Lizette grabbed her cousin's other hand, and both girls hung on to Cole, almost pulling him down, and for the rest of the hot afternoon the clearing resounded with their laughter.

DeWitt Palmer was more than a little disgruntled. He had returned from a week's stay in Charleston and decided to call on Heather at the Chateau, only to discover she was at Tonnerre, and now, after riding all the way upriver he had been met by Heather's Aunt Rebel with the news that Heather and Lizette had gone for a walk.

"Probably to the old swimming hole," Mrs. Dante had told him. "If you'd like to ride out and find them, follow the path that runs north behind the ballroom."

So here he was, on a day that was hot enough to cause heat prostration, riding along this narrow, overgrown path with his clothes sticking to him. He shifted in the saddle and leaned down, patting his horse's neck, Heather was worth it, though. Just remembering her like this brought a warmth to his loins. God, she was a beauty, and untouched. Of that he was certain. She was too shy, too much the lady to have let any man take advantage of her. Yes, she'd make a perfect wife.

He whistled softly to himself as he rode along the narrow path, then suddenly stopped, reining his horse to a halt. From up ahead he could hear soft laughter, then sudden bursts of guffawing.

DeWitt sat astride his horse, then slowly flicked the reins, urging him on. As the horse reached the clearing where the old swimming hole was, he halted him once more and stared ahead to where the river was dammed to make a pool, his eyes wide with disbelief.

There, ahead of him, standing on the bank ready to plunge in, fingers holding her nose, red hair gleaming in the sun, wearing only her camisole and drawers, was Heather. As he watched transfixed, she took a running leap, flew through the air, and disappeared beneath the water before he had a chance to even call her name. He watched in horror as she surfaced, shaking her head vigorously to get rid of the excess water; then he saw Cole and Lizette join her, and the three of them began churning the water into a fine spray that drenched them all.

He had seen enough. His jaw tightened as he dug his horse in the ribs and rode out from the shadow of the trees into the center of the clearing.

Cole was the first to spot him. "Well, look who's come calling!"

"Witt!" Heather exclaimed, wiping a wet strand of hair from her eyes.

He stared at her hard. His hazel eyes, shaded from the sun by his hat, were intense, fiery, and his voice was strained when he spoke. "Just what on earth do you think you're doing?"

She frowned. "I'm swimming."

"Do your parents know?"

"Why . . ." She stared at him, puzzled. "Why, no."

"I didn't think so." His jaw clenched even firmer. "I suppose I can thank your cousins for this," he said angrily. "It was bad enough when it was just Lizette." He glanced quickly at Cole. "I heard you had come home," he said briskly. "I was hoping the rumor wasn't true."

Cole began to move upriver toward the shallow end. "Sorry to disappoint you," he said. "I'm afraid I'm all in one piece, too." He left the water and moved onto the bank, his wet underwear clinging to him. He stood staring at DeWitt Palmer. He had never liked the man. DeWitt had used every means available to stay out of the military, and more than one man had questioned his success at the card tables.

Heather's eyes were on Cole as he stood on the bank, feet planted firmly in the sun-browned grass, and she couldn't help admiring the picture he made, his lean body coppery and sleek, the water making it glisten, muscles rippling the skin. But his eyes were hard and unfriendly as he asked caustically, "What can we do for you?"

DeWitt inhaled sharply. "I came by to see Miss Chapman." Then he turned, addressing Heather, who was still in the water, standing beside Lizette. The water wasn't deep enough to cover their breasts, and their camisoles were plastered against them, outlining the flesh beneath. DeWitt's face turned crimson, but he refused to look away. "I never dreamed I'd find you swimming, Heather," he admonished. "I expected more ladylike behavior from you." He glanced at Lizette, then back to Heather. "I'll excuse you this time," he went on, "since I know your cousin has a way of influencing you. But I think it's time you realized you mustn't go along with all her crazy notions. Swimming! Good heavens, no decent woman goes swimming." He glanced at the pile of clothes on the bank. "All right," he said, "Cole and I'll turn our backs while you get out of the water and get dressed, and if you promise never to do it again, I guess I can see it in my heart to forgive you the indiscretion this time."

For a minute Cole wasn't sure he had heard right, but as he stared at DeWitt he realized the man was serious. He frowned. "Now, wait a minute. Just who do you think you are, ordering my cousin around like that?"

Witt stiffened. "That, sir, is none of your business."

Cole glanced toward the water. "Heather?"

She half-shrugged, not knowing what to say. "I—" she began.

"Miss Chapman is my intended," Witt interrupted crisply.

"I'm no such thing," Heather cried, finally finding her voice.

Witt was taken aback. "No such thing?" he asked. "Haven't we been seeing each other regularly?" he asked.

She only stared at him.

"And haven't I taken you home to meet my father and brother?"

"Yes, but I—"

"And haven't you let me kiss you good night when we parted?"

Even though the kisses had meant nothing to her, to hear him speak of them made her uncomfortable.

"Well, haven't you?" he asked again.

She nodded reluctantly, the water suddenly growing cold, and she felt sick. "Yes," she whispered, "but—"

"Then according to custom, Miss Heather," he said arrogantly, "most everyone would consider that I'd been courting you in fashion and been duly accepted."

"That's not true," she managed to say breathlessly. "And you know it." She began coming out of the water, with Lizette beside her. Cole held out his hand and helped them onto dry ground, and the three of them stood looking at Witt, still in the saddle.

"I admit you've come calling," Heather said, "but not once have you asked me for my hand, and not once have I given you any indication I'd say yes even if you did ask."

Witt's eyes narrowed as they sifted over her full form, now revealed by the sun and her clinging underclothes. The blood ran hot in his veins, and he had all he could do to sit comfortably in the saddle. His eyes moved back to her face. "Don't be absurd, Heather," he said. "A decent woman doesn't let a man kiss her unless she intends to marry him. No man wants a woman who's been used."

"Used?" Cole chided. "A kiss isn't the same as a toss in the hay, Witt," he said. "You know better than that. If it were, you'd have been engaged years ago."

Witt's eyes darkened. "Hold your tongue, Cole!" he yelled.

Cole laughed. "Who's going to make me?"

"I am," said Witt, and he quickly dropped from the saddle.

Cole's eyes gleamed as he stared at his opponent.

As soon as Witt hit the ground, he realized he had made a mistake. The last time he had seen Cole Dante was two years ago, and Cole had been a good six inches shorter. Now, as Witt straightened, tugging at the front of his dark green frock coat, trying to look impressive, he suddenly realized he had to look up to Cole who, barefoot, stood an even six feet to his five-feet-ten.

"You were saying?" Cole asked as he continued to assess Witt thoughtfully.

Witt cleared his throat, reluctant now to carry through with his threat. "I was saying," he said instead, his voice a little less assured, "that Miss Heather and I are practically engaged, and that gives me every right to reprimand her for her scandalous behavior. If her mother knew what she was about, she'd be shocked."

Heather gasped, suddenly remembering that she had a mother. DeWitt was right. She glanced down at herself. The camisole and drawers covered her, yes, but wet like this, there was little left to the imagination, and she flushed, embarrassed. He was right about her mother, but he wasn't right about her engagement. The thought rankled.

"She'd be more shocked, DeWitt Palmer," she said defensively as she started toward where her dress lay on the ground, "if she knew you were standing here ogling me," and she picked up her dress, holding it in front of her. "And another thing," she said scathingly, "I am not nor shall I ever be betrothed to you. Is that understood?"

It was Witt's turn to flush, and for a minute he didn't know what to say, because he was certain she didn't mean a word of it. She was letting her anger at being caught in such a scandalous escapade color her thinking. His eyes softened a little as he stared at her.

"Please, Heather, be reasonable," he said, hoping to help her see the error of her ways. "You know very well how I feel about you, have felt from the very start." He straightened, clearing his throat. "Perhaps I haven't gotten around to asking formally for your hand, my dear, but that doesn't mean I don't plan to," he said. "You say you'd never be my betrothed . . . Well, then explain to me please why you've led me to believe all these months that you felt otherwise. The notion that you didn't know what I had in mind is preposterous."

She didn't know what to say, and stared at him reluctantly. Did she dare tell him that the only reason she let him come calling was that she didn't know how to tell him no? That he was dull and boring, and the only reason she let him kiss her good night was that she didn't know any better because she'd had very little experience with being courted? Good heavens, she'd be embarrassed to have to admit all that. But what could she tell him?

"Well, do I get an explanation?" he asked bluntly.

Heather's jaw tightened. "You don't need one," she finally said, her voice strained. "I let you come calling because you wanted to. If you read more into my actions than that, then I'm sorry. I never meant for you to. And as far as knowing what you had in mind, I'm not a mind reader, DeWitt."

"As simple as that?" he said.

She pursed her lips. "As simple as that."

"So why don't you just leave?" asked Cole.

Witt's eyes narrowed angrily. "I'll leave when I'm good and ready."

"Then I suggest you get ready, because at the moment I don't think my cousin appreciates your presence. Nor do I."

Witt's eyes blazed. "This is all your fault, Cole," he spat venomously. "You and that fat sister of yours."

"Fat?" Lizette yelled. "Who are you calling fat?"

"You!" he said viciously. "And you're nothing but a troublemaker. Every time Heather's done anything unladylike, it's been at your instigation. You're nothing but a spoiled child, and why Bain ever wanted to bother with you I'll never know."

Cole glanced at her in surprise. "Bain?" he asked.

Lizette flushed crimson. "He doesn't know what he's talking about," she said quickly.

"Don't I?" said Witt. He looked at Cole. "Ask her about the horse racing" he said. "And I wouldn't doubt there's been more. I saw the way he looked at her that day." His eyes sifted over Lizette with contempt. "Of course, she was thinner then. If he could see her now, he'd probably turn away in disgust."

Lizette gasped as Cole's arm shot out, his hand fastening on the front of Witt's shirt, squeezing his cravat tighter about his neck. "That's enough about my sister, Witt!" he snarled through clenched teeth. "I want an apology!"

"Or what?" asked Witt, his face livid, both hands clamped on Cole's arm. "I suppose you'll strangle me. I wouldn't put it past you. After all, you are part savage."

Cole's sloe eyes bored into Witt's, and his jaw twitched nervously. How close to the truth Witt was. At that moment Cole would have given almost anything to squeeze the life out of him. "No, I won't strangle you," he said roughly, "but I sure as hell can cool you off."

Witt's eyes shifted from Cole's face to the water, then back again. Unless he wanted to get his clothes ruined, he was going to have to back down, and he wasn't used to backing down from any man. His eyes blazed, lips quivering as he tried to control his temper. "All right," he gasped breathlessly, his toes barely touching the ground as Cole held him in his viselike grip, "all right, I'll apologize to your sister for saying she's fat, but the rest of it's true, Cole, ask her," he said. "Ask her why Bain Kolter decided to leave again so soon after just getting home." He took a deep breath, then went on. "He was running scared, Cole, and I know why. He was afraid somebody might find out he'd been fooling around with her. I was with him enough to see how it was right from the start, so don't go trying to defend your little sister's honor, because I doubt she's got any left."

Lizette and Heather both shrieked at the same time, as Witt suddenly felt himself lifted into the air and hurled from the end of Cole's arm, only to topple onto all fours before sliding the rest of the way down the bank into the water. He hit hard, but luckily he'd managed to close his mouth in time. He sank to the soft sandy bottom, then quickly pushed himself up, settling on his feet in shoulder-deep water. "I'll get you for this, Cole Dante!" he yelled, spluttering, wiping the water from his face. "Someday you'll be sorry."

"You scare me!" taunted Cole. His eyes grew serious and he turned to Lizette, who was watching Witt begin to make his way toward shore. Her face was pale, eyes rimmed with tears. "Well, Liz," he said, studying her curiously, "did I defend an honor you no longer have?"

She bit her lip. She couldn't let him know the truth. If he knew, he'd kill Bain if he ever returned. Witt had been guessing, she was certain. She looked up at her brother. "I raced Diablo against his horse, Amigo, yes, Cole," she answered truthfully. "And Bain Kolter rescued me when my hair caught in the briers, but that's all. If he had any feelings for me, I knew nothing of it," and she felt as if she was telling the truth, because in a way it *was* the truth. Bain had never once said "I love you."

"Then why the tears?" Cole asked.

She flinched. "Who's crying?"

"You are."

"Leave her alone, Cole," said Heather, coming to her cousin's rescue. "Bain's been a sore spot with her ever since the day he caught us at the cockfight and treated her like a wayward child." She slipped her dress on over her head, then walked over to Lizette, putting her arm around her shoulder. "Don't let Witt's stupid accusation bother you, Liz," she said solicitously, then glanced at Cole. "I know there was nothing going on between you and Bain." She saw Cole frown. "There wasn't," she said. "I was there too, most of the time anyway. Sure Bain probably thought she was pretty—most people do—but that gives Witt no right to say the things he did." She glanced over at Witt, who had managed to drag himself from the water. "And you got just what you deserved," she said with conviction.

Witt inhaled sharply, then confronted Heather, face stern, unyielding.

"You ought to be ashamed of yourself, DeWitt Palmer," she said before he could catch his breath to even open his mouth. "Saying those things about Liz. You know very well you have no proof to warrant such slander."

"That's beside the point," he said, blustering angrily. He was still winded from his ordeal. "The point is, Heather Chapman," he continued breathlessly, "that I came to Tonnerre expecting to visit a sweet young lady I've become quite fond of over the past few months, and instead I'm confronted with this . . . this outrageous scene," and he gestured toward her disarrayed appearance. "Your uninhibited behavior and the disgraceful way you were carrying on would be enough to shock anyone, and I think I had every right to voice my disapproval." He paused to take a much-needed breath. "I realize you're not entirely to blame," he went on, "and I also realize you're easily led, a weakness I don't enjoy seeing in you. I imagine your cousins made the prospect of joining them seem exciting, but I sincerely hope that in the future you'll take time to question the propriety of what they're suggesting." He paused for a moment to clear his throat. "For now I'll overlook the incident," he said "because I care for you considerably, but I certainly hope that in the future when I come calling I won't ever be exposed to the likes of something as shameful as this again." He straightened arrogantly. "Now, if you'll excuse me, since Mr. Dante has, as he so aptly put it, cooled my temper somewhat, I'll take my leave and return to Palmerston Grove, but be assured, Mr. Dante"—and he turned toward Cole, who was now tucking his shirt in his trousers—"your savage display this afternoon will not be forgotten. Someday I'll find a way to pay you back, and when I do, you'll regret ever having returned to Port Royal." He slammed his hat on his head as he looked back at Heather. "I'll see you later at the Chateau, Heather," he said quickly. "Good day," and he turned, walked to his horse, mounted, and rode off, leaving them standing half-dressed on the riverbank.

Cole was first to break the silence after the hoofbeats had faded in the distance. "You know, I think he was really mad," he said, half-amused.

Lizette was fastening her dress. She turned toward her brother. "Don't look so pleased, Cole. DeWitt isn't exactly the best person to have for an enemy."

"Why not?" he asked as he sat down to put on his boots and stockings. "Because his father owns the races at Palmerston Grove?"

"No, because since you left two years ago his father, Everett Palmer, has acquired controlling interest in the bank in Beaufort, and he's getting more powerful all the time, with a lot of friends in high places."

Cole frowned as he stood up. "I'm supposed to be worried?"

Heather, who had finished dressing, walked over to Cole. "Maybe you shouldn't have been quite so demonstrative," she said apprehensively. "Liz may be right."

Cole frowned. Had he been a trifle impulsive? He wondered. Could Liz be right when she told him he'd picked the wrong man to have for an enemy? The thought rankled, because he sure as hell didn't want to be the man's friend. He stared off, pensive for a moment then shoved the thought aside. "Oh, well," he said casually, "I'm afraid it's too late now. Even if I wanted to take it back, which I don't, I couldn't, so I guess I'll just have to live with it, won't I? Now"—he smiled, trying to remove the cloud that had suddenly darkened their enjoyable afternoon—"are you both ready to go?"

8

Heather had returned to the Chateau late Saturday afternoon, having reluctantly left Tonnerre. She liked it there and would have stayed longer, but Aunt Nell was irritated enough already with her absences from the Chateau. Her parents didn't seem to mind, though, and hadn't even been home when she arrived. They were still so wrapped up in each other. Of course, when they did get home, they put on a good show of having missed her, but she could see through it.

It was Sunday afternoon now, and Heather sat alone in the library. She stretched and laid the book she'd been reading facedown on the stand beside her, then sighed. The house was so quiet. Except for the servants, she was the only one who hadn't gone to church today. Usually they worshipped every Sunday in the small chapel down near the slave quarters, but it was being painted, so they had all gone to church in Port Royal.

She stood up and walked to the window, staring out at the lazy afternoon. She was restless and bored, fingers tapping nervously on the windowpane.

Her thoughts wandered back to the day she'd gone swimming, and all the questions it aroused. Aunt Rebel had been surprised when they had arrived back without DeWitt, and exclaimed at how eager he had been to find her. The thought annoyed Heather. She didn't like having to answer to him about her comings and goings, and now, since that horrible scene at the swimming hole, she felt even more irritated by his high-handed actions than ever.

Imagine, trying to intimate that she was betrothed to him. When and if she ever did fall in love, it certainly wasn't going to be with anyone as conceited as he was.

She was still staring out the window daydreaming when a movement caught her attention, and she glanced over, staring toward the front of the house.

"Oh, no!" She exhaled disgustedly. It was DeWitt on horseback, and there was no way she was going to be able to avoid him, because he was already dismounting, throwing his reins to the young slave boy who had run out to meet him. And on top of that he had spotted her standing at the library window and doffed his hat, waving a greeting as he ascended the steps to the veranda.

A few minutes later, Heather turned to greet him properly as one of the servants ushered him into the room. She felt ill-at-ease, remembering only too well the last time she'd seen him.

"I was hoping perhaps we might go for a short canter," he suggested. "It's a beautiful day. Not a sign of rain."

"I was reading," she answered.

"You can read anytime, can't you? Besides, there are things we have to talk about that I don't think you'd exactly care for the servants to hear," he said. "Please, Heather. A ride to the pond and back might do us both good."

She wished she could say no, but if she did, there was every chance he'd tell her parents about her little escapade up at Tonnerre. Oh, well, it was just a ride, and as far as what he had to talk about, he could ask her all day and she'd never consent to marrying him. "I'll have to change," she conceded reluctantly.

He nodded, and half an hour later they were on the narrow path that led to the pond where Lizette and Bain had raced their horses. Heather was purposely wearing a brilliant royal-blue silk riding habit that clashed with his bright green coat. As they rode along, she glanced sideways at him, wondering just what he had in mind and why he'd decided to call on her so soon after his humiliating ordeal at Cole's hands.

"I don't suppose you've mentioned your little escapade the other day to your parents, have you?" he asked.

She eyed him warily. "No."

"I didn't think so. Really, Heather," he admonished arrogantly, "I was never so completely shocked in all my life as I was when I rode into that clearing and saw you plunging feetfirst into the water. Whatever possessed you, anyway?"

She inhaled, anger beginning to edge its way into her voice. "That, Witt, is my business," she said.

He shook his head. "Not entirely. You may think others don't care what you do with your life, but I care very much, Heather." He reached out, grabbing her bridle, halting her horse. "Please, we have to talk, darling," he said hastily. "I have to tell you how I feel."

"I think I know how you feel after your outburst the other day," she answered. "And you know how I feel, so I don't know how it'll do any good to talk."

"I know no such thing," he said, "because I don't believe a word you said that day. You were upset because I caught you cavorting like an undisciplined child. Please, Heather. I think you owe me that much."

"All right," she said wearily. "But not here. We'll talk when we reach the pond."

When they did reach the pond and began walking along its edge, he started in at once. "Why did you go swimming the other day, Heather?"

Her jaw tightened self-consciously. "Have you forgotten, it was a hot day."

"Every summer day's hot in South Carolina."

"Really, Witt," she said, "what does it matter why? The point is, I was having more fun than I'd ever had before in my life."

"Heather, Heather," he said unhappily. "Is fun so important to you that you have to risk your reputation to achieve it?"

"No one would have known, if you hadn't come along."

"But I did," he said firmly. "And just the thought that Cole Dante saw you in such a state of undress makes me ill."

"He's my cousin, Witt," she explained quickly, but he didn't agree that it was so innocent.

"He's a man, Heather, and a barbaric one at that. You saw what he did to me. No gentleman would have done such an outrageous thing. Nor would a true gentleman have gone swimming with half-naked ladies either. No, my dear, he may be your cousin, but I pray he doesn't do like most young men his age and brag to his male friends about the episode."

"He wouldn't!"

"Oh, wouldn't he?" He laughed sarcastically. "I see you know very little about men, my dear. I'm sorry to have to say it, but most men are quite adept at bragging about the slightest conquest where ladies are involved."

"You mean like making sure my cousins knew you always kiss me good-bye when we part, only neglecting to explain that the kisses are quite innocent?" she asked.

He flushed. "Now, Heather, you know very well I didn't tell them to be vicious. In fact, I'd forgotten I even mentioned it."

"Well, you did, and I can imagine what they're thinking."

"Then that's all the more reason for letting me announce our betrothal," he said. "Please, my darling. You know by now how I feel, and I'm sure you wouldn't have let me keep coming back if you hadn't some feeling for me."

Heather's violet eyes darkened unhappily as she looked up into his face. Feelings for him? He had always treated her well, she couldn't deny that, but she didn't love him. She was sure of it.

"You're not being fair, Witt, and you know it," she said finally. "My life is still so mixed up I can't really judge my emotions yet. To try to come to terms with my feelings now wouldn't be fair to you or to me. Don't you see? I still haven't come to accept yet the fact that I'm here and that my life is no longer what it used to be. My father accused me of being stubborn because I can't seem to accept the new life he's thrust upon me. But I'm not stubborn, Witt, not really." She paused a moment and her eyes grew misty. "I just don't feel a part of it, that's all. I feel so unsure of the future."

"I could give you an answer for the future," he said.

She shook her head. "But it would be your answer, Witt, not mine. If and when my answer comes, don't worry, I'll let you know," she said. "But for now, don't press me please, and don't try to run my life. I won't put up with it, Witt. If you still want to see me again, it'll have to be my way, not yours. I'm not your betrothed. Maybe I was hasty the other day when I said I never would be. But don't push me, Witt."

He stared at her hard, his eyes caressing her face. "I love you, Heather," he said roughly.

She winced. "Thank you, but I'm afraid at the moment the fact has little meaning for me."

He reached out and drew her to him, his arms enfolding her lithe body, pulling her hard against him. "Perhaps with time," he said huskily. "I'm willing to wait."

Her hands were against his chest as she held back, her head turning as his lips began to descend. "No," she said softly, refusing him.

His lips brushed against her cheek. "I warn you, Heather," he whispered softly, "I'll accept your no now, but this isn't the end of it, my dear. Someday, I guarantee you'll be Mrs. DeWitt Palmer."

She took a deep breath, feeling his lips touching her cheek, his words penetrating her thoughts, and she shivered. Not if I have my way, she thought stubbornly, but said, "That's to be seen. Now, please, if you don't mind, I think we'd better get back to the house."

By the time they arrived back at the house the family was home from Port Royal. DeWitt was asked if he'd like to join them for dinner, but he declined, having a previous commitment.

It was two days later that Heather was completely taken off guard by a conversation with her father. She had been sitting on the back terrace embroidering when he interrupted her.

"Where is everybody?" he asked as he stepped outside.

She looked up from her embroidery. "Grandma Dicia and Grandpa Roth went into Beaufort and Mother's upstairs taking a nap. I don't know where Aunt Nell disappeared to. I think she's upstairs, too."

"Good," he said. "Because I want to talk to you." He sat opposite her on the wrought-iron bench, then leaned forward, watching her fingers plunge the needle into the tight cloth, pulling it taut as the stitches began to make a pattern of flowers on the border of the shawl she was working on. He was dressed in his work clothes, and dust still clung to the creases in his boots. "I was working out near the road most of the morning, helping some of the men put in those new fenceposts, and had quite a talk with one of the neighbors who was riding by," he said.

"Oh?" She wondered what he was getting at.

He looked slightly uncomfortable, and Heather grew even more curious. "He told me a rather interesting story," he said after a pause. "It seems talk's going around Beaufort that my daughter isn't exactly the lady I thought her to be."

Heather pricked her finger as the meaning of his words began to sink in. "What did he say?" she asked apprehensively.

"Well," he didn't know quite how to put it. "It seems word is that you and Cole were supposedly swimming in the nude up at Tonnerre last Friday afternoon."

Heather's face went white. "That's a lie!"

"I imagined it was," Heath said. "At least the part about your being in the nude. But there must be *some* truth in it."

"We were swimming, yes," she said belligerently. "Lizette and I ran into Cole at the swimming hole and he asked us to join him. But we weren't in the altogether."

"What did you have on?"

She blushed and her chin lifted stubbornly. "My chemise and drawers."

He stared at her for a minute thoughtfully, then frowned. "Who knew you were swimming that day?"

"DeWitt came along." She gazed at him sheepishly. "He was mortified at finding me there. You should have heard him. Just because he comes calling at the house, he thinks it gives him a right to order me around," she said. "Cole told him to leave, but when he insulted Liz, Cole threw him in the water."

"He didn't!"

"He did!"

"My God!" Heath shook his head. "Then he must be the one who started the talk."

"Oh, no," she protested. "DeWitt wouldn't have said anything. At least, I don't think he would. That's why he came over Sunday—to make certain no one had found out and to warn me not to let anyone know." She blushed. "He says he's in love with me and doesn't want my reputation ruined."

"Well, at the moment it certainly isn't a reputation to be proud of," Heath said. "I just hope we can counter it with the truth, even if the truth is almost as incriminating. Whatever made you join those two on such an excursion anyway?" he asked.

She shrugged. "I don't know, except it looked like fun. Cole and Lizette never seem to worry about propriety or anything, and they always enjoy themselves. It was the first time I'd ever been swimming."

Heath studied his daughter, realizing again how sheltered her life had been, living in a household of only women. And that was another thing. His parents had ridden into Beaufort. If the tale he had heard was as prevalent as he suspected, there was no way he was going to keep from telling Darcy. And with Darcy adhering to Aunt Nell's rigid behavior pattern, there was certainly going to be an argument the next time Heather decided to go to Tonnerre. What a predicament. His eyes caught those of his daughter. "If DeWitt didn't say anything, then who?" he asked, and saw a knowing look filter into her eyes, yet she denied having any idea who it could have been.

It was only later, after her father had left the terrace, that

Heather put definite thought to the suspicion that was running through her head, and the next afternoon, when she stood on the path that led to the pier, wearing a pale lavender dress with violet trim, and watched Cole ride up the drive and dismount near the stables, only then did she put a definite name to the culprit, remembering DeWitt's warning about men's pride.

Cole had already spotted Heather. It wasn't hard, since her red hair was like a beacon in the warm afternoon sun. After dismounting, he headed for the house, hailing her from a distance. He wasn't in the house long, and when he came out the back door, it took him only seconds to find her again, where she sat on the riverbank throwing pebbles in the water. He walked up and sank down beside her.

She glanced at him for a minute, then turned back abruptly to what she'd been doing, picking up a small stone, throwing it as far out into the water as she could. "Hello," she finally said, but her voice was bristling with antagonism.

He tried to smile, but it didn't come off. "You've heard, haven't you?" he said.

She nodded. "Not only have I heard, but so has the whole household. Why did you do it?" she asked.

He was startled. "Me?"

"Who else! Witt warned me that you'd go bragging to your friends, but I never dreamed you'd tell them we had all our clothes off."

"I didn't tell anyone anything."

"I don't believe you!"

"Now, why would I do anything that stupid?" he asked. "Why?"

'Who knows why? Like Witt said, maybe you were boasting."

"He told you I bragged about it?"

"He warned me you would."

Cole stared at her, shaking his head. "Of all the nonsense. In the first place I'd never brag about something like that, even if it really had happened, and in the second place, I know how the story got around."

"How?"

"Liz."

"Lizette?" Her eyes widened. "You're lying. She'd never tell anyone a story like that."

"She didn't." He picked up a stone and threw it out into the water. "The Kolters came out to Tonnerre for a visit Sunday afternoon, and she confided in Felicia. Unfortunately Felicia has a big mouth and let it slip in front of one of her other friends the next day. By the time it made the rounds, the original tale had been replaced by the garbled version Uncle Heath and the rest of Beaufort heard. That's why I rode down today. I was in town on Monday evening and heard the distorted version myself. When I got home, Liz and I figured out what happened, and I thought maybe I'd better come down and put things straight." He glanced at her. "You didn't really think I told, did you?" he asked.

She flushed. "What was I supposed to think?"

"You could have blamed Witt."

"On the contrary. He was here Sunday to make sure no one had found out."

"Good old Witt!" Cole picked up another stone and threw it, then looked once more at Heather. "Ever been fishing?" he asked suddenly.

She shook her head.

"Would you like to try?"

"Will I get in trouble if I do?"

He laughed, his voice husky. "Only if you don't catch anything." His laughter turned into a smile. "Will you go?"

"When?"

"Now. We'll take a skiff out. Grandfather has some poles, and you can help me get some bait."

"What kind of bait?"

"Worms, of course."

She wrinkled her nose. "Worms?"

"You know, those little wiggly things."

"I know what worms are, silly," she chided him.

He stood up, then reached down to help her. "Good, then let's get some."

The first place they went was into the house to tell Heath and Darcy where they were going and for her to get a straw bonnet so she wouldn't get sunburned, then to the stables to get a shovel, and from there to a pile of manure behind the barn.

"You're going to dig in that?" she asked.

He eyed her curiously. "I see you've never dug for worms," he said. "Now, watch."

The shovel sank deep into the manure, and he turned the first load over, then bent down, probing through it with his fingers, coming up with two fat worms. He had given her a small container earlier. Now he set the worms in it and started to dig more. He kept putting worms in the mug until they had enough.

"What do we do now?" she asked as she followed him back to the front of the barn.

"We get the poles." They went inside the barn, emerging a few minutes later with two fishing poles and a net attached to a long handle. On the way to the boat, Cole explained that the net was to help land the fish.

The whole thing was new to Heather, and excitement caught in her voice as they reached the small rowboat at the edge of the river.

"What if we get caught in the current?" she asked as she struggled, trying to help him launch the boat.

"We won't. We'll anchor just offshore. Besides, even if we did, we'd only end up at the Sound."

When the boat was finally at the edge of the water, Cole helped her in, handed her the poles and the bait, gave the boat a big shove and leaped forward at the same time, landing on the opposite end from where she was sitting. The boat rocked precariously for a few seconds, then righted itself, steadying, and Cole picked up the oars.

Once they were anchored about fifty feet offshore, he began teaching her how to bait a hook, dirtying her lovely lavender dress in the process. Heather was having the time of her life. The weather was warm, the air fresh, and Cole's high spirits were catching.

Not only had Heather never been fishing before, but she'd never been in a rowboat, either. Cole watched closely as she picked a worm out of the mug and put it on the hook at the end of the string on her pole. She was working meticulously, as if performing a ritual. Her lips pursed, then relaxed, tongue darting out, only to disappear as she fought the slippery worm onto the hook. The sight was fascinating to him and he felt a stirring as the sun caught her hair, turning it to fire.

When she finally had the task accomplished, she sighed, blowing a stray curl from her forehead, then flung the bait into the water, clutching the pole expectantly.

He couldn't get over how lovely she was. She had a smudge of mud on her chin, but that didn't matter. She was a rare mixture of beauty and naiveté. He studied her a few minutes longer, then smiled, amused, as she caught a fish, all excited over it; then he watched as she insisted on taking it from the hook herself.

Heather was proud. She had never done anything like this before, and the accomplishment was extremely satisfying.

And besides, she thought to herself, Cole was such a good teacher. She glanced over at him as she handed him the fish she'd just caught. "Did I do all right?"

"For a novice."

"How come you're not fishing?" she asked when she realized he hadn't baited his own pole yet.

"I wanted to make sure you knew what you were doing first."

"And do I?"

"What do you think?" He looked directly into her eyes, and she flushed.

They caught a few more fish; then suddenly Cole turned to her. "How about a ride down the river?"

"Is it safe?"

"With me, cousin, you're as safe as if you were with your guardian angel."

They put their poles aside, letting the string of fish dangle in the water from the back of the boat as Cole pulled up the anchor. Rowing was easy, since they were moving with the current, but he still had to guide the small skiff. Heather watched him and felt a sense of well-being. He had taken his coat off, rolled up his sleeves, and she watched as his muscles flexed, pulling the oars. She had never been around men much before coming to Port Royal, and she was slowly discovering that the male species was far more complicated than she had expected, and very different from what her mother had led her to believe.

Her eyes wandered over Cole's strong frame, watching him maneuver the small boat in the currents. Cole was so different from DeWitt. Witt was blond and thin; Cole was dark and lean, with broader shoulders. And they were two distinct personalities. DeWitt was proud to the point of being haughty. Cole had a different sort of pride. It shone in his warm green eyes and the confident way he carried himself, but it didn't need bolstering by praise or dominance the way Witt's pride did. And Witt always took everything so seriously. When he did smile, it was usually at people rather than with them. Cole smiled from inside, and she liked his smile. It was contagious.

They had been moving downriver for some time while Cole pointed out different landmarks, and Heather had been watching the landscape roll by, admiring the trees and beauty of the area. Sometimes they drifted freely, others he rowed, but all the while, they talked about so many different things.

It was more than an hour after starting their excursion downriver that Cole glanced up at the sky and frowned.

"What is it?" she asked.

"The sky," he said apprehensively. "There wasn't a dark cloud about when we started, but there are some beauties off toward the west, and they look like they're coming this way pretty fast."

"A storm?"

"I hope not, but I thought I heard rumbling a few minutes ago."

"What'll we do?"

He began to work harder at the oars, and as she watched, the small skiff turned halfway around in the water, so the end she was in was pointed toward the shore. "We get off the water," he said quickly as he began to row vigorously. "It probably won't last long. Just a quick summer shower, but sometimes the wind can do more damage than the rain, and I feel it coming up already."

Heather reached up, grabbing her chip straw bonnet that almost left her head as a gusty breeze hit them full force. "I see what you mean," she called to him.

Cole's jaw was tense, teeth clenched, as he heaved against the oars, moving them closer to shore. The water was getting rough, and by the time he ran the small boat up onto the bank, he was breathing heavily.

"Where are we going?" she asked as she took his hand, letting him help her from the boat.

He nodded toward an old building a short distance away. At one time it had been used for tools when the men worked in the fields, so they didn't have to carry them out every day, but now the roof was half caved in and the door was hanging off its hinges. It was the only shelter around. Once inside, Cole ushered her to one corner that seemed sturdier than the others and helped her to sit down, telling her to lean back against the wall. He sat beside her just as the first few drops of rain began beating a haphazard tattoo against the side of the building.

Lightning flashed overhead as the sky darkened, and Heather shuddered.

"Scared?" Cole asked.

"A little."

He reached out and pulled her against him, holding her close. "There, now, if the roof falls the rest of the way in, I'll be the first one hit, how's that?"

She looked up into his face. His eyes were smiling, but behind the smile lines at the corners of his eyes, buried deep in their green recesses, was a strange depth that frightened her for a moment. She had never been this close to a man before. Even when Witt had kissed her, he'd never held her like this. She could feel Cole's heart beating beneath his shirt, and the warmth of his body made her own tingle peculiarly. Her eyes dropped from his intense gaze, and she buried her head beneath his chin while the violent summer storm raged around them.

"Are you cold?" he asked after a few minutes.

She sighed. "No."

"Good."

Silence again, except for the pelting rain. Then: "Do you think it'll last long?" she asked.

He glanced up, watching the branches overhead being buffeted by the driving rain. "I doubt it."

Lightning struck close by, and she jumped.

"All right?" he asked.

"Yes." She snuggled closer. His arms tightened, and silence once more reigned except for the fierce pounding of the storm and the hammering of his heart against her ear.

Another loud crack, and she jumped again. His hand moved up and stroked her hair, then covered her head, his fingers soft against her cheek. "Don't be frightened," he whispered. "I won't let anything happen to you."

The words were no sooner out of his mouth than another bolt of lightning struck close by, and the jolt shook what was left of the roof over them. Heather held her breath, waiting, wondering if it would crash, but instead, Cole's arms only held her tighter. He had put his coat around her, and his face was bent down against her hair.

They stayed like that for a long time while the storm wore itself out. And then after about half an hour, it began to let up. As quickly as it started, it was over. The dark clouds drifted high, dissipating into a sky turning to shades of blue, and the rain subsided. Only a slight breeze blew now, caressing the trees in the wake of the noisy wind that had torn at them barely minutes before.

Cole began to stir. "Heather?" he asked hesitantly as a few leftover drops of rain fell from the edge of the battered roof. "It's over."

She sighed against him and roused reluctantly. It had been so warm and cozy in his arms, and she hated to move. Her eyes had been shut and she had been savoring his closeness, savoring the feelings washing over her. Now her eyes opened as she sat up straighter, and his arms eased from about her, leaving an empty feeling in their place.

He too straightened, then stood up, towering over her. "Come on," he said, noticing the expectant look in her warm violet eyes. "Let's go see what's left of the boat."

"You don't mean . . .?"

He helped her to her feet as he answered, "With a wind like that, I can't be promising."

He held her hand as he helped her over the debris on the floor of the shed, then out into the dripping world.

The rain had been cold; now the sun was hot, and steam began to rise from the ground, swirling through the trees and bushes around them like a thin fog.

Cole headed back toward the river, leading her by the hand, trying to avoid mud as much as possible, but just walking through the long grass soaked their feet and legs.

The river was still choppy, the water churning a muddy brown as they neared the spot where Cole had left the skiff. He looked around, frowning. There wasn't a sign of it. No, that wasn't quite true. He let go of her hand and stooped, reaching down and pulling up what was left of a fishing pole. Then, as he gazed farther down the bank, he spotted two pieces of splintered board, the ends sticking out of the water, but he could tell by the shape of them that it was all that was left of the boat's stern. He stood up, took a deep breath, and sighed. "Well, that's that," he said, the carefree banter gone from his deep voice. "It looks like we're going to have to walk now."

She stared at him, dumbfounded. "All the way back to the Chateau?"

"All the way back to the Chateau."

"Oh, no!"

He looked at her in surprise. "Now what's the matter?" he asked.

Her mouth set stubbornly. "You said I wouldn't get in any trouble."

"You're not."

"I'm not? What do you call this?" She glanced at the sun, low on the horizon, knowing the Chateau was at least five miles upriver. "We'll never get back before dark, and everyone's going to be worried, and . . . and I don't know why I listened to you," she said angrily.

Cole smiled, amused. "Come on, cousin," he said playfully. "Where's your adventurous spirit? I said I wouldn't let anything happen to you, and I won't. Now, come on." He took her hand and began pulling her after him toward the woods. "I know the way, and it shouldn't take long at all."

9

The sun was gone from the horizon and all that was left of the day was the faint light of dusk that hung briefly before night descended. Darcy, standing at the edge of the terrace, glanced off toward the river, frowning as she saw Heath heading toward the house.

"Still no sign of them?" asked Aunt Nell from behind Darcy, where she sat on the wrought-iron bench, her knitting in a sewing basket beside her.

Darcy shook her head and turned back to face her aunt. Nellida McLaren, her deceased father's only sister, had once been a pretty woman. Now her auburn hair was completely gray and the lines in her face made it harsh and demanding. She enjoyed little in life, her one pleasure being the chance to bestow all her love on Darcy and Heather for so many years. She had been like a mother hen with them. Now Darcy was virtually lost to her, having a husband to listen to, so she'd been trying to concentrate all her energies on Heather lately, even though she had had to buck interference from Heath and his parents more often than not. But she had helped Darcy raise Heather, and she intended to have some say in the girl's life. "I told you not to let her go off with that young man," she said. "I had a feeling something would happen."

"We had no idea there was a storm brewing, Aunt Nell," Darcy said quickly.

"Humph!" Aunt Nell's eyes swept the sky quickly, then settled on Heath, who had just joined them.

"I'm getting worried," he told Darcy as dark shadows began descending on the world around them. "It's not like them to be gone this long. I'm sure Cole would have left the river when the storm came up, but even so, they should be back by now."

"Where would you start looking?"

"Downriver, there should be a sign of the boat somewhere."

"I told you not to let her go," piped in Aunt Nell again.

Heath's arm was about Darcy's waist, and he ushered her to where Aunt Nell was sitting. "I know you told us, Aunt Nell," he said, trying not to sound too irritable. "You're always telling us not to let her do things."

"It's for her own good."

"What is?" he asked, his dark eyes flashing. "Never allowing her to enjoy herself? Keeping her cooped up in here reading books all the time? If you had your way, she'd never go anywhere or meet anyone."

"She doesn't need to meet anyone," Aunt Nell countered. "She was perfectly happy in Columbia with just her mother and myself. Why should she suddenly need someone else?"

"Because she's a young woman." He glanced at his wife, who he knew felt the way he did but was reluctant to cross her aunt; then he looked back at Nell. "You saw the look on her face when she told us Cole was going to take her fishing. She was like a little girl being offered a sweet."

"Sweets aren't good for a body either," said Nell belligerently.

Heath was seething. "What harm was there in letting her go fishing?" he asked.

Aunt Nell's brown eyes sparked. "She's not back yet, is she?"

"That's not Cole's fault."

"Words! Just words," she grumbled. "He's a man, isn't he? And part savage at that!"

"My grandson is not a savage," interrupted Loedicia as she and Roth stepped out onto the terrace.

Nell whirled to face the woman whose home had become her own, and her face flushed, but she wasn't about to back down. "Your grandson is part Indian, Loedicia," Nell said, giving in to her feelings. "And Indians are savages."

Dicia's eyes narrowed. "They are not savages," she insisted again. "Indians are people like you and me. Besides, Cole is only part Indian, he's as civilized as any other man."

"That's just the trouble," Nell continued. "He's a man. I saw the way he looked at Heather."

"He's her cousin," said Heath angrily.

"You think that would stop him?" Nell's eyes darkened. "It hasn't stopped men before. They're alone out there somewhere and it's practically dark." She stuffed her knitting in her basket, then stood up, taking it with her, and confronted Heath. "You'd better go after her, Heath Chapman. After all the other gossip, something like this could surely ruin her if anyone found out." She turned and started for the French doors. "I don't know what people are coming to any more, letting young folks do such scandalous things, and never a reprimand either. It's disgraceful." She went inside, shaking her head.

Heath glanced over at Roth. "I think maybe we ought to go looking, Father," he said, his eyes darkening. "Not for her reasons," he went on. "But I have a strange feeling something might have happened. They could be hurt."

Roth nodded. "Storms come up quick. I sure hope to God Cole made it off the river in time."

"Don't even think of it," said Dicia breathlessly. "Just go with Heath and find them, dear, please," she said.

He agreed, then leaned over and kissed her, and both men headed for the stables.

"I'm sorry about Aunt Nell," said Darcy when Heath and Roth had left.

Dicia frowned. "I'm afraid your aunt has little love for your husband's family, Darcy."

Darcy's usually cool green eyes looked at her helplessly. "She doesn't forget easily, I'm afraid. She's so worried that the same thing might happen to Heather that happened to me. Forgive her, please, Dicia," she said hesitantly. "It's just that she loves us so much."

"I love you too," said Dicia solemnly. "And I love Rebel, Beau, Lizette, and Cole. I know my children aren't perfect, Darcy," she said. "But no one is. Cole will take good care of Heather, you'll see."

Dark shadows had crept in among the trees about an hour before, and Heather had watched them apprehensively. Her soft-soled kid shoes were wet and full of mud and her dress was dirty and torn. She glanced sideways at Cole as he sauntered along beside her. His clothes hadn't fared much better than hers, although his boots did look more comfortable for walking than her slippers did.

"Fishing!" she exclaimed again in exasperation as she had a dozen times already. "The next time I trust you, Cole Dante, I hope somebody gives me a good swift kick."

"I don't know what you're so sore about," he replied as they walked along the old dirt road. "You enjoyed the fishing, same as you enjoyed the swimming."

"But I'm not enjoying this."

"You could be." He gestured at the woods around them. "It's a beautiful night, the moon's going to be coming up before long, and the air's full of summer." He put his hand on her arm. "Stop, listen," he said, half-whispering.

She started to pull away from him.

"Listen!" he commanded.

They stood in the middle of the lane holding their breath.

"That's a cricket," Cole said softly. "Now listen . . . a tree frog . . . an owl."

Twigs crackled somewhere off in the brush.

"A fox, or maybe a rabbit," he explained. "The whole night's full of sounds."

His hand was strong on her arm and she stared up at him. Suddenly some of the anger began to ease from her, and the fact that her feet hurt didn't seem important anymore. "How close do you think we are to the house?" she asked after a few minutes.

He gazed on ahead down the lane, his sharp eyes missing little, even though it was dark. "That's the pond up ahead, so we've got about two miles to go."

For the first time since they had started toward home, Heather knew the way. When they reached the pond, they turned onto the bridle path that led toward the slave quarters and headed down it. Cole looked over at her and grinned. She grinned back, and he took her hand in the darkness.

It was thus Heath and Roth found them. The two men were walking their horses along the riverbank near the bridle path, keeping their eyes open and ears alert for any sound, calling out every few minutes, "Heather! Cole!"

"Here! Over here!" came an answering shout, and then the missing couple came into view.

Heath dropped out of the saddle in seconds and ran forward, trying to see Heather's face in the darkness, but it was impossible. All he could see was her vague outline. "Are you all right?" he asked breathlessly.

Now that the worst of it was over, Heather felt strangely content. Walking along beside Cole with the night sky overhead filled with stars had given her a sense of euphoria, and she was just coming down from the clouds she'd been riding. "Yes, I'm all right," she said happily. "You wouldn't believe what happened to us." She didn't realize she was still clutching Cole's hand, but he knew it and his fingers tightened on hers as she laughed. "We caught some fish, then decided to row downriver until that storm came up," she said quickly. "We found an old shack, but the boat got smashed. I'm tired and rather full of mud, but even so, it's been such fun!" She stopped chattering suddenly and stared at her father, then glanced over at her grandfather, who was still astride his horse. "Oh, dear, you were out looking for us, weren't you?" she said, realizing why they were there.

Heath straightened. He wanted to grab her and hold her close, happy she was all right, and yet he could throttle her for acting as if nothing was wrong. "Do you have *any* idea what your mother's been going through?"

Cole moved closer to her, letting go of her hand, putting his arm around her waist from behind instead. "It was my fault," he said quickly. "If you want to blame anyone, Uncle Heath, blame me," he said. "I got tired of fishing and decided to take her for a ride downriver."

"But I agreed," she added.

"Regardless of whose idea it was," said Roth, "the point is, the women at the house are frantic. They have you both drowned or attacked by wild animals, so rather than take any more time explaining, suppose we head back toward the house before they get any worse."

"Heather can ride with me," said Heath quickly.

Roth told Cole to join him riding pillion, and half an hour later the foursome rode up the lane from the slave quarters just as the moon rose from behind the trees.

The women were still waiting on the terrace, and they came running across the lawn as soon as the horses came into view. All except Aunt Nell, that is; she stayed at the edge of the terrace, straining her eyes to see in the dark as their voices carried across to her. Her mouth was still set in an angry line moments later when they all joined her on the terrace.

Nell gasped as Heather stepped into the glow from the hurricane lamp. "Heather, my little girl, look at you," she exclaimed incredulously as she surveyed Heather's torn dress, dirt all over it, and the mud up to her ankles. "Oh, my poor baby!"

Heather let her aunt hug her, then tried to explain. "I'm all right, Aunt Nell, just a little dirty. Really, it was fun."

"Fun?" Nell was horrified. "Fun? What on earth ails you, child? How can you call something so terrible fun? You could have drowned or been killed by wild animals. To go off like that . . . What happened to everything you've been taught? And you!" She turned on Cole, who was standing behind Heather. "How could you do this? How could you let Heather lower herself like this? You ought to be ashamed of yourself."

Cole stared at her, bewildered. "Because I took her fishing?" he asked.

"Because you and your sister are always getting her in trouble," she said blatantly. "If it weren't for you, young man, none of this would have happened." She was incensed. "Cousin or no cousin, unless you intend to conduct yourself like a gentleman in the future, I'm going to have to talk to my niece and your uncle and see to it that you don't associate with Heather anymore. Is that understood?"

Cole was flabbergasted, as were the rest of them.

"Aunt Nell!" exclaimed Darcy in surprise. "You can't order Cole around like that."

She straightened arrogantly. "Well, no one else seems to have courage enough to," she said, bristling. "Someone has to stop the nonsense around here before irreparable damage is done. If you and Heath won't, then it's up to me."

"Really, Nell," Loedicia said, stepping up to stand beside her grandchildren, "if Cole had done anything wrong, believe me, he'd have been told about it. But taking Heather fishing . . . It was just an innocent afternoon that unfortunately had a bad ending. There was nothing wrong in what they did."

"So you say. What about last week?" Nell countered. "What about the swimming?"

Loedicia's violet eyes were vibrantly aggressive. "I swim myself, madam, when I feel compelled."

"In your underclothes?"

"In the nude, if need be."

Nell was speechless, but only for a moment. "Well!" she said indignantly. "If what you just said is true, Loedicia Chapman, you ought to be ashamed of yourself, too. You're *supposed* to be a lady!"

In minutes they were all talking at once, voices rising in

volume as incriminating accusations were thrown back and forth.

Cole glanced over at Heather and shrugged.

Loedicia saw the gesture out of the corner of her eye and suddenly realized how ridiculous they all must look. "Stop it!" she yelled, waving her hands, gesturing for their attention. "For God's sake, stop!"

Nell gulped back the words she was about to fling at them as she inhaled sharply, and her eyes focused hard on Loedicia. "Then you'll concede I'm right?" she demanded belligerently.

Dicia shook her head. "I'll do no such thing, but to carry on like this is insane. We're getting nowhere and only making fools of ourselves, all of us, because when it comes right down to it, there are only two people who have a right to tell Heather what she can or cannot do, and that's Darcy and Heath. And as far as Cole's behavior goes, this is my house, and as long as I'm mistress here, my grandson is welcome." Her eyes darkened as she looked directly into Nell's sharp eyes. "I'll admit that what I said before about swimming in the nude was perhaps going a little too far, but I was angry, and your attitude didn't help," she said. "And perhaps it wasn't in good taste for Heather and Lizette to go swimming in front of a gentleman in their underthings, but there was no crime in the act of swimming itself, just as there was nothing scandalous about Cole taking Heather fishing. But I suggest, in the future, since Roth and I are only the grandparents and you are only Heather's great-aunt, that we leave the decisions on her conduct up to her parents. I'm willing, if you are."

Aunt Nell's eyes narrowed as she stared at Loedicia, realizing the others were waiting for her answer. Loedicia was right, really, but she hated to have to admit it. Her lips pursed stubbornly. "That's it, go ahead," she said haughtily. "Go ahead and let them do what they want, don't listen to me. But mark my words, you'll all rue the day and wish you had listened to me, but by then it'll be too late." Then she clamped her mouth tight and turned, heading into the house, where she went straight to her room and refused to speak to anyone for the rest of the evening.

Darcy felt bad about Aunt Nell's outburst, even though she was inclined to side with her aunt on the subject. After Cole had left for Tonnerre and the household had settled down for the night, Darcy sat on the edge of the bed, thinking.

"What's the matter, love?" Heath asked softly. "You seem troubled."

"I am," she answered, pushing her red-gold hair back off her forehead.

He knelt before her, his face even with hers. "About what?"

She let him take her hands in his, and her fingers twined around his fingers as she looked deep into his eyes, capturing the love that shone there. "What are we going to do about Aunt Nell?" she asked.

"There isn't much we can do, is there, except let her fuss and fume if that's what she wants."

"But she is partially right, you know," Darcy said, surprising him.

"How?"

"She's only trying to protect Heather."

"Protect her? From what?"

"From herself."

"Don't be foolish, darling," he said, frowning. "Heather doesn't need protecting. She needs to learn what life is all about and understand why she feels the way she does. What she doesn't need is an aunt who's afraid to let her breathe." He reached up and touched her face, his fingers stretching out firmly, burying themselves in her coppery hair, and he looked into her eyes. They were beautiful eyes, like the eyes of a cat, intense, mysterious, and they had haunted him so often for so many years. Now they were his to drown in whenever he felt the urge. But now they were wary, unsure. "Why are you so afraid of letting her be human?" he asked curiously.

She sighed. "You don't know?"

His dark eyes bored into hers, and suddenly a twinge of hurt shot through him like a knife thrust, and he understood. His hand dropped from her and he stood up. "For God's sake, Darcy, won't you ever let me forget?" he said huskily. "I was young then. We both were."

"And so is Heather."

"But she's not you, don't you understand? What we did, we did because we were in love."

"And if she falls in love . . . Heath, I don't want her to have to go through what I went through."

"So you'd refuse her a chance to live?"

"That wasn't living," she argued. "It was only existing. Even now there are times when I think back to all those empty years, knowing what love was all about yet denying myself the pleasures of it, and all because I let my emotions control my actions. I don't want Heather hurt."

"And you're not hurting her?" he asked harshly. "You think it doesn't hurt her to have you treating her like a small child? She's a young woman, and yet she's just now beginning to know what it means to be alive. She'd never been fishing or swimming—"

"Neither have I!"

"I'm surprised you and Aunt Nell even let her ride a horse," he went on as if she hadn't interrupted.

"Ladies are supposed to ride, Heath," she answered. "But they don't go fishing or swimming or to cockfights or do any of the other scandalous things your family seems to love."

"For heaven's sake, Darcy," he said angrily. "What did you do in Columbia for fun, read books?"

Her chin tilted stubbornly. "There's nothing wrong with books."

"I didn't say there was, but you can't make love to a book."

"That's just it! I don't want her making love."

"Nobody says she's going to." He was staring at her hard, his dark eyes flashing stubbornly. "What does Aunt Nell think Cole was going to do to her, rape her?" he asked deliberately. "Dammit, Darcy, he's her cousin!"

"And very attractive, Heath. Heather enjoys his company. You saw for yourself how well they got along when they first met. What if she falls in love with him?"

He shook his head. "You're afraid of that? Just because they seem to like being together? Besides, cousins have been known to marry, you know."

"First cousins?" She looked anxiously at him. "Darling, I know there's no civil law against first cousins marrying, just as there are no civil laws against a lot of things people do, but morally they're wrong. I don't want anything like that to happen, Heath, and maybe Aunt Nell's right," she said. "Wouldn't it be better to avoid the situation rather than run blindly into it? Cole's so much older than Heather—"

"Two years, not quite three."

"And he was a soldier. Aunt Nell's right. Heather's a beautiful girl, what if he took advantage of her?"

"Like I did with you?" His jaw clenched stubbornly. "Thank you, my love, for the reminder."

"I didn't mean it the way it sounded."

"The words were enough."

"Oh, Heath, we're getting nowhere with this," she said,

sighing unhappily. "All I know is that I want what's best for our daughter."

"So do I. But that doesn't mean locking her away from the world in a cage like some exotic bird," he said. "Besides, you know yourself that DeWitt Palmer's been courting her, so all this nonsense about Cole is just that—nonsense. He was being nice to her, that's all it was, and it's ridiculous to read something into the incident that isn't there."

She gazed at him hesitantly, not certain what to think, yet wanting to believe him. Her eyes softened. "I'm sorry, darling, but it's so easy to be fearful that Heather will make the same mistake I made."

His eyes filled with hurt again. "Mistake?" he asked abruptly. "Is that the way you look back on our love—as a mistake?"

"No . . . Oh, no, I . . . You know what I mean."

"No," he said firmly, "I *don't* know what you mean. Did you mean it was a mistake for you to love me? Or was the mistake when you let me make love to you?"

"Well, it wasn't right. I never should have," she said. "If I hadn't let you, it wouldn't have hurt so much about Cora and all the rest of it."

"And there'd have been no Heather and we wouldn't be here now. Would that have been better, Darcy, to have just let me go with nothing to remember?" he asked. "If you had, you'd probably be married to someone else now. Could you love someone else enough to compensate for losing what we have now?"

His eyes grew warm, intense, and he walked to her, kneeling once more in front of her on the moss-green carpet, the flickering light from the lamp on the bedside stand casting shadows onto his handsome face. He stared at her, marveling at the way she still seemed so young, so much like the girl he had made love to the first time so long ago.

"Could you, my love? Could you have freely given your love to someone else?" he asked, his voice lowering. "Was it really so horrible a mistake what we did that summer afternoon?" He reached up and touched her lips. "In spite of the unhappiness we've been through, how can you call the love we shared a mistake?"

Darcy's heart turned over inside her as his eyes fastened on hers, and she felt weak inside. He always did this to her, made her feel like she had that long-ago afternoon. It should have been a mistake, but was it? Was Heath right? Love shone in her eyes as she studied him. "It wasn't, Heath," she whispered softly. "Our love wasn't a mistake. It wasn't then, it isn't now," she went on. "But consummating it was. You know that as surely as you know your heart. Even though I loved it, I know it was wrong, and that's what I'm afraid of, darling. That Heather will be like me, ruled by her heart instead of her head."

He frowned, knowing why she worried, yet afraid to hold too tight a rein on his young daughter. "Then guide her, sweetheart . . . help her, but don't forbid her, and don't refuse to let her feel the normal workings of a young girl's heart. Heather's a lovely girl, a daughter we can be proud of, but let her live."

Darcy reached out and touched his face. "I love you, darling," she whispered softly.

He smiled. "I know you do." He leaned forward, his lips touching hers in a caress that warmed him deep inside. "Lie down and I'll blow out the light," he said.

Darcy's eyes followed him as he straightened, standing up. So many times she wondered what she had done to deserve such a love as he bestowed on her, for Heath was the answer to every woman's dreams, yet he was hers. She slid back on the bed, burrowing under the sheet, and waited for him, and when he joined her, taking her in his arms as he always did to kiss away the years that had separated them, she forgot that there was a world around her and lived for just the moment, finding passionate contentment in his arms.

The next few weeks at the Chateau went by quickly. Heather spent her days sewing, reading, and doing all the mundane things she'd always done, and she was bored to distraction. A few times, when Heath caught her pacing restlessly in the parlor, he asked her to go riding with him, and much to his surprise, she accepted. He discovered a great deal about his daughter on those rides, just the two of them. And the more he learned, the less he worried about her behavior. Aunt Nell's strict upbringing had created a built-in resistance to the wild antics that seemed to plague her cousin Lizette. He felt that Heather was both sensible and intelligent. However, she had also inherited her grandmother's stubborn willfulness and her mother's sensitivity, and the combination often waged war on what she knew was wise and prudent, and he sensed, rather than was certain, that with the right persuasion, she could be turned from her straitlaced ways. He wasn't going to worry about it, however, because he also felt certain her head would rule her heart more often than not, if a truly serious decision came along, and he found her a charming companion to spend the time with when Darcy was busy elsewhere.

It was Saturday, June 17, Lizette's birthday, and Heather had been invited to her party, as had all the young people in the area. All except DeWitt Palmer, that is. For one thing, he was somewhat older than Lizette, who was just turning sixteen, and also his altercation with Cole precluded his inclusion in the party. Heather was being escorted by her parents and grandparents, who were to help chaperon the young people. It was a beautiful afternoon as they started for Tonnerre. A little cloudy, but warm and balmy, the scent of summer heavy on the breeze.

The only thing that had marred the day had been Aunt Nell's outburst when they left. They had tried to appease her by inviting her along, but she was her usual stubborn self, and preferred to stay home, pouting. Now, as the carriage pulled up at the front steps at Tonnerre, Heather was glad Aunt Nell hadn't come because the first person her eyes fell on was Cole. He was standing behind his sister and mother, next to his father, leaning lazily against one of the pillars of the veranda and watching Heather as she stepped from the carriage.

She was wearing a dress of white muslin embroidered with deep-hued violets, their tiny green leaves scattered here and there, with violet satin ribbons trimming the bodice. Her deep coppery hair was caught up with more violet ribbons, the curls nestled delicately atop her head beneath a white chip straw bonnet, and small amethyst stones almost the color of her sparkling eyes rested on her earlobes. She looked exquisite with the late afternoon sun turning her hair to flaming red beneath the bonnet, and his eyes followed her intently as she greeted his sister and mother.

"It seems like it's been ages," said Lizette happily as she took Heather's hands in hers, and Heather frowned slightly at the change in Lizette in just the few weeks since she'd last seen her. She tried not to let her concern show, but it was hard. Heather was certain that Lizette had put on a few more pounds. Although her face looked the same, her bosom was trying to explode over the top of her lace-trimmed bodice, and the vague outline of her body beneath the folds of the pale pink silk she was wearing looked more rounded and wider than before, and it was a dress Heather knew had been made for Lizette especially for her birthday.

Heather squeezed Lizette's hands back, greeted Rebel and

Beau, then let her eyes wander to Cole, who she knew hadn't taken his eyes from her since she alighted from the carriage. She dropped Lizette's hands and greeted him as everyone around her started talking, almost drowning out her voice.

He smiled, and she forgot for a moment that Aunt Nell had warned her to stay away from him so she wouldn't get in any more trouble.

"Been fishing lately?" he asked.

She smiled back. "I was waiting for you."

"What would your Aunt Nell have done if I'd obliged?"

She flushed. "Yelled!"

"That's why I didn't." He glanced at the others as Lizette finished greeting her Aunt Darcy, Uncle Heath, and grandparents, then turned back to Heather again and took her cousin's arm, pulling her away from Cole.

"Come on, Heather," she said excitedly, making a face at her brother. "You can talk to him later. I want to show you the cake Liza made before the rest of the guests get here," and Heather let Lizette lead her away, making quick excuses to Cole and the others.

The afternoon was going well. There were some twenty young people at Lizette's party, none of them except the chaperons much over twenty, and to Heather's delight, Felicia came too, escorted by a young man named Alexander Benedict who had been stopping by her parents' home lately to see her. He was a good-looking young man of seventeen whom she'd been chasing for some years now, and she was delighted that he was finally beginning to notice her. Her mood today was carefree and happy, but it was the first the three girls had been together in a long time and Felicia also couldn't get over the change in Lizette, although she didn't mention it to anyone except Heather.

The two girls were standing side by side at the edge of the lawn waiting their turn to bat in a lively game of rounders when Felicia turned to Heather, a worried look on her face. "What do you suppose is wrong with Lizette?" she asked as she watched her longtime friend, who was up at bat.

Both girls watched Lizette closely as she argued with one of the young men on the other team, accusing him of moving one of the bases farther away. The young men were playing against the ladies, and there was an air of conscientious rivalry between the two.

"You mean you've noticed it too?" said Heather as the argument ended and Lizette put the bat on her shoulder once more, ready to hit the ball.

Felicia nodded. "How could I help but notice?" she said. "And so has everyone else. You should hear the comments when she's not around."

"I hope they're not being cruel," said Heather, frowning.

"So far it's been wonderment more than anything else," said Felicia. "But I have heard a few uncalled-for remarks, and it isn't fair. Just because she's gained a few pounds doesn't mean Liz isn't still the same person she always was."

Heather agreed and was about to add to her statement when Lizette hit the ball a good whack, made it to first base, then called over that it was Heather's turn.

Heather straightened, eyeing her cousin dubiously. She had never played rounders, although she had watched it being played. In the first place, she had always understood that it was a man's game, and second, she had no idea what any of the rules were. But Liz had assured her it didn't matter, as long as she could hit the ball and run. At first she was going to refuse, but during the brief moments it had taken her to make her decision, her eyes had met the challenge in Cole's when she happened to look his way, and since he was on the men's team, she felt like a fool saying no.

Now she walked over, picked up the bat where Liz had dropped it, and stepped up to stand in front of what they were calling home base. It was a chunk of flat wood the size of a small pillow.

Cole watched the apprehensive look on Heather's face as she stepped up to the base, holding the bat awkwardly in her hands. He was catching balls the batter missed for the men's team and had his coat off and sleeves rolled up, with his cravat tossed aside and shirt collar open. Heather looked so out-of-place in her fancy dress, and it reminded him of the day they'd gone fishing.

"Relax," he said. "There's really nothing to it."

She blushed, glancing down at the bat in her hands. "I don't even know how to hold this thing."

He smiled, then reached out, grabbing the bat. "You hold it up here," he said. "Like this. Then, when the ball comes, you hit it and run like hell."

Her eyebrows rose at his rough language and her blush deepened. "Cole!"

"Well, you do."

She lowered her eyes from his, then realized she was staring at the front of his shirt where it was open revealing a mass of dark curling hairs. "What if I miss?" she asked self-consciously.

"Then I'll catch it."

She looked up into his eyes again. "I don't know," she said, scowling. "I think Liz can think of the strangest things to do. Why couldn't we have played something simple? Besides, I never heard of ladies playing rounders."

She would have said more, but just then the rest of the guests, irritated with all the time she was taking, started heckling. She turned and glanced across the lawn toward them, embarrassed, then looked down the first-base line to where Liz was urging her to hurry. Heather set her feet firmly so she was facing Felicia's escort, Alexander Benedict, who was pitching the ball. "All right," she said back over her shoulder to Cole. "I'll try, but I feel stupid."

Cole only smiled as he watched her.

She missed the first ball and straightened quickly, flustered from the exertion of swinging at the air. "I told you I'd look like a fool," she said under her breath to Cole.

His smile broadened and he winked at her as he threw the ball back to Alex. "You're doing fine," he told her quickly. "Just swing a little sooner and aim to where you see the ball coming."

She steadied her feet on the ground again, more determined than ever. "You mean like this?" she asked hurriedly as the ball came at her again. And before Cole could answer, the bat cracked, sending the ball between the first two bases, and everyone began yelling.

"Run!" hollered Cole. "Drop the bat and run, Heather," and Heather felt her heart leap into her throat. She had done it. She'd hit the ball. Oh, dear! Now Cole was telling her to run. Quickly she let go of the bat, lifted her skirts, and began running toward the rock base Liz had just vacated, reaching it only moments before the young man who was covering it reached it too, the ball in his hand.

Heather stood with one foot on the base, breathing heavily, and glanced back toward home base, where Cole was watching her. She saw him wink, and smiled to herself. She had done it.

The game went on with a great deal of laughter and merriment, and Heather was having the time of her life. The men won by some ten runs, but Lizette had to concede it was only because the ladies had played poorly, having been too worried about ruining their dresses and hairdos.

They were all having such a good time, but the afternoon went so quickly. It wasn't long before they were feasting on roast pig, chicken, and all the fancy dishes that went along with a good barbecue, washed down with cold cider. Of course there was rum for the guests who were old enough to have it. Heather was happier than she'd ever been, but she didn't know why. Maybe because her parents had been paying more attention to her the past few days. They seemed to have gotten over their preoccupation with each other and were acting more like real parents. She liked that. Or maybe it was just the atmosphere at Tonnerre. Whatever, all she knew was that she felt so good inside.

She was sitting on a bench with a plate in her lap, just finishing some ice cream and cake, when she spotted Cole talking with some of the young men a short distance away. Maybe her exhilaration was because of Cole, she thought, and a sudden surge of warmth swept through her. Could that be it? She had to admit that when he was around it seemed like time simply flew. And he was such fun to be with. She couldn't have wanted a nicer cousin. He never teased her or made her feel out-of-place like some of the other young men. Like today, when they played rounders. He could have just let her get up and make a fool of herself instead of trying to help. And he had made sure she knew what to do during all the other games, too.

She stared at him now, wondering why Lizette's brother should fill her thoughts so much, and as if he sensed her eyes on him, he looked up.

Cole had been talking about some of his army adventures when he'd suddenly looked up to find Heather staring at him. Her eyes were intense, glistening, and he couldn't look away. In fact, he hadn't been able to keep his mind off her all day, and now, as the conversation lulled and one of the other young men began relating a story he'd heard about the war, Cole quietly excused himself and headed toward Heather.

"Hi, cousin," he said as he reached her. He sat on the bench beside her. "Enjoying the party?" he asked.

She nodded. "Immensely."

He gazed over at her. In spite of all they'd done that day, she still looked so fresh and lovely. He remembered watching her learn how to play rounders and suddenly he had a brilliant idea. "Have you ever been hunting, Heather?" he asked suddenly.

She looked at him in surprise. "Hunting?"

"Yes, hunting," he said. "I was thinking you did such a marvelous job learning how to fish and play rounders . . . I bet you'd be fun to have along on a hunt."

"You mean like riding to hounds?" she asked.

He shook his head. "No, I mean tracking a wild animal through the woods on foot, like my ancestors did."

"Oh!" She gazed at him apprehensively. "You hunt like that?"

"Certainly." His eyes sparkled. "How would you like to come along?"

She shot him a startled glance. "Me?"

"Yes, you." His green eyes grew serious, his ruggedly handsome face close to hers. "It'd be fun teaching you how to hunt and track, and . . ." He paused momentarily. "And I'd just enjoy your company."

She frowned. "You really want me to go?"

"I wouldn't have asked you if I hadn't meant it."

She bit her lip, feeling strangely alive and fluttery having him sitting so close. "But ladies don't go hunting, do they?" she asked.

"No, I guess they don't," he said. "Only I thought what ladies do and don't do had nothing to do with what you and I do. At least I rather hoped you'd feel that way."

Her eyes met his again and she inhaled sharply. "When are you going?"

"Tomorrow morning."

"We are staying the night," she said softly.

"I know," he said. "That's what I was counting on."

"You want me to go tomorrow morning?"

"Why not?"

"But Lizette might get mad."

He laughed. "Let her, she'll get over it. Besides, she's been hunting with me before, and she'll be so tired after all the festivities today, she won't care what happens tomorrow. Father has an acrobatic show with tumblers and jugglers for this evening, and afterward there'll be dancing."

"What about me? I'll be tired too."

He smiled. "Not too tired, I hope."

She stared at him. The thought was provocative. To be in the woods alone, just the two of them. It'd be like the day they went fishing. That had been such fun. She sighed. But what would her parents say?

Cole sensed her dilemma. "We won't tell them," he said quickly.

She frowned. "How did you know what I was thinking?"

He laughed lightly. "I was right?"

"Yes."

His eyes held hers. "I always leave just before the break of dawn. By the time we get back, they'll barely be stirring in their beds, so there shouldn't be any worries there. I'll give you some old clothes to wear, and it'll be fun. You will come?"

She didn't know what to say. She wanted to, desperately, yet . . .

He looked deep into her eyes, and something seemed to pass between them that made her shiver.

"Will you?" he asked again softly.

She nodded, and saw his eyes soften to a deep emerald green that seemed to fill her heart with a warmth that was almost frightening in its intensity, and even though she knew what she was doing was against all of Aunt Nell's and her mother's warnings, she also knew it was going to be a day she'd never forget. And for the rest of the evening, as she sat with Lizette watching the acrobats, then danced with Cole, she could hardly wait for this night to be over so she could be alone with him again.

10

The sky was overcast, dark clouds swirling into view, mocking the sun that was feebly trying to make an appearance. For a few brief moments some faint streaks of orange fought to splash their way across the horizon, only to lose the battle and disappear quickly as the dark clouds deepened. Dawn had arrived like a sea of red on the horizon, and Cole knew it would rain soon, but he was hoping it would hold off until they got back.

He glanced over at Heather beside him and smiled. He'd been right. Having her along had been like a tonic, even if he did have to cover her brilliant red hair with a stocking cap so she wouldn't frighten the animals away. He had found some of his old clothes for her to put on, and in spite of the fact that they were too big, he thought she looked enchanting in them. She was wearing her own soft kid slippers and stockings, with his pants rolled up at the ankles and tied at the waist with a piece of rope. And beneath the old buckskin jacket she had on was a faded blue shirt tucked into the pants. He watched her walking lightly through the tall grass, trying to make her steps quiet and stealthy as he'd instructed her; then he glanced again at the sky.

All they needed was about an hour yet and they'd be back at Tonnerre, then it could rain all it wanted and they'd still be able to sneak into the house without anyone knowing. If it rained before then, there was every possibility the rain would wake up the whole household.

They were lucky. The rain continued to hold off as they made their way past the old swimming hole and down the lane toward the house. It wasn't until they were in the house, stealthily making their way up the staircase toward their rooms on the second floor, that the first drops came, and by the time Cole left Heather at the door to the room where she always stayed when she visited, the rain had become a cloudburst.

"Hide the clothes under your bed and I'll get them later," he whispered to her as she started to open the door to her room.

She nodded, then gazed at him shyly, her smile disarming. "I had a lovely time, Cole," she whispered. "Thanks for taking me along . . . only, I hope you're not mad at me for making you miss those shots."

He grinned. "I could never be mad at you. Besides," he said a little more seriously, "I didn't really want to kill anything this trip. I was afraid it might frighten you off and you'd never want to go again. You will go with me again, won't you?"

She stared at him hesitantly. "I don't know. . . . How could we?"

"We could go every time you stay over, and whenever I come down to the Chateau. It won't be that hard to sneak off, and I'll teach you how to load and shoot my rifle."

Heather's eyes lit up. "Would you?" she asked. "I've heard my father say that Grandma Dicia can shoot a rifle as straight as any man."

"She can. And so will you be able to. Is it a promise?" he asked.

Her eyes were intent on his face as they stood in the hall, and she hated for the morning to end. "I promise," she said softly.

He reached out, squeezed her hands, then smiled. "Good," he said. "Now, the rest of them should be stirring any minute. I heard the clock in the hall downstairs strike seven while we were coming up the stairs, and we don't want to take any chances. The servants are already up and about, and we've managed to miss them so far. Let's not press our luck."

She nodded and he reached down, swinging her door open for her.

"See you later," he said as she stepped in, and by the time

she closed the door behind her he was already halfway down the hall to his own room.

That was the start of it. The next few months went by swiftly. No one ever learned of that early-morning escapade, nor the ones that followed each time the opportunity arose. Nor did anyone learn of the days Heather went riding on Jezebel and met Cole on the road between the Chateau and Tonnerre, and the long afternoons they spent together away from everything and everyone, just the two of them.

Heather wished she could have told someone, because her heart was singing inside her. But she remembered her aunt's warning and how upset Aunt Nell and her mother both were the day she went fishing with him, so she kept it to herself. Every Sunday afternoon DeWitt still came calling, and when there was a gathering at anyone's house it was always DeWitt who escorted her, and people began referring to him as her beau, but it was always the quiet moments with Cole that Heather treasured. That finally made her admit to herself she was glad she had come to the Chateau.

It was during one of those quiet moments only the day before Heather's eighteenth birthday that the full reality of why she enjoyed Cole's company hit her.

Cole and Lizette had come down from Tonnerre to spend the weekend and attend the small gathering that was planned for Heather's birthday on Sunday, and on Saturday morning the three of them had decided to go riding. Lizette and Cole had arrived Friday evening in the carriage, leaving their horses at Tonnerre, so were using horses from their grandfather's stables while Heather rode Jezebel. It was a hot September morning, the sun like a ball of fire in the sky, and they tried to stay in among the trees as much as possible to avoid it.

They were almost to the pond, near the road where Lizette had raced Bain on his Morgan horse, when Lizette reined up. "I'm going to have to go back, Cole," she yelled ahead to him. "My horse threw a shoe!"

Cole dismounted and checked her horse, then helped her from the saddle. "You're right," he said reluctantly. "I'll walk him back for you."

"You will not," she said emphatically. "He's the horse I was riding and I'll walk him back. Besides"—she tugged at the waistcoat of her riding habit—"I need the exercise. I swear Hizzie either took the wrong measurements when she made my new riding habit, or I've gained another couple pounds since it was finished. It's so tight I can hardly breathe."

Cole watched his sister straighten, trying to hold herself in, but he knew it was no use. He frowned.

Lizette stared at him, her green eyes snapping. "What's the matter now?"

He flushed. He didn't want to say it, but maybe . . .

"It wasn't Hizzie," he said hesitantly. "You have gained again, Liz." He saw the hurt in her eyes. "I didn't want to say anything because I know how sensitive you are about it, but I didn't want you thinking Hizzie had made a mistake."

Tears fought their way to the corners of Lizette's eyes, and yet she tried to act indifferent. "Well, that settles it, no cake and ice cream for me tomorrow, Heather," she said. "I'll just watch the fun." She tried to smile. "'Now, you two go ahead and have a nice ride. I'll have them saddle me another horse and meet you out by the pond."

"Are you sure?" asked Heather. It was a long walk back to the house.

"Well, if I don't show up, then I'll meet you in the library for a game of cribbage when you get back, how's that?" She turned and started walking back down the trail, stubbornly leading her horse, hoping the two of them hadn't seen her tears.

Cole mounted again, and they watched Lizette for a few minutes until she disappeared around a bend; then he turned toward Heather. "How long has it been?" he asked. "Two weeks?"

"Two weeks and two days," she said. "Not since the day we picked blackberries in Rachel Grantham's pasture."

He smiled. "Ah, yes, those telltale blackberries. You didn't hear what happened when I got home, did you?"

She shook her head as they both nudged their horses, reining them on toward the pond as they talked. "No," she said. "But I can imagine. I forgot my lips would turn blue, and everyone wanted to know how I managed to get off and on the horse by myself without the aid of a mounting block, and where I found the blackberries."

"What did you tell them?"

"That I used an old tree stump to mount. And I told them the truth, that I rode over near River Oaks and stumbled onto a blackberry patch." She eyed him curiously. "What did you tell them?"

"It wasn't quite that easy for me. If you'll remember, I used the excuse that I had business in Beaufort with one of my friends." His eyes crinkled, amused. "Father wanted to know what kind of a friend I had who talked business in a blackberry patch."

Heather giggled, one hand covering her mouth impishly. "What did you do?"

He glanced over at her. "I told him the truth too, in a way—that after my business was over I ran into the most beautiful girl in the world and we raided a blackberry patch."

"He believed you without any other explanations?"

"Why wouldn't he?"

She looked downhearted, and shrugged. "I don't know. I guess you probably do know a lot of pretty girls."

They had reached the pond, and he reined his horse over near it and dismounted, ground-reining him, then turned to Heather. "Help you down?" he asked.

She tried to brush off the melancholy feeling that had begun to tighten about her heart, and threw the reins over her horse's head, leaning over, letting Cole take her from the saddle. How many times before she had felt the strength of his arms when he'd lifted her off Jezebel like this, and each time, as it did now, it made her feel warm all over. However, always before he would let go quickly, as if he'd been burned, and she'd flush, sensing that he was aware of what she was feeling.

But today he held her for a long time while he gazed down into her eyes, his own eyes warm with emotion. "You were right, you know," he whispered tenderly. "I do know a lot of pretty girls, but there's only one girl in South Carolina who's the most beautiful."

She stared up at him, her eyes deepening to a dark violet. "Cole . . . ?"

One hand left her waist and he reached up, cupping her face. "You're beautiful, Heather," he said gently. "So beautiful that I can never keep my eyes from you. Haven't you guessed yet why I always want you with me? Why I've been so patient, teaching you to shoot and track and all the other things? It has nothing to do with being nice to a cousin. It's because I couldn't stay away from you. Because . . . Oh, God, Heather, don't you know what I'm trying to say?"

Heather stared into his eyes, her heart pounding. Could it be? She inhaled sharply, her voice unsteady. "Oh, Cole!"

He pulled her closer in his arms as his fingers held her face so she couldn't look away. "I love you, Heather," he said huskily. "I know that now. I've known it for weeks now but didn't want to admit it."

Heather tried to talk, but no words came out, and she was trembling inside. "Cole, you can't!" she finally gasped. "It isn't right!"

"Right? Wrong? Who's to say it isn't right?" he asked breathlessly.

"But we're first cousins," she reminded him.

"Is that so terrible?"

"Oh, Cole!" She could feel his strong body molded against her own, and it felt good, so good that she wished he could hold her like this forever.

"Well, is it?" he asked again. "Is it so wrong for me to love you, Heather? Is it so wrong for me to want you so badly I feel like I'm dying inside?"

"You can't, Cole," she said, trying to keep the heady feeling that was sweeping over her from taking full control of her heart and her head. "They'll never let us love, you know that."

"Let us love? No one has to let us, Heather," he said. "We either do or we don't." His eyes bored into hers. "You do love me, don't you, Heather?"

"I don't know. I think I do," she whispered passionately, and tears welled up in her eyes. "I've never known love before, Cole," she said. "But I know I'm happy when I'm with you and wish I could stay with you forever."

A helpless groan wrenched itself from Cole's throat as his mouth came down on hers, and she welcomed his lips fervently. The kiss was deep and sensuous, the longing inside them that had built up over the past few months carrying them with it until their bodies were on fire.

"Heather, my love," Cole whispered huskily as he drew his mouth from hers and looked down into her eyes, warm with the desire he'd kindled. "How could I have dreamed I'd find such sweet pleasure loving you?"

She reached up shyly and touched his lips, stopping further words, and her fingers tingled at the touch. "Don't, please, Cole," she murmured softly. "It's no good. We love, yes, but it can go no further, we both know that. I guess I've known too for a long time why I liked being near you. But we both know it's impossible. If it wasn't, we wouldn't have had to meet secretly. I know at first we pretended it was just so Aunt Nell wouldn't complain. But I think deep down inside we both knew."

He stared at her, a deep hurt settling in his breast, the feel of her in his arms warring with what he knew was right. "There's no law—" he began, but she stopped him.

"There doesn't have to be, Cole. It's one of those unwritten laws that no one has thought to make legal yet. But it's a law the churches adhere to, and so does society."

"We could go away . . . no one would know."

"I'd know." Tears trickled down her cheeks. "We'd both know, Cole, and knowing would destroy us." Her hand moved across his face, and she caressed it as she gazed deep into his eyes. "Don't ruin what we have, Cole," she said hesitantly. "We can't love openly, but we can love. There's no way all the laws in the world can stop my heart from feeling."

"Nor mine," he said. He raised both hands and took her face in his, then kissed her tenderly on the lips, letting the kiss draw her heart to him. "I'll make a vow, now, here, while your eyes look into mine and tell me of your love," he said. "I'll never marry, Heather, sweet Heather, unless I can someday marry you."

"And I, my love," she answered, her voice barely above a whisper, "shall never marry either, unless it be to you." With her words the pledge was sealed, and the kiss that followed was filled with all the love Heather had to give.

They stayed there by the pond talking for a long time, holding hands and wishing things could be different, yet knowing their situation was impossible and avoiding the issue purposely. They sat on the soft grass and Cole leaned back against a tree, drawing Heather into his arms, and there were no words needed to make the time pass as she lay back against him, her head on his shoulder. It wasn't until they heard the distinct sound of Lizette's horse on the path that they were forced to break apart, their eyes anxiously searching each other's face for a sign of the love they had just shared.

The next day was torture for Heather and Cole, although no one seemed aware of it but the two young lovers. Heather had to force herself to be nice to Witt and felt her heart tighten bitterly inside every time she saw Cole talking to one of the girls who'd been invited to her birthday celebration. It hurt and she wanted to scream, yet knew she had to accept the fact that it would be like this forever. And Cole cursed to himself every time he saw Witt treating Heather as if she belonged to him. That was why he cornered her early the next morning after the party and made her promise to meet him the following day near Rachel Grantham's pasture again. And so the affair went on.

September gave way to the falling leaves of October, and

the countryside saw summer bow out in a flourish, relinquishing its warm sunny skies to the cooler days of fall and winter, and before long, Christmas was at hand. With Christmas came a new spirit of excitement at the Chateau. The holidays were always filled with merriment and entertaining. And for the first time in years, possibly because he could now claim a wife and daughter to his credit, Heath was finally welcomed into the homes of the families of Port Royal and Beaufort, and that meant Heather was invited to a round of parties that staggered her imagination. She had never dreamed life in Port Royal could be so exciting.

She and Cole were still madly in love, but she didn't get to see him as often as she would have liked. However, the few precious moments snatched from the weeks and months helped soothe the hurt of pretending to the world that he was only her cousin. Yet at every party they both attended, he managed to dance with her as often as was respectable, and she tried to keep the happiness from showing in her eyes. Things seemed to be at a standstill in her life. She kept refusing DeWitt's offers of marriage with excuses that she was still too young and wanted to enjoy her new life for a while longer. And she spent a great deal of time with Lizette, who, perhaps because she was Cole's sister as well as Heather's cousin, became the closest friend Heather had, but even to her Heather dared not confide her secret love.

As the girls' friendship grew, Heather became increasingly concerned as Lizette's continuous weight gain began to change her life. In spite of the fancy dresses and her past flirtations, the young men seemed to be avoiding her, and the ones who did get up enough courage to talk to her, did just that, only talked. She stood alone most of the time and watched others dancing the quadrilles and reels, and her only escort seemed to be her brother, who was slowly becoming an enigma himself. Since returning from the war, Cole had become one of the most eligible young men in the area, yet it was quite obvious that he was avoiding any serious entanglements with the young ladies. Consequently he didn't mind escorting his young sister to all the festivities, a dilemma that kept all the young ladies guessing and talking and vying for his attention, a fact that bothered Heather. She tried not to be jealous, but it was so hard.

The holidays were going fast. Christmas was spent at the Chateau with presents exchanged all around in an atmosphere of warmth Heather was unused to. She received a new saddle from her parents, a new wrapper from her grandparents, a set of books from Aunt Rebel and Uncle Beau, an embroidered shawl from Lizette, and, much to her surprise, a small fur muff from Cole, made with furs he had caught and cured himself. It was beautiful, soft and fluffy, the lining made of rich brown silk with a small pocket sewn inside where she could tuck a handkerchief. Her present to him was a set of six white linen handkerchiefs with his name embroidered in silk thread, and to his surprise, she had also embroidered the Bourland family crest beside his name, since officially he was really the Duke of Bourland. The crest had been Lizette's idea, and she had helped Heather get a copy of it from the third-floor attic at Tonnerre.

Even Aunt Nell enjoyed Christmas Day—maybe because she found herself suddenly surrounded with presents, or maybe it was just the fun and laughter that got to her. Whatever the reason—rum in the egg nog or something else they didn't even know about—she was all smiles most of the day, even when Cole presented her with a small gold locket. They had no way of knowing that her happiness was due to the fact that she was certain her worry over Heather's earlier fascination with her cousin was over. After all, Cole was so busy on his father's plantation that the two young people hardly got to see each other anymore. She had no way of knowing that what she had suspected was a passing fancy had blossomed into a forbidden love.

After Christmas Day, the rest of the week was so full of parties and dinners that there was little time for Heather to be alone with Cole. It wasn't until New Year's Eve that they managed to find some time together, and that was snatched shortly after midnight at the annual New Year's ball at one of the neighbors'. While everyone was still yelling and laughing and drinking in the new year of 1816, they managed to slip away to the garden outside and found a spot where no one would see and spent a few cherished minutes in each other's arms.

When the holidays were finally over and the long wait for spring began, things finally quieted down and Loedicia watched her granddaughter closely. Heather had changed. She no longer tried to do things to irritate everyone, as when she had first arrived, and there was an air of confidence about her. She was still seeing DeWitt, and Dicia was certain the young man was madly in love with Heather. There was something about DeWitt Palmer that she didn't like, a cruelty and hardness about his eyes, so she hoped that Heather would continue to be cautious in her dealings with DeWitt and see other young men.

No, it wasn't Heather she worried about anymore. Unfortunately, it was Lizette. On Sunday, the tenth of March, they had all taken a ride up to Tonnerre to have dinner. A quiet celebration this year to celebrate Loedicia and Rebel's birthdays, which were in the middle of the week. They had decided to have a small dinner party instead of a big ball like last year, and Loedicia had felt her heart quicken in dismay when Lizette came down the steps to greet them that day.

Her hair was still lustrous and beautiful, face as lovely as ever, but the bulges beneath the blue silk dress she wore were impossible to hide, and although she had been a little heavier than normal during the Christmas holidays, the last few months had added even more pounds, affecting not only her looks but also her temperament. She was quieter, more sensitive, and although Dicia tried not to let her see that she had noticed any difference, she sensed that Lizette knew.

The next afternoon, back at the Chateau, Loedicia had talked to Heather about it, trying to find an answer so she could perhaps help her young granddaughter.

"It isn't that Liz doesn't try, Grandma Dicia," Heather said as they sat on the back terrace sewing and talking, just the two of them. "She told me she rarely even eats breakfast anymore. And she's cut out all the pastry. The only thing is, like she said, when she goes without one meal, she gets so hungry later it just makes matters worse and she ends up eating too much again."

Loedicia frowned. "I noticed her putting on a little last spring, but I guess I hadn't paid too much attention for a while. But I did notice during Christmas that the young men seemed to be avoiding her."

"And it hurt," said Heather. "She used to be so popular, all the young men crowding around her. You'd think she'd gotten leprosy or something instead of just putting on a little weight, the way they act. Some of the remarks they make are really cruel, too. I wish I could do something," she went on.

Loedicia's frown deepened. "Maybe you can," she said thoughtfully. "It's been a long time since you've spent a few days at Tonnerre. Why don't you ask your mother and father and go up this weekend? I know Lizette would like that, and it might help."

So it was arranged. A letter was sent to Tonnerre stating that Darcy and Heath would like to bring Heather up that Friday evening, and if it was all right with Aunt Rebel and

Uncle Beau, she'd stay until Monday afternoon, or longer if Lizette wanted. The answering message confirmed the plan.

Heather was excited. She hadn't seen Cole for some time now. His father had sent him to Charleston on business the third week in February, and he hadn't gotten back in time for the birthday dinner for his mother and grandmother. But he must be back by now, and the prospect of seeing him again had turned her insides to butterflies.

The ride up to Tonnerre in the carriage with her parents did nothing to quiet her fluttery feeling. It was spring again. The flowers were all blooming, the trees covered with green again, and the air was fresh with their scent. It was enough to make anyone glad to be alive, and being in love made it seem even more special.

They arrived early in the evening, and as Heather took her father's hand and stepped from the carriage, lifting the skirt of her pale green silk, she glanced up, looking for Cole. Her heart sank. He wasn't there. Aunt Rebel and Uncle Beau were waiting, arms stretched out to welcome her; and Lizette, dressed in a dark green velvet dress with shirred bodice, was waiting beside them with some servants standing about, but no Cole. She swallowed her disappointment and greeted the others.

It wasn't until they were in the house, seated in the parlor, that she learned Cole had gone into Beaufort earlier in the day and wasn't back yet.

"I think maybe he's finally courting someone," said Beau. "He's been gone every night since he came home."

Heather listened to the words but didn't want to believe them.

"I hope it's someone you approve of, Beau," said Heath. "And not just some doxy he's become fascinated with."

"Heath!" said Rebel, admonishing him. "Just because you and Beau led a less-than-exemplary life when you were younger doesn't mean your sons are going to."

"What sons?" said Heath. "So far our only claim to parenthood is a daughter." He turned to Darcy and took her hand, squeezing it. "Of course, that doesn't mean we're not trying."

Rebel looked at Darcy. "You're not seriously hoping to have another child now?" she asked.

Darcy blushed. "Well, we had hoped." She glanced over at Heath. "I know it's been a lot of years since Heather was born, but I've always wanted to have more children."

Rebel smiled reassuringly. "Then I hope you do," she told her sister-in-law. "But believe me, I certainly hope I don't have any more. It's been enough trying to raise the two I did have." Her face suddenly saddened. "But I did lose a son, you know. He would have been a few years older than Lizette."

"I heard," said Darcy, then glanced over to where Lizette sat beside Heather. "But I'm sure the children you did have, have really been a blessing to you."

Lizette smiled. "It's a wonder Mother doesn't have a head full of gray hairs," she said. "I'm afraid Cole and I are anything but a blessing." She turned to Heather. "By the way," she said quickly. "Speaking of getting in trouble, I've been dying to show you what Cole brought back from Charleston for me." She stood up and grabbed Heather's hand. "Come on," and Heather glanced back hesitantly as she let Lizette drag her from the room.

Upstairs, Lizette led Heather down the hall directly to her room. "You're going to die when you see it," she said cheerfully. "I never dreamed they even had such things," and a few minutes later Heather stood in front of a strange contraption set up at one end of Lizette's huge bedroom. It was a weird conglomeration of wood, ropes, pulleys, and weights.

"What is it?" asked Heather as she stared at it, bewildered.

"Cole had it made special for me," Lizette answered quickly. "It's supposed to help me get rid of some of this weight I've put on."

"How could that thing help you lose weight?"

Lizette walked over to it and climbed on, standing on the wooden platform that seemed to be the main part of the contraption, and sat on a seat built into it. When she was firmly seated she braced both feet against a board at the bottom, then reached out and grabbed two wooden handles at the front of the machine, pulling on them as hard as she could. As she pulled and strained on the handles, slowly bringing them out toward her chest, the structure began to creak and moan. She began to struggle even harder, forcing and tugging, muscles straining with the effort, and slowly little by little as she pulled, the weights hanging at the end of the ropes that rode the pulleys began to rise.

By the time she had successfully lifted the weights halfway to the top, her face was flushed and red and the veins in her neck stood out almost like a man's. She was still straining to get the weights higher, but couldn't, when suddenly her arms gave out and she eased up on the wooden handles, letting the weights fall back into place. She leaned back on the little seat and took a deep breath. "What do you think of it?" she asked Heather breathlessly.

Heather shook her head, amazed. "My heavens, how is that going to work?"

"I don't know really, but Cole said he's seen similar machines where men train for fisticuffs to build up their muscles and keep in trim, and he said he can't see why something like this wouldn't work to give me extra exercise instead of just sitting and embroidering all the time. Riding helps, but I can't ride all day." She stood up and patted the machine hesitantly. "The only problem I've found with it is that whenever I'm through exercising on it, I'm hungrier than I was when I started. Cole says it's because I don't eat right. But I haven't had a piece of cake or any of Liza's other gooey desserts for ever so long, and still it doesn't seem to help. Look at me," she went on bitterly. "I can't even wear a thing I wore last year. The clothes Hizzie made for me just after Christmas still fit, but they're going to be getting tight too before long." Tears rimmed her eyes. "How do you do it, Heather?" she asked, her eyes sifting over her cousin's slim, yet curvaceous figure. "How come Mattie's cooking doesn't seem to have bothered you?"

Heather shrugged. "I don't know, I never paid much attention. They put the food on the table and I just eat, that's all."

Lizette sighed. "I wish I could be like that," she said angrily. "But it seems like I just don't know when to stop. And it all started with that horrid sprained ankle last year. Oh, I could strangle Bain for what he did to me that night!"

"Bain? You blame Bain for this?"

"Who else? If he'd just let me alone I'd have made it to the house by myself and wouldn't have hurt my ankle and spent the next week sitting around stuffing my face. Oh, I could kill him!"

"If he wasn't hundreds of miles away."

Lizette glanced furtively at Heather. "How do you know where he is?" she asked.

Heather sensed rather than actually saw the anxiety in Lizette's eyes. "Grandpa Roth saw Mr. Kolter in town the other day, and the last time they heard from Bain, he was somewhere in a place called St. Louis, but he didn't say anything about when he'd be home. Oh, but Stuart's coming home," she said quickly. "That's Bain's older brother, isn't it?"

Liz nodded. "He's the one who was just elected senator. I didn't know he was coming home for a visit."

"It isn't just a visit," said Heather. "According to Grandfather, he's bringing his family to live in Beaufort. It seems his wife's whole family is here and she doesn't like living in the capital."

"I bet Felicia's glad," Lizette said. "She fairly dotes on Stuart. Thinks he's some kind of saint or something. At least she used to, although like she said before, he's probably changed since he got into politics."

"What's he like?" asked Heather.

Lizette frowned. "Stuart?" Her frown deepened. "I really can't remember. I was only about ten when I last saw him, and I guess I didn't pay much attention to what he looked like. All I can remember is that he seemed terribly tall and grown-up." She looked back at the machine Cole had brought home from Charleston. "But tell me, what do you think of my present?"

Heather glanced at it skeptically. "If it works, I think it'll be marvelous, Liz," she said, not wanting to discourage her. "I know how self-conscious you've been lately because of your weight, and I think it was terribly grand of Cole to get it for you."

"That's Cole," Lizette said proudly. "You know, I couldn't want a nicer brother."

Heather gazed at her cousin thoughtfully. "Do you think your father's right, Liz?" she suddenly asked, watching her closely. "I mean, when he said Cole was courting a girl?"

Liz laughed. "I wouldn't doubt it," she said. "After all, he was twenty-one in February, and it's about time he started showing an interest in something besides roaming the woods. The ladies are beginning to think he's a little weird, always escorting his sister to the socials."

"Has he ever told you why he doesn't take any of the local ladies out?" asked Heather hesitantly.

Lizette shook her head. "All he says is there's plenty of time for that and that the day he finds someone worth spending his time with who's nicer than his sister, he'll gladly escort her. I think this time maybe he has, though, because he's sure been closemouthed about where he's been going since he got back," she said curiously. "I know Merrilou Phillips was being terribly nice to him the last time we ran into her in town. But then, so was Felicia Kolter." She glanced quickly at Heather, not noticing the strained look on her cousin's face. "Felicia! My God, I hadn't thought of Felicia!" she cried enthusiastically. "Cole's always been so nice to her. Wouldn't it be something if Felicia ended up being part of the family?"

"Just delightful," Heather said sharply, wishing she could

bite back the words, but Lizette didn't notice, so enthralled was she with the notion that Cole might have fallen madly in love with Felicia.

As they left Lizette's bedroom, heading back downstairs, Heather was in a terrible state, and remained so throughout the evening.

Ordinarily Heather would have settled down to sleep with the rest of the household, but tonight, because her heart was so filled with hurt, anger, and frustration, she was still up staring out the window of her room when she saw Cole cantering down the drive close to midnight.

Cole's jaw tightened and he cursed softly to himself as he rode his mare into the stable and dismounted. He expected to have to unsaddle the horse himself and was surprised when the big Watusi, Aaron, came out of the harness room at the back of the stables.

"Aaron, you startled me," he said abruptly.

Aaron smiled. "I couldn't sleep. Just one of those restless nights," he said as he took the reins from Cole. A lantern was hanging a few feet away, and the flickering light fell across Cole's face. Aaron looked at him sharply. "What's the matter?" he asked, concerned.

Cole glanced up at Aaron, one of the few men he had to look up to anymore, and wished he could confide in someone. "I'll live through it, Aaron, don't worry," he answered instead.

"A little too many spirits?" Aaron asked.

Cole nodded. "That's part of it." He put his hand on his horse's neck and felt the dampness. "Could you rub her down good too, Aaron?" he said. "I'm afraid I rode her rather hard."

Aaron eyed Cole curiously. "You sure you don't want to talk about it?" he asked helpfully. "You always used to tell Aaron your troubles before you went off to do your soldierin'."

"These aren't little-boy problems, Aaron," Cole said sadly. "I'm afraid you can't fix up the hurt this time. It's not like putting a broken toy back together."

Aaron's eyes darkened. "Maybe not," he said affectionately, "but I've lived too, boy, don't forget that," he said. "And I know a lot about what goes on in people's minds and hearts. If you ever need me, I'm here."

Cole put a hand on Aaron's shoulder. "I'll remember, Aaron," he said softly. "But there's no way anybody can help me solve the problems I've got now. I'm afraid it's something

I'm going to have to take care of in my own way." His hand dropped from Aaron's shoulder. "Just say a prayer for me, Aaron," he said unhappily. "Pray that somehow, some way, it'll all work out. Now I'd better get in while I can still walk up the steps. Good night."

Aaron nodded, then watched Cole head for the house, and he wondered what torments the young man was going through.

Cole's heart was heavy as he entered the house and headed up the stairs. Heather must have arrived hours ago, and he'd planned such a delightful surprise for her. Now it was all over, and he knew it, and he hadn't even been here when she arrived to explain. What a fool he'd been. What a stupid fool to think it would work. Well, it was too late tonight; he'd have to tell her tomorrow.

As he started down the hall, trying to think of the right words, words that would ease the pain some for her, he suddenly stopped, staring at the doorway to her room. Heather was standing there in the open doorway, a lamp flickering low in the hallway falling on her figure, making it look almost ethereal. They stared at each other long and hard; then slowly Cole stepped forward, Heather's name on his lips, and she waited apprehensively until he reached her.

"Where were you tonight?" she asked hesitantly. He frowned, and she smelled the ale on his breath. "You've been drinking."

"What else is there?" he said bitterly.

"What is it, Cole? . . . What's the matter?"

He reached up, touching her face, then sighed. "I have to talk to you alone," he said quickly. "Let's go inside. No one will know I'm here."

She stared at him for a few minutes longer, then nodded. "All right." She backed away from him into the room, and he came in after her, closing the door.

The room was in darkness except for moonlight coming through the window, and Cole stood just inside the door, staring at Heather. She was standing in the moonlight and the effect was striking. He held his breath momentarily, then let out an agonized sigh. "Heather! Heather!" he cried passionately. "What are we to do? I can't go on with you, yet I can't live without you!"

They were close enough to touch, and she reached out, her hand moving to his face. "Where were you tonight, Cole?" she asked. "Your father said you've been gone every night since you came home. He thinks you're courting some girl, and Lizette thinks it's Felicia."

"What?" he asked incredulously.

"Lizette thinks you've fallen in love with Felicia," she repeated.

He exhaled. "Oh, my God!"

"Where were you?" she asked again.

He took her hands in his and pulled her into his arms. "I went to talk to the priest in Beaufort," he said huskily.

She was surprised. "But we're not Catholic."

"I know," he answered. "He was my last resort. I've been to every minister and priest in Charleston, Beaufort, Port Royal, and towns all along the way. I was trying to find someone who'd marry us."

"Oh, Cole!"

"They said no, Heather," he said angrily. "Every damn one of them said no. There's no law that says I can't marry you, yet everyone says it's wrong." His eyes darkened. "I thought maybe I could find someone who wouldn't care about tradition, who wouldn't care whether we were first cousins or not, but they all say the same thing." He reached up, caressing her face. "I love you, Heather, and there's no one else, you should know that, but I'm having a hard time living with it. Every time we've been together I go home hurting inside." He flushed, her nearness making him begin to ache again. "Every time I take you in my arms it's torture, darling, and I don't know how much longer I can keep telling myself not to touch you."

She stared at him and he saw the puzzled expression on her face.

"I love you, Heather. I want you," he explained vehemently.

Her voice was barely a whisper: "You . . . you mean like Liz told me about?"

"It all depends," he whispered. "What did Liz tell you?"

"About making love." She shivered as she said it, and strange tingly sensations flowed through her as they always did when he kissed her and held her in his arms. Her eyes held his. "Is that the way you want me, Cole?" she asked tremulously.

He swallowed hard and pressed her closer to him as he felt himself hardening. "Yes," he said breathlessly, and felt a wave of heat sweep over him. "Oh, God, yes, Heather," he went on. "Whenever I look at you, whenever I hold you like this, all I can think of is how wonderful it would be to feel your flesh against mine, to touch you and caress you," and while he talked, his hands began to move up her body, over the silk of her wrapper, kneading the warm flesh beneath it.

Wherever Cole's hands touched, Heather suddenly felt hot and flushed, and a warm weak feeling began to penetrate her body. For a moment she fought against it as she had so many times before when Cole had kissed her, afraid to let herself feel, but then suddenly, in a rush of longing as he bent his head and began to kiss her throat, his lips whispering her name, his breath hot and sensuous, all the fight was gone from her and she melted against him.

She didn't care anymore what was right or wrong. All she cared about was that Cole was holding her in his strong arms and that he wanted her. "Love me, Cole," she whispered softly, fervently in his ear. "Love me now," she said. "Please, I need you, I hurt so inside."

"Heather . . . do you know what you're saying?" he asked breathlessly, looking deep into her violet eyes.

She sighed, her eyes soft with desire. "The last time we were together, when we parted I thought I'd go mad," she murmured passionately. "I never knew before loving you that I could feel like this," she said. "And . . . and I want you, Cole." She reached up, her hands stroking the back of his neck, her mouth close to his, her sweet breath hot on his lips. "Show me what it is to be loved, Cole," she whispered softly. "Please!"

He held his breath, trembling inside with want of her, his heart fairly bursting inside him. He eased her back away from him so he could reach the ties to her wrapper, and with slow, deliberate movements untied them and slipped it from her shoulders. She quivered with anticipation, and he saw her nipples hard and firm, pushing against the sheer silk of her nightgown. The sight was intoxicating, and he reached down, lifting the nightgown, slowly drawing it up higher and higher until it was free of her body, and let it slip to the floor.

She was lovely. So lovely. His hands touched her shoulders, the fingers caressing the delicate curves. "I love you," he cried tenderly, dropping his hands to cup the full mounds of her breasts.

"I love you too!" she sighed.

He leaned forward, his lips claiming hers in a lingering kiss, and as the kiss lengthened and deepened, his hands slipped from her breasts, moving down her body, and he gathered her up in his arms. It was only a few steps to her bed, and as he laid her on it, shoving the quilts aside, his lips left hers and he straightened just long enough to shed his own clothes before climbing in beside her.

Heather couldn't take her eyes from Cole as he stripped off his clothes. She had seen him naked from the waist up the day they'd been swimming, but tonight as the rest of his body was revealed to her in all its youthful vigor, she felt a frightening sensation run through her. Her body was throbbing with the strength of her desire, and yet tears filled her eyes.

Cole saw them as he stretched out beside her on the bed, lying on his stomach, looking down into her eyes. "What is it?" he asked softly.

She shook her head. "I don't know. I know I want you and need you, Cole, but deep down inside, I'm still a little afraid."

He caressed her face, then began to kiss her softly over and over again, and a short while later, when he finally moved over her and entered, thrusting deep, all the fear was gone from her and only love remained.

Cole made love to her with every fiber of his being, bringing her body alive, nurturing it, feeding it with a vibrant love that carried her to heights of rapture. She moaned ecstatically as he thrust into her over and over again; then, with his lips crushing hers, she felt a throbbing crescendo that suddenly exploded, filling her whole body with an unbridled ecstasy that made her cry out.

Cole felt the strength of her climax, and his heart swelled. He loved her so very much. He had pleased her, he knew, and with this thought filling him he knew he could hold back no longer. With wild abandon, softly whispering her name, he thrust into her with all his strength, then felt his body begin to convulse as his own release began, and trembling, holding her close against him, he let the feeling carry him to its complete end, leaving him weakened and spent.

11

Heather stirred, stretching slowly. She had fallen asleep in Cole's arms sometime after their lovemaking, and now, as she felt the warmth of his naked body against her, she sighed. Her eyes opened and her face flushed as she realized he was already awake, staring at her.

"I look terrible when I sleep," she said self-consciously, but he didn't agree.

"You look beautiful," he said.

She laughed softly as his arms went around her, and he kissed her lovingly, making her tremble.

"It's breaking dawn," he said suddenly, and she frowned.

"You have to go!"

"I know."

"I don't want you to."

"I know that too." He kissed her again.

"Cole, what are we going to do?" she asked.

"Oh, God, I wish I knew," he answered. "But one thing for sure, I can't be found in your bed." He kissed her again, then sighed. "Let me make love to you before I go," he whispered softly. "Please."

"Is there time?"

"We'll make the time!"

Her hands answered him, stretching across his broad chest,

running through the curling hairs until they reached his face, and she pulled his head down until their lips met in a burst of passion that filled them both to overflowing.

Afterward, she watched him slip from the bed and put on his pants. "I'll carry the rest," he said as he gathered his clothes up into a bundle in his arms.

She started to leave the bed to help him, but he shook his head. "No, stay there. I'll be fine," he said quickly, trying to keep his voice down. The first rays of the sun were beginning to come through the window as he walked over to the bed and gazed down at her. "This won't be the last, Heather—you know that, don't you?"

She nodded. "I'm glad," she said fervently. "Because I don't want it to be the last, I want to go on loving you forever, Cole."

His eyes softened and he smiled. "I'll see you later at breakfast," he said quickly, then headed for the door.

Beau had been restless and woke earlier than usual, watching the dark shadows in the room dissipate with the coming of dawn. He glanced at Rebel curled up beside him still asleep and felt like the luckiest man in the world. Their feelings for each other were still just as strong as they had been those long years ago when they first fell in love, and the only thing that marred their happiness now was the children. He worried about Lizette. All her life she had been thin, never worrying about anything. Enjoying life and enthusiastic about everything, but lately she had been melancholy, her usual zest for fun lost in her obsession with her thickening waistline.

And Cole worried him too. Cole had been acting so strangely since he'd come back from Charleston, running off every night to God knows where, with no explanations, no hints even as to where he was going or who he was spending his time with.

It worried Beau that he hadn't heard Cole come home last night. Beaufort and Port Royal were both port cities, and Beau remembered when he and Heath had been shanghaied once. The thought brought a tightening to his insides and he suddenly felt an urgent need to make certain Cole was all right.

Beau didn't make a sound as he left the bedroom and tiptoed quietly down the hall to Cole's room and opened the door. He stuck his head in and stared. In the dim light from the approaching dawn he could see that Cole's bed was still made, pillow in place, covers undisturbed. A chill ran through him and he tried to tell himself it was foolish to worry. Cole could take care of himself. Yet the nagging fear wouldn't let him rest. Maybe Cole had been drinking, he told himself as he stared at the empty bed. Maybe he'd been too drunk to make the stairs. He shut the door and descended the stairs, determined to still the fears that gripped him. Cole might be in the stable, sound asleep, and he was worrying for nothing. He had to know.

A few minutes later he was back inside, walking slowly through the quiet house. He was perplexed. It had taken only a few minutes for him to find Cole's horse in the stall and determine that he had arrived home, yet there was no sign of him. Not a trace. Where the hell was he?

Beau reached the top of the stairs and was just about to step up off the last step when a slight noise down the hall caught his attention, and he stopped, one hand on the top rail of the balustrade. As his eyes adjusted to the dim light, he saw the door to Heather's room open, then held his breath as Cole stepped out. Cole's coat and shirt were draped over his arm, boots in one hand, and he was wearing only his trousers. His feet were bare. He stepped furtively from the room, closing the door quietly behind him, then hurried down the hall to his own room.

As the door shut behind Cole, the breath left Beau's body and a feeling of disbelief began to take hold. He shook his head, trying to grasp what he had seen. Cole in Heather's room? How could this be? It was obvious that he hadn't just been having a pleasant chat with his cousin.

Beau straightened, his knuckles white from gripping the balustrade, and stepped up the last step. He pulled the sash on his robe tighter, knowing full well what he had to do, and with long determined strides he headed for Cole's room.

Cole tossed his clothes on the chair beside the bed, then leaned over and pulled back the covers. He stared down at the empty bed, remembering with bittersweet delight how wonderful it had been to share a bed with Heather. Damn! Why couldn't things be different? How grand it would be to be able to sleep beside her every night. He sighed, stripping off his trousers, and climbed in.

His head had no sooner hit the pillow than the door to his room flew open and his father strode into the room, slamming the door behind him.

Beau stared at Cole, his eyes blazing, mouth rigid, and Cole felt his stomach begin to churn.

"Well," asked Beau harshly as he moved toward the bed, "what do you have to say for yourself?"

Cole stared at him, unable to say anything.

"I want an answer, Cole," Beau said furiously. "And I want it now. Why were you just sneaking from Heather's room, and how long has this been going on?"

The churning in Cole's stomach tightened into a fiery ball. "You saw . . . ?" he asked, his voice breaking.

Beau nodded. "I saw!"

Cole sat up and smoothed the covers out in front of him. How could he explain? How was he going to tell his father he was in love with her? He couldn't, and yet he had to. "I'm in love with Heather, Father," he said bluntly. "And it's been going on for months. Not what you saw this morning. Last night was the first time."

"And the last!"

"No," countered Cole. "I want to marry her, Father."

"You can't!"

"I'll find a way somehow!"

"There is no way, Cole," Beau said forcefully. "She's your first cousin."

"So what's wrong with that?" he asked. "There's no law says I can't."

"Society says you can't."

"White man's society. If I lived in the world you came from, I could. Indian law says a young woman can marry the son of her father's sister, a young man the daughter of his mother's brother."

"Only if they're not in the same clan. Otherwise it's still forbidden. Even the Tuscarora knows that when blood ties are too close the seed is tainted." Beau's eyes hardened. "For God's sake, son, why?" he asked.

"Because I love her."

"Why didn't you stop before it came to that?"

"It was like that from the start," Cole yelled angrily. "There was no such thing as stopping it."

"Well, it's going to stop now," shouted Beau. "It has to. Good God, Cole, this can't go on!"

Cole kicked back the covers and stood up, facing his father. "It can if I find someone to marry us!"

"You won't!" Then suddenly Beau understood. "Is that what you've been doing these past few days?" he asked. "Trying to find someone to marry you?"

"Yes."

"It won't work, Cole," he said, suddenly seeing the pain in his son's eyes. "Good Lord, who did you ask?"

Cole took a deep breath. "Don't worry, I told them I was inquiring for a friend."

"Oh, fine," said Beau. "That's the oldest ploy in the world."

"Don't worry, Father, I'm sure they believed me."

"I hope so," said Beau. "Because if they didn't, the whole of Port Royal and Beaufort will know what you're up to."

Cole stared at his father. "How do I tell my heart to stop feeling, Father?" he asked unhappily. "Could you stop loving Mother simply because someone ordered it?"

Beau's eyes darkened. He knew Cole was right. Once the love was there, you couldn't just say it didn't exist. He had tried to do that once and had discovered it was impossible. And now he was going to have to ask Cole to do the impossible. "Cole, listen to me," Beau said firmly. "I can't make you stop loving her, but dammit, you're going to have to give her up whether you want to or not!"

"I can't."

"You can, and you will!"

"If I don't?"

"I'll talk to Heath and make sure he takes Heather away where you'd never see her again."

"You have no right!"

"I have every right. I don't want to do this, Cole, but I have to," he said. "I want a promise from you that you'll put an end to this affair here and now."

Cole trembled with the violence of his anger. He didn't want to give her up, especially now that she had become so much a part of him.

"Cole?" Beau demanded.

Cole's lips quivered. He knew his father was right. That was just the trouble. He knew it, and the reality of it was killing him. "All right," he groaned helplessly. "All right, I'll give her up!" There were tears in his eyes. "But, my God, how do I tell her?"

Beau was relieved. "You'll find a way. If you want, I'll tell her."

"No," said Cole acidly. "I'll tell her!"

"Today, Cole," said Beau.

Cole nodded. "Today."

Beau reached out and put his hand on his son's shoulder. "I'm sorry, Cole," he said, his voice unsteady.

Cole stared into his father's eyes long and hard, dark green eyes that were so like his own. He had promised he'd give up the woman he loved. Oh, God, now to find the strength to do it.

Beau saw the torment on Cole's face, and his hand dropped from his shoulder. "I'll leave you alone now," he said softly, trying to keep the pain from his own voice. "Just remember, your life isn't over. There's a big world out there and it's full of women, all kinds, Cole, and there's no law says there's only one woman in the world you'll ever love."

Cole's eyes narrowed. "And how many women have you loved, Father?"

"Touché," Beau conceded; then his eyes hardened. "But your mother was not my first cousin, Cole."

Cole stared after his father as he left the room. He swallowed hard. He had promised, but could he keep that promise? Slowly, as if in a daze, he sank down on the bed. How? How was he going to tell her? He lay back, staring at the ceiling, trying to think of the right words so she'd understand. There were none.

The sun had been hiding behind the trees at her back, and now it peeked over them, settling its warmth on her whole body as Heather sat on the bank of the river a few hundred yards from the slave quarters, trying not to be seen in the tall grass. She was alone and had been for the past half-hour now, ever since she'd watched Cole ride down the long drive at Tonnerre, heading toward town.

Her thoughts were in a turmoil, her heart broken in little pieces, and her hands shook as she plucked a small wild daisy from the grass beside her and brought it to her nose, trying to catch a fragrance that wasn't there. Funny, she thought all flowers smelled. All this one did was tickle her nose. She lowered it from her face and gazed absentmindedly out to the river, trying to make her heart accept what her ears had heard from Cole's lips.

It was over. A year of happiness and snatched moments of bliss, then one night of love, and it was over. Uncle Beau had found out, and now, if they didn't end it on their own, he'd see that it was ended. Tears welled up and rolled down her cheeks at the thought of losing Cole. How could she? How was she going to tell her heart to stop loving him simply because the world said so?

Her shoulders shook, and she was crying so hard she didn't hear Lizette approach until she had already reached her.

Lizette stared at Heather in surprise. She had wondered

where she had wandered off to. She and Heather had been in the music room earlier when Cole had come in and told Heather he had to talk to her about something important, and the two of them had walked off. She had tried to join them, but Cole had become terribly upset with her for some reason and demanded she leave them alone. Then she had seen Cole take off down the driveway on his horse as if he'd been stung by a bee, and Heather hadn't come back to the house. Instead, she was sitting here on the riverbank crying. It didn't make sense.

"What is it, Heather, what's happened?" she asked as she stared down at her.

Heather wiped a hand across her nose and looked up at Lizette. "Oh, Liz," she cried miserably. "What am I going to do? What am I going to do?"

Liz dropped to her knees beside her, a little awkwardly because of the weight she'd gained, but kneeling to be close to her. Her hands were spread across the front of her embroidered green muslin. "About what?" she asked curiously.

Heather stared at Lizette with red-rimmed eyes. Did she dare tell her? Her stomach churned with the violence of her hurt. She had to. She had to tell someone. Nothing mattered anymore. She sighed. "About Cole!" she blurted tearfully. "How do I stop loving him, Liz? How do I tell my heart not to feel?"

Lizette stared at her hard, the words confusing her as she tried to make some sense from them. "Cole?" she asked hesitantly. "Heather, what are you talking about?"

Heather shook her head, the tears streaming from her eyes as she told Lizette about her brother and the stolen trysts and everything that had led up to last night. "And then last night when he came home late and told me he'd been trying to find someone to marry us . . . I can't forget last night, Liz," she sobbed passionately. "He made love to me last night, and I can't forget that!" With a helpless wail, she flung herself toward Lizette, whose arms went around her protectively.

Lizette held her close, letting her cry herself out while all sorts of crazy notions flooded her thoughts. In the first place, she'd never suspected anything was going on between her cousin and her brother, and now . . .

As soon as Heather's tears began to subside, Lizette stroked the hair from her cousin's face, but let her keep her head buried against her shoulder. "You and Cole," she asked, half-whispering as she tried to soothe Heather, "you mean you really made love? Like the way I told you that day?"

Heather nodded, reluctantly murmuring an assent, and Lizette's arms tightened about her.

Lizette stared straight ahead, shocked by Heather's confession, yet concerned for her. "Don't cry anymore, please, Heather," she said softly. "I understand, I do."

Heather gulped back the sobs that were still trying to free themselves, and raised her head, pulling it back to look into Lizette's face. "How can you understand, Liz?" she said sadly. "How do you know . . . how could you possibly know how I feel inside?"

Lizette's eyes held a faraway look for a moment as she remembered another time, another riverbank, and Bain's body covering hers; then she made her decision. "I do know how you feel, Heather," she said softly. "Because I lost someone I love too."

Heather wiped the tears from her eyes as she stared at Lizette. "You?" she asked breathlessly.

"Me," answered Lizette. "I haven't seen Bain for a year."

"Bain?" Heather momentarily forgot about her own pain as she saw the hurt in Lizette's eyes. "You're in love with Bain?" she asked.

"Yes."

She studied Lizette for a few minutes; then tears once more rimmed her eyes. "But it isn't the same, Liz," she said quickly. "Bain's never made love to you."

"Hasn't he?"

"Liz!" Heather's eyes widened, the tears glistening.

"Remember the day my hair got caught in the briers?"

Heather nodded. "He made love to you?"

"Yes." Lizette's voice was hushed. "But I didn't dare tell you, Heather," she said. "I didn't know you as well as I know you now. Besides, I was barely fifteen—if anyone had found out, they'd have tarred and feathered Bain and run him out of town."

"Does Bain love you?" asked Heather hesitantly, trying to sniff back the tears.

Lizette's eyes fell and she stared down at the front of Heather's pale yellow dress, watching her bosom heave emotionally. "I don't know," she said after a short silence, then glanced back up at her cousin. "I think he cared. He never really said how he felt."

"But he went away."

"And I died inside!" Lizette's eyes were on Heather's again. "Don't say I don't know how you feel, Heather," she said unhappily. "I do!"

"But if Bain comes back, there's nothing to stop you from loving him," Heather said. "I'll never be able to have Cole, Liz. If we don't stop seeing each other, your father has threatened to have my father send me away."

Lizette's body went slack at the hopelessness of their situation, and she stared hard at Heather. "There's no way?" she asked.

Heather shook her head. "None."

Lizette frowned, trying to think of some way to make Heather feel better. "Where did Cole go?" she asked.

Heather shrugged. "To get drunk, I guess. That's what he said he was going to do."

"That isn't going to help matters."

"That's what I told him, but he said he didn't care anymore. And neither do I, Liz."

"You will, Heather, believe me, you will," Liz said stubbornly. "You'll find out you'll not only go on, but you'll want to go on. You're lucky in one way, at least. Even if you can't be alone with him, you'll still be able to see him once in a while. I don't know if I'll ever see Bain again, or if I can ever love anyone else."

Heather stared hard at Liz. "Help me, Liz," she pleaded unhappily. "Tell me what to do, tell me how to live with the pain."

"I wish I could, but I haven't discovered the secret of that yet myself," and she reached out to hug Heather again, and it was a long time before both girls came back up to the house.

A different Heather returned to the Chateau on Monday, but neither Darcy nor Heath had any inkling of what had changed her. She was quieter than usual and seemed sad to leave Tonnerre, and they suspected it was because, in Lizette, she had found a friend and hated to leave her, especially after watching the warm good-bye the girls exchanged.

Cole hadn't been there to say good-bye. In fact he hadn't spoken to her, but had avoided her since Saturday when he had sworn he was going to get drunk. He had, too. She had heard him come home late Saturday night. The whole household had, and Monday morning, after sleeping off a hangover most of Sunday, he left to go upriver to do some work for his father in the fields. So Heather returned to the Chateau.

The following Sunday afternoon DeWitt Palmer was on the doorstep of the Chateau to take Heather riding, and life resumed its usual pattern. However, there were no more rides alone on Jezebel; there was no need, because Cole wouldn't be waiting anymore. And when the opportunity to go to Tonnerre overnight rose again, there was no need for excitement because Cole was seldom there; he usually found some reason to be gone—to the cockfights, the races, or working someplace on the plantation for his father.

Heather was going crazy. If she could see him just once, she felt it would help. Easter Sunday came and went, and she couldn't take it any longer. She had heard rumors that Cole had been seen around town with a number of different young women, and it hurt terribly. The week after Easter Beau stopped at the house and during the conversation at dinner happened to drop a remark about Cole having to ride into Beaufort for him the next afternoon. Heather latched onto the information with relish.

The next day, dressed in her deep green riding habit, she sat astride Jezebel near where the main road to Beaufort intersected and watched nervously up the road toward the direction of Tonnerre. Her fingers were fidgeting with the reins and her anxiousness was making her breathing erratic. She only hoped she hadn't missed him.

Jezebel nickered and shifted restlessly beneath her each time a carriage or someone on horseback came along the road, and it was all she could do to quiet her and keep her from revealing where they were hidden among the trees.

She had been waiting for almost an hour when she glanced up and saw dust in the distance.

"Please, let it be him," she whispered softly, then strained her eyes, watching as the rider drew near.

Her heart leaped and she exhaled excitedly as she recognized his tall muscular frame in the saddle, and after making certain no one else was on the road with him or coming from any other direction, she spurred Jezebel hurriedly, urging her forward, crashing out from behind the bushes and trees just as Cole reached the turnoff to town.

Cole hadn't been riding fast. He'd been moving at an easy gait, his thoughts miles away. He had been trying so hard to forget Heather, but it wasn't easy. Every time he rode down from Tonnerre, he remembered the afternoons spent with her, the secret meetings that had given him so much pleasure. And his mind was remembering now, when suddenly he heard a noise off to his right and gazed across the field to where a rider was approaching, her horse at a hurried gallop.

He halted his own mount and waited spellbound as she reached him and reined her horse across the shallow ditch and onto the road beside him. She was breathless, and neither of them spoke, but just stared at each other. Then Cole found his voice. "Heather!"

"Don't be angry with me, Cole, I had to see you."

He shook his head. "I'm not angry. How could I be, when all I've done is dream of being with you again."

She flushed. "That's not what I've heard."

"What do you mean?"

"Can we talk?"

"Not here." He gazed about, then motioned down the road toward Beaufort. "No one'll be at the racetrack at Palmerston Grove this time of day. Come on."

It took a good fifteen minutes to reach the racetrack, and Cole checked it out closely first before they rode in, just to make sure it was deserted, then tethered their horses at the hitching rail and helped her from the saddle.

She was light in his arms, and when he looked into her face he realized she was thinner. "You've lost weight," he exclaimed.

"I've been upset."

Her feet hit the ground, but he didn't let go. Instead, he gazed tenderly into her eyes and his heart lurched inside him. "It's so good to see you."

"Then why haven't you?"

He winced. "Because it hurts." He pulled her closer against him. "I thought if I didn't see you I could forget," he said unhappily.

"Have you?"

"You know better than that!"

"Do I?" she asked. She stared up at him. "I've heard about all the women you've been seen with, Cole."

He shook his head, then reached out and touched her face, his fingers playing lightly along her chin line. "Heather, I'll never stop loving you," he said huskily. "Yes, I've been seeing others—what am I supposed to do? I can't have you, I need someone."

"You've made love to someone else?" she asked incredulously.

"Yes . . . no—not the way you think. I'm not celibate, darling, I never claimed to be," he said. "How can I make you see?" he whispered softly. "I thought the only way to put you out of my heart was to take another woman in my arms, but I've discovered it isn't the same." He looked deep into her eyes. "I've been seeing other women, yes, and I've slept with a few."

"Oh, Cole!"

"It wasn't the way you think, Heather," he said painfully. "I used them, that's all. I used their bodies to find the release I couldn't find any other way because you weren't there."

"That makes it right?" she asked bitterly.

"I didn't say it was right."

"How could you?" she cried helplessly. "How could you share yourself with someone else?"

"You have DeWitt!"

"I haven't slept with him!"

"Heather, please," he said anxiously. "Try to understand."

She tried to push herself away, staring at him angrily. "Understand? What am I supposed to understand? When I think of you touching another woman and doing the things with her you did with me, I feel sick inside. Those things were mine, Cole, mine, and you had no right to let another woman feel them. Oh, God!"

He took her by the shoulders, his jaw tightening. He shouldn't have told her, he should have kept her ignorant of his pitiful attempts to get her out of his system, but he wanted no lies between them.

"Heather, I didn't give them anything that belonged to you," he tried to explain. "Dammit, no one has ever taken from me what you took. You took my heart and left me empty, and I tried to find it again, but couldn't. What I did, I did in desperation." He pulled her to him again, his breathing heavy, eyes blazing. "If I could have you, I'd never look at another woman again, believe me. Oh, Lord, Heather, if I could have you . . ." and suddenly his mouth came down on hers in a grinding kiss that sent her senses reeling.

As the kiss deepened, his mouth eased on hers until only the warmth of his love for her remained, and when he finally drew away, he was trembling. "Understand, darling, please understand," he whispered, his voice breaking as he tried to control himself. "I don't want anyone else but you, only it can't be!"

She stared at him, trying to understand, her lips tingling from the force of his kiss, her body aching for him. And yet, even as she yearned to be his, the bitter thought of what she felt was his betrayal in the arms of someone else made her shrink from him. "I can't . . . I can't understand," she cried passionately, her heart breaking inside as she glared at him. "You gave someone else what should have been mine alone. You shared the love we had with someone else, and I'll never forgive you, Cole."

"Heather, please!" he pleaded, but she brushed his hands aside, wrenching herself from his arms.

"No," she yelled furiously. "I wanted to see you just once more, to know in my heart what we did was right and what we've had together was real. But I can't accept this!"

"Then let me love you, Heather, don't turn me away," he cried, his voice lowering seductively. "Let me make love to you now and whenever we can, and I'll never touch another woman as long as I can have you."

"What about your father?"

"To hell with my father! We kept it from them before. We can do it again."

She wanted to say yes, yet knew the folly of it and shook her head instead. "I just can't, Cole," she answered breathlessly. "What if I got pregnant, then what would we do?"

"I could use something, find some way to try to prevent it."

She shook her head. "The risk is too great. It could destroy us."

He straightened, eyes darkening savagely as he gazed at her. "Then don't tell me what to do, Heather," he said, frustrated. "You won't let me live with you, then let me live without you."

She bit her lip, trying to hold back the tears. "Then I guess our talk is over, isn't it?" she said, her voice shaking. "Will you help me back onto my horse, Cole?"

His breathing was labored, frustration deepening his anger as he turned, walking toward where the animals were tethered. She followed hesitantly, then avoided his eyes as he turned, put his hands on her waist, and lifted her to the saddle.

For a brief moment she forced herself to look into his eyes. "Good-bye, Cole!" she said, her voice breaking.

He swallowed hard, but before he could reciprocate her farewell, she reined her horse about and galloped down the lane that led to the main road.

Cole stood for a long time watching the trail of dust left in her wake, his heart heavy. Maybe it was better this way, he thought. Maybe this was the best thing after all. Now she could go on with her life the way it should be before he had blundered into it. Slowly he untied his horse's reins and mounted, and as he cantered easily down the lane, turning off onto the main road toward Beaufort, he took one last look behind him, and all he could see through misty eyes was a tiny speck of dust in the distance as she rode out of his life.

For the rest of the week Heather walked about in a daze. She was listless, overly sensitive, quick to anger, and wasn't eating well.

"You can't afford to lose any more weight, young lady," Aunt Nell admonished one morning at breakfast. "You were thin enough as it was before you started leaving most of your food uneaten. I don't know what's gotten into you unless you're afraid you'll get fat like that cousin of yours." Aunt Nell was mortified when Heather broke into tears and ran from the room.

"Let her go," said Loedicia. "You never seem to know how to be tactful, do you, Nell?" she said. "Heather's grown fond of Lizette, and with the mood she's been in lately, you making fun of Lizette didn't help."

"I didn't make fun of her," protested Nell, but Loedicia didn't agree and cautioned her to tread easier until they discovered just what was ailing Heather and found a way to perk up her spirits.

Unbeknownst to them, there was no way anyone could have made Heather feel better, and one night in the middle of May as she stood upstairs in her bedroom, staring out her open window, smelling the scent of cape jasmine that was heavy on the breeze as it gently moved the sheer curtains that hung beneath the heavy pink draperies, she knew she could deny it no longer. One night with Cole, one careless happy night filled with love, and she was pregnant. Why?

She swallowed back a sob and straightened stubbornly. She wasn't going to cry, not again. She had cried herself to sleep almost every night the past few weeks, and it hadn't changed a thing. She hung on to the velvet draperies, then stared down at herself, her eyes filtering over her lace-trimmed nightgown, wondering if anyone else had noticed that although she had lost weight, her breasts had gotten larger. But then, who would notice? she asked herself. No one ever saw her undressed, and she'd been careful not to wear anything sheer or tight-fitting. No, no one suspected a thing. But what was she going to do?

At first she had thought of telling Cole, but after the pain of their last meeting, she had decided against it. He must never know. But how was she to keep it from him, from all of them? If she just hadn't been so stupid, she would have known what was happening to her when it started. But it wasn't until she had missed her second time of the month and the sick feeling had started that she began to realize what her body was trying to tell her.

Her hand dropped from the curtains and she walked to the bed, sitting on the edge, pondering what to do. There was no way she could stop the baby from growing, and no way Cole could become her husband.

There was only one thing for her to do. Dread swept over her as she made her decision. One way out of this trap—and she didn't want it. Oh, God, she didn't want it, but it was the only answer—the only way to get through the next few months without anyone finding out that Cole was the father of her baby.

Her decision made, she stood up, walked to the dresser, blew out the lamp, and returned to the bed, climbing in under the covers.

She felt her life was over, yet it had only begun.

12

The wedding of Heather McGill Chapman and DeWitt Palmer was to be held in the chapel at the Chateau, with a barbecue afterward and dancing in the evening on the back lawn under the stars, and Roth, as one of the wedding gifts, offered to let his private ship, the *Interlude,* carry the newlyweds on their wedding night to Charleston. At first DeWitt thought they should get married in August, but after some urging from Heather, along with a coyly seductive plea that she didn't know how she could wait so long, he willingly changed it to the second week in June.

DeWitt was overjoyed, considering himself the luckiest man on the face of the earth. But no, it wasn't luck, he told himself that evening as he rode his horse down the drive, heading for home. His gamble had paid off, as he had known it would. He had proposed again, and she had come to her senses and accepted. It was his destiny. After all, didn't he always get everything he wanted?

Heather stood at the door and watched him go, wishing she could tell him never to come back again, but that would be madness.

She had made up her mind that this was the way it had to be; now she had to accept it. Aunt Nell was happy she had made a good match, her parents hadn't objected too strenuously, and Grandma Dicia and Grandpa Roth were the only ones who seemed displeased. However, even they came around in the end, and now there was no going back. No way to undo what she was doing.

The hardest part of the whole ordeal was the day Heather rode up to Tonnerre with her grandmother to ask Lizette to be her maid of honor. It was early afternoon when they arrived, and Lizette was in her bedroom exercising on the machine Cole had brought from Charleston.

"But it isn't doing much good," she told Heather after greeting her exuberantly. She was wearing her drawers and chemise to exercise in, with stockings covering her legs and kid slippers on her feet, and her hair was tied with a ribbon to keep it from getting in her eyes. She finished counting as she pulled the weights, then sighed, sitting back on the seat of the contraption to catch her breath. "My heavens, where have you been keeping yourself? We haven't seen you for so long."

"I've been seeing a great deal of DeWitt," Heather said cautiously.

"Good," said Lizette. "That ought to serve Cole right."

Heather glanced at Lizette furtively. "I'm going to marry DeWitt, Lizette," she said quickly.

"You're not serious!"

"That's why we came up to Tonnerre today," explained Heather, trying to stay calm. "To ask you to be my maid of honor."

"But you can't!" Lizette exclaimed in dismay.

"Why not?" she asked, perturbed.

Lizette stared at her. "Because you're in love with Cole, you ninny!"

"Not anymore, I'm not."

"Oh, Heather . . ." Lizette shook her head. "Don't be crazy," she said, exasperated. "You can't fall in and out of love so easily. If so, then you weren't really in love in the first place."

"Maybe I wasn't!"

Lizette's eyes narrowed. "What happened, Heather?" she asked, her playful manner gone. "When did you see Cole long enough to quarrel with him?"

Heather returned her stare. "We didn't quarrel."

"Didn't you? When did you see him?"

"The week after Easter. I met him on the road to town. I had to, Liz," she said when she saw the look on Lizette's face. "Everyone was always talking, speculating about all the women he'd been seen with lately. I couldn't stand to think that he had forgotten about me so soon."

"Had he?"

She looked miserable. "Oh, Liz, not only did he forget me, but he's made love to other women too!"

"He told you that?"

"Yes!"

Lizette couldn't believe it. It didn't conform with Cole's actions the past few weeks. He had been so moody and on edge. He hadn't forgotten Heather, and Lizette knew it. His easygoing attitude had been replaced by a sullenness that had fired tempers at Tonnerre lately.

"He actually told you he didn't love you anymore?" Lizette asked.

Heather shook her head. "He didn't have to," she answered. "When . . . when he made love to me, I thought it was something special for him, just like it was for me, but he admitted he's made love to other women since then. Don't you see, Liz," she said angrily, "if he really loved me, he wouldn't have wanted anyone else!"

"Oh, goosefeathers!" exclaimed Lizette. "Is that why you've decided to marry Witt? Because if it is, it's the stupidest thing you could do. Cole still loves you."

"What about the other women?"

"Heather, be sensible," she tried to explain. "He was trying to forget you, to find someone to take the hurt from him. You said he doesn't love you. I bet if he were allowed to be with you, he'd never touch another woman the rest of his life."

"That's what he said."

"Then for heaven's sake, believe it. He's a man and he's human, Heather. You don't have to be in love with a person to sleep with them, at least a man doesn't. Attraction's enough for a man, that's why they're willing to pay whores. So if you're just marrying Witt because you're mad at Cole, forget it."

Heather's eyes faltered and she looked away.

"What is it now?" Lizette asked quickly. "Are you afraid to tell Witt you've changed your mind?"

Heather bit her lip. "I haven't changed my mind, Liz," she said.

"What do you mean, you haven't changed your mind? Now that you know why Cole did what he did, there's no reason anymore for you to marry Witt."

"Yes, there is," she cut in quickly.

Lizette frowned. "What are you getting at?"

"Liz, if I tell you something, you have to promise not to tell anyone, not even Cole," Heather demanded unhappily.

Lizette's frown deepened. "I promise," she said, wondering what on earth this was all about.

"I mean it, Liz," Heather went on, seeing the skepticism in Lizette's eyes. "If you do, I'll kill myself."

"Oh, for heaven's sake, Heather, don't be so dramatic," Lizette replied. "I told you I won't tell anyone."

Heather took a deep breath, then exhaled. "I'm pregnant, Liz," she half-whispered.

"Pregnant? Oh, my God!" Lizette gasped.

Tears welled up in Heather's eyes. "I can't marry Cole, Liz," she said. "You know that, we both know it, so the only way I can keep anyone from finding out is to marry DeWitt."

"Holy Jesus!" cried Lizette. "No wonder you don't look well." She studied Heather closely. "But to marry DeWitt? Why don't you just tell your mother?"

"She'd never understand."

"How do you know? She was in the same predicament once."

"I just know," said Heather stubbornly. "Besides, Cole tried before to find someone to marry us. It's impossible."

Liz tried to help think of a different solution for Heather, but there didn't seem to be any. She had heard through gossip, as most people did, that there were places where a woman could go to get rid of unwanted babies, but she wouldn't even know how to go about locating anyone like that, and besides, Heather refused to go even if she could find one. So while Lizette redid her toilette, fixed her hair, and slipped back into a lemon-yellow frock she'd been wearing before she had decided to do some exercising, the two young cousins reluctantly made plans for Heather's wedding.

Downstairs on the back terrace, Loedicia stared reflectively at Rebel as she sipped at a cup of tea. "What's the matter, Reb?" she asked. "Ever since I told you of Heather's plans to marry DeWitt, you've been getting that faraway look in your eyes."

Rebel finished her tea, then set the cup and saucer down. She stood up, walked to the edge of the terrace, and stared off toward the river, then turned back. "Mother, if I tell you something—and I feel I have to tell you—will you promise not to tell anyone?"

"I hope that doesn't include Roth."

"You know what I mean," said Rebel.

Loedicia nodded. "Yes, I know what you mean. All right, I promise," she said. "Now, what's the matter?"

Rebel sat on one of the wrought-iron chairs beside her mother. "Do you remember the week after our birthdays this year, when Heather came up to stay at Tonnerre for the weekend?"

Loedicia nodded.

"Cole wasn't here when she arrived, and he came home late that night. The next morning, Beau caught Cole coming out of Heather's bedroom."

Loedicia sat motionless.

"It seems the two of them had been in love for some time, and being under the same roof was too much."

Loedicia finally found her voice. "Then why is Heather marrying DeWitt?" she gasped incredulously.

"That's what's been bothering me," Rebel confessed. "I think she's marrying him on the rebound, to spite all of us. We never said anything to anyone because Beau made the two of them break it off, but Cole's been miserable to live with ever since. He blames us for what's happened."

"Then he's still in love with her?"

"Of course. He's his father's son, isn't he?" She stared at her mother anxiously. "Mother, what bothers me is, what is he going to do when he finds out, and on top of it all, why has Heather decided to marry DeWitt? She can't be in love with him."

"Maybe she feels it'll help her forget Cole," Loedicia tried to reason.

"Maybe." Rebel wrung her hands. "Oh, for God's sake, Mother, why does society have to put so many taboos on everything? If you could just see what this whole thing is doing to Cole, and now this."

"Now what?" asked Cole from the edge of the terrace, and both women glanced up, startled. He was standing at the edge of the flagstones, his work coat slung over his shoulder. His sleeves were rolled up, boots dusty. He was staring at the two women, green eyes intense. "Hello, Grandmother," he said, walking closer, then addressed his mother. "I asked you what, Mother," he said again.

Rebel's eyes wavered. She glanced at her mother, then looked up at her son nervously. He seemed to tower over her. "Heather's getting married," she murmured reluctantly.

Cole's eyes narrowed. "What did you say?"

"She said your cousin Heather's marrying DeWitt Palmer

on the eighth of June," Loedicia answered for Rebel, and they both held their breaths at the explosive look in Cole's eyes.

"Where is she?" he asked.

Rebel motioned inside with her head. "Upstairs with your sister."

He didn't say another word, but walked toward the open French doors that led into the parlor, and as he stalked inside, heading for the stairs in the foyer, he was oblivious of his mother and grandmother calling out to him.

Of all the crazy, stupid things to do! He knew why she was doing it. She was trying to get even with him for what she felt he'd done to her, but this wasn't the way. Not like this! When he reached the door to his sister's room he hesitated, but only for a second, then took a deep breath and knocked.

Lizette answered. "Who is it?"

"Cole!"

There was mumbling from the other side of the door, and what sounded like protesting; then the door suddenly burst open.

Cole stepped into the room, his eyes falling instantly on Heather, who was trying to look inconspicuous near the window, her back to him.

"Well?" asked Lizette. "What do you want?"

"I want to talk to Heather."

"Fine, go ahead." Lizette gestured toward Heather. "There she is."

Heather turned to face him. It was the first she had seen him since that day at Palmerston Grove, and as her eyes fell on him her heart skipped a beat. But she had to be strong. Oh, God! For the sake of the baby, she had to be strong. "Hello, Cole," she said unsteadily.

He scowled, his mouth rigid. "Why?" he asked, and she flinched.

"Because my life has to go on," she said quickly. "Because I'm through trying to hold on to a fantasy. The world's real, I'm real, and I have to have someone to love me, too."

His eyes darkened. "So you had to pick DeWitt?"

"I'm in love with him."

"Liar!"

"Prove it!"

Suddenly he grabbed her shoulders, pulling her toward him. His kiss was rough, demanding at first, then softened into a sensual pleasure that made Heather shiver.

"Have I proved it sufficiently?" he asked as he drew his mouth from hers.

"Take your hands off me!" she gasped.

Instead, they tightened. "I want an answer, Heather," he said acidly. "Why did you promise to marry DeWitt?"

"I told you!"

"I can tell you," said Lizette from behind him. They had ignored the fact that she was there.

Heather's eyes wrenched from Cole to Lizette. "No!" she screamed helplessly. "Don't, Liz! You promised!" Her eyes grew wild. "I'll kill myself if you tell him!"

Lizette stared at Heather, seeing the savage anger in her eyes, and a fearful panic seized her. My God! If she did tell Cole, there was every chance the shock would drive Heather to doing what she threatened. She should have kept her mouth shut. She bit her lip. Maybe she could bluff Cole. "Heather's marrying DeWitt because . . . because it's the only way she knows of to get even with you," she said, and saw Heather relax.

"Is that true?" Cole asked her anxiously.

She drew her eyes from Lizette and looked up into his face. "Yes," she whispered agonizingly. "Yes."

"Then tell him you've changed your mind," he said angrily. "Tell him it's off."

"I can't!"

"You can!"

"Why?" she asked helplessly. "So I can go on being miserable without you? Watching you court all the women in Port Royal and Beaufort? I won't do it, and you don't have any right to ask me to."

Cole stared at her hard. She was right. He had no right to ask anything of her, but Lord how he loved her. Pain shot through his chest at the thought of giving her up to DeWitt. It was bad enough he had to give her up, but to him!

The pain eased into his eyes. "Does it have to be DeWitt?" he asked bitterly.

She bit her lip. "He asked me."

His hands tightened on her shoulders. "Wait, wait for someone else to ask, someone worthy. Dammit, Heather, I can't have you, but Jesus, do you have to give yourself to him?"

She stared up at him, wanting to give in, yet knowing she didn't dare. "Yes," she whispered, trying to keep her voice steady. "I'm going to marry DeWitt, Cole, and nothing you or anyone else says will make me change my mind."

His eyes blazed, and he wanted to shake her, make her give in, but he knew it was hopeless. With an agonized groan he practically threw her back against the window as he released her. "Go ahead, then, marry him," he yelled savagely. "Ruin your life if you want, see if I care, but you'll never stop loving me, Heather, no matter how many men you give yourself to." And on those bitter words, he turned and went out the door, slamming it behind him.

There was a momentary silence. "I should have told him the truth," Lizette said unhappily.

Heather shook her head, her eyes glazed with sadness. "No, Liz, it's better this way." She straightened the skirt of her pale blue afternoon dress, then squared her shoulders, trying to keep her composure. "Now, shall we finish our plans for the wedding?"

Later that afternoon, on the way back to the Chateau, Loedicia glanced over at Heather beside her in the buggy. She still looked unhappy, not beaming like a future bride. "I know all about Cole, Heather," Loedicia finally said as they rode along through the countryside.

"I don't know what you mean."

"I mean I know you're in love with him."

This time Heather glanced over at her grandmother. "Aunt Rebel told you?"

"Yes."

"And now you hate me?"

"Good heavens, child," said Loedicia. "What makes you think I'd hate you? No one hates you."

"Isn't it customary to hate someone who does something so evil?"

Loedicia gazed at her sympathetically. "I see nothing evil about you loving Cole," she told her. "It's everyone else who thinks it's wrong. Believe me, if I had my way, dear, I'd say marry him and the devil with the rest of the world. You see, love isn't bound by limits, it just happens, and whether you fall in love with your first cousin or second cousin isn't something you can decide ahead of time. However, unfortunately, or fortunately, however you want to look at it, I don't run the world, dear."

Heather studied her grandmother carefully. She was sixty-one, yet there were few wrinkles in her face, and her violet eyes were always warm and caring. "You really love Grandpa Roth a great deal, don't you, Grandma Dicia?" she asked.

Loedicia nodded. "I love him more than you could ever imagine, child," she answered. "That's why I can understand how you must feel loving Cole and not being able to share your love. Only I don't like to see you marrying DeWitt simply because you can't have Cole."

"I'm not."

"Why are you marrying him, then?"

Heather hesitated. She almost felt her grandmother would understand. Yet fear kept her from telling the truth. "Because he asked me, and I couldn't see any reason to refuse. I can't forget what I feel for Cole by sitting around all the time moping about it. The only way I'm going to forget it, Grandma Dicia, is by turning my thoughts to someone else. I like Witt. We've had fun together. He's been kind, thoughtful, a bit arrogant at times perhaps, but no one's perfect . . . so I'll marry him and try to make a life for myself that doesn't include Cole."

Loedicia watched the hurt in Heather's eyes as she spoke and wished to God things could be different, because deep in her heart she had a strange foreboding that Heather was making a terrible mistake. But she didn't disagree with her; for now, she'd accept the explanation, even though it sounded shallow and contrived. She reached out and squeezed Heather's hand. "If that's the only explanation you want to give, then I guess I'd better quit being a meddling old grandmother and let you live your own life," she said affectionately. "But please, dear," she said as an afterthought, "if you ever need anyone, or want to talk for any reason, I can be very understanding when I want to be. Will you remember?"

Heather nodded.

"Good!" Loedicia patted her hand. "Now, since we barely have three weeks to prepare everything, I suggest you and I put our heads together and come up with the best shindig these parts have seen for a long time. How's that?"

Tears welled up in Heather's eyes as she stared at this remarkable little woman sitting beside her. They said she'd fought in wars, survived capture by Indians, and who knew what all, and still she had such a zest for life. Heather prayed for all she was worth that the baby inside her, the child that would be Loedicia's first great-grandchild, would be a child Grandma Dicia could be proud of.

The next three weeks were more than just hectic, they were a whirlwind of activity. DeWitt's brother, Carl, was to stand up with him during the ceremony, and that necessitated Heather having dinner at Palmerston Grove. She had been there before with DeWitt, but not formally as a future member of the family.

Everett Palmer was a widower and the house was all male except for a slave who served as housekeeper and a few younger ones who did the work. The housekeeper was a tall, slender woman with light skin, and Heather knew by her blue eyes that probably more than one of her ancestors had been white. Her name was Oleander and she ran Palmerston Grove with an iron hand. Heather felt a little intimidated by her.

Palmerston Grove was an old plantation, older than the Chateau. It had been handed down to Everett Palmer from his father, and his father before him, and the land had been in the Palmer family since the first settlers. The house was big and rambling, sprawled amid moss-covered oaks, the verandas enhanced by trellisses of wisteria and honeysuckle that kept out most of the sun.

Everett Palmer was a wealthy man and had made the plantation prosper. His only concern now was seeing to it that his sons married and produced sons and heirs so that all his work wasn't in vain. Unfortunately, Carl had let him down. He was twenty-seven and had married five years earlier. His wife, Charity, had been seventeen at the time. All seemed to go well at first. However, five months after their marriage, Charity miscarried. She had been only three months pregnant, but it had been a tremendous blow to her. During the next four years, after one more early miscarriage and two stillborn sons, Charity's mind began to wander. It was little things at first—forgetting to do her hair, wearing the same dress over and over again until Carl finally had to tell her to change, not keeping up with conversations going on around her. But as time went on, she became worse, eventually reverting to the years before she was married. When it became quite obvious that her mind was really gone, Carl finally consented to let her leave Palmerston Grove and return to her parents' home, where she lived as a perpetual child. Charity had been Catholic, and her parents refused, as her present guardians, to sign papers that would dissolve the marriage, so Carl was left with a mentally unbalanced wife who could no longer be called a wife and Everett Palmer's one chance for an heir now rested solely on DeWitt.

Witt had told Heather briefly of Carl's tragic history, but as she sat across from him at the table during her first formal dinner at Palmerston Grove, for some reason she couldn't feel sympathy for him. There was a hard, unyielding air about Carl Palmer. His hair was red-gold and his hazel eyes were much like DeWitt's, but most of the time they were unsmiling, although they raked over her often, making her feel uneasy.

Everett Palmer was a combination of both his sons. His gray hair had once been blond like DeWitt's, and like Carl, he spent little time outdoors, leaving the running of his land to an overseer, so his complexion was drab and lifeless. He was a hard, unyielding man with an inflated image of his own importance and was quite pleased that his son had chosen the granddaughter of an ex-congressman to marry, even though he did disagree on almost every political issue Roth had favored over the years.

The dinner went well in spite of Heather's discomfort in the presence of these two men, but it did have an adverse effect on her when she realized that after the wedding she and DeWitt would be making Palmerston Grove their home. She dreaded the thought, but it was just something else she had to make up her mind to do for her baby's sake, regardless of her own feelings.

The day of the wedding arrived sooner than Heather dreamed it would, and that morning as she opened her eyes, watching the sun streaming in at the window of her room, she felt sicker than she had felt in days. Maybe it was the excitement of the wedding or the fear that lay dormant inside her at the thought of letting DeWitt make love to her, or maybe it was just the baby protesting. Whatever it was, she felt so nauseated she wished she could dic. It took supreme effort to push back the covers and get up, but she finally did, sitting on the edge of the bed with her head in her hands.

For an agonized moment she felt her stomach lurch at the thought of what lay ahead for her today. Oh, God! She couldn't throw up, not today. She gulped back and swallowed repeatedly, trying to keep her stomach from upheaving, and it was like this that Lizette found her.

Lizette had stayed overnight, and as she walked into the room without bothering to knock, she shook her head sadly, shutting the door quickly behind her. "Oh, Lord, don't get sick now."

Heather shook her head. "I'm trying not to," she whispered.

Lizette pulled the ties on her crimson wrapper tight as she stared at Heather. "I'll be right back," she said quickly, and turned, leaving the room without any explanation to Heather, but a few minutes later she was back with a large mug of hot cider and a slice of dry bread. "It's the only thing Mattie could think of that'd settle your stomach," she explained to her cousin.

"You told Mattie?"

"I told her you were excited because of the wedding and your stomach was doing flips." Lizette watched anxiously as Heather sipped at the cider and nibbled the bread. "Are you sure you can really go through with this?" she asked, frowning.

"I have to, Liz," she said emotionally. "I just have to, for the baby's sake." She swallowed hard, setting the half-empty mug down on the stand. The bread was gone, and she put a hand on her stomach, pressing lightly. "Now, thanks to you, I think I have things back under control again." She sighed. "But we'd better get moving, don't you think? There's still a lot to do before everything's ready this afternoon."

Their morning was filled with hair washing, bathing, a few alterations on their dresses, and all the other last-minute things that always have to be done, while Darcy, Loedicia, and Aunt Nell ran around seeing to it that everything went smoothly. Long tables had been set up at the back of the house to serve as a buffet. Other tables with chairs were put up about the lawn for the guests, and servants bustled around hurriedly, checking on everything. Overhead, lanterns had been hung, because the celebrating would go on well after dark, and the slaves had built a large wooden platform for dancing, with a stage at one end for the musicians. The chapel was filled with flowers.

By late afternoon, Heather was in a dither as she stood upstairs in her underclothes waiting to slip into her wedding dress. She, her mother, and Grandma Dicia had all had a hand in designing it, but Aunt Nell had insisted on doing all the work on it herself. The dress was a filmy illusion of white gauze over white satin, the high waist girdled and tucked in with Irish lace and satin ribbons. The satin sleeves were off the shoulder and shirred to just below the elbow, where flounced layers of Irish lace and gauze formed ruffles. Then, across the low neckline, were rows of lace and gauze that stood about two inches high, forming a ruffled edge. The gauze veil that hung to the floor in back was held in place with more starched ruffles of lace and gauze, with satin ribbons adorning the sides.

Heather was fortunate that empire waistlines were still the

style, because that way Aunt Nell didn't have to measure hers and wouldn't notice the change. It wasn't much of a change at this stage, only an inch or two, but she was pleased anyway. As Heather turned now toward the bed where the dress lay and watched her maid Tildie, a plump young girl of about fifteen, lift it up to help her on with it, she sighed. There was no going back, no changing her mind, no chance to undo what had been done. She lifted her arms and let the girl help raise it up over her head, letting it slip down.

The young girl gazed at Heather rapturously as she began fastening the back. "You're going to look mighty pretty, Miss Heather," she said happily.

Heather smiled wanly.

Tildie had almost finished, when the door opened and Lizette walked in.

Lizette's dress was every bit as delicate as Heather's. It was yards and yards of pale apricot-colored panels hung over a skirt of burnt-orange satin, and as the panels floated about, the darker skirt beneath was glimpsed only momentarily, making an unusual effect. The waist was caught just below her full bosom with a band of Irish lace the deep color of the underskirt, and the satin off-the-shoulder sleeves had pale gauze and deep lace trimmings similar to those on Heather's dress, with satin ribbons decorating the lace and gauze flounced ruffles at the elbows.

Heather's bouquet was white roses and cape jasmine, with narrow white satin ribbons falling from it. Lizette's bouquet was of cape jasmine only, the ribbons adorning it in the same coppery color as the satin in her dress.

Heather saw that Lizette too was excited. Everyone was coming, all the important families, and as Heather turned once more to look out the window, she gave thanks for one thing at least. There had been no rain for the past few days and today had dawned warm and sunny. The ceremony was to take place at four o'clock. She glanced at the dainty porcelain clock on the dresser. It was almost three-thirty already, time to add the veil to her hair, which had been set in curls atop her head, and take one last look in the mirror to be certain everything was all right.

Her mother had come to talk to her the night before, but it hadn't helped much. Darcy had tried as best she could to explain to Heather what she was to expect, but it wasn't easy, especially after all the years of pretending that physical love didn't exist. It was only recently that she had admitted to herself that there was no terrible sin in enjoying the pleasures of her body. So her talk with Heather was a stilted, embarrassing attempt to explain to her the part a woman played in marriage. Heather listened stoically, wishing she could tell her mother that the talk wasn't necessary, that she knew what marriage entailed, including the intimate act of making love, but all she could do was nod her head occasionally and assure her mother that everything would be all right.

Now, as Heather let Tildie fasten the veil to the top of her curls, she wasn't quite as certain things were going to be all right. She was getting cold feet, and on top of it, her stomach was acting up again. She closed her eyes as Tildie put in the last hairpin, then opened them again and gazed at herself in the mirror. It was done. She took a deep breath and turned to Lizette as the door opened and Loedicia came in.

Loedicia was wearing a dress of deep purple silk with lace trimming that brought out the silver highlights in her hair, and gracing her throat and pierced earlobes were clusters of amethysts. She looked stunning as she stood in the doorway staring at her two young granddaughters. "Are you both ready?" she asked.

Heather looked from her grandmother to Lizette then back to her grandmother again. "I'm ready," she said.

Lizette echoed her answer. "So am I."

"Then we'd better get downstairs. The guests are all waiting, the carriage is ready to drive you down the lane to the chapel, and it's almost time."

Heather took one last look in the mirror, then set her jaw stubbornly and followed her grandmother out of the room, with Lizette close at her heels. They met Roth outside the bedroom door, and his eyes were beaming at the sight of them. He escorted the three of them down to the foyer, where Heath and Darcy were waiting. Heath and Roth were both wearing black frock coats and buff trousers, and Darcy was in pale green, the color of her eyes, and they all seemed almost as nervous as Heather.

Heath smiled at his daughter; then, as he handed her the bridal bouquet and looked into her eyes, he frowned momentarily. He had grown to love Heather very dearly and often was able to read her moods better than even her mother, and this afternoon he sensed a sadness about her. "Is everything all right, dear?" he asked affectionately.

She nodded. "Yes, just a little nervous."

"I guess perhaps all brides are a little wary of the venture." He wrapped his hands over hers as she held the bouquet and pressed them warmly. Her hands were as cold as ice. He looked into her eyes and was about to question her again, but changed his mind. "I hope you'll be happy, Heather," he said instead, and thought he saw a tear at the corner of her eye.

She forced a smile. "Thank you, Father." She took his arm, letting the tear roll down her cheek as she turned her head away. "If you're going to give me away, we'd better get started, hadn't we?" she asked, and they all headed for the door, where the carriage awaited.

As the carriage moved along, the closer they got to the chapel, the more upset Heather became. Her insides were in a turmoil, and in spite of the perpetual smile she was forcing to her lips as she nodded here and there to guests, she felt panic seize her. She couldn't throw up, not now!

The crowd was milling about, whispering among themselves as the carriage pulled up in front of the small chapel and everyone got out. They moved up the steps of the white wooden building in unison, and it was torture for Heather because her knees were shaking so badly she could hardly walk. That she made it at all was a miracle, and as she started down the aisle to the organ music, the scent of all the flowers almost overpowering her in the heat of the summer afternoon, her eyes fell on DeWitt where he stood with Carl in front of the altar, and a new wave of terror swept over her. She clutched her father's arm tighter for moral support to keep from turning and running toward the door. DeWitt was smiling, and even though she had seen him smile a hundred times over the past year, there was something frightening about the way he was smiling now.

His eyes were riveted to her, the strength in them unfailingly dominant, and with his head held high, shoulders thrust back, it was as if he had suddenly sighted prey rather than his bride. By the time she and her father reached the front of the chapel and stood before the minister, Heather had shaken the feeling somewhat, because when Heath handed her over to DeWitt, his smile softened and his eyes grew less intense. She was relieved, but her relief didn't last long, when she suddenly realized a few minutes later that the ceremony was almost over and that she remembered nothing of what she had said or done during those few moments. It was more as if the whole thing was happening to someone else. And it wasn't until she had lifted her mouth to meet DeWitt's for the proverbial kiss, then turned to walk back down the aisle, that the impact of what had happened struck her, for there, standing in the open doorway at the back of the chapel, waiting silently to meet the newly married couple, his body tall and erect in a dark green frock coat and buff trousers, hat in hand, his coal-black hair ruffled by the breeze that was blowing outside, was Cole.

13

The overhead lanterns cast flickering shadows through the crowds of people scattered over the lawn. The festivities had been going on for hours now, and still everyone was having fun. Dancing had begun after the lanterns were lighted, but people were still milling about the tables filling their plates with food, and there had been so many toasts raised to the newlyweds that it was a wonder everyone wasn't inebriated.

Heather had weathered Cole's unsmiling presence and reluctant congratulations at the door of the chapel in spite of the emotional upheaval it was causing her, although she had to admit to herself that DeWitt's attitude had helped her through it. She had no idea whether he did it for her sake or simply because he didn't want to make a scene, but DeWitt actually accepted Cole's congratulations graciously, and it helped ease her discomfiture.

Now, as she sat at the bridal table next to DeWitt, watching all the merrymaking, she glanced off toward the dancers just in time to see Lizette wander off into the crowd. For a moment Heather forgot her own troubles as she realized she hadn't seen Lizette dancing with anyone all evening except her father, brother, and grandfather. It was sad to see her being left out; even Felicia had remarked on it earlier in the evening. Heather tried to see through the crowd, but Lizette had disappeared.

The night breeze was warm against Lizette's face as she crossed the walkway that led to the pier, then moved down toward the river, where a maze of flower gardens had been laid out. She glanced back. Everyone was having such a good time. The only other person at the wedding as miserable as she was, was Cole. She had seen him ten minutes ago forcing himself to listen to Merrilou Phillips tell about the trip she had taken to Charleston last week, and she knew his mind wasn't on what she was saying because all evening his eyes had been glued to Heather, the pain in them transparent enough for anyone with the slightest suspicion to see.

She maneuvered around a large bed of flowers, lifting the skirt of her fancy dress so it wouldn't get dirty, then turned once more toward the river, following a flagstone walk that led between the flowerbeds to a bench at the end of the gardens, where she often sat when she came to visit so she could watch the boats go by. As she sat down, she realized she could still hear the music and laughter from the wedding party.

She bit her lip, trying to hold back the tears. It was so lonely out here, yet it had been lonely back there too. Lonelier perhaps, in a way, because here there was no one to snub her and treat her cruelly. Here she was by herself through her own choice. She stared out over the water, watching the moon coming up over the trees downriver turning the water to a ribbon of silver, and she sighed, remembering the last night she had seen Bain. There hadn't been any moon that night, but the river had been just as beautiful then.

Many of the things about that night were still hazy in her memory, but one thing was clear. She remembered those few precious moments just before he left her when she knew he was doing all he could to keep from making love to her again. His hands and lips had made love to her, and he had wanted her that night, as much as he had that day at the old swimming hole. And now she wished deep in her heart that he hadn't come to his senses, that he had finished what he had started and made her his again, just once more. She had wanted it so badly. And even now, thinking back on that night brought a sweet ache.

She sighed, then turned, startled as she heard a footfall behind her. She stood up and stared into the shadows made by the oak tree.

"Who is it?" she asked anxiously.

She heard someone inhale; then a deep masculine voice asked, "Do you mind if I join you?"

Liz stared, her heart pounding as a tall figure stepped from the darkness into the moonlight, and for a brief moment, the voice, familiar with its mellow tones and the way he stood . . . Could it be?

"Bain?" she asked breathlessly.

"You know my brother?" the man asked as he walked over and stood directly in front of her, and Lizette stared in awe.

It wasn't Bain, but the resemblance was strong. The same dark brown hair, waves turning silvery bronze where the moon caressed it, the jawline . . . He even wore a short clipped beard and mustache. His nose was a shade wider perhaps, the brows heavier, and he was older than Bain, but it was remarkable.

"Stuart?" Lizette asked in surprise. Heather had told her he was coming back to live in Beaufort, and earlier today Felicia had said he and his wife would be along later. She had never dreamed that anyone could be so much like Bain.

"Oh, you know me, then," he said, smiling. "Have we met?"

"Not for a long time."

"I see."

"I'm Lizette Dante."

His eyebrows rose. "Aha, the other granddaughter."

"That's right."

"And you're hiding out here all by yourself?" He glanced about at the long expanse of lawn beyond the walkway and over to where the lanterns hung. "Felicia said you were maid of honor today."

"I was."

"Then shouldn't you look happier?"

"Who says I'm not happy?" she asked.

His mouth tilted cynically. "A beautiful woman prefers a lonely bench by the river to the company of all the most eligible young bachelors from Beaufort and Port Royal all bunched together in one spot? It doesn't quite make sense, now, does it?"

She stared up at him, wishing she could see the color of his eyes, because the expression in them reminded her so much of the way Bain had looked at her when they had first met after all those years. But she couldn't, and could only guess at what lay behind the look he was giving her.

"I'm not a beautiful woman," she said quickly.

A frown creased his forehead. "Who told you a ridiculous thing like that?"

"No one, I just know it," she answered. "I'm fat and ugly and . . . I'd rather be out here alone, if you don't mind."

He stared down at her, then reached out and put a hand below her chin, tilting her head to the right so that the moon was full on her face. "Ugly?" he said, bewildered. "I remember you as a child, Lizette Dante—you were beautiful then, you're gorgeous now. You mean the young men around here haven't noticed?"

She pulled her head away from his hand, but her eyes still bored into his. "Don't make fun of me, Stuart," she said bitterly.

His frown deepened. "You think I'd do that?"

"Others have."

"I'm not cruel, Lizette."

Her eyes lowered self-consciously. "I'm sorry, then," she said.

Stuart Kolter's eyes moved from her face down to the front of her dress. The moon brought her full bosom into view, and it looked like velvet above her neckline, all soft and cushiony. He took a deep breath. She had said she was fat. He had to agree that she weighed more than most young women her age—what was she, fifteen? sixteen? But her weight was all in the right places, and there was a sensuous quality about her that bothered him. She was young and lonely, and he felt a strange warmth toward her.

"Would you care to dance, Lizette?" he asked suddenly, not really knowing why he had asked, except there was something about her that intrigued him.

She gazed at him in surprise. "Here?" she asked curiously.

He glanced about again. They could still hear the music above the laughter of the crowd. "Why not?"

"Your wife—shouldn't you be with her?"

He smiled. "Right now I imagine she's still trading recipes with one of the ladies she was talking to," he said. "Besides, she doesn't like to dance." He lifted his arms. "Shall we?"

Lizette was hesitant. The more she looked at him, the more he reminded her of Bain, and she had just been thinking of Bain in a rather reckless way. This wasn't right, she told herself as she stared up into his face. He was too much like Bain.

"Please?" he coaxed.

How could she refuse? Besides, she wanted to dance with

him. To dance with a man for a change who wasn't her brother, father, or grandfather. With a man who had the power to make her feel like a woman again. Slowly, deliberately, she stepped forward until she was almost touching him. "All right," she half-whispered, and his smile faded, replaced by an intense gaze she couldn't quite fathom as his arm circled her waist and he pulled her even closer.

He began to move to the strains of the music, and she followed his lead as he danced away from the bench and began gliding along the flagstone walks that separated the flowerbeds. Magnolia and other flowering trees were interspersed among the flowers here and there, and although they weren't blooming this time of year, they cast delicately laced shadows along the walks. He moved in and out with the rhythm, holding her close in his arms; then, as the tempo of the music slowed and the song changed, he drew his head back and looked down into her eyes. "How old are you, Lizette?" he asked curiously.

She was a bit breathless. Not from the dancing, but from the shock of his remarkable resemblance to Bain—and having him hold her so close like this wasn't helping. "I'll be seventeen on the seventeenth," she said unsteadily.

"Of this month?"

"Yes."

"I see." He smiled slightly.

"You're making fun of me again," she warned him.

He shook his head. "I told you before, that's one thing I'll never do is make fun of you. I was just remembering when I was seventeen. It seems like ages ago."

"Somehow I can't imagine you being seventeen," she said.

"Oh, but I was." He drew his eyes from her face, then leaned forward, resting the lower side of his cheek against her hair and smelled the sweet scent of cape jasmine that seemed to surround her as he continued dancing. "That was fourteen years ago, and you were only about three then, and look at you now," he said. His arms tightened a little and Lizette felt a strange warmth spread through her at the sound of his voice so close to her ear. "I wish I were seventeen again, Lizette Dante," he said unsteadily as they swayed to the music. "Because if I were, you'd never spend another evening alone again."

Lizette's feet faltered and she missed a step. His arms loosened about her momentarily. "I'm sorry," she said, rather flustered. "I . . . I guess I'm not very good at dancing."

Stuart's face was flushed as he stared down at her, and suddenly he felt a strange shock run through him. There was something about her, something that warred with all his good intentions. He had just meant to be friendly. She was young and looked so alone.

"Why did you walk over here away from the others?" she asked him, and he didn't know how to answer.

"I don't know," he finally said. "I saw you earlier talking to one of the guests and then I saw you standing watching the others dance, and when you wandered off by yourself, you suddenly looked so forlorn."

"In other words, you felt sorry for me."

"No, not exactly." His eyes locked with hers and he felt a warm quickening deep in his loins. "I wanted to know who you were and find out why you wanted to be alone, so I followed you."

"You had no idea who I was?"

"None whatsoever. Julia and I arrived only about an hour ago—we couldn't make it to the wedding earlier."

"I see."

"I'm sorry if I've upset you in any way, Lizette," he said softly. "I only wanted to try to make you feel better. It seemed everyone was having a good time except you."

"Now you know why," she said. "I can't even dance without making a fool of myself."

"That was my fault." He flushed, feeling weirdly incompetent in her presence, like a bumbling schoolboy. "I shouldn't have said what I said, I suppose," he went on, "but I meant every word. You're absolutely lovely, Lizette," he said huskily.

Her eyes were still locked with his, and she trembled. "Thank you," she said softly. "It helps."

Her hands were on the front of his coat, and he reached up, covering them with his own as he studied her face. Never before in his life had he ever felt this way with any other woman than Julia, and lately he hadn't even felt this way with Julia. She was always too busy with the children or her organizations, and it seemed as if she never found time to just let him look at her anymore. Or was he the one who couldn't find time for her? He went over it briefly in his mind. No, he was right the first time. Even now, earlier, when he had asked her to dance, she had refused, finding conversation and the local gossip more interesting than his arms.

He felt a sweep of passion rush through him and tried to

suppress it. What he was doing was utterly insane, and yet he couldn't seem to break the spell this lovely young woman seemed to have cast over him.

"Shall we finish our dance, Lizette?" he asked.

She nodded, and once more his hand secured her waist, moving deftly across her back, and he drew her to him until she filled his arms, soft, yet firm. He loved the feel of her against him and the scent of her filling his nostrils, and as he gazed up at the moon, chiding himself for playing the fool, she too stared up at the stars, her eyes closed, cursing herself for accepting his invitation to dance, because now, after feeling what it was like in his arms, she didn't want it to stop, yet knew it had to.

They danced in silence for a long time after that; then suddenly the music stopped and they too stopped, only he still held her.

"You're not unhappy anymore, are you?" he asked, his breath warm against her ear.

She sighed. "No."

"Good." His arms tightened for a brief second; then he drew away abruptly and turned from her, gazing out over the river. "Will I see you again after tonight?" he asked huskily.

She shrugged. "I don't know. I suppose we'll run into each other in town on occasion."

He nodded. "It's likely."

"I hear you're living in Beaufort now," she said.

"We bought the old Sheldon place, about two miles from my parents'."

"But being a senator, don't you have to spend a great deal of time in Washington?"

He sighed. "It'll work out."

"I hope so."

He straightened, his broad shoulders flexing, and turned to look down into her face again. "So much for the chitchat," he suddenly said, and his eyes looked bewildered. "I guess I'd better not see you anymore," he said deliberately. "I'm sorry, Lizette. You're right, I'm a married man, I have no right even being here."

"But you came."

"Yes, dammit, I came," he said. "I came because . . . God help me, I don't know why I came. Can you understand that?"

She nodded meekly. "I'm sorry," she said, close to tears.

"Don't be sorry. I'm the one who's sorry. Look," he said,

trying to extricate himself from an explosive situation, "we'll pretend it didn't happen. All right?"

"If that's what you want."

"No, it's not what I want." His eyes grew pained. "It's just the way it has to be. As I said before, if I were seventeen again . . . But I'm not, Lizette. I'm almost thirty-one, with a wife and two children, and that's the way of it. I didn't mean for any of this to happen when I followed you, I just wanted to help."

"You did," she said.

"Did I?" he asked, and saw a softness fill her eyes.

"Didn't you?" she asked him in return, and he tried to smile.

"Well, then, maybe we'd better join the party now," he said. "Someone might have missed us."

"I doubt it," she said. "Not me anyway, but that's all right, I'm starting to get used to it."

She turned from him and started back up the flagstone path.

"Lizette?" he called softly.

She turned back, then stopped and waited for him to join her.

"I don't want you walking back alone," he said, and without another word they left the gardens, crossing the walkway and joining the rest of the wedding guests, and as they reached the others, Lizette glanced up, her eyes looking into his under the light from the lanterns overhead and she saw the color of his eyes for the first time. They weren't gray like Bain's, but blue, a beautiful deep shade of blue. She smiled at him self-consciously; then, without saying a word, he winked, and she turned away, beginning to hunt for Cole in the crowd.

Cole had listened to Merrilou's prattling as long as he could, then wandered off hoping to lose himself in the crowd. He hadn't seen so many people in one place for years, and the more he drank, the more he seemed to see. It wasn't the liquor that was making him see double, it was the pent-up anger. She had done it. Heather had gone ahead and married DeWitt even though he had begged her not to. It wasn't fair, none of it! He sat at one of the tables now, brooding, staring off toward where Heather was sitting talking with Grandma Dicia. He had seen DeWitt wander off with his father a few minutes earlier, and now he watched Heather excuse herself, stand up, and head for the house.

His eyes followed her covetously as she reached the terrace, and he suddenly realized she was probably heading for her room. He slammed the half-empty mug of ale on the table in front of him and stood up, straightening his frock coat, then smoothed back his hair. He had to talk to her. If he didn't, he was going to go berserk.

He started working his way through the guests toward the house. Once inside, he knew where to go. The house was so quiet, and no one seemed to be around. Quickly he moved to the stairs and took them two at a time, then stopped abruptly in front of the first door on the left. He hesitated, then reached down and turned the knob. He didn't knock, because if he did, she'd probably refuse to let him in.

Tildie let out a small cry, and Heather turned toward the door, startled. He stared at her, his eyes alive with anger, but he addressed Tildie. "Get out of here, Tildie," he said quietly. "I want to talk with my cousin."

Tildie glanced furtively at Heather, then looked uncertain.

"It's all right, Tildie," said Heather quickly. "Please do as he says." Tildie started to leave the room. "And don't tell anyone he's here, Tildie, please," Heather demanded as a last thought, and Tildie nodded agreement, then hurried out.

Cole stared at Heather, his eyes glazed with passion, an ache settling in his chest. "It hasn't helped, you know," he said boldly. "Just because you're another man's wife now doesn't mean I don't love you."

"I know!"

He moved toward her slowly, then stopped, staring down at her, his eyes devouring her. "You should have been wearing this for me," he whispered softly, and touched her veil. "What am I to do without you, Heather?" he asked huskily.

She reached up, her hand covering his, bringing her fingers around so her lips touched them with a light kiss. "And I without you?"

He leaned down, and she knew he was going to kiss her, but didn't care. She needed his kiss more than she had ever needed it before. His lips were soft yet firm, and at their touch she felt a sweet pain shoot through her. She melted against him and he held her close as his lips clung to her mouth. They cherished the rapture of the moment, and yet each knew deep down inside that it had to end.

Cole's mouth started to ease on hers, but she moaned deep in her throat, and he pulled her even closer. He couldn't let go, not just yet. Then, slowly, as he kissed her, he felt salty tears on the tip of his tongue as it searched, opening her lips to his. This time he did draw back, staring down into her glazed eyes.

"Oh, Cole, don't torture me like this," she gasped breathlessly. "You know nothing can come of it."

"Then you do still love me?" he asked.

"I never stopped!" she cried.

"Then why did you do it?"

"I told you . . . Please, Cole, don't make it any harder for me."

He took her head in both his hands and stared down into her eyes, his own gentle and loving, all anger gone from them. "He'd better treat you right, Heather," he cried passionately. "If he ever hurts you, I'll kill him."

"He won't," she said. "He loves me too, Cole," she reminded him. "He wouldn't have asked me to marry him if he hadn't."

"He could never love you as I do," he said, then saw the hurt in her eyes. "I want you to remember one thing, Heather," he said anxiously. "I can't have you—they've made that clear—but if you ever need me, if anything goes wrong, let me know, do you understand?"

She nodded, unable to find her voice.

"Do you know how hard this is for me?" he asked helplessly. "To know he'll be making love to you?"

She reached up again and covered his hands that were on each side of her face. "It has to be, Cole," she said. "We had no right to fall in love, and this is the only way I know to make things right. It's hard for both of us, I know, but say good-bye now, Cole, please. Say good-bye and walk out of my life while I still have the strength to watch you go."

For an instant she thought he was going to refuse; then, as if finally admitting the futility of it all, he whispered softly, "Good-bye, love," kissed her lingeringly on the mouth, then turned quickly, leaving the room.

She stood for a long time staring after him. It was all over. Well, not quite all. She couldn't have Cole, but she was going to have his baby. That would just have to be enough.

Heather stood on the deck beside DeWitt, listening to the creaking of the rigging and the snap of the sails in the night breeze. She was still dressed in her wedding gown. Most of the guests had left already, but those that had stayed were lined up along the pier waving and wishing them well.

Witt's arm searched for her waist, drawing her closer to

him. "At last," he whispered passionately, "I have you to myself."

Her stomach tightened nervously. That's what had been bothering her all day. She knew this time had to come, yet dreaded it. But she had to go through with it. It wouldn't be too bad, she tried to convince herself. At least she knew what to expect; all she had to do was bear with it. However, she did have to pretend some feeling for Witt. After all, he had married her in good faith. She forced what she thought was a loving smile to her lips and turned to him as the ship began to inch away from the pier.

"How long do you think it'll take for us to reach Charleston?" she asked.

"Who cares," he said, his voice deepening. "We have all the time in the world." He smiled at her triumphantly.

The ship gave a heave beneath them as it slipped into midstream, and she waved one last time, watching the moonlight playing across all the people who had stayed to say good-bye, watching them get smaller and smaller in the distance. This was her wedding night, the start of her honeymoon, and she was scared to death.

The crew was shouting and wind continued filling the *Interlude*'s sails as it began to drift downstream, and in a short while even the pier was lost from sight. The moon went behind a cloud, and DeWitt looked down at Heather, turning her toward him in his arms. "It's over, Heather," he said softly. "All the noise and commotion. Everything that's left now is just for us." He reached up and brushed a stray hair back from her face, wishing it was light enough to see the color of her eyes. They were always so beautiful. "I imagine you're tired?" he said affectionately.

She inhaled sharply. "No, not really," she said, trying to prolong the inevitable as long as she could, but it did little to dissuade him.

"Come, now, Heather," he said. "It's terribly late and I do want you to be able to enjoy the rest of the evening." His arm was still about her waist and he began to lead her away from the railing, off toward the doors that led belowdecks to their cabin.

Roth had turned the master cabin over to them for the journey and Captain Casey had assured them when they boarded that Loedicia had made sure everything was in order. There were flowers everywhere and their trunks were set neatly at one end of the cabin, with their nightclothes already laid out on the wide bunk.

DeWitt closed the door behind them, then watched Heather move into the room, where she stood motionless beside the bunk. The only light was the faint glow of a lantern on the side wall. His eyes traveled the length of her body, and he held his breath for a moment before walking up behind her. "Here, let me do that," he half-whispered, taking the pin from the ruffle that held the veil atop her head and tossing the veil aside. She started to turn, but his hands on her shoulders stopped her. "I'm not finished," he went on, and leaned forward, kissing her neck as his fingers started unfastening the dress.

This is it, she thought apprehensively. Oh, God, I hope I can go through with it. She closed her eyes, letting his fingers continue to fumble at the hooks, and she prayed they wouldn't give. But they did. She felt the dress fall to her feet, and she stood before him in her chemise and underdrawers.

DeWitt stared at the smooth skin at the nape of her neck, then slid his hands beneath her arms as he pressed close against her back and covered her breasts in front, pressing them firmly. "This is what I've been waiting for, my sweet," he whispered softly in her ear.

She swallowed hard, trying to ignore the strangely familiar tinglings that were beginning to invade her body. She wasn't supposed to feel like this. Cole was the only one who was supposed to be able to make her feel like this, and yet as Witt's fingers gently kneaded her breasts, she felt a stirring inside that she knew had nothing to do with love. Somehow it had to do only with touch and movement and soft words in her ear and warm breath on her neck. For a moment it was as if Cole was there with her, yet she knew it was Witt's lips on her neck, nuzzling behind her ear and telling her how much he loved her.

She held her breath as his hands left her breasts and turned her to face him, then pulled the chemise up over her head.

Instinctively her arms moved up to cover the quivering mounds of flesh, but as quickly DeWitt brushed them aside. "No!" he cried passionately. "Let me look at you, Heather." His eyes widened, glazed with passion, and he licked his lips in anticipation. He leaned forward and kissed her on the mouth; then his lips moved to her throat and on down, his tongue tracing the outline of her nipple.

Witt trembled. Lord, he had to have her, he couldn't wait any longer. He drew his mouth from her breast and grabbed her underdrawers with both hands, beginning to strip them roughly from her body, dropping to his knees before her.

She started to protest, but he glanced up at her, and the look in his eyes stopped her. His eyes were filled with naked desire, and as his hands shed the underdrawers from her body, she could feel his breath close against her skin, and suddenly he pressed his head against her flesh.

She felt him pull the last leg of her drawers from her foot, then gasped as he ordered her to lie down on the bunk. Then, seconds before she backed away, she felt his lips touch her skin just above the patch of coppery red hair that lay between her legs.

She quickly climbed onto the bunk and squirmed beneath the covers, trying to hide from his prying eyes. But there was no place to hide, and as she saw him begin to loosen his cravat, all she could do was look the other way so she didn't have to watch. Her knuckles were white as she gripped the sheet that was the only cover on the bed.

It was hot in the cabin, and she felt the gentle sway of the ship while she waited, then gritted her teeth as he crawled in beside her. He wasted little time in continuing what he had started only moments before, burying his head against her neck while his hands dipped beneath the covers and began teasing her effectively.

Heather avoided looking at Witt—she had to, it was the only way she was going to get through this charade. Her body was responding, but her heart wasn't, and it was killing her inside.

Witt's hands explored every inch of Heather's body, and while they were caressing her, his lips found her mouth and kissed her hard, his passion fired by a response he hadn't expected.

Heather didn't want to respond, but his hands, his fingers . . . He hit a nerve, a spot that sent a flame piercing through her, and she was lost. Her hips moved instinctively, arching upward, and Witt pulled his hand away, replacing it with his body full length over hers, and as he poised, then entered her, she let out a reluctant moan that tore into him with a strange, violent pain.

He froze for a few seconds, then slowly began to move in her, brushing aside the knowledge of what he had just discovered, fired on by the wanton thrusting of Heather's hips, and in a quick answer to her response he felt a swelling peak of pleasure begin sweeping through him, throbbing and pulsating, and with an agonized groan he shook spasmodically, then lay still.

Heather gasped beneath him, her body still quivering with

need, her hips still trying to reach a caress that was no longer there, and abruptly, without saying a word, Witt slipped from her and rolled over on his back.

Heather opened her eyes, the shock of his action like a glass of cold water thrown on her, and she bit her lip as her body stopped writhing. She stared at the cabin ceiling, the ache in her loins like fire, the promise of release stolen from her.

"Who was he?" Witt suddenly asked from where he lay.

Heather was stunned. "Who was who?" she asked breathlessly.

He laughed, a deep mocking laugh. "The man who got there before I did," he said bitterly. "And don't try to tell me you were a virgin," he went on. "I'm not that gullible, Heather!"

She felt sick. How did he know? Then she remembered the quick stab of pain when Cole had first entered. Oh, God! She had forgotten about it.

"Well?" he asked when she didn't answer.

"I don't know what you're talking about," she said defensively.

His laugh turned cruel. "Don't lie!"

"I'm not lying. Please, Witt, I . . . There hasn't been anyone but you!"

He rolled to the side of the bed and got up, grabbing his nightshirt off the foot of the bunk. He slipped it on over his head, then turned back to face her. "I can wait," he said, jaw clenching obstinately. "I can wait a long time, Heather. Because someday you're going to tell me, and then I'm going to kill him. But tell me first," he went on as he grabbed her nightgown off the bed and threw it at her, "did you give it to him or did he take it without your permission?"

She shook her head. She couldn't tell him, not ever; she had to keep trying to live the lie. "You're wrong," she yelled at him helplessly. "There's no one, Witt!"

He glared at her. She was lying. There had been no obstruction. A tightness, yes, but nothing to interfere with that first thrust. It wasn't possible she could still have been a virgin.

"Put your nightgown on and let's get to sleep," he said angrily.

She picked up the nightgown, untangled it, and slipped it on over her head. This done, she moved to the far side of the bunk, against the cabin wall. Witt walked over to where the lantern hung and blew it out, then came back and climbed into the bunk.

The cabin was dark now except for moonlight that filtered in.

They lay quietly, both of them, and Heather stared up at the ceiling, her insides twisting viciously. No matter what he said or how many times he accused her, she was determined to keep denying it. It was her word against what he thought he had felt, or not felt. She lay still, waiting for him to say something, anything, and finally he did, his voice harsh, unsympathetic.

"You weren't raped, were you, Heather?" he said, but didn't wait for her to answer. "I know you weren't," he went on. "You know how I know?" Again he didn't wait for her to answer. "Because you've been made love to before," he said arrogantly. "You see, you gave yourself away, my dear," he said. "No woman acts so wanton the first time. In fact, no proper woman enjoys a man's body the way you were enjoying mine. And I treated you so prim and proper all these months, when all the time I could have been enjoying you myself."

"I don't know why you're doing this, Witt," she said tearfully. "I don't know what you think I've done, but you're wrong," she insisted.

"Oh, shut up!" he said disgustedly.

She started to answer, but again he stopped her.

"Good night!" he shouted forcefully, and turned with his back to her.

Heather lay next to him in the dark, tears streaming down her cheeks. She had tried. It wasn't her fault things weren't going right. Witt wasn't supposed to act this way. He was supposed to love her and protect her, and later, when she told him she was expecting a baby, he was supposed to be happy about it. Nothing was going like it should, nothing! Her tears rolled onto the pillow as she glanced over in the dark toward the vague outline of his back turned to her. He was angry with her . . . no, he was more than just angry, he was incensed. All right, so he was angry. Well, so was she. Angry with society for forcing this on her, angry with God for making her love Cole and taking him from her, and angry with Cole for making her pregnant. But she wasn't angry enough to throw it all way. Witt could hate her, turn on her, never touch her again, but there was no way he'd ever learn about her and Cole and no way he'd ever get her to admit anything other than what she'd already told him. If he never touched her again because of tonight, she'd be happy. And with that thought in mind, she turned away from him as he had from her, and with the gentle rocking of the ship to lull her, finally drifted off to sleep.

The next morning, Witt opened his eyes and turned, staring down at Heather beside him. She looked so young and innocent. She was everything he'd always dreamed of having in a wife, and he had wanted her from the moment he had first set eyes on her. He thought over everything that had happened the night before. Her reluctance to go to bed, the shy way her eyes met his when he mentioned it, and the flush on her cheeks when she tried to cover her breasts so he wouldn't see them. Was it possible she could have been telling the truth? His frown deepened as he remembered how easily he had penetrated her, and yet she had been tight. What was the matter with him? He wanted to believe her, and yet reason told him it shouldn't have been that easy. But he loved her, dammit, and if she loved him, there was every chance that she might have responded the way she had.

What a predicament to be in. If she was telling the truth and there was some strange reason for there to have been no obstruction when he entered, then he was doing her an injustice. He wanted this to be true, because he wanted this marriage to work. It had to work.

He reached out and ran the back of a knuckle along her temple and saw her take a deep breath; then she stirred, and the covers dropped from her shoulder. He hadn't slept well last night, but it looked like she had. The sleep of the innocent? he wondered.

Heather felt the fluttering along her temple, and her breathing deepened as nervous fear gripped her. It had to be Witt; he was awake. Well, she had to face him sometime, it might as well be now. She opened her eyes and let them focus on his face. He was gazing down at her with a puzzled expression. "Who was it, Heather?" he asked softly.

Tears welled up in her eyes. "It wasn't anyone," she lied. She had to; there was no way she was going to tell him the truth, no matter how gently he asked.

His hazel eyes hardened as he watched her. "I wish I could believe you," he said. "But I don't know how."

She looked into his eyes. At least he was being honest with her. She wished she could be honest with him, but it was impossible. "Witt, why are you doing this to me?" she asked, her voice unsteady. "I don't even know why you're accusing me," she continued lying. "I did just what Mother told me to do, and instead of pleasing you, all I did was anger you. Why?"

"You don't know?" he asked, frowning. "You mean you really don't know?"

She shook her head. "I thought you loved me."

"I do."

She turned her head from his piercing eyes and stared off at the window, where the morning sun was streaming in as the small three-masted sailing ship cut the waters. It had passed through the sound during the night while they were asleep, and was heading up the coast already, and she felt the heaving as it plied the waves.

"If I knew what was wrong, maybe I could explain," she said, trying to act ignorant, yet still avoiding his eyes. "I know Mother said what happened last night would hurt, but it didn't," she said coyly, and as if she ordered it, her face flushed a deep crimson. "If that's why you're angry, I'm sorry, Witt, but I couldn't pretend something I didn't feel." She drew her eyes from the window and looked up at him again shyly, her face quite crimson. "But believe me, Witt, there's been no one but you."

He inhaled sharply, then ran a hand through his pale hair, sweeping a lock of it back off his forehead. "If you're lying, Heather—"

"Oh, Witt!" she cried helplessly.

Her mouth formed a provocative pout, and a twinge of desire shot through him. One thing was certain: whether he believed her or not, he still wanted her. His jaw clenched stubbornly as he tried to fight the effect she was having on him, but he couldn't. Well, dammit, she was his wife, wasn't she? He could have her whenever he wanted, couldn't he? His eyes darkened passionately while he stared at her, and as the ship tacked full into the northeasterly wind that had blown up with the new day, Witt leaned over and kissed Heather a long, lingering kiss, trying to convince himself that last night had been nothing more than a terrible mistake.

14

While Heather was in Charleston on her honeymoon trying to make Witt believe her lie, Lizette was back in Port Royal trying to find something to do with herself, and watching Cole try to go on with his life. Before Heather's marriage, Cole had tried to forget his unhappiness in carousing and other women; now, instead, he suddenly took to the woods. At one time Lizette would have joined him in some of his excursions, but her added weight and the fact that she was older precluded it, and life picked up where it had been before Heather arrived. Well, almost. Things would never be the same as they had been before Heather arrived; in fact nothing was the same anymore, not even Lizette.

It was Sunday, June 16, the day before her birthday, and Lizette stood in front of the mirror in her bedroom stark naked and stared at her body. She had been trying, but she just couldn't seem to lose the forty some excess pounds that had crept onto her frame over the past year and a half. She had been a svelte hundred and ten pounds when Heather arrived at Port Royal; now she had to be at least a hundred and fifty, and at five feet, five inches tall, she felt miserable.

Why? she asked herself silently as she looked at herself from all different angles. Well, one thing in her favor, at least she had gained everywhere and not just in the hips and bosom.

She glanced at the wooden contraption Cole had had made for her to exercise on. A lot of good it did. All she had done was start to put muscles where the fat had been, and the fat was still there. So now the ridiculous machine was collecting dust. It was bad enough being fat; the muscles she could do without. She glanced back in front of her into the mirror again and continued to stare at herself, wanting things to be different, wishing she could just snap her fingers and things would be like they were before. That Bain would be back and she'd be thin again. Even if he did come back now, he wouldn't want her. Not someone who looked like this.

She wrenched her eyes from the mirror and walked over to the bed and began putting on her clothes, and as she slipped her chemise over her head, then pulled up her underdrawers, she thought back to the night of Heather's wedding, and to Stuart Kolter. She stopped dressing for a minute and stared off into space, remembering. What a strange evening that had been. Was it only last weekend? It seemed like ages ago. Maybe because this wasn't the first time she had reminisced about that night. Stuart Kolter had been on her mind more than she wanted to admit. He had made her feel like a woman that night. It was the first time in months that anyone had treated her with such warmth and feeling. He was probably being kind to her simply because she was the daughter of family friends.

She sighed. Regardless of why, he had made a lasting impression on her. Of course, the fact that he looked so much like his younger brother didn't help. And the fact that she was in love with his younger brother didn't help either, nor did the fact that Stuart was married.

She fastened her underdrawers, then continued to ponder. Her dance with Stuart that evening hadn't been just a simple dance. His words and actions were puzzling, to say the least, and she wondered: was he just another married man trying to prove he was still able to attract the ladies, or had he truly been sincere? He didn't seem like the former, yet she couldn't imagine him being the latter because he didn't seem the type to cheat on his wife. Yet he had been there, and he had said all those things to her.

He was too much of a puzzle, and rather than tax her brain trying to understand all that went on, she brushed all thoughts of him aside for now as Pretty came in carrying her new dress over her arm. It had just been pressed, and she was to wear it today on her ride into Beaufort.

She wasn't having a party this year for her birthday, but Felicia had invited her to spend a few days, so she was going in to the Kolters' tonight, would stay until Friday, and spend her birthday tomorrow with Felicia.

She slipped on her petticoat, then let Pretty help her on with her light blue silk dress while she tried to think of all the things she and Felicia would be able to do tomorrow.

Rebel and Beau rode into Beaufort with Lizette, staying for dinner and enjoying a visit with Rand and Madeline, while Felicia helped Lizette get settled in. She had brought a small trunk with her, and after it was carried upstairs, Felicia helped her unpack it in the guest room.

It was a lovely room, with a huge canopied bed, the covers and draperies in deep red velvet with a Persian rug on the floor, its design characterized by delicate red flowers. Greens and golds were mixed in with the flowers, and the walls of the room were golden beige, several framed landscapes decorating them. It was a pleasant room, neither feminine nor masculine, but not as large as Lizette's room back home.

While they unpacked, they made their plans for the next day. They'd have a late breakfast on the back terrace, then get dressed and head toward some of the shops in town. After shopping for a while, they'd return to the house for a light lunch; then Madeline would accompany Felicia to her music lessons, and Lizette would rest at the house until their return, at which time they were all going for afternoon tea at the home of one of their other friends. Then in the evening, after an early dinner, they were to attend a performance of Sheridan's *The School for Scandal* given by a traveling theater troup.

At one time Lizette would have preferred to do something a little more daring, but for some reason she seemed to have lost the devil-may-care attitude she had always nurtured. Maybe it was a sign she was growing up. Whatever it was, it served to dampen all thoughts of perhaps doing something outrageous to celebrate her birthday.

The next morning went as planned. Both young women slept late, then enjoyed breakfast on the back terrace, where the morning sun filtered through the leaves of the many trees that decorated the gardens. When breakfast was over, Felicia slipped into a dress of pale green embroidered muslin, and Lizette put on a rose-colored satin brocade, and both girls wore chip straw bonnets with velvet bows and artificial flowers adorning them; then they joined Madeline, who was to accompany them.

The shops were crowded, but they managed to find everything they wanted, including a present for Lizette. It was a beautiful trinket box, carved and painted, the petals of the flowers inlaid with mother-of-pearl, the leaves gilded. It was a gift Lizette would treasure for years, and Felicia was glad she had waited for Lizette to pick it out herself, rather than buying it ahead of time.

By the time they arrived home, it was a little past one. Felicia's music lesson was at two-thirty, so they ate a quick lunch, and Madeline and Felicia left. Lizette told them she'd probably rest while they were gone, since they had stayed up rather late talking the night before. But after they left, she changed her mind and decided to do a little reading.

The library at the Kolters' was extensive, and Lizette loved some of the poetry books on the shelves. She had the maid, Susu, bring her a glass of lemonade; then, with a book tucked under her arm, she headed for the summerhouse in the middle of the formal gardens at the back of the house.

It was lovely here in the summertime, with the scent of flowers filling the air, an occasional bird gliding from tree to tree, and the lazy afternoon, when the world seemed almost to stand still. She wished they had a summerhouse at Tonnerre, but back home she usually strolled down to the riverbank to read, or just sat in the garden under a shade tree. This was much nicer, because she could sit on the bench that cirumvented the inside wall, lean against one of the support columns, and put her feet up on the bench, making a stand with her knees to rest the book on. The lemonade she set down on the top of the railing that was partially screened by the wisteria that hung from the roof. It was secluded here, yet the sun peeked in between the wisteria vines, giving plenty of light to read by.

She was propped up, still wearing her rose-colored dress, sipping on her lemonade and enjoying one of the poems, trying to memorize some of the words, whispering them softly to herself. " 'O, my love is like a red, red rose,' " she intoned. " 'That's newly sprung in June. O, my love is like the melody that's sweetly played in tune!' "

" 'As fair art thou, my bonnie lass, so deep in love am I. And I will love thee still, my dear, till all the seas go dry,' " said a deep voice from the arched doorway to the summerhouse.

Lizette whirled quickly and looked over her shoulder. "Stuart!"

He began walking toward her. He was wearing a deep blue frock coat, buff trousers, and highly polished boots that clicked on the wooden floor of the summerhouse, and he continued reciting the rest of the poem as he approached. " 'Till all the seas go dry, my dear, and the rocks melt with the sun. I will love thee still, my dear, while the sands of life shall run. And fare thee well, my only love, and fare thee well a while! And I will come again, my dear, tho it were ten thousand miles.' " He stopped at her side, gazing down at her.

She flushed. "You know all the words," she exclaimed in surprise.

"One of my favorites. It's too bad the man who wrote them was such a bounder."

"Why do you say that?"

He smiled. "Don't tell me you didn't know that Robert Burns had quite a reputation with the ladies."

Lizette shook her head. "I guess I'm not much of a one for reading about other people's lives," she said. "But I like the poem. It has a feel about it, describing love as being like a beautiful melody."

"And is it?" he asked.

Her blush deepened. "I wouldn't know."

"You've never been in love?" Something about the look in her eyes made him tread softly. "I hope you don't mind my coming out to say hello," he said, changing the subject. "I stopped by to tell Mother that Julia and I'll be able to make it this evening, and Susu told me you were out here."

"You and Julia are coming tonight?" she asked.

"Didn't you know?"

"Felicia didn't say a word. But I'm glad," she said. "I think your wife's pretty, Stuart."

His eyes warmed. "Thank you, so do I." But as he said it, he was thinking to himself that Julia's plain brown hair and soft, even features couldn't compare to the vivacious dark-haired beauty Lizette possessed.

"Of course, I didn't get too much chance to talk to her at the wedding," Lizette went on. "But the little I did, she seems quite nice."

Lizette wasn't aware of the confusion inside Stuart, but she did sense the interest hidden behind his deep blue eyes, and she felt self-conscious.

"Are you coming to the theater with us too?" she asked,

trying to ignore the strange feelings that had gripped her since he'd appeared.

"That was the idea."

"Oh . . ." She turned, slipping her feet from the bench, putting them on the floor. "I didn't mean to make that sound as if I didn't want you along," she tried to explain.

His eyes darkened. "But you don't."

"I didn't say that."

"You didn't have to." He gazed down at her. "Lizette, no one knows about last weekend, believe me," he said, his voice lowering vibrantly.

"I know," she said. "But for some reason, I feel strange inside at the thought of you being there." She was still blushing.

"I didn't mean to upset you that night," he said softly. "I'm sorry."

"Don't be," she said unsteadily. "You didn't upset me, it's just that . . ." Her eyes locked with his. "It's just that I can't seem to forget the things you said, and I don't feel I have a right to them."

He reached out and touched her face, looking deep into her eyes. They were such a beautiful shade of green. He hadn't been able to see their true color that night in the garden, but here in the summerhouse with the sunlight making everything warm and light, they were alive with passion and she looked so vulnerable. "You have a right to far more than I'm able to give, Lizette," he answered. "That's just the trouble. I wish I could give it all to you, and that's why I'm the one who's going to feel awkward tonight, not you. I know I shouldn't feel this way, I know I should just walk away right now and never look back, but I can't, and I don't know why. You frighten me, Lizette," he said softly. "Because I've never had anything like this happen before."

She continued to stare up at him, not knowing if it was his resemblance to Bain that was causing it, or the yearning inside her for someone to care, but whatever it was, something was making her feel strangely giddy inside. "I . . . I don't know what to say," she whispered. "Maybe you shouldn't come tonight."

"I have to," he replied. "What excuse could I give? How would I explain it to Julia or my mother?"

"Stuart . . . I'm sorry I said that."

"Now you're sorry," he said, and turned from her gaze out beyond the purple wisteria. "All right, let's make a bargain, Miss Dante," he said. "I've never claimed to be a saint,

I don't think there are many of them running around in this world, but I'm having a terrible time coping with something new to me. However, if you'll try not to look at me too often with those big green eyes of yours, then I'll try not to make you feel uncomfortable, and maybe I'll get through this in one piece."

She frowned. "Aren't you making more of it than it deserves?" she asked as she studied his profile.

His head turned and their eyes met again. "Am I?" he asked. "Be honest with me, Lizette. Can you sit there and truthfully say that you feel nothing when we meet?"

She couldn't answer.

"Well, can you?" he asked again.

She shook her head. "No."

"That's what I thought." He took a deep breath. "Under the circumstances, young lady, I think from here on in you and I had better keep as far from each other as possible. Agreed?"

She continued to stare at him. "Agreed," she said. "But isn't that going to be rather hard tonight, since you'll be a part of the festivities?"

"Think you can ignore me?" he asked.

An impish smile played about the corners of her mouth. "If you want, I can pretend you don't even exist," she said. "How's that?"

"Don't overdo it," he answered quickly. "Just treat me like . . . like Felicia's big brother, like you treated Bain when he was here."

"Bain?"

"Why not? After all, there is a family resemblance."

Her eyes narrowed. "You have no idea how I treated Bain," she said curiously.

He smiled. "Well, seeing as he hasn't been home for almost two years, and you must have been fairly young at the time, I imagine you treated him rather obnoxiously."

"That's what you think?"

"Well, didn't you?"

She bit her lip. "I guess I did at that," she said, hoping she sounded convincing. She stood up and reached onto the rail, retrieving her lemonade, the poetry book in her other hand. "Maybe I should start right now," she said. "When do you have to return to Washington?"

"Not until December, but I have to go back to Columbia right after the Fourth of July. For a few weeks anyway.

We're still working hard trying to get that tariff legislation ready."

"What legislation is that?" she asked as they left the summerhouse.

"As soon as the war was over, Britain started flooding the market with everything salable," he began to explain. "With a tariff, we can cut down the imports and give the manufacturers in this country a break."

They talked a little longer, keeping the conversation political, and when they reached the house, Lizette promised to tell his mother that he and Julia would be there in time for dinner.

"Good-bye, Lizette. We'll see you tonight. And . . . happy birthday," he said, and winked at her quite mischievously, then stepped outside, closing the door firmly behind him.

Lizette stared at the closed door for a long time, trying to understand why he had done what he had just done, then shook her head, frowning, and went upstairs to her bedroom to lie down and rest until Mrs. Kolter and Felicia returned. Only her thoughts were in such a turmoil after his visit that she never did fall asleep, only lay there.

That evening Stuart and Julia arrived well ahead of dinnertime, and everyone gathered in the parlor to exchange small talk. Lizette was late coming downstairs. Felicia had stopped by her bedroom to wait for her, but nothing seemed to be going right. Lizette was wearing a white embroidered satin that she hadn't had on for a while, and was having a terrible time with the hooks in the back. Felicia did them up for her, but Lizette's hair hadn't been styled yet either, so Lizette insisted Felicia go down without her, hoping she could sneak into the parlor quietly so no one would notice. However, it didn't work out that way. At the moment she walked in, there had suddenly been a lull in the conversation, and all eyes had automatically turned toward the doorway.

She stood there hesitantly, feeling like a stuffed goose in the fancy white dress, wishing she could look pretty and knowing full well she looked atrocious.

Felicia looked lovely in a dress of bright blue watered silk with the new huge puff sleeves, ribbon and lace trimming the bodice. Madeline had on a dress of crimson gauze over matching satin with the same new sleeve style, and Julia wore a dress of deep pink brocade with diamonds at her ears and about her smooth throat. The men were dressed in their evening best, white trousers and frock coats with ruffled shirts and fancy silk cravats. Rand's coat was black, Stuart's was a rich deep coffee brown. They all looked so elegant, and Lizette just knew she was going to be out of place with them. But surprisingly, it was Julia who was the first to notice her discomfiture and try to make her feel better.

For a moment Julia couldn't figure out why Lizette was standing there so awkwardly; then it dawned on her. She remembered Felicia talking about the weight her friend had gained lately, and now, seeing her again . . . Last weekend it had been dark outside and she hadn't paid too much attention to the fat young girl whom she had been introduced to. This evening, seeing her standing alone in the doorway, was like having her put on display, and her voluptuous figure was revealed for all to see. Julia walked over and caught Lizette's arm, smiling at her warmly. "Well, here's the birthday girl herself," she said happily. "It's so good to see you again, Lizette," she went on as she led Lizette farther into the room. "When Mother Kolter said it was your birthday we were celebrating, I was so pleased. I know we didn't get a chance to talk much at the wedding last weekend, but I'm sure we can make up for it tonight," and with her words, everyone else clustered around Lizette too, wishing her well and telling her how nice she looked.

Of course Lizette knew they were only saying it to make her feel better, but it worked, and for a while she forgot how fat she was and how terrible she just knew tonight was going to be.

To her surprise, the dinner went well, the play was enchanting, and the only time she felt uncomfortable was when she caught Stuart staring at her during the performance, when the lights in the theater were low and she knew he thought no one would see. At first she wished he wouldn't do that, but then, as a warm tingling sensation went through her, she was suddenly glad he did, because once more he was making her feel like a normal human being.

Stuart wasn't staring at Lizette because he wanted to. He was doing it because he couldn't help himself, and it was scary. She really looked beautiful tonight, all white and angelic. He tried to appraise just what it was about her that excited him. He had made a bargain with her that he suddenly wondered if he was going to be able to keep. Flickering shadows from the lamps in the theater were cast across her face as she sat next to Felicia, a few seats away, and he studied the exquisite lines of that face, the rounded curves of her arm where it left the small puff sleeve and gracefully rested against her body. Julia had whispered to him earlier while they were leaving the house for the theater that she was pleased they were helping Felicia's fat friend have a nice birthday, and remarked that it was a shame someone so lovely had let herself get so fat. The comment had bothered him, although he hadn't let Julia know, but now, as he gazed at Lizette, he began to wonder why the aspect of her weight had never entered his head. Not the way it seemed to preoccupy everyone else around him.

He remembered when he had first noticed her at the wedding. She had been standing off by herself near one of the tables not far from the dancers, and light from the overhead lanterns was playing across her face. He and Julia had been talking to some old acquaintances, and for a moment he had totally lost the thread of the conversation as he stared at her. She was only a few tables away from where they were sitting, and he could see the look on her face so clearly. For a moment he had thought she was going to cry, but she didn't. Instead, she had lowered her head unhappily and wandered away, and his eyes had continued to follow her retreating figure until it was lost in the darkness of the gardens beyond the walkway that led to the pier. And not once while he was watching her, not once while he was dancing with her later on, had he even thought of her as being fat.

He remembered Lizette's words that night by the river. She had said she was fat and ugly. Her eyes softened intensely as he stared at her, watching her laugh at something funny on the stage. Fat and ugly? Lord no! And for a brief moment he had the weirdest sensation, wondering what it would be like to make love to her, to feel her warm and softly sensual beneath his hands. At that moment Lizette's eyes left the stage and she turned to him, the laughter on her lips suddenly stilled by the intense look in his eyes.

Lizette caught her breath and forced the laughter to continue as it had started, while her eyes fastened on his violently, hoping no one around them would notice.

Stuart swore softly to himself, dragging his gaze away, and tried to concentrate on the stage as Julia spoke his name and pointed something out to him that one of the characters, Lady Sneerwell, was doing. He pretended to find the performance amusing, but if reality could be known, he didn't even know what was going on. He straightened in his chair for a moment as the laughter in the theater died down; then he closed his eyes for a second and chastised himself for being such a damn fool. You've been tempted before, Stuart Lyle Kolter, he thought silently to himself as he opened his eyes again and stared once more at the stage. There have been a good many beautiful women in the world you could have had if you wanted, but you didn't. Julia has been enough, and it should end there, so don't let this young woman get to you. She doesn't have to, you know. You're quite happy with things as they are. You have a lovely wife, two wonderful children, and a new career ahead of you. The last thing in the world you need is to be acting like a love-struck young ass over the likes of a girl barely old enough to be called a woman. He took a deep breath, determined to thwart the ridiculous feelings he'd been letting sway him every time he looked at her. He reached down, taking Julia's hand in his, and smiled at her. She drew her eyes from the stage and returned his smile, then they continued watching the play.

Once more Lizette felt lost and alone, just like she had the night of her birthday when they had been at the theater. Stuart Kolter had been looking at her so strangely that night, his eyes warm and caring; then suddenly he had wrenched his eyes from hers and concentrated on what was happening on the stage before turning to his wife, taking her hand, and smiling at her. Lizette had never dreamed that such a simple gesture could have such an effect on her, but it had. She had felt cut off from him somehow, and even though she had promised not to do anything to cause problems, she didn't like the feeling. Now suddenly the feeling was there again—the desolate certainty that no one cared, that if she died tomorrow there'd be no one to mourn her except her family.

She had arrived back at Tonnerre a week ago Saturday afternoon with the unhappy feeling that life was passing her by. While at the Kolters', she and Felicia had visited various friends, and she had tried once more to fit in where she used to, but the snubs had been even worse this time. The crushing blow, however, had been when Alexander Benedict came to see Felicia one evening and Lizette inadvertently overheard part of their conversation in the foyer shortly after his arrival. It seemed Felicia had asked him to bring a friend along for Lizette. The contention was that he couldn't find anyone gullible enough to join him.

"Of course, I suppose if I had paid them enough they probably would have consented," she had heard him tell Felicia.

The remark had sent her back upstairs, and she had

feigned a stomachache rather than come back down again that evening.

Now, just a few days before the Fourth of July, which was on a Thursday this year, she stood on the back terrace of Tonnerre, gazing out across the long expanse of lawn and garden toward the Broad River, and there were tears in her eyes. She was dressed in a plain yellow cotton dress with small puffed sleeves that left her arms and shoulders bare, letting the heat from the afternoon sun turn them a golden bronze. Strange, she thought as she stared at her tanned arm, all the other young ladies made sure they stayed out of the sun to protect their skin. But she loved to see her arms tan and golden. Maybe because she felt somehow the tan covered the marks where her skin had stretched and kept the fat from looking so flabby.

She ran her right hand down her left arm, then turned abruptly as Cole came out of the house. He had ridden down to the Chateau earlier that morning, and was just arriving back, and she had watched him walk up from the stable a few minutes ago, wondering if he felt as left out of things as she did.

"Well, Liz, you were right," he said as he walked over and stood beside her, his eyes intense. "The newlyweds arrived home almost a week ago."

"And yet we haven't heard a thing."

"You didn't think we would, did you?"

"Did they get in touch with Uncle Heath and Aunt Darcy?"

He frowned. "Not really. At least they haven't come calling at the Chateau yet. Uncle Heath ran into Everett Palmer in town last weekend, and he said they arrived home on the twenty-fifth."

Lizette looked bewildered. "The twenty-fifth! My God, Cole, it's the first of July already. Surely Heather would have tried to reach us by now to let us know she's back."

"Would she?" he asked. "I doubt it, Liz. After all, we aren't part of her life anymore."

"We're still her cousins. And why didn't she get in touch with her parents? Surely she should have told them she was home."

"Maybe she's glad to get rid of the lot of us," he said defensively.

"You know better than to say something like that, Cole," she said. "You know she wishes things could be different." Her eyes met his. "Brooding about it won't really do any good either, you know, Cole," she went on. "Why don't you see if you can find someone else to love? There are so many nice girls in Port Royal and Beaufort."

"Like Felicia?"

"Well, why not? What's wrong with Felicia? I'd rather see her married to you than Alex Benedict."

"Oho, and what did Mr. Benedict do to earn your disfavor?"

Her jaw clenched. "Nothing special, I just never did like him, that's all."

"So you want me to maneuver him out of the picture."

"It'd be nice. I think Felicia already likes you."

He sighed. "Well, I'll think about it." Then his eyes grew distant. "By the way," he added, "speaking of the Kolters, I met Stuart at the cutoff to town earlier. He was on his way to the Chateau to see Grandfather."

"Did he say what it was about?"

"Politics, naturally. Something about exports and imports. Poor Grandfather, he's on both ends of the stick, what with shipping companies in England and over here. I hope he can keep his head above water until everything's cleared up about all this tariff stuff."

"He will," insisted Lizette. "Grandfather always manages to come out on top." She sighed. "I wish I could say the same thing for myself. Maybe I don't live right," she said. "Do you suppose, Cole? Could God be getting back at me for all the trouble I put everyone to when I was younger?"

"You mean because you gained weight?"

"It's not impossible."

"But it's improbable," he said. "Liz, for heaven's sake, you heard Father, he said his mother was anything but thin, and his sister too. Maybe this is the way you're supposed to be."

She wanted to cry. "Then why wasn't I fat to start with?" she admonished him. "No, Cole, I'm fat because I'm being punished."

"Punished for what?"

She exhaled disgustedly. "Oh, never mind, you wouldn't understand." She pursed her lips, then stared thoughtfully off toward the river. "You know, I think I'll go calling on Heather," she said suddenly, and he looked at her in surprise.

"You think that's wise?"

"Why not?"

'You know DeWitt doesn't like you any better than he likes me. He only let you be Heather's maid of honor because she insisted."

She straightened stubbornly. "Well, like me or not, he's going to have to put up with me once in a while," she answered. "Heather and I are not only cousins, but best friends." She started toward the French doors that led to the parlor.

He watched her disappear into the house. In a way, he was glad she was going, because he'd been wondering how Heather was, and if anyone could find out, Lizette could. She was just spunky enough.

Lizette liked to exercise Diablo every day, and this would give her the chance. She let Aaron help her into the sidesaddle, then waved to him as she flicked the reins and started down the long drive.

She had changed from the cotton dress into a riding habit of bright green silk with green satin frogging down the front, and her hat was the same green satin with small matching feathers in a cluster near her ear on the right side. The rest of the hat was pinched and tucked into fancy folds.

As she started down the main road, holding Diablo back so he wouldn't tire himself in the early-afternoon sun, she had no idea of the lovely contrast her dark-haired beauty and bright clothes made with the pale coloring of her horse. All she knew was that it became more awkward riding all the time, and if she gained any more weight she wouldn't be able to get into the saddle, even with help.

She hadn't paid any attention to the clouds in the sky when she left Tonnerre, nor did she now as she neared the cutoff that led to Beaufort, but she reined in, stopping curiously as she saw a familiar figure astride a horse coming in her direction from downriver. "Well, hello," she said cheerily, surprised at how pleased she was to see him.

Stuart's eyes took her in quickly and he half-smiled. "You just coming from Tonnerre?"

"Yes."

"Good," he said. "Then I won't have to worry about keeping our bargain while I'm there, will I? Not if you're not around."

"You're headed for Tonnerre?" she asked.

"I have to see your father on business."

"Father and Mother aren't home," she said, eyeing him boldly. "They rode upriver to see some land Father's interested in buying and took the ferry across the Coosaw, so they won't be back until after dark."

"Then I guess I won't ride up to Tonnerre," he said. "Are you on your way to the Chateau?"

She shook her head. "I'm going to see Heather. They came home last week and I haven't heard a word from her."

"Well, your father's the only one I had left to see on this side of the island," he said. "I've already talked to Rachel Grantham and the others closer toward the sound. I've even been to Palmerston Grove already, but I'll be glad to ride that far with you, if you like."

"Are you sure you'll be safe?" she quipped testily.

"Don't play with me, Lizette," he said seriously. "Maybe what happens whenever we meet means nothing to you, I don't know, but I don't like having to fight feelings like this. You're a beautiful woman, and dammit, I'm not a schoolboy."

"Nobody said you were."

"Then quit teasing me!"

"I didn't know I was."

"Well, you were."

"I'm sorry!"

He watched her gentling her horse to keep it from pawing the ground as thunder broke off in the distance. "Come on, I'll ride as far as Palmerston Grove with you," he said huskily, and she didn't argue, but reined her horse around, ready to follow beside him down the main road that led to Beaufort.

The sky had been darkening the whole while they had been talking, and now as she dug her horse in the ribs, a sudden gust of wind caught her hat, freeing it from her head, hatpin and all. She slid quickly from the saddle to go after it, but Stuart yelled, telling her to stay put, and he was out of the saddle and away across the dusty road in pursuit of her fancy chapeau that was now completely airborne and sailing across a split-rail fence into a field overgrown with wildflowers and weeds.

He scaled the fence quickly, trying to keep his eye on the clump of green satin and feathers he was chasing. Stepping away from the fence, he stumbled, almost falling as his foot hit a rabbit hole, but he caught himself and straightened, watching as the bit of fluff he was chasing caught on a low tree branch and stuck there. He made his way through the field, retrieved the hat, then turned to go back just as a drop of rain collided with his face.

"You're going to get wet!" Lizette yelled to him, but he waved her hat in the air to show her he had it, then headed back across the field at a fast pace.

The wind was whipping at him now, and drops of rain hit

intermittently as he made his way through the weeds, then climbed the fence once more, dropping to the other side. He hurried to where Lizette stood waiting.

"Thank you!" she said, fastening it back on her head; then she glanced at the sky. "But we're both going to get soaked."

"Not if I can help it," he said, and glanced around, frowning.

"There's no shelter anyplace," she yelled above the wind, but he shook his head.

"Yes there is," he replied, then helped her back on her horse. "Come on," he said quickly as he too hit the saddle, and they moved down the road a few hundred feet, heading back toward the Chateau, then cut into an overgrown trail off to the right that led to a dilapidated old barn hidden far back among the trees.

"But this is River Oaks property!" Lizette exclaimed as they rode through the open doorway just in time to beat the rain.

He turned, looking at her curiously. "It's dry, isn't it?" he asked.

She nodded. "Well, yes, but . . . if Rachel Grantham finds out, she's going to be mad."

"She won't find out," he assured her. "If you'll notice, there's not that much left of it, and it hasn't been used for years for anything more than storing odds and ends. Besides," he said, his eyes twinkling mischievously above his dark brown clipped beard, "I'm a senator now, remember. I don't think she'd begrudge my coming in out of the rain." He dismounted and reached up, lifting her from the saddle.

She stared up at him. "What made you think of it?"

"You," he answered thoughtfully.

She listened to the rain hitting the sides of the weather-beaten old building. "Me?" she asked.

"Surely you know the story of this barn," he said.

She frowned. "This particular barn?" she asked, and gazed at the small barn that was missing boards here and there and smelled of musty hay.

"My father told me about this barn a long time ago," he said, then looked at her inquisitively. "Lizette, you do know the story of your mother's first marriage, don't you?"

She nodded.

"Then you should know about this barn. This is where the duke had his men keep her when he kidnapped her, until he could come for her," he explained.

She froze. "Oh, my God!" she exclaimed in surprise. "I've

always stayed off River Oaks land. I never even knew the barn existed anymore."

"This is it," he said. "Quite a few years back, when I was about eighteen, Father and I were on our way back from Tonnerre one evening when another storm blew up. While we were in here weathering it, he told me the full story of your family, as told to him by your father. It all happened shortly before my parents came to Beaufort, but it was such a fascinating story, I never forgot it."

"I see," she said, then realized he still had his hands on her waist. She was looking up directly into his eyes, and suddenly she shivered.

"Cold?" he asked.

She shook her head. "On the contrary, at the moment I feel rather warm."

"So do I," he whispered roughly. He took a deep breath as he gazed down into her eyes, the scent of cape jasmine that always clung to her filling his nostrils.

Neither could look away, both feeling the same emotions that always seemed to draw them together. To Lizette it was like looking into Bain's eyes. The color was different, but the depth in them was the same, as was the hidden desire. To Stuart, it was like drowning in a sea of green.

He sighed. "Lizette, Lizette," he said, his voice trembling. "What am I going to do about you?"

"What do you want to do?" she asked breathlessly.

He pulled her closer against him. She felt good in his arms, so good that it was hard not to forget everything. "You're teasing again," he cautioned her.

"I only asked—"

"I know what you asked." He reached up and cupped the side of her face with his hand, his eyes moving to the fancy little hat atop her head before settling again on her eyes. "And I wish I had the answer," he said softly. "I know you don't mean to tease, and I don't mean to respond to it either, but I do." He studied her face, his thumb gently caressing her temple, his fingers buried in her hair. "You don't know what it does to a man, Lizette," he went on huskily. "How could you? Right now I feel light-headed, as if I'd had too much to drink, and yet every nerve in my body is so alive I feel like I'm ten feet tall, and I shouldn't feel like this, not with you or anyone else but Julia."

Mentioning Julia's name seemed to jolt Stuart back to reality, and he drew his hand from Lizette's face, backing away from her, then turned and walked to the open door, where he stood staring out at the pounding rain.

She felt a sharp loss at his withdrawal, maybe because she knew what his arms could bring to her, what she could feel in them. She remembered what it had been like in Bain's arms, the fire and passion, the driving force that warmed her and made her weak all over while filling her with such pleasure. It had been so long since she had known the thrill of love, the enchanting, sensual gratification of being made love to. And at the rate the young men in Beaufort and Port Royal were responding to her, she'd never feel it again, ever! Yet here was a man who seemed to want her. And she wanted to be loved so badly.

Somewhere in the back of her conscience the thought of his wife sprang up. What was she thinking of? Stuart didn't belong to her, he belonged to Julia. She had no right to think of him like this. And yet her body felt so strangely alive whenever he was near. If she could only borrow him, just for a little while. She laughed at herself. What a dreamer! After all, he already had made it clear to her that he wasn't about to let anything happen. Tears misted her eyes as she watched his silhouette in the doorway.

Stuart stood for a long time trying to cool the fire in his veins, hoping the plunging rain would put a damper on the craving for this young woman that was making him ache inside. What was it about her that set him off like this? Even Julia hadn't done this to him. Their love had grown slowly and been nurtured by mutual interests. He had nothing in common with Lizette Dante—she was fourteen years his junior.

He tensed, suddenly feeling the prickling awareness that he was being stared at. He turned and walked back to where Lizette stood, and when he saw her tears, his resolve to do things right faded, and his heart constricted inside him. "Don't cry, Lizette," he said softly. "It's not your fault."

"I can't help it," she sniffed. "I feel so lost, so alone and unloved."

He reached out slowly and pulled her into his arms and held her tight, his eyes shut, savoring the feel of her. He couldn't let her cry, he just couldn't. He wanted to see the laughter in her eyes again the way it always was when she teased him, and the vibrant glow that had held him spellbound when they'd danced the night of the wedding.

His hands pressed onto her back and he began to caress

her. "Hush!" he whispered, his voice breaking. "There's no need for tears."

"You don't know," she gasped breathlessly, her voice unsteady as she pressed her face against his shoulder. "You have no idea what it's like to see everyone around you being loved and knowing no one will ever love you."

"There'll be someone someday," he tried to assure her.

"No there won't," she cried angrily. "I'm too fat and ugly!"

He stopped stroking her back and straightened, then took her by the shoulders and held her away from him. "No . . . no, you could never be ugly," he whispered softly. He let his hands move down her arms slowly, caressing them, and he wished there was no material between his fingers and her flesh. Now suddenly his hands couldn't stop, and they moved to her waist, then slowly began to rise until they covered her full breasts, and he felt her nipples harden beneath the material.

Lizette stared at him mesmerized, the tears still glistening on her lashes, but no new tears joining them. Her mouth opened in awe at his touch.

"So lovely," he whispered huskily, and as their eyes clung precariously and she held her breath, he began unfastening the front of her riding habit.

His eyes devoured her as he loosened the hooked frogging, then let the dress fall away, slipping it back onto her shoulders, sliding it down her arms to reveal her tanned flesh all golden and warm. He leaned forward, his head bending, and kissed the velvety skin on her right shoulder, then moved his lips up to her ear, tickling it sensuously.

Lizette's head was tilted up toward the loft of the barn, but she didn't see it. Her eyes were closed so she could enjoy his touch more keenly.

His lips left her ear and she knew he was gazing into her face once more, yet she kept her eyes shut, afraid to open them, afraid to see disappointment that was certain to cross his face when his fingers finished their work of letting her riding habit fall to the floor at her feet.

Stuart stepped back, giving the riding habit room to settle on the floor, then reached out to pull the chemise up over her head.

Lizette's eyes suddenly flew open and she grabbed his wrists, holding them tightly as she looked into his eyes, her own unsure, terrified. "No," she whispered helplessly. "You don't want to see," she begged, but he shook his head.

"I want to see all of you, Lizette," he said, and when his eyes captured hers again, boring into them, she felt all weak and warm inside and her hands eased on his wrists.

She was still staring directly at him as the chemise came off over her head, and to her surprise, she saw a look of profound pleasure fill his eyes. He sighed, hands trembling, and touched her bare breasts, beginning to stroke them as if he were touching something rare and precious.

"How can you say you're not lovely," he whispered breathlessly as he bent to kiss her breasts. When his head came up again, he stared into her eyes, his own hot with desire. "Let me love you, Lizette," he pleaded huskily, and saw the wonder in her eyes. "I can't stop now . . . not now," he whispered.

She balanced between rapture and reality; then she caught her breath sensuously "Yes . . . oh, yes," she murmured, eyes shining. "Love me, Stuart!" she gasped, and as the words left her lips, his mouth covered hers and he drew her close against him, his body exploding in a hot flurry of desire.

The kiss was deep, making them both tremble, and when it ended he took her hand and led her farther into the barn, to a stall where hay covered the floor; then he turned to her, his eyes glazed with passion. "The hay is rough," he said, but she wasn't discouraged.

"If you spread my riding habit . . ."

He shook his head. "I have a better idea." He left the stall for a moment, then returned with a blanket he found in one of the other stalls and spread it on the hay.

She was hugging her arms self-consciously, covering her breasts, so afraid she was going to see disgust in his eyes. Instead, he looked pleased as he stepped toward her and cupped her face between both of his hands. He kissed her mouth, a fiery, passionate kiss, then let his hands move down her body, where they stopped long enough to unhook her petticoat, letting it fall, then unfastened her underdrawers.

"Take them off, love," he whispered softly, and felt her tremble again. "Have you changed your mind?" he asked.

She swallowed hard. "No, it's just that . . ."

"Don't be frightened, Lizette," he said fervently. "I won't hurt you."

"I know," she replied, her voice hushed. "It's just that . . ." Her face turned crimson.

"Don't be embarrassed, either," he said, looking down into her eyes. "I want you, Lizette. God! I've wanted you ever since first laying eyes on you."

He began to loosen his tie as he watched her slowly begin to step out of her drawers. He remembered her condemning words. No, she wasn't fat, she was rounded and voluptuous, her hips padded enough so his hands as they caressed them could feel the flesh beneath instead of hard bone. His clothes were gone now too, thrown aside with his good intentions, and he drew her to him, against him, until the warmth of her skin touched his, then he pulled her down with him to the blanket.

His kisses fed her like wine, intoxicating her and bringing memories of Bain back to her in all their splendor, yet she kept telling herself this wasn't Bain, it was Stuart. It was Stuart loving her as Bain had loved her for a while. For a little while. . . .

She responded to his hands, reveling in their touch, and gently caressed his face with her own hands. Then, as she enjoyed the feel of his muscles beneath her fingertips, he moved over her to enter. She arched up, reaching for him, and with one forceful plunge he was inside her. For a second he hesitated, then went on, fired by her wanton pleasure and her urgent need.

Lizette moved beneath him eagerly, reaching for the stars, and was rewarded quickly as her body suddenly exploded in a peak of ecstasy that made her shake all over and cry out. Then, as she began to gasp for air, throbbing sensations pulsing through her, she felt him tense inside her, and his release began too as he shook spasmodically, then grew still.

He lay over her, the warmth of her body beneath him, filling him with content; then slowly a frown creased his forehead. She hadn't been a virgin. He had expected to be the first, and that he wasn't came as a complete surprise. Yet she was tight, too tight to have had a man regularly. In fact, except for the fact that there had been no obstruction in his way, her embarrassment, everything else . . .

His lips caressed her neck in a tender kiss, then he raised his head. "Who was it, Lizette?" he whispered softly as he stared down into her eyes.

"Who was what?" she asked.

"Who was the first?"

She bit her lip, then turned her head away, her face turning bright red as she avoided his eyes. "You wouldn't want to know. It was a long time ago, and just the once."

"Did you tell your family you'd been raped?"

"It wasn't exactly rape, no more than this is," she murmured. "It ended the day it began, without ever really beginning."

"You loved him?"

"I thought I did."

"You must have been very young."

"You're angry with me?" she asked.

He reached out and brushed a stray hair from her face, feeling her breasts pressing into the curling hairs on his chest, and it was a nice sensation. "Why should I be angry with you?"

"Because you weren't the first."

"Will I be the last?"

"That's up to you," she said, her voice breaking. "Will I see you again?"

"Do you want to?"

She nodded shyly, suddenly overwhelmed by the passion she had aroused in him. He was still hard, and still inside her, and somehow it was forging a bond between them. She wasn't sure it was love—maybe it was, she had no way of knowing. But she did know that she didn't want it to end, not yet. She needed Stuart and what he could give her. Her eyes looked deeply into his, and she sighed. "What of Julia?" she asked unexpectedly, and saw sadness veil his eyes.

He wanted to say Julia didn't matter, Julia had no part in this, but that wouldn't be true. Lizette's question brought him back to reality, and he winced as he slipped from her and reached out to grab his clothes. He sat up, his back to her, and pondered her question. What of Julia? "I don't intend to leave her, if that's what you mean," he said quietly.

"I didn't think you would," she said as she sat up beside him. "Will you hand me my petticoat and underdrawers?" she asked politely, then added, "So where does that leave me?"

He handed her things to her, his eyes intent on her face. "What do you want me to say?" he asked.

"That you care." She hugged her underclothes to her, covering her breasts self-consciously with them.

"I do care, Lizette, that's just the trouble," he said. "I care . . . and I shouldn't."

"You said we could see each other again."

"We can, but we're going to have to be careful." He sensed her withdrawal. "I don't want it to be like this," he went on, "but what else can I do?"

Tears sprang to her eyes and she looked down at the clothes in her hands, then began slowly putting on her underdrawers. Stuart watched her for a minute, then began getting into his own clothes. She stood up and pulled on her petticoat, then left the stall and retrieved her chemise and riding habit. She was standing in the main part of the barn near their horses, fastening the frogging on the front of her riding habit, when he joined her, his cravat in one hand, her shoes, stockings, and hat in the other.

She took the things from him and sat on an overturned box, starting to put them on.

He tied his cravat, then walked over, taking her hand, pulling her to her feet. She avoided his eyes and played with the lapels on his frock coat. He had hoped to see the laughter back in her eyes; instead he had only caused her more sadness. A twinge of regret gripped him, and an ache settled in his breast. He wished he could explain his actions, even to himself, because as he stared at her now, he suddenly realized he didn't want this to end any more than she did. "Are you all right?" he asked.

She nodded, trying to hold back the tears.

"I'm sorry, Liz," he whispered huskily. "I wish it could be different."

"I know," she said bitterly. "Like before, it ends before it really begins."

"It doesn't have to."

"You'd be willing to risk a scandal?"

His eyes darkened passionately. "No one need know." He reached up and put his hand beneath her chin. "Look at me, Lizette," he ordered softly. "I can't give you up," he whispered against her mouth. "Say you will—"

She drew back and stared at him, trying to understand just exactly what he wanted her to do. "You . . . you want me to go on seeing you like this?" she asked.

"I want you to let me love you," he answered.

"To be your mistress?"

He shook his head and pulled her closer into his arms. "No, my dear. A mistress isn't loved, she's used," he said. His eyes deepened as she gazed up into them, realizing again how much he was like Bain. "I intend to love you, Lizette, whenever I can, whenever the opportunity arises," he went on. "Would that be enough for you? The world could never know, but you and I would know. Please . . . today was more than I dreamed it could be. Don't let it end now."

She studied his face. She should say no, and every decent spark within her urged her to follow her instincts and end it here and now. But would saying no end it? And if she did try to end it, what then? More lonely hours with no one to share them? Never to feel the thrill of being touched or kissed, the joy of knowing someone cared? Never again to let her body find pleasure in a man's arms? To say no would relegate her to the sterile existence she'd been suffering since Bain left. Is that what she wanted? God, no!

She had come alive today, and all because of Stuart, a man she had no right to, yet a man she suddenly realized she needed as surely as she needed the air she breathed. The bitter lines about her mouth softened, and her eyes grew languid, their green depths surrendering to him. "Will we see each other often?" she asked unsteadily.

He held his breath, hardly daring to believe he had heard right. "As often as I can manage," he said. He sighed. "Oh, my love, does this mean yes?" he asked anxiously.

She ran her hand along his beard, feeling the short, bristly whiskers, then moving it to the back of his head, pulling it down until their lips met. "A kiss before we go?" she asked tearfully. "After all, I don't know when I might see you again."

When they finally drew apart, her tears were gone and the laughter had returned again, but it wasn't the same careless laughter that had been there before; it was a warm, deep laughter that responded to his look with the knowledge of a secret only they shared.

The rain had stopped some time ago, and the sun was out, the dark clouds gone. He helped her onto her horse, and as he mounted and they rode out of the barn into the newly washed afternoon, the smile she gave him made his heart turn over. This was right, it had to be, he told himself, and he smiled back, a smile that lit up his deep blue eyes.

15

The rain had only served to make the air muggy rather than cool it, and Heather sat in the parlor at Palmerston Grove, glad the sun was out again, yet wishing it wasn't so hot. Her clothes were sticking to her in spite of the wisteria vines that kept the sun from entering the house, and she wondered what it must be like outside. Thank God the last few months of her pregnancy would be in the winter, when it was cooler.

She hadn't as yet told DeWitt about the baby. It was too soon. They had been married on June 8, and she had told him her menses were due the end of the month. The time had come and gone and he hadn't seemed to notice, so she hadn't said anything. The baby was due in December, so she figured if she gave it another month, then told him just before the first of August, that would give her almost five months before the baby came. By then she hoped it would be too late for him to deny that the baby was his, at least to the rest of the world. What he accused her of in private would be different. She had to take the chance.

She tried not to think of it, and concentrated harder on the scarf she was embroidering, leaning toward the window to get a little more light. Everett Palmer insisted the lamps weren't to be lit until sundown, and there were times, like earlier today when it was raining, that it was so dark inside Heather could barely see.

That was a surprising aspect of life at Palmerston Grove that she had learned since her marriage. Everett Palmer, for all of his flash and extravagance to the outside world, was a frugal man where his family was concerned. Oleander was instructed that unless company was expected, there would be no leftover food. Only enough to feed the family was to be cooked. And there were a dozen other ways he was thrifty to the extreme in one way and extravagant in others. Expensive paintings hung in all the rooms, and the furniture in the house was the best, but the slaves were always being reprimanded for wasting too much beeswax to shine it, or too much soap keeping the linens clean.

Thank God neither DeWitt nor Carl was anything like him. Both hated their father's miserly habits to the point of being rather careless with money, and Heather had discovered that DeWitt was fond of gambling. Even on their honeymoon he had spent hours at the gaming tables, insisting that she stay by his side for luck.

He hadn't made further mention of the incident that had marred their wedding night, and she was hoping he had forgotten it, but sometimes when male friends happened to drop by, he'd get a strange, haunted look and watch her closely. She shoved the thought aside as one of the servants came in and announced company.

"For me?" she asked in surprise.

The servant nodded, his dark face impassive. None of the servants at Palmerston Grove seemed to smile much, at least not when any of the family was around.

Heather stared at the white-haired slave. "Who is it?"

He stood stiffly, his black suit hanging loosely on his frame. "The young lady said her name was Mistress Dante."

Heather stared at him in surprise. "Lizette?" She smiled. "Oh, please, do show her in."

"He doesn't have to," said Lizette from behind the servant, and Heather stood up, shoving her embroidery aside, holding her arms out to her cousin.

"Oh, Liz, it's so good to see you!" Heather exclaimed as she felt Lizette's soft, warm body in her arms, hugging her back. "You don't know how I've missed you!"

Lizette pushed herself back to look into Heather's violet eyes. "Then why didn't you let us know you were home?" she asked.

Heather eyed her strangely. "I did," she said. "We got back

on Wednesday, and the next day I sent one of the servants to Tonnerre with a note for you, telling you I was home. I sent one to the Chateau at the same time, but I never got any answers. I thought maybe you were away for a while or something."

Lizette extricated herself from Heather's arms, straightening her riding habit. "None of us received any messages," she said, and watched Heather's reaction.

"But I know I sent them," she said stubbornly.

Lizette smirked. "Did you hand them to the servant yourself?" she asked.

Heather thought back. "Yes. Why?"

"Then I suggest you find out what the servant did with them. For a minute I thought maybe if you gave them to Witt he might have thrown them out."

"And not sent them?"

Lizette shook her head. "I see marriage hasn't changed you all that much—you're still terribly naive."

Heather made a face. "I thought we were friends."

"We are," said Lizette. "But I still think you're naive." She took Heather's hands and made her sit back down, then turned around, surveying the room. "Not a very cheerful place, is it?"

Heather shrugged. "It's all right. At least the vines on the upstairs gallery and veranda out front keep it a little cooler."

"And darker," added Lizette.

"I'll get used to it."

Lizette stopped appraising the room and turned her attention to Heather. "Well, maybe it was just some kind of a mix-up," she said. "Anyway, how is everything going?"

Heather's lips pursed. "What do you expect me to say?" she said. "I guess I'm not unhappy. Witt's attentive, thoughtful."

"But you're not happy either, are you?"

"Please, Liz," she cautioned. "Not so loud. The servants are everywhere."

Lizette frowned. "So?"

"So they all report everything to the housekeeper, Oleander, who keeps Witt's father informed about everything that goes on here!"

"How pleasant! But you're right, I probably would have put my foot in my mouth."

Heather was wearing a yellow muslin dress with the new bouffant sleeves, and she folded her hands in her lap, resting them on the soft material as she gazed at Lizette. "Everything at home's fine?" she asked a trifle breathlessly.

Lizette knew why she had asked. "Everything's fine," she offered. "Mother and Father are both well, and Cole is the same as ever. Still doesn't have a steady lady."

Heather tried to look indifferent at the mention of Cole's name. "Have you seen my parents?" she asked.

"Not for a little over a week. I went over there a few days after I got back from the Kolters'."

"That's right, Felicia did invite you in for your birthday, didn't she? I remember you mentioning it the day of the wedding. Did you have a nice time?"

Lizette had let her mind wander at the mention of the Kolters, and as she stared toward one of the windows, watching the dappled sunbeams trying to elude the vines outside, she remembered the hungry look on Stuart's face when he had left her at the gates of Palmerston Grove, and his promise that as soon as it could be arranged they'd be together again.

"I asked if you had a good time," Heather said again, cutting into Lizette's daydreaming.

Lizette blushed. "Oh, I had a lovely time."

Heather eyed her curiously. "Liz, what's the matter with you?"

Lizette shook her head. "Nothing."

"Come, now, you look like you're pleased about something. Did Bain come home?"

Lizette straightened, the warmth in her eyes suddenly vanishing. "No, he hasn't come home," she replied.

"But you have met someone, haven't you?" Heather cried anxiously. "Oh, I knew it. I could tell when you came in . . . there was something different about you."

Lizette stared at her, frowning. "What makes you think that?"

"You. You don't seem as restless and discontented as usual."

"Oh that," she said, hoping to change the subject and sound nonchalant. "I've decided that I'm not going to let my weight bother me anymore, that's all," she said. "If people don't like it, that's their problem."

Heather wasn't so sure. "I could have sworn I saw something else in your eyes when you first walked in here," she said, then flushed. "But I guess I was wrong." She was about to say she was glad Lizette wasn't going to fret anymore about her weight, when they were interrupted by a voice from the doorway.

"Well, and what do we have here?" asked Witt as he entered, staring hostilely at Lizette.

"Isn't it marvelous, Witt," Heather said quickly. "Lizette stopped by for a visit. I'm so pleased."

Witt studied Lizette disdainfully. He didn't like her being here, not at all. He had warned Heather that he wasn't going to put up with any nonsense from her cousins now that they were married, and that included visits. He wondered if Heather had mentioned the notes she had written.

In her next breath, Heather answered his silent question. "Liz said no one ever received those messages I sent, Witt," she said, frowning. "I think you'd better speak to the servants. I distinctly remember giving them instructions."

Witt's eyes narrowed. "I'll take care of it, dear," he said, then addressed Lizette. "All's well at Tonnerre?" he asked stiffly.

She returned his hateful glare. "Do you really care how things are at Tonnerre?"

He sneered. "Not really, but it is customary to make small talk when relatives drop by, isn't it?"

"Witt!" Heather exclaimed. "What a thing to say."

Witt's eyes hardened. "Let's face it, my dear wife," he said, gazing first at Lizette, then turning to Heather. "There has never been any love between your cousins and myself, and you of all people should know why. For your sake, I had to put up with them at the wedding, but this is my house, and I can't see being forced to entertain either Lizette Dante or her crude brother here."

"It's my house too!" cried Heather angrily. "For heaven's sake, Witt, what's gotten into you? I know you've never gotten along, but insulting Liz like this . . ."

Lizette laughed. "I think I understand what you're up to, but it won't work, Witt. As Heather said, this is her house too, and as long as she wants to see me, I intend to drop by, welcomed by you or not."

"And if I give the servants orders to keep you out?"

"You would, wouldn't you?" she said.

He smiled cruelly. "I intend to, Miss Dante, just as soon as you leave the premises."

Lizette's jaw tightened as she stared at him. This was the man Heather had promised to spend the rest of her life with? She took a deep breath, then turned to Heather. "Don't worry, Heather," she said gently. "I think your parents will have something to say about that."

"Her parents will have nothing to say about it, Miss

Dante," he countered, without giving Heather a chance to answer. "Heather's not their daughter anymore, she's my wife, and if I choose to keep her from associating with the likes of you, then that's my business and not theirs."

"Witt, you can't be serious," Heather cried as she stared at him, but Witt was very serious.

"If you think I'm going to let you risk your reputation being close to the Dantes again, you're sadly mistaken, Heather," he insisted. "I married you, not your cousins." He paused for a moment, then turned to Lizette. "For today, I suppose I'll have to put up with your being here because I neglected to tell the servants to keep you out," he said abruptly. "But don't try to return. You won't be welcome." Then he turned and walked out.

Lizette was mortified. "He's serious, isn't he?" she exclaimed.

Heather shook her head in disbelief. "Oh, Liz, I'm so sorry."

Lizette stared at her in awe. "You mean you're going along with it?"

"I have no choice, Liz," she answered, her fingers twitching nervously in her lap. "He's my husband, what can I do?"

"You're not a slave, Heather," Liz said angrily. "Good God, don't you have any backbone?"

"Liz, please," she said, and lowered her voice to a whisper. "I'm in no condition to demand anything from him, you know that." She glanced around quickly to make sure no one was close enough to hear, then lowered her voice again to barely a whisper. "I don't dare cross him, Liz," she confided hurriedly. "As it is, he knew I wasn't a virgin, and I've had to lie my way through that. If he finds out the truth, I don't know what he might do."

Lizette studied Heather's face. She was beside herself with worry. "I know, I know," Lizette said, calming down a little as she tried to soothe her. "It's just that he makes me so angry."

"We can still see each other, Liz," Heather assured her. "We'll see each other in town once in a while, and I'm sure he won't say anything if I go to the Chateau. We can meet there."

"I suppose so," said Lizette. "But I still think it's ridiculous."

Heather bit her lip. "It's hard enough for me as it is, Liz," she whispered. "Please, don't make it any worse."

"What do I tell Cole?"

Heather's eyes filled with tears. "That I'm happy," she said. "He won't believe it."

"Then I guess you'll have to try to convince him."

"Not me," said Lizette. "I went along with all of this for your sake, and his too," she went on. "But that's as far as I go. If you want him to think you're happy, then you're going to have to do the convincing yourself." She straightened, patting her hat in place and smoothing the skirt of her riding habit. "Now, I guess I'd better be going. It's getting late and I want to get home before dark."

Heather stood up, and they headed for the front door. "I'm surprised you didn't get wet on the way down," she said, to make conversation. "That storm came up so quickly. I don't know how you missed it."

"I didn't," said Lizette nonchalantly. "I found some shelter and waited for it to pass." She turned to Heather and took her cousin's hands in hers, wishing she could tell her about Stuart, but knowing it was impossible. They had reached the large foyer, and both women looked at each other, their eyes strained. After a brief pause, Lizette said, "I hate to leave you here like this."

Heather tried to smile. "I'm all right, Liz, really I am. Witt's good to me . . . and it's what I wanted."

Lizette squeezed her hands. "Good-bye," she said affectionately, and gave Heather a big hug, which was returned; then Heather watched solemnly as Lizette hurried down the front steps, walked to the hitching post, unhitched her horse, then went quickly to the mounting block, and climbed into the saddle. She waved to Heather, then spurred Diablo down the drive, heading for home.

Heather watched her go, an ache in her chest. It had been so good to see her. She had thought everyone had forgotten about her, since there had been no answers to her messages. And that was another thing. Why hadn't they been received? She made a vow that if Witt didn't talk to the servants about it, she would, and was just ready to turn from the door when Witt's voice startled her.

"Well, what did she want you to do this time?" he asked sarcastically.

She whirled around. "Oh! You scared me. I didn't know you were standing there." She frowned as his words sank in. "What do you mean?" she asked curiously.

His eyes narrowed. "My dear, sweet, wife, isn't it obvious? She's always coming up with some harebrained idea to get the two of you in trouble. Thank God she no longer has any influence on you." He walked toward her and reached out, pulling her into his arms. "I know you're disappointed, Heather," he said, trying to make up for his treatment of Lizette. "But I can't take the chance that she might talk you into doing something ridiculous and bringing scandal to the Palmer name. I'm sorry, sweetheart. Please, you do understand, don't you?"

She looked up at him, both hands on his chest. His hazel eyes were hard, unyielding, and she knew this was the closest thing to an apology she'd ever get for his uncalled-for treatment of Lizette. Her heart rebelled and she was just on the verge of telling him to take his hands off her, when a sudden fluttering in her stomach made her catch her breath, and she held back the words. The baby was moving. They were only tiny movements, like a butterfly in distress, but they were enough to remind her that she needed Witt, and why.

"You didn't have to be so brutal, Witt, did you?" she said after a brief pause. "Couldn't you have tried to be just a little more tactful? After all, Lizette isn't a child anymore, she's a young woman . . . and she is my cousin."

"That's just the trouble. Because you're cousins, for some reason the two of you seem to think you should be inseparable. Heather, you're my wife now—the little-girl fun is over." His eyes suddenly grew more intense, and she saw the flickering passion flood them. He bent down and began kissing her throat below her right ear as he continued to plead his case. "If you happen to meet her or any of the rest of the Dantes away from Palmerston Grove, I won't stop you from saying hello, but I don't want them here, and I don't want you at Tonnerre, is that understood?"

"What about Aunt Rebel and Uncle Beau?" she asked unsteadily.

"They weren't the ones who talked you into doing all those crazy things," he said, lifting his head and looking into her eyes. "Naturally, if they come calling, they won't be turned away."

"And if Lizette's with Aunt Rebel?"

He smiled. "I'm sure she won't be planning any forbidden escapades with her mother listening in," he said. "Circumstances alter things a great deal, but I just hope you stay as far away from your family as possible, my love," he said, trying to discourage her. "Because I'm not any too fond of any of them, really."

"Then why did you marry me?" she asked, puzzled.

"Because I love you," he said huskily, and once more his

eyes took on that intense glow that precipitated his lovemaking. He leaned over again and began kissing her neck, his lips close to her ear. "Besides," he whispered breathlessly, "I married you, not your family."

As she surrendered passively to his arms and tender caresses, she stared off over his shoulder and suddenly froze. Carl was watching them. He was standing at the other end of the foyer, leaning against the doorframe, an amused look on his face.

"Witt, please," she protested weakly. "Not here, your brother's watching!"

She felt Witt tense; then his arms released her and he turned to face Carl, who was now walking toward them. "Do you have to stand around watching every time I kiss my wife, Carl?"

Carl's mouth twitched slightly. "Father saw you come home and wants to know if everything went all right in town."

"Certainly," replied Witt, his jaw beneath his low sideburns tightening. "Why wouldn't it?"

"He was afraid maybe they'd give you a little trouble."

"Nothing I can't take care of. By thc way, I met Stuart Kolter on the road a short time ago. He was just returning from the Chateau."

Carl looked surprised. "So he went to see Chapman too," he mused. "I guess it figures. I just wonder which side Roth is on."

"You can bet he'll be on the side where the money is," Witt remarked. "I heard tell he's going to divert his British trade to the South Seas and Canada"

"That's one way to beat it. Well, you'd better go in and tell Father all about it," Carl said. "He's been up in arms ever since this business started. He'll be glad to hear it's finished."

Witt turned to Heather and excused himself, then went into the library.

"What was that all about?" she asked.

"None of your business," retorted Carl.

Heather glanced at him in surprise. "Well," she snapped testily, "you don't have to be so snippy. I was just curious. Just because you don't like me, Carl, doesn't mean you have to be rude."

"Who said I don't like you?" he asked.

"I just assumed it because it seems you always have something nasty to say when Witt's not around."

"It isn't because I don't like you," he answered.

She scowled. "Then why?"

"Did you ever think that maybe it's hard for me to see my brother enjoying such romantic bliss when I'm denied the pleasure myself?"

Her flush deepened. "Oh . . . I hadn't thought."

"No, I don't suppose you had."

"I'll say something to Witt about keeping his amorous little gestures more private," she said, embarrassed.

"No, don't do that!" he said harshly.

"Then why did you just say . . . ?"

His mouth curved sardonically. "Sometimes the forbidden can be enjoyable, dear sister-in-law," he half-whispered, and without another word walked to the door Witt had closed moments ago and joined his father and brother in Everett Palmer's office library.

Heather was dumbfounded. Carl had always seemed rather strange, but now she really began to wonder. Ah, well, it wouldn't be much longer and she'd have her baby to keep her company, and then she wouldn't care what anyone else at Palmerston Grove did.

The Fourth of July arrived cooler than the two preceding days, but still it felt like a hundred in the shade. It had drizzled a little the night before, but the road was dry now, and dust clouds billowed around the two carriages, which kept an even pace so the second carriage was far enough behind not to eat the other's dust.

Roth, Loedicia, Heath, and Darcy were in the first carriage; Rebel, Beau, and Lizette in the second. Some distance behind them, Cole tagged along on his piebald mare, wearing his usual buckskins, which he knew were going to be out-of-place. But he didn't much care; he hadn't wanted to come today, because he knew Lizette was going to throw Felicia at him, but he wanted to see Heather so badly, and Uncle Heath said she and DeWitt would definitely be there. Cole had attended two parties over the past weekend and the newlyweds hadn't been at either one, but Everett Palmer was one of the chairman for the annual picnic and barbecue that always kicked off the political rallies in Port Royal on the Fourth of July, so the Palmers were obliged to attend.

The picnic grounds, near the waterfront on a section of land between Beaufort and Port Royal, were teeming with people by the time they arrived. There was swimming and fishing in the sound, carriage and horse races, a chase for a greased pig, games of chance, horseshoe tournaments, rounders, and later in the day, before the dancers began to glide over the rough ground to the music of a string band composed of slaves from various plantations, the men always secreted themselves off somewhere for a rousing cockfight or sometimes even a bout of fisticuffs.

It was late in the day, during the cockfight in which DeWitt's prize bird was participating, that Cole finally found Heather alone.

She was wearing a fancy dress of bright blue silk, with one of the new wide-brimmed hats trimmed with contrasting blue flowers, and was keeping the sun from her face with a lace-trimmed parasol. He had a hard time keeping his eyes off her. They didn't say much, only gazed at each other longingly while he tried to remember that she belonged to someone else. It was hard to appear casual, and harder still to hide how they really felt.

They talked about so many things, yet left so many unsaid, but it didn't matter. The important thing was that the anger between them had evaporated, and only love remained. A love that would never die, yet one they could never acknowledge openly.

Cole tried not to spend too much time with Heather so Witt wouldn't get suspicious, so after leaving her when he saw the cockfights breaking up, he took Lizette's advice and joined the Kolters, whisking Felicia expertly away from Alex Benedict. Felicia seemed enchanted with this new turn of events and Cole was surprised. He decided maybe Lizette was right after all. Felicia wasn't Heather—no one could be—but Felicia was fun to be with, and that's what he needed now more than anything else. Someone to help him forget.

While Cole was with Felicia at the refreshment tables, Lizette wandered off by herself. The day had been the same as always. Everyone said, "Hello, Lizette," "How are you, Lizette," "Glad to see you, Lizette," but not one person said, "Come on, Lizette, I'll buy you something cold to drink" or "Would you care to join our group, Lizette?"

She was wearing a dress of pale pink muslin with an overskirt of pink gauze that flowed freely from the high waist with no frills. The sleeves were short and puffed with delicate lace inserts, and pink satin ribbon binding them. Above the waistline, the bodice was shirred and tucked, exposing the top of her dusky bosom, and the white straw bonnet atop her head was held in place with a ribbon the color of her dress, with small green-leaved pink flowers decorating the crown. She had brought a parasol, as had most of the other women, but had left it back in the carriage, preferring to feel the sun on her face, and using a lace-and-irory fan when the heat became intense. She was dressed in the best of fashion, so she knew that wasn't the reason for the snubs. It was because of her weight.

The fan was attached to her wrist by a ribbon, and she toyed with it absentmindedly as she strolled along, thinking back to everything that had happened earlier in the day. They had arrived with a flourish, everyone recognizing them, and were greeted by a jubilant crowd. There were still people who thought Roth shouldn't have given up politics, Stuart among them, and many of Roth's old constituents were on hand to greet them, as was Andrew Pickens, candidate for governor, who had just recently opened his campaign.

Her grandparents and parents shook hands all around, as did Uncle Heath and Aunt Darcy, while she and Cole both tried to stay in the background, and she was just starting to relax a little, staring off toward where some friends of hers were talking, when a voice broke in on her reverie.

"Well, hello, Lizette," Julia said.

Lizette straightened abruptly and turned toward the voice. Julia was standing next to the carriage, her hair tucked beneath a gray silk bonnet with bright red flowers clustered on each side. Her dress too was gray silk, with bouffant sleeves that ended at the elbows in deep red lace. The underskirt of her high-waisted dress was the same red lace, and the skirt was split in front to let the lace show. A red lace parasol was in one lace-gloved hand. Her other hand was resting on the shoulder of a girl about six or seven who had russet-brown hair, big blue eyes, and was wearing a dress to match her eyes, with a bonnet the same color. Next to her was a little boy of three or four, dressed in a brown tunic suit, white stockings, and a brown cap on top of dark brown curls. His big gray eyes gazed up at Lizette inquisitively, and her heart sank. It was the first time she had seen Stuart's children, and a pang of guilt ran through her.

Lizette looked into Julia's pale blue eyes, trying to keep her own from giving away her discomfiture. "Hello, Mrs. Kolter," she said.

Julia smiled. "I thought you might like to meet the children," she said as she pushed them forward a little, urging them to say hello. The children were shy, but they smiled at her and greeted her politely.

Lizette would never forget that conversation, especially when Stuart joined them and she had to pretend he was just

Felicia's older brother and nothing more. It had been one of the hardest things she had ever had to do in her life.

As she walked along now, moving through the crowds, she wished she could just find someplace where she could sit down and cry. It was starting to get dark already, and the day had been nothing but a disappointment for her. Two years ago she had been in all the games and joined her friends in races and relays. Even last year she had had more than one young man following her around, trying to buy her sweets, and had danced almost every dance. This year she had done nothing except wander about, talk to a few people, and try to entertain herself.

Disgusted with the whole thing, she sighed and moved back toward where the food and the refreshments were. She had eaten a good breakfast at home that morning, then purposely stayed away from this area of the picnic grounds, but now her stomach was twisting miserably, begging for something, anything, to still the dull ache.

She stopped in front of a table where some women were slicing ham and slapping it between slices of brown-crusted bread, and she watched them longingly. She was just ready to step up to the table to buy one when a familiar voice sounded behind her.

"Why don't you? The treat's on me," said Stuart.

She whirled around, her stomach suddenly turning its aching hunger into a taut bundle of nerves as she looked into his dark blue eyes. She didn't know what to say, and just stared at him. All around them people were talking and laughing.

He stepped up to the table, and the women greeted him cordially by name. She watched him order two sandwiches and two mugs of cider while the women fawned over him and told him how much they had enjoyed his speech earlier, commenting on how pleased everyone was that the distinguished senator and native son had decided to make Beaufort his home. She listened and watched, her heart beating wildly, wondering what he thought he was doing.

He paid for the food, then turned to her, handing her one of the sandwiches.

She finally found her voice. "Stuart, what on earth are you doing? Someone will see!"

"I'm buying the daughter of a friend a sandwich," he said quickly as he started to usher her away from the table. "Just like I've been doing off and on all day with other young ladies and gentlemen. It's a politician's prerogative, and, it's a lot more fun than kissing babies. You know, I think I've bought sandwiches for some dozen or more young ladies already today just in order to have an excuse to be with you."

He led her off away from the worst of the crowd, to where they were practically alone, then moved under a huge willow tree, where they stood in the darkest shadows. "Eat your sandwich," he said, looking down at her thoughtfully.

She swallowed hard. "I don't think I can."

"Nonsense, you haven't had a thing to eat all day, and you'll have the vapors if you don't have something."

"How do you know I haven't eaten?"

"Because I've been watching you." He reached out and nudged her hand with his, pushing the sandwich toward her mouth. "Now, take a bite!" he ordered.

She tore off a piece of the sandwich, having trouble with the tough crust.

He laughed as he followed suit, and for a few minutes they both ate in silence. It still wasn't completely dark, although it was becoming harder every minute to distinguish one face from another in the crowd, and as Lizette sipped the last of the cider in her mug, staring out from the deepening shadows beneath the tree, she was still very aware of the chance Stuart was taking, in spite of what he had said earlier.

"Feel better now?" he asked.

She nodded. "Yes." She looked over at him, watching as he finished his own sandwich. He was dressed in a dark gray frock coat with Wellington boots, the strap on the bottom of his buff trousers hugging the arch of the boots, and his white silk cravat was tied at the collar of a ruffled shirt, a high beaver hat covering his dark russet hair. He looked very handsome and distinguished, and at the moment, very much like Bain. The thought made her shiver, and it also reminded her that his little boy's eyes had been the same color of gray as Bain's.

"Your children are really lovely, Stuart," she said softly. "I'm glad I got to meet them earlier." Her voice broke on the last words.

"I would have liked the meeting to be a little less upsetting for you," he replied gently. "I knew you hadn't been expecting it, and when I saw Julia start toward the carriage, I wished I could have shouted a warning."

"I had to meet them sometime."

"But they don't really have anything to do with us, Lizette," he said.

She frowned. "How can you say that? They're your children."

"And I love them, but it has nothing to do with how I feel about you." He gazed at her, watching one of the dark curls near her cheek, realizing how young and inexperienced she was. "The other day when I got home, Lizette," he said, his voice low and hushed, "I looked at Marie and Adam, and at first I castigated myself, then I vowed I was going to tell you it was over, and for the next two days I kept arguing with myself, thinking of you and changing my mind, then changing it back again. Until last night. I knew I'd be seeing you today, and I thought the best way to keep from falling under your spell again was to remind myself that Julia was here for me whenever I wanted. Only I'm afraid it didn't work out the way it was supposed to."

"What happened?"

His eyes grew hard. "I guess I can't really blame Julia," he said. "It was probably part my fault too. Maybe I was expecting too much, but . . ." He hesitated briefly, then went on. "Let's just say that when it was over I felt incomplete. There was something missing, something that had been there when I was with you, Lizette . . . and God help me, I need whatever it is." His eyes caught hers and softened. "That's why I couldn't just tell you good-bye and end it." He didn't wait for her to answer, but looked off toward the people beginning to gather where the band was tuning up. "I'm leaving for Columbia Saturday," he suddenly said.

She searched his face in the growing darkness. "How long will you be gone?"

"Three or four weeks."

"That long?"

"I'm going to try to be home before August fourth. Felicia has some silly notion that we should celebrate our birthdays together this year, since mine's on the fourth and hers is on the sixth."

"When will I see you again?" she asked hesitantly.

He turned to her, his eyes holding hers passionately. "I have to see you alone before I go," he said, trying not to let the anxiety show on his face.

She frowned. "How . . . if you're leaving Saturday?"

"Shhh . . . listen. I have to go see your father tomorrow. Is there anyplace up at Tonnerre where we can meet and be alone?"

She shook her head. "I can't think of anyplace," she said, her frown deepening. Then stopped suddenly, her eyes faltering beneath his steady gaze. "There is a place," she said, flushing. "But it's not at Tonnerre."

"Where is it?"

"At the southern tip of Port Royal. It was used years ago by some pirates who used to meet there and plan their forays along the coast."

"How did you find out about it?"

"Cole has been all over Port Royal hunting," she answered. "He took me with him a few times and we ended up there."

"You're sure you know the way?"

"Positive. There's an old trail just past the wooden bridge downriver from the Chateau. It's hard to see if you don't know it's there. I could meet you and lead the way in. It's really isolated." She looked at him sheepishly. "The slaves claim it's haunted, and the land around it is too wooded to clear for planting, and not wet enough for rice. It's just a small stone building, but there are vines almost covering it completely. I think most people have forgotten it's there."

"You'll meet me there?"

"By the bridge. When are you supposed to be at Tonnerre?"

He cleared his throat. "Your father said we could talk over lunch."

She looked back out toward the milling crowd. "Then I'll leave Tonnerre right after you get there and ride down to the Chateau and visit with my grandparents for a while. When I leave the Chateau, I'll ride downriver instead of up."

"Leave the Chateau at three o'clock," he said. "I'll make sure I reach the bridge in time."

She turned to look at him again, and the look in his eyes sent a shock through her. "You won't change your mind?"

The passion in his eyes deepened, the light in them intense. "I won't change my mind," he said, then sighed. "Oh, God, Lizette, I wish I could be with you this evening," he said. "I wish things could be different."

"I know," she replied.

He reached over and took the empty cider mug from her, his hand covering hers, and their eyes met for a few moments, the air between them vibrant with emotion. "Lizette . . . ?"

"Go," she told him quickly. "Please, until tomorrow . . ."

He squeezed her hand, taking the mug from it, and turned, walking out of the darkening shadows of the tree, heading back toward the table where he'd bought the cider.

She watched as people stopped him here and there, shaking his hand, then she turned away and walked deeper into the shadows where no one could see her tears. She stood under the tree for a long time, leaning back against the gnarled trunk, trying to pull her emotions into some kind of reasonable perspective. It wasn't until the dancing was well under way, the lamps flickering into the darkness casting deep shadows all around her, that Lizette felt composed enough to leave the shelter of her tree, and the first two people she ran into were Felicia and Cole.

"Well, where the devil have you been, Lizette?" Cole asked as he cornered her.

She glared at him. "For heaven's sake, Cole, I haven't tried to keep track of where you were all day."

"He was with me," said Felicia proudly, holding on to Cole's arm tightly as she gazed up at him and smiled.

Felicia was wearing a lavender dress of watered silk, but had taken her white hat with its violet ribbons off shortly before the dancing started, and her dark amber hair was slightly ruffled.

"I can see that," said Lizette sarcastically. She was glad Cole had finally taken her advice and was paying some attention to Felicia, but at the moment it rankled her to think that Felicia had someone to spend the evening with and she didn't.

Cole studied his sister curiously. "What's the matter, Liz?" he asked.

She shrugged. "Nothing, I've just been feeling sorry for myself, I guess, that's all."

"Well, come on," he said, and motioned with his head toward where most of the people were. "Mother's been worried about you. Said she hasn't seen anything of you for a couple of hours."

As they neared where her parents were sitting, Lizette's heart suddenly started pounding and she wished she hadn't come with Cole and Felicia. Her parents were talking to Julia. Stuart was nowhere in sight. Grandpa Roth was watching the dancers, and there were a few other people about, but she didn't see Aunt Darcy or Uncle Heath either. However, as they drew near, the music stopped and she searched the edge of the dancers where Grandpa Roth was staring, then frowned, feeling her stomach tighten again into vicious knots.

It was Grandma Dicia, and she had been dancing with Stuart. They were talking seriously about something as they walked, and suddenly Stuart looked up and saw Lizette. His face became a cold mask, and she looked away quickly, hoping no one would notice her nervousness. She wasn't at all prepared for what happened next.

Felicia had been trying to think of a way to make Lizette feel better all the while they'd been walking across the picnic area, and now suddenly she grabbed Lizette's hand, pulling her toward Stuart.

"Where are you taking me?" protested Lizette, trying to hold back.

"I'm going to get a smile back on your face!" Then she hailed her brother.

He and Loedicia both stopped, and Lizette blushed.

"Stuart, who were you going to dance with next?" asked Felicia anxiously.

He stared at her in surprise, then shrugged. "I hadn't decided, really. Why?"

"Because Julia can't dance right now with Adam asleep on her lap, and I don't want to dance with you, so why don't you dance with Lizette?" she suggested cheerfully.

He looked at Lizette, and there was a guarded look about his eyes.

"Felicia!" Lizette said between clenched teeth. "He doesn't want to dance with me. Please!"

"Don't be silly," said Felicia. "You don't mind dancing with her, do you, Stuart?" she said quickly. He started to say something, but she didn't let him get the words out. "And I'm sure Julia doesn't mind either, do you Julia?" she asked, turning to her sister-in-law.

"I think it would be a fine idea," Julia said congenially.

"Then quit arguing," said Felicia as she turned to Lizette and pushed her forward, almost shoving her into Stuart's arms.

"I think it's a fine idea," said Loedicia, seeing how unhappy Lizette looked. "Go ahead, dear," she urged her granddaughter.

"Shall we, Miss Dante?" Stuart asked.

When they reached the area where the dancers were, he took her in his arms, starting to move to the music. She glanced up at him furtively. He looked almost angry. "Is something wrong?" she asked shyly.

"That depends," he said.

"On what?"

"You."

"Me?" She was certain he was upset now.

"We'll talk about it tomorrow."

She frowned, puzzled. "If you say so."

They danced awhile longer in silence; then "You could look a little more like you were enjoying yourself," he retorted coldly.

She sighed. "I am, only I didn't think you wanted me to look too happy."

"Well, you don't have to make everyone think I'm some kind of ogre, do you?"

"Sorry!" she snapped.

His eyes flashed. "Just dance!"

Something was wrong, drastically wrong, she thought as they moved in and out among the other couples. Something had happened to make him angry with her. But what? Any other time she would have given anything to be able to dance with Stuart, but now she just prayed for the dance to end.

It was almost over, and he looked down at her, feeling rather guilty. "I'm sorry," he suddenly said. "I didn't mean to be so brusque a few minutes ago."

"Then why were you?"

"Tomorrow," he said, and he was still unsmiling.

She wanted to scream. Instead, as the music stopped, she said, "Thank you for the dance Senator Kolter."

"Not at all," he answered politely. "My pleasure," and they returned to the others.

The next afternoon when Lizette arrived at the bridge, Stuart was already there waiting. It had been a long night and she hadn't slept well. She was wearing the same riding habit she had worn the first day he'd made love to her, and as his eyes sifted over her, she wished she could ask him right away what had happened, but only said, "Hello."

"Hello yourself," he answered. He nudged his horse close to her and stared into her eyes. "You look lovely," he said, but his eyes told her something was still wrong.

"I thought maybe after last night you had decided to back out," she said.

"I told you I wouldn't change my mind. Now, let's get off the road. Someone might come along."

"This way," she said quickly, and dug Diablo in the ribs. She rode across the bridge, and he followed; then, some ten yards farther on, she reined her horse off the road, past some bushes, and was soon on an old path barely visible in the thick woods. It had been a long time since any horses had been along here, and the bushes and weeds were dense. Once they had to ride around a fallen tree, and there was a small stream to ford.

Half an hour later, they reined up and dismounted in front of an old crumbling stone building covered with moss and ivy. It was just one story, and half the wall on one side had caved in, but the roof was intact.

They stood for a few moments saying nothing. "What's wrong, Stuart?" she finally asked. "What have I done?"

"I asked you once before, that first day, Lizette," he said, trying to keep his voice steady. "And you said I wouldn't want to know. Well, now I have to know . . . you have to tell me, Lizette. Who was it?"

She couldn't seem to find her voice.

"You said you were young!" he yelled at her. "Fourteen? Fifteen? How old were you the last time Bain was home, Lizette?" he asked, his eyes blazing.

She felt sick. "Stuart . . . I . . ."

He took a step toward her. "Your grandmother said she thought you were infatuated with Bain. It was him, wasn't it?" he shouted.

She didn't want to answer, but his eyes were sparking dangerously.

"How old were you, Lizette?" he asked again. She shook her head, and he grabbed her arms, shaking her violently. "How old were you?"

"Fifteen!" she yelled at him. "I was fifteen!"

"And it was Bain?" He shook her again when she didn't answer. "I asked you, dammit! Was it Bain?"

"Yes!" she yelled, tears flooding her eyes. "Yes, yes, yes!"

He glared at her furiously, and for a minute she wasn't sure what he was going to do; then suddenly the rage in his eyes began to smolder, and a burning passion filled them. "Damn him!" he cried heatedly. "Damn him all to hell!" and in one quick movement he pulled her close against him, his arms engulfing her, and held her tight, rocking her back and forth in his arms as if she were a baby. "I knew it," he said, his voice breaking. "I just knew it. The minute your grandmother said it, I knew. That's why he didn't stay the last time he was home, isn't it?"

Lizette couldn't answer. She was sobbing softly against his chest.

"You don't have to answer, my dear," he whispered tenderly, then added, "I could kill him." He began to stroke her back. "I'm sorry, Lizette," he whispered. "Please forgive me for hurting you so, but I had to know." He continued letting his hands caress her back while he held her against him and let her cry. "I didn't mean to get angry with you last night, but all I could think of was you in his arms, letting him take what he wanted and giving him your love as you gave it to me, and I wanted to lash out!"

Lizette felt the strength of his arms about her. She had been telling herself she was a woman, but at the moment she felt very like a little girl again. She stopped crying, and he stepped back just enough so he could look down into her face. Her lashes had tears in them, and he reached into his pocket, handing her his handkerchief.

He studied her closely. Her soft full mouth quivering slightly, the oval face with a tear still clinging at the side of her cheek; she was so beautiful. He swallowed hard. "Lizette, do you still think you love him?" he asked gruffly.

She twisted the handkerchief in her hands, staring down at it, then raised her eyes to meet him. "I don't know," she answered. "It's been almost two years, and I honestly don't know what I feel anymore," she whispered, and saw his eyes darken. "Now I've angered you again."

He shook his head, his jaw tightening. "Not anger, Lizette. Jealousy," he said roughly. "I can't stand the thought that you might be with me only because of him."

"What do you mean?"

"I know there's a strong resemblance," he said, his voice vibrating emotionally. "And I don't want you to be using me as a substitute for Bain. I want you to be mine, and only mine, Lizette," he said. "All of you, even your heart."

"And if I'm not free to give it yet?"

"Then I'll take it!" he cried passionately. "I can't give you up, Lizette. In spite of what Bain did, I want you. God, how I still want you!"

She shivered at the violence of his passion. "And I want you," she whispered fervently.

He leaned forward and kissed her until she went weak all over; then with a violent shudder he wrenched his mouth reluctantly from hers and drew her slowly to him. They walked toward the old abandoned building, where he took her deep into its cool shadows and made love to her again as he had once before, and everything was all right again.

16

On Saturday morning, July 6, Stuart left for Columbia and Julia was glad. There were a number of reasons why she had wanted to move back to Beaufort: her parents were here, as were many of her old friends, and she liked it here much better than at Columbia, but the most important reason was that she knew Stuart wouldn't be able to stay here with her all the time. It was the hardest part of her decision, but the most important one really. She loved him so very much, yet separation was the only sure way to guard against pregnancy. As it was, she was going to have to wait out the next few weeks, anxiously wondering if it was already too late.

She didn't want another baby, not now, not ever! Stuart hadn't known about the one she had rid herself of shortly before his election last year. She had been fortunate not to have had any complications, but the thought of going through that horrible experience again and trying to keep it from him was terrifying, but then, so was the thought of carrying another baby to term. Marie and Adam were enough for her, and Stuart had been thoughtful enough to understand, trying not to bother her too much, and never coming inside of her anymore when they did make love. Once in a while though, he'd get carried away and forget, and every time he did, it frightened her. Like the night before the Fourth—he had forgotten then, and now she'd have to worry and wonder. She prayed hard that she wasn't pregnant already, then sighed, relieved that at least she wouldn't have to give herself to him until sometime in August when he came home again.

If only there was some way for him to make love to her without the worry of babies. She adored his lovemaking and missed it terribly, yet she hated being pregnant more. Yes, this was the best solution, she told herself calmly as she waved good-bye to him that morning, and when he was out of sight, she closed the door and breathed a sigh of relief.

Lizette felt differently about Stuart's leaving. She had the same fears, worrying about whether her menses would show up this month or not. But every time she thought of the lonely month ahead without him, she wanted to cry, and her only recourse so she wouldn't get too lonely was to try to make Heather's life a little happier for her, if she could. So she met her sometimes at the Chateau, where they had long talks together, and it made the month go by more quickly.

It was the first week in August when DeWitt finally learned about the baby. It had rained all the night before, and as Heather stirred in the huge bed she shared with her husband in the mansion at Palmerston Grove, she was conscious that he was still beside her. Usually by the time she woke he was up and gone downstairs already.

This morning he was still beside her, and when she opened her eyes she found him staring down at her, his hazel eyes narrowing inquisitively.

She flushed under his gaze and glanced over at the window. It was still raining. Her eyes moved back to his face and she studied his sharp features. He was unsmiling, his blond hair ruffled, and for a moment his gaze frightened her.

"Is something wrong, Witt?" she asked, her voice dulled from sleep.

"I don't know. You tell me."

She frowned.

"Heather, just how ignorant were you when we got married, and just how much do you know about babies and the like?" he asked curiously.

She flushed. "You've guessed, haven't you?" she said, trying to act innocent.

He stared at her shrewdly. "I've been waiting for you to say something. Isn't it customary for a wife to tell her husband?" he asked.

"Yes, but . . . well, at first I wasn't sure, I thought maybe it was the excitement of the wedding and all, but then in July

I started to feel rather sick a great deal, and . . . Oh, Witt, I didn't know how to tell you. We never discussed children, and besides, I wasn't certain even then. But I'm sure now, Witt," she added.

"When did you flow last, Heather?" he asked curtly. "You haven't since we've been married, I know that."

Now came the big lie. "On the twenty-sixth of May," she said hesitantly. "Just before the wedding."

A slow smile began to play about the corners of his mouth, and he looked relieved. "Well, fertile little thing, aren't you?" he said playfully.

"Fertile?"

"You evidently got pregnant on our honeymoon." He put his arms around her and pulled her close against him, a position she dreaded but tolerated. "Now, let's see, when will it be due?" he mused.

"I don't know," she said sheepishly. "I don't know how to figure those things out."

He thought for a while. "March," he said reverently. "I'd say sometime in late February or early March, wouldn't you say, Mrs. Palmer?" he asked.

"I guess it sounds right," she said, trying to act as if she was sure of herself, but wondering to herself what he was going to do when it showed up in December instead. Oh, well, she wouldn't worry about that now. This was August and she could still have a few months left to enjoy before she had to account for what she had done.

"It is right," he said tenderly, then leaned down and kissed her forehead. "Just think, I'll have a son," he fantasized.

"What if it's a girl?"

"It won't be," he said convincingly. "At least not the first. It has to be a boy, that's the way I have it all planned." He gazed down at her, his eyes shining. "You didn't know that, did you, Heather?" he said, pleased with himself. "I've been planning this ever since I first laid eyes on you. Carl threw away his inheritance when he married that weak-minded bit of fluff he called a wife, but I'm not going to lose out, not me, and someday, Heather, my darling, our son is going to be heir to Palmerston Grove and everything will be mine." And with the light of greed in his eyes, he pulled her even closer against him and began to make love to her with a violent passion that frightened her.

Sunday, August 4, was the day of the big party Felicia had talked Stuart into having to celebrate both of their birthdays, and they had decided to hold it at the senator's new home on the outskirts of Beaufort. It was a beautiful place on rolling hills, with iron gates at the entrance and brick pillars holding the gates in place. A long white fence ran the length of the property in front, with split-rail fencing bordering both sides. The house, of brick and frame, was two floors, with L-shaped wings on each side, and at the back between the wings was a conservatory. A gallery ran the length of the upstairs at the front of the house, with a colonnade beneath it, and in the middle of the house, on the roof, was a widow's watch from where you could look out over the city and Port Royal Sound in the background.

Stuart had loved the place for years, and was pleased that when he decided to move to Beaufort, it had been available. He stood now in his best frock coat of deep purple velvet, with Julia, dressed in pale yellow silk and diamonds at his left, and Felicia in white satin and pearls at his right. They were greeting the guests as they entered the huge drawing room in the east wing of the house.

He had been accepting birthday wishes from everyone and had been shaking hands vigorously as people went by, and it was no surprise when he found himself shaking hands with Everett Palmer, his sons Carl and DeWitt, and the new bride. He had seen little of them since the wedding in June except for the picnic on the Fourth of July.

He shook hands with DeWitt; then his eyes strayed to the young red-haired woman beside him. She looked lovely in pale green gauze over white satin, and he could see her family resemblance to Lizette about the full mouth. For a moment it made him uneasy. She had made a beautiful bride, and now he listened as DeWitt informed him she was going to make an equally beautiful mother. Stuart congratulated them both, then shook hands again with DeWitt before turning his attention toward the next group of people coming through the door.

Heather felt self-conscious as she held on to Witt's arm, letting him usher her farther into the room, already half full of people. She wished he hadn't said anything to any of the others about the baby just yet, because people were bound to watch her more closely now.

She remembered the day they received the invitation to the birthday party. Cole was going to be there, she was certain, and she had stared at the invitation for a long time, wondering whether to go or perhaps pretend she was ill and beg off. Lizette had told her that Cole had been courting Felicia Kolter, and even though she wanted to see him so badly she ached inside, she wasn't certain she could stand to watch him fawning over Felicia all evening.

Now she stopped a short way into the room and stood beside her husband, scanning the people already there. She didn't see Cole anywhere, and was suddenly drawn into conversation with another couple who had cornered her and Witt, pleased to see them again. She shoved thoughts of Cole to the back of her mind and tried to act natural, joining the conversation.

Outside, as the carriage she was in made its way up the circular drive in the front of the big brick-and-frame house, Lizette too had mixed feelings about being here. She wanted desperately to see Stuart, yet hated the prospect of having to contain her feelings all evening behind a mask of indifference. Her time of the month had come along as usual and she knew that worry was behind her, and she had actually managed to lose a couple of inches on her waistline for a change, so decided to be daring and had Hizzie make her a dress of deep violet lace over white satin, the neck very low-cut, sleeves slightly bouffant but short so she could show off her tanned arms. She wore white lace gloves and carried an ivory fan with violets painted on it, and had sprigs of purple and white violets adorning the clusters of curls atop her head. A satin-and-lace shawl was draped over her shoulders, and she tightened it about her as the carriage began to slow, then stopped in front of the small white-columned portico.

She watched her father leave the carriage first. He almost always dressed in a black frock coat for formal affairs, and tonight was no exception, and she realized how it made his swarthy good looks even more dominant, especially beside her mother's fair beauty. Rebel was wearing white tonight, and the contrast between the two was intriguing. She looked across the seat from her to where Cole sat waiting for his mother to finish getting out of the carriage. For a change, he wasn't wearing those ancient buckskins, but was dressed in a fancy green frock coat trimmed with the same color satin, his white trousers neatly strapped over Wellington boots, a beaver hat covering his dark hair. His green eyes were intense as she watched him, and she knew why. He had been seeing a great deal of Felicia lately, and although Lizette knew he enjoyed her company, she also knew he was still in love with Heather, and both of them would be here tonight. The prospect had made him extremely irritable, and she felt almost as sorry for him as she did for herself.

By the time they reached the large drawing room where the party was being held, Lizette's heart was pounding wildly. Others were still arriving too, and she was glad they weren't making a grand entrance; still, it was going to be upsetting. Stuart was shaking hands with one of the other new arrivals, and she inhaled sharply as she realized he too was wearing deep violet. A strange coincidence. She had learned that he had arrived home two days ago, but she had heard nothing from him. That wasn't unusual, though, since there was no way for him to reach her without someone finding out, and he couldn't take the risk.

She watched furtively as he smiled at the man with whom he was shaking hands, and then suddenly, for some reason, he glanced up and their eyes met. She held her breath as she saw the slight hesitation in his eyes, then let her breath out again as he looked away quickly, pretending nothing had happened. Lizette hoped she had been the only one to see his reaction. She had been looking for it, others weren't; so it was most likely it had gone unnoticed.

In the meantime, she tried to keep her eyes off him, and consequently Cole had to nudge her when Felicia greeted her with an enthusiastic hello. Her parents were already greeting Stuart and his wife, and Lizette hugged Felicia, wishing her a happy birthday, then took a deep breath as she forced herself to look at Stuart. He had just released her mother's hand, and he took her hand as she extended it.

"Lizette, delighted to see you, my dear," he said briskly. "So glad you could come . . . and your brother, too."

He released her hand quickly and shook Cole's hand, and Lizette meekly said, "Happy birthday, Senator Kolter," then stepped along hesitantly, shaking hands, saying hello to Julia. It was over. The worst part of the evening. Now it was just a matter of avoiding him as much as she could so she wouldn't have to worry about giving herself away.

Behind Lizette, Cole was surveying the room. He had promised Felicia they'd spend some time together as soon as she was through greeting the guests, and now his only interest was in seeing if Heather was here. His eyes faltered, then stopped as he saw a glint of coppery auburn hair across the room. The woman had her back partially turned to him, but he couldn't mistake the hint of a jawline that was visible, and a shock ran through him. He still cared, dammit! All this nonsense with Felicia, trying to let her assuage his wounded heart, and he knew it wasn't working.

He straightened as his eyes moved to the man beside

Heather. DeWitt was a strange one. For all his arrogance and conceit, he did really seem to care for Heather. That was one consolation. After some of the remarks Cole had heard Bain make about DeWitt over the years, he had a notion that DeWitt might possibly make a lousy husband, but so far, from what Lizette told him of her conversations with Heather, he was treating her well. Although once Lizette had remarked that Heather seemed a little afraid of her husband. "Not that he's ever done anything to her," Lizette had said. "But then, she's never crossed him as yet, either."

He remembered that conversation now as he studied DeWitt's sharp features. God, why couldn't things be different? He sighed as Lizette turned to him and said something, and he had to ask her to repeat it.

The evening was going quite well. Lizette was managing to stay out of trouble, but then, that was easy for her nowadays. In spite of the inches lost on her waistline, she was still being ignored by the males in attendance. However, it wasn't the other men at the party who bothered her. There was only one man she cared about, and only one who could get her in trouble, and so far he seemed to be avoiding her as much as she was avoiding him. How wonderful it would be if she could just let her guard down and not have to keep pretending.

She was standing alone and began to fan herself, sighing, turning from the others in the room, catching a glimpse of French doors behind her where the draperies came together. Making certain she wasn't seen, she slipped behind them, cautiously pushing one of the doors open a little farther, then stepped outside. Only it wasn't outside. As she stared into the darkness, then glanced upward, she realized she was in what looked like a conservatory. She had never been in Stuart's house before, and the greenhouse was a surprise.

Large tropical plants of all kinds lined the walls, and above them skylights in the roof brought in the fresh air and moonlight. This was better, much better. She began to stroll along slowly, admiring some of the flowers. There were orchids, hibiscuses, and a number of other tropical plants, including a sweet-scented frangipani. She stopped for a moment, sniffing in the intoxicating fragrances that filled the air.

It was quiet out here away from the chattering people, and she walked over, touching one of the blossoms gently, her fingers tracing the petals.

Suddenly a noise behind her made her fingers stop. She turned, startled, then saw the familiar breadth of Stuart's shoulders as he approached.

"You like my orchids?" he asked as he stopped in front of her.

"They're beautiful," she replied.

His voice dropped until it was barely a whisper. "So are you," he said.

"Stuart!"

"Don't stop me, please," he said softly. "I have only a few minutes. If I'm gone too long I'll be missed." He reached out and drew her to him, pulling her into the shadows of one of the large plants, and his lips came down on hers, sending little shocks through her. Gradually his mouth eased, but only after a long demanding kiss. "I have to see you again," he murmured, his lips caressing hers. "Tomorrow? The pirates' lair?"

"Yes," she whispered against his lips. "Yes, darling, yes."

He kissed her again, savoring her lips with a rapturous longing that made him tremble. "Now, I have to go," he said breathlessly. "But I'll see you tomorrow . . . about three?"

"About three."

The worst part of the whole evening for Cole was that he had discovered Heather was expecting a baby. The news had shattered him completely. Her marriage had been hard enough to take, knowing she was obligated to give herself to DeWitt, but it had seemed almost like a dream, and there were times when he was sure he'd wake up and discover the nightmare was over. But now the dream was over and reality was all that was left. Well, fine, he'd grab all he could out of what was left for him, and with a determination fired by passionate anger, he confronted Felicia. "Let's go for a walk," he said, his face grim.

She rolled her eyes at him. "Now?"

"Now."

"Where to?"

"Where we can be alone."

Felicia stared up at Cole. For years she had practically chased Alex Benedict, thinking he was just wonderful, then suddenly Cole had quit treating her like a little sister. He had invited her to go riding with him, had picked her up and taken her for buggy rides, and escorted her to a couple of soirees. And tonight he had been constantly at her side. She stared into his green eyes, their sloed slant making them so intriguing. She had to admit he was ruggedly good-looking in a wildly sensual way. "We can be alone in the conservatory," she whispered softly.

His eyes grew intense. "Lead me!"

She smiled mischievously and took his hand, leading him sedately across the crowded room, trying not to look too obvious. When they reached the gold draperies that hid the French doors, they both looked about furtively to make sure they weren't being observed; then Felicia found the opening in the center, pulled them back, and pushed the door open farther just as Lizette started to enter.

"Liz!" Cole gasped, startled.

Lizette tried to appear calm, but her face was flushed, eyes still warm with desire, lips still quivering slightly from the kisses Stuart had bestowed on her, and she backed up a step into the conservatory.

Felicia and Cole stepped in with her, and Cole studied her face. "Are you all right, Liz?" he asked.

"I'm fine," she said quickly, her voice breaking slightly, then smiled at them. "I . . . I was just admiring the flowers."

Cole straightened and looked behind her, his eyes searching the moonlit shadows. "Alone?" he asked.

Her face reddened. "Certainly alone," she retorted. "Do you see anyone else?"

Cole's eyes narrowed shrewdly. "Not at the moment, dear sister, but it is a possibility."

She laughed. "Oh, come on, Cole, you know very well I can't even find a man to talk to, let alone walk me in the moonlight," she said cynically. "Be realistic. I'll leave that to you and Felicia," and she moved around them, slipping in through the open French doors.

Cole stared after her, and Felicia glanced up at him. "What is it, Cole?" she asked.

He took a deep breath. "She wasn't out here alone, Felicia."

She looked surprised. "Are you sure?"

"You saw the look on her face." He smiled. "I wonder."

She sighed. "I thought you wanted to be alone."

"I do," he said huskily, and his hand reached out, grabbing hers, and he started to walk to the back of the conservatory, where the shadows were dark, the flowers smelled sweet, and he hoped Felicia could help him forget that Heather was expecting Witt's baby.

The next afternoon Lizette met Stuart at the bridge again and was in his arms the minute they reached the old stone building.

"I missed you terribly," he said as he held her against him, kissing her over and over again.

She sighed, relishing his lips on her throat, her eyes, and they sipped at her mouth until it opened, and he explored its sweetness before he once more took her into the deep shadows of the old stone building and made love to her.

Stuart didn't leave for Columbia until the first week of September, and during the month of August he and Lizette met every chance they had, which wasn't often. It was hard for Stuart to get away, and there was no way for him to send word if he did want to see her. All he could do was ride to the little stone building in the hopes she might be there, and wait. Occasionally they left notes for each other in the building beneath a loose rock so that one would know when the other would be there, and it helped. Sometimes they would make love until it was time to go, afraid something would happen and he'd have to leave Beaufort before they could see each other again. Then other times after their lovemaking they'd dress and sit in the doorway of the building and just enjoy each other's company, discussing everything except politics. Every moment was precious for them because there were so few.

Then one day Stuart said he'd be leaving again, and once more the loneliness began. Time went slowly. The leaves began to turn color, and the intense heat of summer gave way to cooler breezes.

By the time the leaves started to fall, covering the ground with a blanket of color, Thanksgiving was just around the corner, and with the races no longer running at Palmerston Grove, DeWitt had more time to spend with his wife. Heather's pregnancy had blossomed considerably, and since she was eight months along instead of five, the last few weeks had been miserable for her. More and more she found Witt staring at her curiously, although he hadn't said anything so far.

Then one afternoon, a few days before Thanksgiving, Heather put a green knit shawl on over her gray silk dress and stepped outside for a short walk. There were no formal gardens at Palmerston Grove, but there was a long expanse of lawn, and close to the house, in the back, was an arbor of honeysuckle. It was long, and there were benches inside the arbor. Heather often spent the afternoons there. Today there was a slight chill to the air, and the naked branches of the dormant honeysuckle vines looked bleak, but it was a quiet place where she could sit and get away from the rest of the household.

She had seen hardly anything of Lizette for the past two months, because since Witt had found out about her pregnancy, he had refused to let her ride Jezebel, and it was harder to get someone to ride over to the Chateau with her in a buggy. Witt wouldn't let her go unless one of the slaves was with her, and Oleander was reluctant to let any of them leave. Heather had made up her mind that she was going to ask Grandpa Roth if she and Witt could buy Tildie from him, and then she'd have a slave of her own whom Oleander wouldn't be able to order around.

Oleander was a strange woman, and the longer Heather stayed at Palmerston Grove, the more she was convinced that the dusky-skinned woman was not just Everett Palmer's housekeeper, but his mistress. The looks that passed between the two when they thought no one was around were too revealing. And another aspect of Palmerston Grove that brought a chilling suspicion to Heather was the fact that there was a large number of young light-skinned Negroes here. She often wondered: was it Everett himself, or was Carl the one? It could even be DeWitt, although since their marriage she was certain he'd had no need to turn to anyone else. His appetite for her seemed insatiable. At least it had been up until her pregnancy had become so obviously advanced. Lately, however, he had begun to treat her rather indifferently, and it had been a little over two weeks since he had even kissed her. The thought was troubling. Not that she wanted his kisses. She dreaded them more and more with each day, because no matter how hard her heart fought against responding to them, her body paid little heed to the fact that he wasn't Cole.

The thought of Cole brought tears to her eyes. She hadn't seen Cole either since the night of the party at Senator Kolter's, and the only words that had passed between them the whole evening were his stiff, formal congratulations on her coming motherhood, and he probably wouldn't even have said anything then if his grandparents hadn't been standing beside him. That night he had seemed so infatuated with Felicia, who was, after all, of marriageable age now. How damning if she had to live the rest of her life here so near to him and know he belonged to someone else. She wondered if perhaps that was why Cole was doing what he was doing—to hurt her the way he thought she had hurt him. If so, then he was succeeding, because she had never felt emptier inside.

Suddenly she straightened as she heard a door open and close, then the grating of heavy footsteps along the flagstone walk. She glanced toward where the arbor turned, to see DeWitt striding toward her. He was wearing a casual brown frock coat, white shirt open at the throat, and brown trousers tucked into top boots. His blond hair was rumpled and he carried his hat in his hand. She watched him approach, then frowned. "I thought you were going to be over at the lumber mill all afternoon," she said flatly.

He hit the side of his pants with his hat as he stopped next to her. "One of the slaves was hurt," he said. "Both of his legs crushed. We shut the mill down for the rest of the day." He glanced around. "You like it out here, don't you?"

She nodded. "It's nice. Especially when the weather's warm and the honeysuckle's in bloom. But even like this, there's something peaceful about it."

He glanced down at the huge protrusion in front of her. She was resting one hand on it, and he frowned, then sat down on the bench beside her. "Heather," he said, his eyes searching her face, "I think it's time we had a long talk, don't you?"

She stared at him warily. "About what?"

He cleared his throat. "I think I'm being taken for a fool," he said harshly.

Her jaw clenched. "What do you mean?"

"Oh, don't be so namby-pamby," he blurted angrily. "You know very well what I'm talking about." His face was hard, like granite. "I tried to believe you that night, Heather," he said bitterly. "It was our wedding night and I loved you so damn much, but I can't believe this! I'm not that stupid!"

"Witt, will you make sense," she pleaded.

He took a deep breath. "All right, I'll be a little more specific. I said you weren't a virgin, you said you were. I knew you weren't, and yet I told myself maybe there was a mistake somewhere. Well, there was a mistake," he said viciously. "The mistake was when I fell for your clever act. Tell me, my dear, if I hadn't been so eager to marry you, which other gentleman in Port Royal or Beaufort would you have hoodwinked into marrying you to give your baby a name?"

Her teeth were clenched tightly. She didn't know whether to admit anything to him or not. She stared back at him, unable to think of an answer.

"There's only one thing I want to know," he said, his thin lips pressed into a grim line. "Why didn't you just marry the baby's father? Why me?"

"You *are* the baby's father," she finally said, deciding not to give in to him.

"The hell I am!" he yelled angrily. "I've been watching you getting bigger and bigger every day. How far along were you on our wedding day, Heather?" he asked, eyes blazing furiously. "Two . . . three months?" He reached out and grabbed her wrist, his long lean fingers cutting into her flesh. "Whose is it?" he asked again, and his voice lowered ominously. "Damn it, you'll tell me or I'll—"

"You won't touch me," she cried, her eyes boring into his. "My father'll kill you if you lay a hand on me."

"Then tell me, damn it! For God's sake, Heather, I have a right to know whose bastard I'm giving a name to!"

She took a deep breath, refusing to give in to him. "The baby's yours, Witt," she insisted stubbornly. "I don't know why I'm so big. Maybe twins run in my family, I don't know!"

His eyes narrowed and he stared at her hard. He knew she was lying, and yet, unless he used physical force, she was going to hold to her lie. "All right," he half-whispered, "protect your lover, whoever he was, but I'll find out, don't you worry. If not before, then when the baby's born, because it sure as hell won't look like me, and then I swear I'm going to kill the son of a bitch!"

He let go of her wrist, throwing her hand from him as if it was filth, and he stood up.

"Where are you going?" she asked, her voice trembling.

He laughed cynically. "Do you really care, Mrs. Palmer?" he asked. "I doubt it, but for your information, I'm going to go in the house, clean up and change my clothes, then go into town, find a woman to lay, and get drunk!" and he whirled, walking off, leaving her sitting alone.

Her hands trembled as she pulled the shawl tighter around her. It wasn't cold out, yet her body felt as if it had been submerged in ice, and she was shaking all over. She wasn't going to tell him, ever, no matter what he did or how much he threatened, and all she could do now was pray that when the baby was born it would look like her instead of Cole.

She sat for a long time staring off beyond the arbor, through the dried vines, watching a couple of yellow warblers chase each other through the branches of a small oak tree, then lose themselves in the shiny green leaves of a holly hedge near the drive. Soon it would be over and all the world would know that she had been pregnant when she was married, but even DeWitt knew that in spite of the fact that the baby would be born early, no one would suspect it wasn't his, because as far as anyone knew, DeWitt was the only one courting her before her marriage. So unless the baby ended up looking like Cole, the world would never know the truth, because she wasn't about to reveal it.

The sun was shining the day before Thanksgiving and the weather had warmed again. Lizette was in the best mood she'd been in for weeks. She had received a note the day before: "I'm home, two o'clock tomorrow."

Now she stood in front of the mirror in her room, primping with her hair. She was wearing a new riding habit of rick dark brown velvet. The collar and cuffs were of fur—the latest style from Paris, so she had read in the dress shop. It did make her look older and more stylish. She was hoping the dark color would hide the two inches she had put back onto her waistline since Stuart had been away. It was probably from sitting about mooning over the fact that he was gone. She finished fussing with her hair and grabbed the hat off her dresser, fitting it neatly on top of the curls. The hat was also deep brown, with a fur brim and satin ribbons that tied under the chin.

Her eyes went quickly to the small porcelain clock on the stand next to her bed. If she didn't get started, she'd be late, and she couldn't miss him. It had been so long. She grabbed a pair of brown silk gloves from the dresser, along with her riding crop, took one last quick look in the mirror, then left the room. But when she reached the stables, no one was in sight. She stuck her head in the door and called, then listened as a voice answered from somewhere in the back. Picking up her skirts, she headed for the farthest stall in the rear, where she found Cole and Aaron putting a poultice on the fetlock of one of the horses.

"I figured someone should be around," she said as she stood watching them. "But what are you doing here?"

"What does it look like we're doing?" retorted Cole.

"I didn't mean that," she said, motioning toward the horse's leg. "I meant you. You were supposed to go upriver with Father this morning."

"I decided not to. He was leaving early and I wanted to sleep, so I've been out back helping them load the ship until Aaron here needed a hand."

"Oh." She glanced around. None of the stableboys were anyplace in sight. "Well, then, how about saddling Diablo for me?" she asked. "Since no one else seems to be about."

He grabbed a cloth from where it lay in the straw and began wiping his hands as he stood up, straightening. "Where are you bound for?" he asked.

She shrugged. "Oh, just for a ride. I thought since it had warmed up again, it'd be a good chance to get some exercise."

He stared at her riding habit, knowing it was brand new. "All right, come on," he said, and she followed him to Diablo's stall where he saddled the horse, then helped her into the saddle, handing her the reins. "Be careful riding alone," he cautioned.

She laughed. "Don't worry, I'm always careful," and she gave Diablo a quick nudge to get him started, then headed down the drive.

As soon as she was out the stable door, Cole turned quickly and headed for his own horse in another part of the stables where he'd had her saddled and waiting. When he had mounted, he called a quick good-bye to Aaron, then left the stables.

At first he hadn't planned to follow her, but the temptation was too great. He had been home late yesterday afternoon when his sister received the message from town and had seen the look on her face when she read it. She said it was from Felicia, but he didn't believe her. He had had a suspicion for a long time, ever since the party at the Kolters', that she had found herself a beau, and he was dying to find out why she was keeping it such a secret. He had left the room right away after she received it and managed to catch the young man who brought the message, but it didn't do any good. The boy said another boy had given it to him to bring, and that the first boy got it from yet another boy who had three gold pieces and said they each got one if they saw to it the message was brought out to a lady named Lizette at the Tonnerre plantation. "I don't know where it come from, mister."

Lizette had gone straight to her room after getting the message, and later last evening, while she was down in the sewing room having Hizzie help Pretty put finishing touches on the riding habit she was wearing today, Cole stole up to her room and searched it until he found the note tucked into the pages of a poetry book; then he made up his mind that he was going to find out once and for all what the hell she was up to.

He kept behind her now all the way as she rode the dusty road downriver past River Oaks. When she reached the Chateau, she spurred her horse into a quick canter, riding by as fast as she could, as if hoping to get by without being seen.

Cole did the same, then reined in so she wouldn't see him. It was hard to stay back far enough to keep out of sight, yet not lose her; however, as a precaution, he had used a file this morning and marked a deep gouge in one of Diablo's shoes to ensure that even if she did manage to get too far ahead, he could still find her.

It wasn't until she stopped at the bridge to look around a few minutes, then headed across it and cut off the road into the woods, that he realized where she was headed, and he knew if he followed her too closely on the trail she'd surely see him. So instead, he waited until she was out of sight, then hurried across the bridge, heading for another way in that he knew. It was longer this way, and he knew she'd reach the old stone building before he did, but it was the only way he could approach without letting her know he had been following. When he knew he was within a few hundred yards of the building, he reined up, tied his horse to a tree, and went the rest of the way on foot.

It didn't take long to reach the place he was looking for, and he climbed up, lying on his stomach on top of a large boulder that overlooked the whole area. Moving forward a little, he raised his head slightly, peeking over the top of the huge boulder. It was quiet, but not deserted. Two horses were ground-reined a short distance from the front of the building, and that meant she was inside already. He'd just have to wait. He wasn't about to barge in on them; all he wanted to know was who, and why she was keeping it a secret.

His arms crossed beneath his chin, and he rested it on them, preparing to wait it out. The sun grew hotter as the afternoon wore on, and it was like sitting in a deer blind. Occasionally a bird would land nearby, eye him curiously, then fly off. From inside the crumbling stone building he'd hear an occasional laugh, sometimes light and airy, other times low and vibrant, but most of the time it was quiet, except for a few outcries that were all too telltale of what was going on. He should stop it, but that wasn't what he'd come for. He continued to wait.

The warmth of the afternoon made him drowsy and a couple of times he almost nodded off. He must have been there well over an hour when suddenly Lizette came to the doorway, stretching her arms high as if reaching for the sun. Then she lazily began fastening the buttons on the front of her riding habit, which had been open wide, revealing her chemise. Her hat was no longer on her head and her hair was disheveled, but she didn't seem to care. She buttoned the last button, then turned toward someone who stood in the shadows.

Cole strained his eyes, but all he could see was the vague outline of a man; then, as he continued to watch, squinting, a hand shading his eyes so he could see better, the figure moved forward and he almost gasped out loud as he watched Stuart Kolter grab Lizette playfully, twirl her around in his arms, then stop, kissing her hungrily.

It had been a long time since Stuart had felt so carefree. When he was with Lizette, all his worries fell away. All he cared about was seeing the light in her eyes and feeling the warmth of her near him. Now he drew his head back and looked down into her eyes. "I'll be leaving the day after Thanksgiving," he said unhappily. "The new session of the Senate convenes in Washington December 2, and I have to be there."

She clung to him desperately. "But it's so lonely when you're gone."

"I'll be back."

"When?"

He sighed. "We'll have a short vacation over Christmas, and I've already made plans to sail home. That's one advantage of living in a port town. I can get here quicker by ship than overland, but even then it'll only be a few days."

She reached up, touching the side of his face. "Then today's the only day we'll have until Christmas?"

"I'm afraid so." He kissed her again, then gazed hungrily into her eyes. "I wish I could take you with me," he whispered softly.

Her eyes lit up. "You could," she said eagerly. "I could go to Washington—we could travel separately, and you could find a place for me to stay where we could be together."

He shook his head. "It wouldn't work," he exclaimed unhappily. "I wish it would, but there's too much risk for both of us. I couldn't let you take the chance. Besides"—he smiled, his teeth gleaming against his deep russet beard—"if you were there, I'd never have my mind on my work. As it is, I think about you more than I should." His eyes softened. "Just let it be like it is now. Don't let it change, love," he said. "I need you."

Her eyes glistened passionately. "Then I'll be here, if that's what you want."

He drew her closer in his arms and kissed her again hungrily, while Cole watched from above them on the boulder, still in a state of shock. He couldn't hear what they were saying, but it was more than obvious that they were lovers. He watched them separate, and Stuart went back into the building, bringing out her little fur trimmed hat and his own high beaver hat. Lizette straightened her hair, then tied the hat on while they talked some more. Then, before saying good-bye, they kissed again, a long lingering kiss that brought heat to Cole's loins as he watched and made him feel guilty for even being here. Then the senator put his arm around Lizette's waist, walked her to her horse, and helped her into the saddle. She leaned over, kissing him once more; then, without looking back, she dug her horse in the ribs and headed back down the trail that led to the road.

Stuart watched her go, then mounted his own horse, but instead of following close behind her, he moved slowly, giving her a good head start so that by the time he reached the road she'd be out of sight ahead of him.

Cole saw Stuart's horse disappear down the trail, then sat up and shinnied down from his perch on the rock, his mind still reeling from what he had just seen. Senator Kolter and his little sister? It didn't seem logical. Yet he had seen it with his own eyes.

He took a deep breath as he hit the ground, then stood up, heading toward his own horse. Lizette was crazy to get mixed up in something like this. How long had it been going on? As he reached his horse and mounted, he remembered the night of the birthday party. Had Lizette been in the conservatory with Stuart? He also remembered the flushed look on her face and knew the answer almost before he finished asking it. The crazy fool! Why? It didn't make sense. He clenched his jaw stubbornly and headed back down the trail he had taken earlier, trying to decide whether he had a right to interfere or not.

17

Lizette arrived home from her rendezvous with Stuart later than she had planned, but by the time she reached Tonnerre she had accepted the fact that she wouldn't see him again until the Christmas holidays, and even then they'd have to snatch whatever moments they could.

She stood in her room now, fixing her hair. They were all supposed to go down to the Chateau this evening and stay overnight, having Thanksgiving dinner there the next day. Their bags had been sent down earlier, and Lizette was almost ready to go downstairs and join the others when there was a knock on the door.

"Who is it?" she called.

"It's Cole."

"It's open."

Cole stepped into the room.

Lizette finished putting the small emerald teardrops in her earlobes, then put a little perfume behind each ear while Cole watched her.

In the mirror she saw the way he was studying her. "What's the matter, something wrong with the dress?" she asked.

His eyes narrowed. "Not exactly."

She turned. "You haven't stopped by just for a chat in a long time."

"Maybe I should have," he said.

"What's that supposed to mean?"

"It means I think you and I should have a long talk."

"About what?"

He took a deep breath, his green eyes steady on her. "Stuart Kolter!"

Lizette froze. The carefree tilt to her full red lips disappeared and her face paled. "I don't know what you're talking about," she replied, her voice shaking unsteadily.

"You don't have to lie, Liz," he said. "I followed you today."

"You what?" she yelled in disbelief.

"I said I followed you!"

"You had no right!"

"How long has it been going on, Liz, two months, three?" he asked angrily. "He's only been here since the first of June, or did you meet him while he was down here looking for a house?"

"It's none of your business when I met him!" she countered.

"For God's sake, Liz," he cried, his eyes filled with rage. "Whatever possessed you?"

"Whatever possessed me?" she asked furiously, and tears were rimming her eyes. "Look at me, Cole," she cried. "Take a good look at your little sister." She gestured down her figure with both hands. "She's not so little anymore, is she?" she said. "You don't like what you see, do you? I've never seen you courting a girl who weighs anything near what I weigh. Men don't like fat women, you included, and you know it! They have some strange notion that we don't have hearts under all this fat." The tears flooded her eyes now. "Well, I do. I hurt and I feel, and I can love like anyone else. And yes, I can enjoy a man's arms just as much as I did when I was thin. The fat doesn't make me a female eunuch, you know!"

"Nobody said it did."

"They don't have to say it," she ranted angrily. "They shout it every time they snub me at a dance." Her dark head tilted stubbornly. "Well, Stuart didn't snub me," she said, choking back the sobs. "He doesn't care that I'm not slim and sylphlike. He makes me feel alive, and that's more than I can say for any other men I've met for a long time, and I think I deserve love as much as anyone else, including you!"

"But he's so much older than you!"

"I don't care. He loves me and I'm not just existing anymore!"

"Damm it, Lizette, he's a married man!"

"You think I don't know that?"

"So what happens if you get pregnant?"

"Then I'll do the same thing Heather did," she yelled angrily. "Marry the first man I can find who'll have me, even if I have to lie to do it!"

Cole's mouth fell open and he stared at her, stunned. He tried to breathe, but for a second the air just wasn't there; then suddenly he gasped breathlessly, "What did you just say?"

Lizette stared at him, her eyes wild, the tears still clinging to their corners, and suddenly her mouth quivered as she realized what she had done. "Oh, God, Cole," she cried miserably, "I'm sorry. I . . . I didn't mean . . ."

He strode toward her, grabbing her wrist, holding it so she couldn't get away. "Repeat it!" he demanded through clenched teeth.

She shook her head. "Please, Cole. I didn't mean it . . . I . . . You heard wrong."

"No I didn't," he said heatedly. "You said you'd do like Heather did and marry the first man you could find who'd marry you." His eyes darkened. "Is that what Heather did, Liz?" he asked. "Is it?"

Her eyes filled with tears again and she wanted to die. "I promised!" she pleaded.

"I don't care what you promised. I want the truth. Heather's pregnant. Was she pregnant when she married Witt?"

She bit her lip, her eyes pleading with him. "Please, Cole . . ."

His sloe eyes grew wildly savage. "Damn it, Liz, I have a right to know!" he yelled furiously, trying to keep his voice down. "Was Heather pregnant when she married Witt?"

She inhaled sharply. There was pain in Cole's eyes and she didn't know what to do.

"The truth, Liz," he went on, then added viciously. "Either you tell me the truth right now, or the whole world's going to hear about you and your precious senator!"

"No, Cole, you can't!" she gasped, half-shrieking.

"I can and I will!"

"Cole!"

"Was she?"

"Yes," she finally whispered unwillingly, giving in to his threat. "Yes, she was pregnant."

He was breathing heavily, his heart pounding. "And the father?" he asked.

"Cole, don't do this, please," she begged.

"It's mine, isn't it, Liz?" he said.

She nodded reluctantly. "Yes," she answered, her voice unsteady. "She didn't want you to know."

His fingers eased on her wrist and as he dropped it, she saw his jaw tense, the lines in his face deepen. Without another word he turned and headed for the door.

"Where are you going?" she called unsteadily.

He stopped with his hand on the doorknob but didn't answer.

"I said, where are you going?"

"Don't worry," he called back. "Your secret's safe with me, little sister. I won't tell on you and your precious senator!" and with that he left the room, slamming the door behind him.

Cole was incensed. He was going to be a father and Heather hadn't even wanted him to know. He practically ran down the stairs, meeting his father at the bottom.

"Is Liz ready yet?" Beau asked.

Cole's eyes snapped. "Who cares!" He brushed past his father and headed for the front door, grabbing his hat from the rack.

Beau frowned. "Where are you going?" he asked. "We're almost ready to leave."

"I'll ride down by myself and meet you there," he called back.

"But we've made plans to go together. Your mother's waiting—"

"Tell her I'm not in the mood for a carriage ride. Tell her anything you want," he barked furiously.

Beau's eyes darkened. "What's the matter with you?" he asked heatedly.

Cole glowered. "Nothing, Father," he said bitterly. "At least nothing you'd want to know," and he walked out, banging the door shut loudly behind him while Beau stared after him.

It didn't take Cole long to saddle his little piebald mare, and just as the rest of them came out the front door, he was disappearing down the drive.

"Are you certain you don't know what's gotten into him,

Liz?" Beau asked his daughter as they started down the front steps.

Lizette stared after Cole, her insides fluttering like butterflies. "I'm certain," she answered stiffly. "Cole doesn't confide in me much anymore, nor I in him. Who knows, maybe he had a fight with Felicia."

At first Cole rode fast through the dark night, the warm breeze hitting his face. After a while he slowed to a walk and let the full impact of Lizette's confession sink in. He was going to be a father.

For a few moments he allowed himself to think back to that night at Tonnerre when they had shared their love. So wildly free, so wonderfully new. From that night had come the baby she was going to have. A baby DeWitt Palmer was going to claim as his. Suddenly the warmth drained from Cole and he shuddered at the thought of his child having a man he hated for a father. He couldn't let it happen! And yet . . .

His jaw tightened furiously as he realized that his hands were tied. He swore out loud. If she had only told him. Maybe under the circumstances everyone would have relented and let them marry anyway. He reached up and felt his throat. And then again, maybe they wouldn't have, and bastardy was a hanging offense.

He rode along, running the whole thing over in his mind, trying to understand why Heather had refused to tell him. It was obvious, really. She had known he'd never let her marry Witt under the circumstances, and yet she didn't have the courage to leave with him and start somewhere else. Damn her! he cried silently to himself.

A short while later, when he reached the intersection where the main road branched off toward Beaufort, he suddenly stopped, staring down it.

Palmerston Grove was down that road. Palmerston Grove and Heather. He stared for a long time, then suddenly reined his horse to the left, and instead of heading for the Chateau, urged the little mare on toward Palmerston Grove, his face set with determination.

Cole had passed no one on the road so far, and now he reined his horse over toward the side of the road where Palmerston Grove property began. When he reached the lane that led back to the racetrack, he turned onto it, riding easy in the dark until he reached the clearing where the deserted buildings stood. They looked bleak and forlorn this time of year, and the absence of a moon made them seem even more so. As he looked about, he could almost imagine he could hear the shouting and excitement that lingered here even after the season was gone.

He straightened in the saddle, shaking his head to clear it of the old memories, then veered off to the right down another lane he knew led past the slave quarters and toward the house.

The house looked quiet. Bright lights glowed from the kitchen area, and he assumed the servants were getting things ready for Thanksgiving dinner the next day.

He wanted so badly to talk to Heather, but how? He had no idea which room was hers, or where she'd be in the house if she wasn't in her room. He frowned as he stared at the place, every nerve in his body tense, alert. He was so restless he felt like he could explode.

Suddenly he straightened, eyes straining as he saw movement in the back at one of the doors. Watching intently, he saw a figure step into the light from one of the windows, and his jaw clenched as he recognized DeWitt's familiar walk. Cole frowned as he saw Witt stroll purposefully down the walk toward him. He held his breath, hoping his little mare wouldn't decide to give him away.

Curious, wondering what Witt was up to, Cole waited until Witt was far enough past him so he wouldn't hear the creak of the saddle; then he dismounted, tying his horse to the fence. He moved along the fence, then bent down and ran swiftly across the road toward the slave quarters, where he flattened himself quickly against a tree. He scanned the shabby buildings and spotted Witt quickly. There weren't too many people around, and Witt's white shirt and blond hair were easy to pick out among the slaves.

There was a small hut in the middle of the cluster of shacks, and in the bright light from the lamp in its window, he saw Witt stop and say something to a young black woman sitting on a bench beneath it. Cole couldn't see her face, but he could see Witt's, and the man's eyes were hard. Witt said something else and reached down, pulling the woman to her feet, and Cole saw that she was younger than she had looked at first, her body slight but full.

He saw Witt put an arm about her waist, and a minute later they disappeared into the shadows at the side of the building, moving off toward the barn.

Cole took a deep breath. He had heard rumors about the Palmers. Tonight left no doubt in his mind that they were true, and he wondered if Heather knew about it. Remembering Heather, he glanced back toward the house. If he could just get close enough. It was obvious DeWitt was going to be busy for a while. There was an arbor at the back of the house, and he eyed it anxiously. Lamps in the windows of the house cast enough light that he could see it was long, the leafless vines covering it, thick.

He glanced back toward where the slaves were, then straightened against the tree. He'd never know unless he tried. He pulled on his coat cuffs nervously, then hesitated for just a second before crouching down and starting to sprint quickly across the drive, up onto the lawn. He reached the vine-covered trellis and ducked beneath its tangled web. He glanced about cautiously. The backyard was still quiet and deserted. Turning toward the house, he made his way to the far side of the arbor, looking out between the bare honeysuckle vines. If he could just get into the house.

Inside, Heather watched Oleander straighten the roses in a vase on the middle of the dining-room table, then check the good silverware for the next day. The dark woman looked up and saw Heather standing in the doorway to the room. She pursed her lips, resenting Witt's wife, knowing that when Everett Palmer was gone DeWitt's wife would be mistress of the house, and she'd be relegated to taking orders from her, and she wasn't used to taking orders from anyone except Everett. She had made her mind up years ago when he had bought her as a young girl of sixteen that she wasn't going to end up in the fields, and she hadn't. She had learned to survive by using her body, but DeWitt was a young man, and when Everett was gone, he'd go to the young girls out in the shacks rather than to her. Just like he was doing now.

Her eyes rested on Heather's big belly and she smiled to herself. So the snooty young lady hadn't been all that innocent before her marriage. Five months! She was eight if she was a day. Her eyes shifted to Heather's face.

"You look tired," she said, her voice showing little emotion. "Why don't you go in the parlor and rest awhile. Or better yet, tomorrow's going to be a big day. It's not too early to retire."

Heather sighed. "It's warm outside. I think I'll go out and sit in the arbor," she said wearily. "By the way, did you see where DeWitt went?"

Oleander's eyes narrowed slightly. "No, ma'am," she said.

"Then I think I will go out," Heather said, and walked through the dining room, past Oleander, into the kitchen, and on to the back door.

Cole saw a movement at the back door and froze, leaning into the side of the arbor, hoping he wouldn't be seen. He didn't know who might be coming out, and held his breath; then his heart began to pound as the lights from inside the kitchen fell across Heather's red hair, bringing it into fiery relief. As she turned toward the arbor, her stomach was in full view, and he felt a strange warmth as he saw how large it was pushing out beneath the folds of the pale green embroidered muslin she had on. To him she looked beautiful.

A tree between the house and arbor cast shadows into the other end of the arbor, and Cole moved deeper into them as Heather began walking toward the arbor.

She was strolling slowly, favoring her stomach, gazing off toward the slave quarters, and he wondered if she knew where Witt was. He watched her reach the arbor and start through it, her feet barely making a sound on the flagstones. She reached the bench and sat down.

It was so peaceful here. Heather thought back to the argument she had just had with DeWitt upstairs in their room. He had accused her again, and again she had refused to admit anything; then, when he had tried to make love to her, anger rather than ardor behind his passion, she had frozen him out with indifference, and he had become infuriated, shouting at her that he didn't need her, that he could get what he wanted whenever he wanted it, and she had stood at the window a few minutes later, watching his shadowed figure head across the lawn. She knew where he had gone, yet it was strange, she didn't care. He could go to them whenever he wanted, and she'd welcome it.

She leaned her head back against the latticework of the arbor, then suddenly jerked it erect as a noise from deep in the shadows brought her to attention.

"Heather?" Cole whispered breathlessly, not wanting to frighten her.

She strained her ears, her eyes searching the darkness, hardly able to believe she was hearing right. "Cole?" she questioned softly.

He crouched low, moving out of the darkness, and dropped down beside her on the bench, his hands grabbing hers quickly as he spoke. "Shhh! I don't want them to know I'm here," he whispered.

She stared at him in wonder, letting him hold her hands close against his chest, and suddenly tears filled her eyes. It was the first she had been this close to him for months, and her heart fluttered wildly.

"I have to talk to you," he went on, keeping his voice low. "Can we talk here?"

She finally found her voice. "Witt's outside somewhere," she answered.

He nodded. "I know, but he'll be busy for a while. Where are your father-in-law and Carl?"

"They went away earlier this afternoon. Should be home anytime now."

He glanced toward the drive. "I'll keep watch." He squeezed her hands, then looked into her face, his eyes meeting hers. "Why didn't you tell me, Heather?" he asked tenderly.

She bit her lip. "Tell you what?" she asked, unsure of what he meant.

"Heather, I still love you," he whispered fervently. "I always will. If you had just told me about the baby, we could have worked something out."

The tears that had rimmed her eyes rolled onto her pale cheeks. "Oh, Cole, who told you?" she asked helplessly.

"Never mind how I found out," he said. "The important thing is that I know." He frowned. "Why didn't you tell me?"

"I couldn't." Her heart warmed as she looked into his green eyes, seeing the love that was still buried there.

"We could have gone away, just the two of us. There's a big world out there to hide in."

Her eyes lowered. "I'm a coward, Cole," she whispered. "I could only think of what would happen if people found out. I couldn't let that happen to you, Cole. I love you," she said.

"So you sold yourself to DeWitt!"

"He asked and I accepted. I thought it would solve everything."

"Has it?"

"No." She sighed. "He knows I'm farther than five months. So far he's done nothing except threaten, trying to get me to tell him who the father is, but I'm so afraid sometimes. Like tonight. He started to raise his arm once and I thought for certain he was going to hit me. I don't know what stopped him . . . he had such hate in his eyes." She trembled. "I'm afraid, Cole," she said helplessly. "He says he'll kill the father when he finds out."

"He doesn't have to know."

"And if the baby looks like you?" She pulled her hand from his and reached up, touching the side of his face. "How could you deny a son or daughter if he or she has eyes like yours?"

He grabbed her hand, bringing it to his lips and kissed it, then reached out and took her face in both his hands. "And if it has red hair and looks like you?" he asked.

She tried to smile, but his lips stopped hers in a softly sensual kiss that made her whole body ache with want of him.

He drew his head back and reached down, putting a hand on her stomach just as the baby kicked. His eyes widened. "It moved," he whispered.

She nodded and put her hand over his. "It does that all the time." She felt it kick again and knew he felt it too. "Oh, how I wish I could tell the world it was your child," she said passionately. "I love you so terribly much, Cole," she went on. "I wanted to tell you so badly. You don't know how hard it's been for me to watch you courting Felicia when I wanted your heart to belong only to me."

"Oh, my love!" he cried softly, and this time his arms closed tenderly about her and his mouth found hers waiting eagerly.

It felt wonderful to be in his arms once more, but as his kiss deepened, neither of them saw DeWitt step out of the shadows at the far end of the arbor.

He had finished with the slave girl quickly and had decided to come back to the house to try once more to get the truth from Heather. And now here he was listening to the truth—listening in disbelief. Cole! No wonder she was so reluctant to name her lover! His mouth trembled as he stepped forward, and his voice cut into their embrace. "Well, well, well! What a remarkable display!" he snarled explosively.

Cole's head jerked up, his lips leaving Heather's abruptly, and he held her back, trying to shield her in the crook of his arm.

Witt laughed viciously. "Cousins!" he yelled angrily, his eyes blazing. "I should have guessed! Damn me for a stupid fool!"

Cole stood up, standing between DeWitt and Heather, and once again DeWitt realized he had to look up to Cole, and in spite of his anger and the threat to kill the father of Heather's baby, he backed off. "I might have known you'd be the one," he said angrily as he stared at him. "I always knew you were perverted!"

"There's nothing perverted about it," said Cole defensively. "I'd have married her, but they wouldn't let us."

"So instead you told her to trick me into marrying her just to give your bastard a name."

"It was my idea, Witt," Hearther burst in. "Cole didn't even know the baby was his until tonight!"

"Liar!" Witt's eyes were cold, deadly.

"She's not lying," Cole said furiously. "If I had known, you'd never have gotten your hands on her."

"Oh, no? What would you have done, Cole?" he asked. "Or have you forgotten that they hang men for bastardy?"

Cole's eyes narrowed. "We could have left the Carolinas," he answered. "I'd have taken her away, anything rather than let her marry you!"

Witt laughed. "That's funny," he said, mouth twitching nervously. "That's really funny. I knew you didn't have any scruples, Cole, but I just never realized before what a low snake you were."

"What are you going to do?" Heather asked anxiously as she studied her husband's face, remembering his threat.

Witt's eyes bored into Cole's as he ran her question through his mind. What *was* he going to do? What could he do? If he called him out, the whole world would learn he had been made a fool of; if he didn't, if he just let him leave and pretend the child was his . . . There was a chance the little bastard would look like its mother and not its father. "What do you want me to do, my dear wife?" he asked.

"Nothing," she gasped breathlessly. "Please, Witt. Cole and I never meant to fall in love, it just happened. We never meant for any of this to happen."

He stared at her, the hatred so strong in his soul he wanted to strangle her, yet his hands were tied. There was nothing he could do, not without jeopardizing his reputation, at least not at the moment. Cole Dante would pay, that he silently vowed, and he'd pay with his life, but tonight wasn't the time. It had to be done in a way that wouldn't involve him. No, tonight he'd do nothing except make the man crawl.

Witt's mouth twisted into a sneer. "So I'm supposed to be the accommodating husband, is that it?" he said. "All right," he went on in a quiet, deadly tone, "I'll be the forgiving husband, but I swear, Cole Dante, if you ever so much as talk to my wife again, I'll see you hang for bastardy whether my wife likes it or not. Is that understood?"

Cole wanted to grab Witt by the throat and wipe the sneer from his face, but he felt Heather trembling against him. Bucking Witt wouldn't help her, and she was too close to her time. The best thing he could do tonight was walk out of her life, at least until the baby was born. Then maybe they could run away where Witt would never find them.

Cole straightened and started to say something.

"I said get out!" yelled Witt, trying to keep his voice down so the household wouldn't hear. "Get out of my sight, and don't ever set foot on Palmerston Grove again!"

Cole glanced down at Heather, his eyes worried. "You'll be all right?" he asked.

She nodded, anxious for his safety, knowing that Witt was close to losing control completely. "Yes," she said softly. "Now go, please, before he changes his mind."

Cole looked at Witt, his green eyes steady. "I'm going, Witt," he said reluctantly. "But not because of your threats. I'm going because Heather is in no condition to go through any more pain. But, by God, you'd better treat her right, or so help me, I'll come back and kill you!"

Witt's eyes narrowed viciously.

Cole stared at Witt for a brief moment, then stepped past him and disappeared into the darkness.

DeWitt watched over his shoulder until he heard the faint creak as Cole hit the saddle, then he turned to Heather and they stared at each other while they listened to Cole's horse galloping down the lane.

As soon as the hoofbeats faded into the night, Witt stepped toward her, his eyes blazing. "You slut!" he yelled furiously. No one was around to stop him now. "You damned whore!"

Heather cringed under his outburst, her hands automatically spreading over her stomach to protect it.

"I should have known!" he cried, his eyes wild with rage. "I could kill you for what you've done to me!" and before she had a chance to see it coming, he thrust out, smashing his hand across her face. Her stomach retched as his hand flew across her face again, and she felt a gush of blood from her nose.

She choked, sobbing, and a shriek tore from her lungs as his hand came at her again, missing her face this time and catching her shoulder. She raised her arm, trying to ward him off, but it was ineffectual. He was too strong.

What DeWitt had no way of knowing was that the farther Cole galloped down the lane toward the racetrack, the more he began to worry about the savage look he'd seen in DeWitt's eyes. He had seen that look before on men who were ready to explode, and it bothered him. He urged his little mare off the road onto the grass where she'd make less noise, then turned and headed back toward the house. He reined up at the same spot as before, and just as he hit the ground, he heard a shriek of pain. He ran for the arbor as Heather screamed again.

Cole wasn't the only one who heard Heather scream. The servants in the kitchen stopped what they were doing, staring at each other in startled bewilderment, but it was Oleander who ordered them to keep working as she moved to the back door and slipped outside. She reached the end of the arbor just as Cole crashed into Witt from the other side and grabbed him by the shirt, pulling him off Heather and driving a fist into his gut.

Witt, taken completely by surprise, lifted his arms, swinging his elbow, trying to keep Cole away, but it did little good. Cole was taller and more powerful, and with one quick thrust he gripped Witt's clothes, lifted him halfway off the ground, and threw him bodily against the other side of the arbor, where he crashed through the trellis, falling backward. Suddenly Witt's eyes opened wide, mouth gaping, and he let out an agonized scream.

Cole breathed deeply, waiting for Witt to move, but all he did was groan, his arms twitching slightly.

Oleander let out a shriek and rushed toward Witt, dropping to her knees beside him, and stared in awe as she saw the bloody tip of one of the pieces of splintered lattice sticking up through a tear in his shirt. Witt was impaled on the broken lattice, but he was still alive. Oleander leaned down, trying to talk to him, telling him to lie quietly. "I'll get the others to help," she said quickly.

His face was contorted with pain, but he gasped, voice raspy. "No," he cried fearfully. "Must listen . . . Cole . . . Heather . . . lovers!" The words spewed forth in vicious gasps. "The baby . . ." He choked some, then went on, his voice faltering with the unbearable pain. "The baby . . . not mine . . . Cole's . . ."

Oleander leaned close, her eyes hard on his face, her fingers reaching for his hand, holding it in hers as she stared at his broken body.

Witt sighed. "Tell Carl . . . my . . . my father . . . he threatened me. He . . ." Suddenly Witt began to choke again, and this time his eyes rolled up in his head as a trickle of blood flowed from the corner of his mouth. He made a few gurgling sounds, then went limp.

"He's dead!" yelled Oleander as she set Witt's hand down and turned, staring up at Cole and Heather, who'd been watching her. "You killed him!"

"He can't be dead!" yelled Cole. He couldn't see the piece

of lattice poking through Witt's chest. "I didn't hit him that hard!"

"He broke the lattice and a piece went clean through him," she stated grimly, and stood up, staring at Cole. "Only he told me, you heard him," she went on, her eyes shifting angrily from one to the other, then settling back again on Cole. "He told me about you and his wife and the baby . . . and you gonna hang, Mr. Dante," she said. "You killed Mr. Witt, and they gonna hang you!"

"No!" cried Heather. "It was an accident. He didn't mean to kill him!"

"But he did! Mr. Everett and Mr. Carl gonna be home real soon now, and they gonna see you gets yours, and I'm gonna keep you here till they do." She started toward the house, calling to someone.

Heather looked up at Cole quickly. "Oh, my God, Cole! She'll get the other servants. You've got to get away," she cried.

"But I can't leave you here."

"Yes you can." She looked back toward Oleander. "I'll be all right. They won't do anything to me, but she's right. Everett Palmer won't be satisfied until he sees you hang."

"Heather!"

"Go, Cole, please . . . hurry!" she begged. "Get out of Port Royal, go as far as you can, then send word to me when this has all quieted down. Please, darling, quickly, before she gets back. I hear them coming already."

Cole knew she was right, yet had to tear himself away. He took one quick glance at Witt's body, broken on the lattice, then kissed her quickly, oblivious of the blood from her nose still on her lips, and he took off into the dark shadows at the other end of the trellis as Oleander reached Heather, the rest of the servants beside her.

Heather sat down on the bench again in relief as she heard the hoofbeats from Cole's horse fading in the distance. She was in a daze. Blood covered the front of her dress, and a little still seeped from her nose. She lifted her hand and felt the side of her jaw. It was swelling as she touched it, and her eye hurt too. In fact, both eyes had received the full brunt of Witt's hand, and her head was throbbing. Then suddenly, as she licked her lips, trying to moisten them because they felt parched and sore, she felt a pain begin deep in her loins, roll up into her belly, and her belly constricted hard. Her eyes widened and she gasped with pain, letting it wash over her; then she began to cry huge salty tears as another pain followed close behind it. The baby wasn't due yet for almost two weeks. It couldn't come now. Oh, God! She needed Cole. It couldn't come now!

By the time Everett Palmer and Carl arrived back at Palmerston Grove to see Witt's body hanging on the lattice in the arbor, it was covered with a sheet from one of the beds, and upstairs, Heather had given birth to a little boy. Although he failed to breathe on entering the world, and got no help from those around him, babies have a miraculous way of surviving on their own, and in spite of the fact that Oleander told Heather the baby was dead, it was a lusty-lunged, squalling bundle that Everett Palmer took secretly from the house that night, down the lane to the slave quarters, where the sloe-eyed baby joined a small dark child at the breast of a black woman. Everett wasn't about to let Cole Dante's son present himself to the world as his grandchild, and the tiny casket that would be buried in the small cemetery at the far end of Palmerston Grove next to his supposed father, unbeknownst to Heather, was to contain only rocks.

Cole's heart was pounding as he reined his little piebald mare down the lane, past the silent racetrack, and toward the road. He hadn't wanted to leave Heather, but she had been right. No one would give thought to the fact that he was protecting Heather from Witt. All they would care about was that there had been a quarrel and Witt was dead. And what chance would he have in the courts? A lover innocent and the husband guilty? That was a laugh! Just by loving Heather he was guilty. My God, what was he going to do?

He reached the cutoff and reined up, trying to decide which way to go. Downriver to the Chateau to let his parents know, or upriver to get his things? He chose the latter. Digging his mare in the ribs, he took off at a fast gallop, and in spite of the darkness, reached Tonnerre in record time.

Aaron was in the stables as he rode in. "Now what did you do, boy?" he asked as he saw the look on Cole's face.

Cole was still breathless from the hard ride. "I really did things up right this time, Aaron," he said, choking on the words. "This time I killed a man."

Aaron stopped stark still and stared at Cole. "You're lying boy!" he exclaimed.

Cole shook his head. "I wish to God I were, Aaron," he said quickly. "I didn't do it on purpose, but no one's going to believe me."

"How can you be sure?"

"Because it was DeWitt Palmer!"

Aaron's eyes narrowed knowingly. "Where will you go?" he asked.

Cole shrugged. "I don't know, leastways not right now." He handed his horse's reins to Aaron, then headed for the door. "All I want to do now is get far enough away where they can't put their hands on me."

Hizzie was still up when Cole burst into the house, and the first thing she did was question him on why he wasn't at the Chateau. "And why are your clothes like that, Cole?" she asked as he headed for the stairs.

He gazed down into Hizzie's dark eyes. He couldn't lie to her. Besides, Aaron would only tell her the truth when he was gone. He reached out, taking her hands in his and his eyes softened. "Hizzie, I'm in trouble," he whispered gently. He squeezed her hands. "I've killed Heather's husband." He saw the fleeting pain in her eyes. "It was an accident, but the law won't care."

"Oh, Lordy!" she gasped. "Oh, Lordy!"

He pulled her to him and hugged her, remembering all the times she had done the same for him when he was feeling bad.

"I'm going away, Hizzie," he said quickly. "I don't have much time . . . I don't know how soon they'll be coming for me."

She hugged him against her, his big lean frame so different from that of the little boy she had cradled as his wet nurse. "You go, then," she said hurriedly, and pushed back so she could look up into his face. "You get your things from your room, child," she said firmly, the tears resting in her eyes. "I'll get you some food to take along. And when you get to where you's goin', you let us know." She squeezed his arms. "Your mama don't know yet, does she?" she asked.

"No."

"You gonna have time to go by the Chateau?"

"I'm going to try." His hands clasped her shoulders. "Now, I've got to hurry, Hizzie," he exclaimed.

She nodded. "Yes, yes. And I'll hurry too. You come through the kitchen when you get your things. Now, hurry, child, hurry," she said.

Cole ran up the stairs three at a time. Half an hour later he was on the road again, dressed in buckskins this time. He rode fast, yet was cautious. It had been two hours since he had ridden out of Palmerston Grove, and he had no idea if the authorities had been alerted yet.

When he reached the cutoff into town, he stared down it straining his eyes, but saw nothing. Good, no sign of them yet. He still had a little more time. A quick flick of the reins, and he galloped on downriver, past River Oaks, until he finally turned into the gates of the Chateau, where he could see the lights were still on in the parlor.

Inside the huge plantation house, Lizette was fidgeting nervously as she paced back and forth across the parlor floor. Both of her parents were angry with her, and she didn't blame them. She had refused all evening to tell them what she and Cole had quarreled about.

Rebel sat on the sofa beside Beau, her violet eyes snapping with anger as she stared at Lizette, trying to reason out what they could have been arguing about that could have upset Cole so badly that he would disappear like this, making them worry. And Rebel was worried. She ran her hands across the skirt of her bright red dress and looked over at her husband. "I think you should have gone looking for him," she said heatedly.

Beau shook his head. "He's a grown man now, Reb," he insisted. "He's twenty-one, not a child. He'd never forgive me if I went chasing after him."

"But you said he was upset."

"He was."

"And you know why, young lady," she said, addressing Lizette.

Lizette stopped her pacing and stared at her mother, but it was Loedicia who spoke.

"Don't be too hard on her, Rebel dear," she said quickly. "Maybe Cole made her swear to secrecy. You know how brothers and sisters are."

"I'm sure Dicia's right," said Roth, hoping to help soothe things over.

Heath stood by the front window with one arm about Darcy where they had been watching the drive. Suddenly he turned and smiled at Rebel. "Well, you won't have to wonder any longer, sis," he said, nodding toward the window. "Your errant son just rode up the drive as if the devil was on his tail."

Rebel sighed. "Thank God!" She turned and faced the door, waiting, trying not to appear too anxious, and they were all staring at the parlor door a few minutes later when Cole rushed in.

He stopped on the threshold, his eyes wildly alert, and Loedicia knew right away something was drastically wrong. She gasped in dismay. "What happened, Cole?"

They continued to stare at Cole, waiting.

"DeWitt Palmer's dead!" he stated bluntly, and the silence in the room was frightening.

"My God!" cried Beau, staring worriedly at his son. "How?"

Cole's eyes darkened. "I killed him!"

Rebel screamed, and for the first time since it happened, tears welled up in Cole's eyes as he realized he wasn't leaving just Heather behind—he was leaving everything behind.

"Witt was hitting Heather," be began to explain, his voice shaking. "I couldn't stand it. I didn't mean to kill him . . ."

Rebel's legs were shaky, but she stood up, moving toward her son, and flung herself into his arms, burying her face in his buckskin shirt as tears rolled down her cheeks. "Oh, God, Cole, why?" she asked helplessly. "Why did you ever go there?"

"I had to, Mother," he answered softly, then took her by the shoulders and looked into her face. He saw the puzzled look in her eyes, then glanced over to Lizette. "You didn't tell them?"

She shook her head. "I didn't know if you wanted them to know."

"They have to know now!" he replied, then looked down into his mother's worried face. "The baby Heather's expecting is mine," he said softly, and saw the startled look on her face as everyone else gasped incredulously.

"Yours?" she stammered.

"My God!" Heath cried, staring at his nephew. "What have you done, Cole?"

"I loved her, Uncle Heath!" Cole cried helplessly. "I still do," he tried to explain to him. "I didn't mean to hurt her."

"What did I tell you!" shrieked Darcy. "Didn't I tell you this would happen!"

"Shut up!" Heath demanded angrily. "For heaven's sake, Darcy, let's find out what this is all about." He looked at Cole, beseeching him. "What did you do to my daughter, Cole?" he asked hesitantly.

Cole swallowed hard as he stared at his aunt, then looked to his Uncle Heath. "All I did was love her," he whispered tearfully. "And she me." He turned to his father. "It happened that night up at Tonnerre," he said softly. "But I never knew about the baby until today, I swear, Father. I had to go see her, and Witt found us together, and . . . It was an accident. I only meant to stop him from hitting Heather, but the trellis broke and he fell on it."

"He knew about you and Heather?" asked Beau.

"He overheard us talking, and he told Everett's housekeeper before he died." Cole looked weary. "They'll never believe I didn't kill him on purpose, Father, to silence him from charging me with bastardy."

"If only I had stopped you and Heather in time," said Beau, frowning.

Heath stared at Beau, his face troubled. "You knew about this, Beau?" he asked.

"I knew they were in love, yes."

"For how long?"

Beau flushed. "Since the morning I caught Cole coming from her room while she was visiting," he answered.

"And you said nothing?"

"What was there to say?" He grabbed Heath's arm. "The damage was already done, Heath," he said quickly. "I didn't know she was already pregnant. I thought I had stopped it in time, and I had Cole's promise that there would be no more."

"His promise!" cried Darcy. "Oh, my poor Heather, why didn't she tell me?"

"Because she knew you wouldn't understand," said Lizette from behind her.

Darcy whirled around. "Not understand? Why wouldn't I understand?"

"Because she loved her cousin and no one seems to understand," she said. "Would you have let them marry?"

Darcy's eyes fell before Lizette's bold gaze. "No . . . I guess I wouldn't have," she said.

"Nor would my parents. What else was she to do? You loved Uncle Heath and could have married him. Heather loves Cole, but was denied that right. Except for one night, she wasn't even allowed to admit she even cared. And why? Because the world says it's a sin to love your first cousin. Well, tell me, which is the worse sin, for her to love her cousin or give herself to a loveless marriage and subject Cole to a life without her? Damn it, Cole," she cried, her eyes filled with tears. "I tried to talk her into telling you and going away with you. I wanted you to know, and now I'm sorry I didn't tell you."

"What will you do?" asked Loedicia, staring at her grandson, tears rimming her eyes.

"I won't stay here to hang!" he cried. "I've already been up to Tonnerre, and I have all my things. I only stopped to say good-bye."

"Good-bye?" cried Rebel, and her hand flew to her mouth.

"You can't go," she cried miserably. "Oh, my God!" She turned to the others. "What are we to do?"

"Where do you intend to go?" asked Beau.

He shrugged. "I don't know. Anywhere."

"You'll never get out of Port Royal," said Roth quickly, then straightened, nodding his silvery head toward the back of the house. "Take the ship," he said, and Loedicia looked relieved.

Roth called for Mattie, who was usually puttering around somewhere until all hours. "Go find Jacob," he said when the big black woman hurried to him. "Tell him to run to the dock and alert Captain Casey. I want the ship ready to cast off as soon as possible. We'll be down to the pier shortly. Is that understood?"

Mattie nodded, then disappeared down the hall.

Roth turned again to Cole. He was only a step-grandson, but Roth loved him dearly, and he wasn't about to have him hang for the likes of DeWitt Palmer. "I'll give Casey instructions to take you wherever you want to go," he said. "But think on it. Remember it's winter up north. You may want to stay in the south."

"You brought your horse?" asked Beau.

"She's in the stables."

"I'll get her," he said, "and meet you all down at the pier. You're going to need a horse when you hit land again."

Heath stared at Cole, watching the bewildered look on his face. Now, after listening to Cole and Lizette, and searching his own heart, his initial outrage vanished and he felt sorry for him, for both Cole and Heather. Heather loved him, and knowing her the way he did, he knew she'd never forgive him if he didn't help Cole. He looked at Darcy. Her face was pale, and he knew she had been shaken too, but he also sensed that she didn't want Cole hurt any more than he already was. He looked at Cole; the young man's eyes were dark, intense.

"I love her, Uncle Heath," Cole said again unsteadily.

Heath reached out and took Cole's hand, squeezing it. "I just wish the two of you had come to me when this all started. Maybe we could have worked something out. But that's neither here nor there now. The important thing is that you need help. Cole, there's a friend of mine, his name's Eli Crawford. He should still be around out there. He can usually be found this time of year trapping up on the Scioto River. Have Captain Casey drop you off down near Savannah and head up the Savannah River into the Chattahoochee.

When you reach there, set your sights dead north. If you manage to keep your horse, you should be able to reach him in about a month. He's about twenty miles north of a small settlement called Franklinton where the Scioto and Olentangy rivers meet. The settlement's on the west back of the Scioto, and if you stay along the riverbank, he'll be easy to find. He's got sandy hair and a beard. I'll tell you what to look for on our way down to the ship. In the meantime . . ." He straightened, and looked over at Beau. "I've got warm skins upstairs. He can take them with him," he said. "He'll need them up there."

"You think you can do it, Cole?" asked Beau.

Cole nodded. "I made it home from New Orleans, didn't I?"

'This is different, son," said Beau. "You're not used to the cold, and you knew where you were headed then."

"And I know where I'm headed now. Just make sure Everett Palmer doesn't find out."

Heath went upstairs, and Beau left for the stables, while they all headed for the foyer, giving Cole advice, and Roth went into the library, bringing some money from his safe. "Here, take this," he said, handing it to Cole. "It might come in handy."

Cole tucked the money into a leather pouch tied about his neck, then tucked the pouch back beneath his buckskin shirt, and a few minutes later Heath joined them, carrying a wolfskin robe and fur leggings laced into a roll so it would fit with Cole's bedroll behind his saddle.

"Do you have food?" asked Loedicia anxiously.

He nodded. "Hizzie stuffed my stomach full, then insisted I take a whole bag of food."

She smiled at him, trying to hide her tears, as they all headed for the back door and started down the walk. They met Beau halfway to the ship, leading Cole's piebold mare.

Rebel was crying, and so was Loedicia. Even Lizette could hardly see where she was going. She thought back to their argument earlier this evening, wishing now it had never happened, knowing if it wasn't for her own indiscretions, she wouldn't have gotten angry and blurted out the truth, and Cole wouldn't be running for his life now.

When they finally reached the ship, silence settled over all of them for a moment. Then slowly Cole began to say his good-byes. It was hard to do, worse than when he had left for the war, because he knew he was leaving them to face all the scandal and talk.

"Watch over Heather, Mother," he whispered softly. "See if maybe she can leave Palmerston Grove and have the baby at Tonnerre or the Chateau. You wouldn't really mind having her at Tonnerre, would you?"

Tears streamed down Rebel's face. "I'll love the baby like my own, Cole," she answered anxiously.

He kissed her, then turned to each of the others. His father was the last, and Cole hugged him hard, then took the reins of his horse, tied the bundle onto the horse's back behind his bedroll, and turned quickly, heading for the gangplank. He turned the mare over to one of the men on deck, then watched as the gangplank was pulled on board.

He moved to the rail and stood quietly, searching the darkness, barely able to make out the vague outlines of his family standing silently waving good-bye. The rigging creaked, the sails unfurled, and Cole felt the ship give a heave. Then, as the wind hit the sails, snapping them briskly, the ship lurched again and they were on their way.

18

Thanksgiving Day of 1816 was one of the most puzzling in Port Royal's history. When the sun broke on the horizon, it brought with it a sadness Heather had never dreamed she could ever experience and live through.

The first thing they told her was that her baby had been born dead; the second was that Cole Dante had disappeared with a price on his head, and when caught, would be hung for murder.

Oleander had told Carl and Everett Palmer everything she heard from DeWitt's lips only moments before he died, but the authorities were never told. Instead, they were told that Cole Dante had forced his way onto Palmerston Grove property, attacked his cousin, beating her savagely, then killed her husband when he tried to protect her, and the results were that she had lost her baby.

Both Beaufort and Port Royal were up in arms. Cole Dante was Roth Chapman's grandson, and Roth and Cole's father, Beau Dante, were two of the most respected planters in the area. To think that Cole would attack his own cousin was heinous enough, but killing her husband on top of it. Most people just shook their heads in disbelief, and it wasn't until wanted posters with Cole's name on them began circulating about town that they accepted it as fact and not simply rumor.

DeWitt Palmer was dead. His funeral was the day after Thanksgiving, but his widow was too ill to attend, and her infant son, not even having been named, was buried beside his father at the same time. There wasn't a dry eye at the gravesides, nor was there anyone from either Tonnerre or the Chateau. It hurt Loedicia not to see her great-grandson laid to rest, but it hurt more to know her grandson was being blamed for the child's death, and a few days after the funeral, with Darcy by her side, she decided it was time someone brought the nonsense to an end.

Roth wanted to join her, but she said no, feeling that a man's presence was more intimidating, so shortly after lunch the first week in December, her carriage, driven by Jacob, turned off the main road to Beaufort and moved up the winding drive at Palmerston Grove. She was angry and upset, and with good reason. Twice Heath and Darcy had ridden to Palmerston Grove to see Heather, and twice had been turned away. She wouldn't be.

For all her dainty looks, she carried a pistol in her reticule, a fact she had neglected to tell Roth, and it was loaded. When the carriage stopped, she motioned to Darcy, and Jacob helped them both out.

"Are you sure we're doing the right thing?" asked Darcy timidly. "Maybe we should have brought one of the men."

"Nonsense," stated Dicia, her violet eyes sparking with anger. "Now, come along!"

The skirts of Loedicia's deep violet walking dress swished briskly as she headed toward the front door of the long rambling house, her daughter-in-law at her side. Darcy's face was pale beneath her red hair. As they reached the veranda, she dropped a few steps behind Loedicia, who grabbed her arm and pulled her forward. "You must be up beside me, Darcy, dear," she said quickly as she pounded with the doorknocker. "After all, you're Heather's mother."

The door was opened by a tall black servant with white hair, who looked like he had been at Palmerston Grove for centuries. Loedicia didn't even wait for an acknowledgment from him, but simply walked in past him, with Darcy at her side.

"Who's there?" called a voice from the library.

The servant looked perplexed. "It's two women, sir," he said unsteadily. "They came in before I had a chance to tell them otherwise."

Everett Palmer stuck his head out from the library, then straightened, grabbing his black frock coat off a chair beside the door inside the room, and he slipped it on as he hurried toward them. "What are you doing here?" he asked curtly.

Loedicia fumed. "Good God, Everett, what else would we be doing here?" she said angrily. "I've come to see my granddaughter."

His chin tilted stubbornly. "You can't see her."

"Her orders or yours?"

"Hers!"

"Liar!" She straightened, trying to look taller. "I intend to see my granddaughter, Everett," she insisted. "You have no right to keep us away."

"The doctor has given strict orders—"

"Rubbish! I talked to the doctor in town yesterday, and he said she's perfectly capable of receiving visitors. That it would do her good."

"I can't let you go up."

Loedicia's eyes narrowed, and she reached into her reticule, her hand curling about the handle of the pistol she carried there. She lifted it out firmly, holding it aimed directly at Everett.

His eyes widened. "You don't really think that thing is going to frighten me, do you?" he asked.

"It should."

He laughed. "In the first place, Loedicia Chapman, if you kill me, you'll be joining your grandson on the gallows, and in the second place, you wouldn't have the courage to pull that trigger."

She smiled. "Try me!"

"Don't be ridiculous. You don't really mean you intend to kill me?"

"Did I say that?" she asked. "No, I don't have to kill you, Everett. Did you ever see what a bullet in the knee can do to a man, or how neatly it can shatter an elbow?"

"You mean you intend to wound me?" He snorted in disbelief. "That's attempted murder."

"Is it? Not when I know what I'm doing."

"I'll bring charges. You wouldn't dare."

She laughed, a light laugh filled with malice. "Have it your way, Mr. Palmer, if you insist," she said smugly. "But I don't think sending me to jail will compensate for ending up without the use of your legs. I have two bullets in this gun, one for each knee, and at this close range I'd hate to think of the damage that could be done. Now"—she lowered the pistol so it was pointing at his right knee, and cocked it—"do I see my granddaughter, or do you end up with two useless legs?"

Everett stared at her, his eyes narrowing. She meant it. She really meant it. He could tell by the look in her eyes. He swallowed hard, then cleared his throat. "You win," he said stiffly, and turned to the slave, who was still standing waiting to be dismissed. "I'll take them up," he said.

Loedicia took a deep breath. It had worked. Of course, there might be repercussions over it, but she'd let Rand Kolter handle that for her. The important thing was that she and Darcy were going to see Heather. She kept the pistol in her hand until they reached the room; then, as they entered, she slipped it quickly into her reticule again, where Heather wouldn't see it.

Neither Darcy nor Loedicia was prepared for what they encountered in Heather's room. The shades were low, and they had to strain their eyes to see.

Heather was lying against the pillows, staring at the ceiling. Some of the swelling had left her eyes, but the bruises hadn't, and they were now a purplish yellow with small blackish-red streaks running through them. Even her nose was one huge bruise. She was awake, but her eyes had little life in them, as she looked up at them. "Mother?" she asked.

Darcy reached out, taking Heather's hand. "My dear . . . oh, Heather . . ." She started to cry.

"We'd have been here sooner, Heather," Loedicia said, "but your father-in-law said the doctor didn't want you to have visitors!"

"But I wanted you here," Heather said feebly. "I prayed and prayed you'd come." She licked her lips. "He hit me," she said, tears welling up in her eyes. "Did you know he hit me? That's why Cole hit him—"

"She doesn't really know what she's saying," Everett cut in sharply. "I'm afraid we've had to give her laudanum, and it's made her mind a little hazy."

"Liar," said Loedicia, looking across the bed to where Everett stood. "She knows very well what she's saying. Your son did this to her because he found out she was expecting Cole's baby. All Cole did was try to protect her."

"Tell it to the magistrate, then, if that's what you think," said Everett, challenging her. "He'll never believe you. You see, Oleander has already sworn, as have all the other servants, that it was Cole who did it."

"Has the magistrate heard it from Heather herself?" asked Loedicia.

"There's no need. It's all been taken care of."

"I know," said Loedicia. "I know exactly how it was 'taken care of,' as you put it."

She watched Darcy and Heather as they talked, trying to think of something she could do to help. There was no way they could move Heather when she was in this condition, that was certain, but she disliked leaving her here with these people. Everett Palmer had a way of being intimidating, and Heather was in no condition to stand up to him. Loedicia bit her lip, thinking. Suddenly she looked across the room. "Mr. Palmer," she said thoughtfully, her eyes unyielding. "I've noticed that you don't have a full time servant with Heather, and she should have someone with her at all times. I assume you can't spare one, so I'm going to send her personal maid over as soon as I return to the Chateau. She's experienced with sick people, and will be a big help."

"There's no need, Mrs. Chapman," he said irritably.

She brushed his protest aside. "Nonsense," she said stubbornly. "Might I remind you, Mr. Palmer, that I carry the pistol in my purse at all times. Don't buck me in this or I assure you I'm not afraid to take my chances in jail just to see you having to crawl for the rest of your miserable life."

Everett stared at her hard. The woman was insane! But clever. And she was just reckless enough to carry through her threat. All right, let her send over one of her slaves; he'd control her the same as he did Oleander and the rest. "If you wish," he said quickly. "Now, as I said, my daughter-in-law needs rest."

They talked for a few minutes longer; then Loedicia could see Everett was right: Heather did need her rest. "We'll be back, my dear," she said as they both kissed her, then left, but as they walked slowly down the stairs, with Everett Palmer following at their heels, Loedicia was quite sure she wasn't going to be allowed inside the front door again.

Roth was furious when they returned to the Chateau and he learned about Loedicia's escapade, but he was even more furious when told of Heather's condition, and that evening Tildie, bag and baggage, was sent over to Palmerston Grove. At first Loedicia worried that perhaps the young slave girl would be sent back, but Everett had kept his word, and she took up her duties nursing Heather back to health.

As the days went by and the search for Cole proved fruitless, life in Port Royal and Beaufort began to settle back to a semblance of normalcy. Christmas came as it did every year, but there was no laughter with it this time. Both Loedicia and

Rebel tried to have things go on as usual, but nothing was the same. Houses were decorated, presents bought, but the joviality that had always lifted their spirits this time of year was missing.

Friends tried to sympathize but didn't know what to say. Some believed the vicious way the Palmers had twisted the truth, others felt Cole had been justified in what he did. Rumors ran rampant, and no one seemed to know what the truth was.

The only bright part of the whole Christmas season for any of them was when Stuart arrived home. But even his coming couldn't cheer Lizette completely. As she lay in his arms once more in the little stone building, and gave herself to him with a wild abandon, made even more keen by their long weeks of separation, she felt guilty because she was here and Cole was somewhere away from his love, without hope of ever seeing her again.

Stuart tried to make Lizette feel better, and he did for those few precious moments they were together, but before the new year set in, he had to leave again, and once more she was alone.

There was no ball on New Year's Eve this year for the Dantes to attend, nor the Chapmans either. They had been invited, as usual, but declined, preferring to spend a quiet evening at the Chateau, where they toasted the new year of 1817 alone, hoping it would be better than the last. While the others raised their glasses in the parlor, Lizette stood on the terrace by herself, listening to the ringing bells up and down the river and wondering where Cole was and what he was doing.

Cole had spent Christmas Day making his way slowly through the Cumberland Gap, and now, as the new year was getting ready to dawn, he found himself heading north toward a settlement called Portsmouth, where the Scioto flowed into the Ohio River. It was a long way yet through what used to be Shawnee territory, and the farther north he rode, the colder it was getting. Although the sun was shining, the air was crisp and the ground hard beneath his mare's hooves. Dark clouds were rolling in from the west, and he expected the sun to be gone by noon, with snow before nightfall.

For almost a week now, he had been wearing the fur robe Uncle Heath had given him, but hadn't put the leggings on yet. The furs were warm, sometimes too warm, but today he huddled down into them a little farther than usual, hoping the beard he was growing would be thick enough by the time the weather got really nasty.

So far, the journey had been without incident. Now he rode along, his eyes scanning the trail for a sign of any kind that might show someone ahead of him. There was nothing. Few people were foolish enough to head into this territory this time of year. Farther south he had crossed the trail of a good many wagons heading west, settlers moving into territory that had once been the Indians' exclusive domain.

It was surprising sometimes how he forgot that he was part Indian too. It was times like this that reminded him. He had a feel for the wilderness, a sense of belonging that somehow seemed to be missing when he was back in civilization. Except when he was with Heather. He thought of her as he rode along.

The baby would have been born already. Would it be a son or a daughter? He couldn't imagine himself having a daughter. They were such fragile little things. It was probably a boy.

It was late afternoon, and he hadn't realized how intently he'd been daydreaming as he rode along until he heard voices up ahead and suddenly reined in, staring ahead on the trail.

There was a passel of boulders to one side; then the land beyond it sloped downward. Beyond the drop-off he could hear shouting occasionally, then silence, then voices again, but he couldn't distinguish what was being said. Cautiously he pulled the horse to a stop and left the saddle, rubbing her nose to reassure her. He moved forward stealthily, hugging the boulders, then stretched his body out, neck extended as he looked down the incline toward a valley up ahead. Off in the distance, at the foot of a hill, was a group of about eight or ten men. They had oxen hitched to ropes and chains, and they were trying to pull the stump of a large oak from the half-frozen ground.

He gazed farther out across the valley, toward where a small river wound its way through the trees, disappearing into the distance. There was a cluster of log buildings a short distance from the river, with a few cleared fields nearby. It was a small settlement, perhaps on its second or third year. Cole had purposely been avoiding any settlements, but if he'd kept track of the days right, it should be New Year's Eve. A time no man likes to spend alone. Besides, his staples were getting low. He might be able to buy some cornmeal, and it had been weeks since he'd had a fresh egg. His eyes wandered to where a few hens scratched in the hard ground not far from one of the houses. From here they looked like ants.

Reaching out behind him, he whistled softly for his little mare, then felt her hose hit his hand. He turned back to her and leaped into the saddle once more, just as a few flakes of snow began to drift down from the dark clouds overhead.

The men below had been yelling at the oxen and arguing about which way to pull the stump, pushing and tugging, and at first as Cole rode in, they were oblivious of him. Then suddenly one of the men spotted him and reached toward a rifle leaning against a nearby tree. He lifted it quickly, cocking it, and pointed it toward the trail as Cole reached the edge of the clearing and all of them stopped what they were doing.

"That's far enough!" the man hollered.

Cole reined up. "No need for the rifle," he called over, settling lazily onto the saddle. "As you can see, mine's still on my back. I come in peace."

The man eyed him dubiously, while the others stared warily. "Where'd you come from?" the man asked.

"South. I'm up from Savannah. Heading toward the Scioto."

"You're a half-breed!"

"Not exactly," answered Cole, a little miffed at the man's remark. "My father was Tuscarora and French, my mother English. I'd say that makes me American."

The man studied him hard for a minute. "All right, ride in," he finally said, and Cole nudged the mare, easing her forward toward the group of men as the snow began to fall a little heavier. "The name's Baldridge," the man said when Cole reached him. "Nate Baldridge."

Cole leaned down, offering his hand. He had decided when he left Port Royal that he'd have to use a different name. "Duke Avery," he said convincingly.

The man studied him curiously. "You come a long way," he said. "I ain't never been to Savannah, but I know it's a lot warmer down there this time of year. What brings you north?"

"Business," said Cole, knowing the man was combining his curiosity with small talk.

"Well, I guess you look all right," said Nate, rubbing his chin. "And you sound like a gentleman, in spite of the beard and all." He motioned the others over, introducing them.

Cole dismounted and shook hands all around. He was sure he wouldn't remember all their names, but two of them did stand out. They were Nate's sons. Ezra and Ezekiel Baldridge were obviously twins. They were about the same height as Cole, but stockier, with grips like iron, their hair a plain brown, but with beards almost as red as Heather's hair. They appeared to be close to Cole's own age.

By the time they had finished shaking hands, it was snowing so hard you could hardly keep your eyes open against it. Nate seemed to be the leader of the group, and he ordered the others to unhitch the oxen and head back to the barn before it got any worse. There was one huge barn where they all kept their livestock in out of the weather, and six cabins, one larger than all the others, where Nate's family lived.

"We all stayed here when we first arrived," he said as he ushered Cole in. It was almost like a tavern inside, with a huge fireplace at one end, a kitchen at the back, and all but one of the sleeping rooms upstairs. "Been here a year and a half," he said easily. "Built this here place the first spring, and this is the second year for crops. It's been a good year." He closed the door behind Cole and ushered him inside, while Zeke and Ez stayed out at the barn helping bed down the livestock to weather the storm. "This here's my wife, Fiona, and our daughter, Lily," he said introducing Cole.

Cole nodded to them both, noticing when he did that Lily looked to be about the same age as Liz, maybe a trifle younger, and was rather plump. She smiled at him flirtatiously, trying not to be too obvious in front of her parents, but her big brown eyes held just a hint of interest. Cole frowned. It had been a long time since he'd held a woman in his arms. He brushed the thought aside quickly as Fiona Baldridge, a well-rounded woman with graying brown hair, asked if he was staying for a while.

Nate brought her attention to the fact that it'd be getting dark in another hour or so, and with a blizzard kicking up its heels, he'd be a damn fool to go on. So Cole consented to stay the night, settling down to supper with them when the boys returned from the barn, and since it was New Year's Eve, according to the calendar Fiona had made and hung on the wall, their neighbors were walking over tonight for a visit.

As Cole waited for supper, he glanced about the cabin. There was a small fir tree in the corner with pine cones painted red and white, some strings of popcorn, and a couple of fancy store-bought ornaments Fiona had probably brought with her from back east. Over the fireplace were some pine boughs with red velvet ribbons, another luxury Cole figured Fiona had salvaged from her other world, and in the center of the boughs was a small porcelain figurine of an angel. The rest of the log cabin held only the bare necessities, the furniture a mixture of handmade benches and tables alongside fancy chairs with needlepoint seats and carved legs. It was obvious that they had saved little from their previous life.

The meal they fed Cole was the best he'd had in a long time. Cabbage, potatoes, some pork from a pig they had brought with them and slaughtered, and dried-apple pie, all washed down with cider. Then later in the evening, as the other five families joined them, there was more food, including cakes, strudels, and homemade bread and smoked ham from the newly built smokehouse down near the barn.

The older women quilted, the younger women, including Lily and seven other girls ranging from eight to about twenty, had a taffy pull, and three young women with small babies sat in a corner of the room discussing their children's latest accomplishments. The men whittled, played checkers, and Zeke and Ez entertained them on a guitar and fiddle. Sometimes they sang songs, most of the time in unison; then occasionally one of them would sing by himself.

Cole watched it all with interest but didn't join in. Finally Lily slipped over to sit beside him. "You're mighty quiet," she said as she gazed up at him.

He sighed. "A few memories . . ." he said, and his voice broke on the words.

"Pa says you talk like a southern gentleman. I never met a southern gentleman, so I wouldn't know. We're from New York originally. The city, that is. Pa and my brothers were in the army, and when they came home, Pa said he heard there was land out here just for the taking. Ma didn't want to come, but Pa made her." She smiled demurely. "I miss the city, 'specially at Christmastime. This year was our second Christmas out here, and it just doesn't seem the same."

"I know what you mean," said Cole, and he was remembering last Christmas, his first Christmas home from the army.

"Pa thought you were a half-breed when you rode in," she said innocently. "You are part Indian, aren't you?"

He nodded.

"That must be something. I hear tell the Indians around here were real bad just a couple years back."

"Don't fool yourself," said Cole quickly. "There are still a few disgruntled Indians about." He didn't want to scare her, so he added, "But you're right—most of them have moved farther west."

"Is that where you're going?" she asked.

He looked down at her, sensing the warmth in her voice. "I might, eventually," he said.

They talked for a while, and the friendly atmosphere took some of the edge off the anger that still burned inside him. Lily was easy to talk to, and reminded him a little of Heather in her innocence.

They all toasted in the new year with a bottle of blackberry wine Nate had made for the occasion, then one by one the families left for their own cabins, and the huge log house settled down for the night.

They gave Cole one of the upstairs bedrooms to sleep in, and it was the first time he'd slept in a bed since leaving home.

He stayed with the Baldridges two days, while the storm swirled around them. He helped the men with their chores, and swapped tales of the war with them. It wasn't until the night before he left that he realized Lily had started to form an attachment for him. He had tried to treat her the same way her brothers treated her, but had inadvertently been more charming. Her brothers never carried the water for her, or helped her carry in the wood, or complimented her on her cooking or the way she fixed her hair. To Cole, these things came naturally. They always had. To Lily they were like salve on a wound. There were few men out here to court her, and unfortunately she didn't like any of them; therefore, Cole was the answer to all her prayers.

The snow stopped shortly before dark on his last evening with the Baldridges, and as the dark clouds that had been overhead for the better part of two days moved on, they left behind a full moon, with the temperature slowly dropping at nightfall. The family had been sitting around the fire, letting the warmth from the flames make them drowsy, when Fiona remembered she had promised Ezra's wife she'd send an extra blanket over tonight, because their little one had complained the night before about being cold. Ezra and his wife and little boy had their own cabin at the edge of the clearing, not too far from the barn.

Fiona poked Zeke, who was stretched out on a quilt before the fire, staring into the flames. "Here, take this to your brother," she said, a patchwork quilt bundled in her arms.

Zeke gazed up at her reluctantly. "Why didn't Ez come get it earlier?" he complained. "I don't feel like movin'."

"I'll take it over for you, Mrs. Baldridge," offered Cole, who had been sitting at the table working on his horse's bridle, repairing one of the leather straps that had been ready to break in two. "I have to take a walk down to the barn and check out this halter to make sure the fit's all right anyway. I'd hate to get ready to leave in the morning and discover it won't fit over her ears. I'll be glad to take the quilt over."

"You sure you don't mind?" asked Fiona.

He insisted he didn't mind at all. "The fresh air will do me good."

Lily had been sitting at the table watching him. "May I go with you?" she asked.

He eyed her curiously. "It's cold out there."

"I know," she said. "I love to walk when the snow crunches under my feet."

"Then come along," he said. "That is, if it's all right with your mother."

Fiona had no objections, although she did make sure Lily bundled up.

"She's always afraid I'm going to catch something," Lily said as she and Cole left the cabin, heading across the snow-covered path that led down the row of cabins. "That's because my sister, Rose, died from a fever the first year we were here. I tried to tell Mother it was because she was sickly in the first place, but you probably know how mothers are."

"How old was Rose?" he asked.

"Two years younger than I am."

"So that made her how old when she died?"

"Fourteen." She eyed him curiously. "Why didn't you just ask how old I am," she said, "if that's what you wanted to know?"

He smiled. "A gentleman never asks a lady's age, Lily," he replied seriously.

She flushed. "I wouldn't know. I've never met a gentleman before," she said. "Besides, you don't look much like a gentleman, Duke, in that old fur robe, beard, and all."

Cole laughed. "I guess I don't at that," he said.

They didn't go in when they reached Ezra's cabin, just handed the quilt to Ezra at the door, along with some biscuits Fiona had made for morning and sent along. It wasn't far from Ezra's place to the barn, but the snow had drifted in places during the storm, and paths had been shoveled through the drifts.

Cole stepped into the dark barn, then sighed. "I forgot a light," he said as he stood looking around.

"Want me to go get one?"

He shook his head. "No need," he said. "You stay here and make sure the door stays open. I know her stall. It'll only take a few minutes to fit the bridle on. I can do that in the dark."

He moved farther into the big barn. Moonlight coming in at the door gave just enough light so he could make out his little mare. After tapping her gently on the rump to move her over, he stepped to the other end and felt in the dark, slipping the bridle on over her head, fitting it over her ears, checking to make sure the strap wasn't too long or too short.

"It fits fine, doesn't it girl?" he whispered softly to the mare, and she nickered. He gave her a few extra pats as he took the bridle off, then hung it up on a peg near the saddle and started for the door.

Lily was standing outside, leaning against the huge door while she gazed before her at the beautiful moonlit night. She could see her breath on the air, but she wasn't cold. Not deep inside. She was thinking of Duke. There were so few travelers who passed this way, and none like him. Most of them were old men with teeth missing who smelled to high heaven. Duke was different from any man she'd ever met before, and she loved the lazy way he talked.

She glanced toward the open doorway as she heard a noise, then watched Duke walking toward her. He was so tall and lean. Her eyes softened as he strolled up and stopped, looking down at her.

"You look cold," he said.

"I'm not." She straightened. "Do we have to go back yet?"

He caught the plea in her eyes. "I guess not," he answered. "You don't want to just stand here, do you?"

"We could go up to the loft in the barn, and open the door and see the whole valley," she said, her voice hushed. "It'd be warmer up there, if you're cold."

"I don't think that would be a good idea," he said quickly.

She flushed, her voice low. "Why not?"

"Let's just say that haylofts have a way of getting too comfortable." He nodded outside. "Since you're not cold, we could take a walk."

"Could we go to the hill?"

He knew where the hill was. It was the hill he had come down the first day he rode in, and the huge boulders he had ridden around were the start of a natural formation of small caves.

"All right," he conceded. "Let's take a walk to the hill."

They shut the barn door and followed a line of trees, trying to keep out of the large drifts that had blown onto the trail. The night air was crisp, snow crunching as they walked, and Cole marveled at its beauty. He had never seen snow like this before. At home it rarely snowed, maybe once or twice every couple of years, and then barely enough to show on the ground. This was facinating, like a beautiful painting.

"Are you sure you're not cold?" he asked Lily, trudging along beside him.

She shook her head. "I love to walk in the snow. Especially on a night like tonight. I remember once back when we lived in the city. I had to go out after dark on a night like this to run some errands for my mother, and I don't think I ever saw the city looking so pretty. It had snowed earlier in the day, and the moonlight made it look like something in a dream. Even the people riding by in sleighs didn't look real." She hesitated, then went on. "But the next day, when the sun came out again, it didn't look any different than it ever was. Like here." She glanced about them as she struggled through the snow. "Tonight it looks so . . . oh, so beautiful, and tomorrow after you're gone, it'll be the same old place again."

"What does my going have to do with it?" he asked.

She avoided his eyes, looking straight ahead at the rock formation looming before them in the moonlight. "It won't seem the same with you not here," she said. "I'm glad you came along." They reached the caves, and she stepped into the edge of one, then looked back out at the still night. There was even a myriad of stars overhead, bright and clear. "Why do you have to go?" she asked suddenly.

Cole took a deep breath, staring out at the same fairy-tale world, so quiet and stark. "You don't know anything about me, Lily," he said softly, knowing why she had asked him.

"Does that matter?" she said.

He drew his eyes from the scene before them and looked down at her. The moonlight was on her face, and she looked so much like a little girl, with her fur hat tied beneath her chin and a scarf about her neck to keep the cold out. Then, quite abruptly, she looked up at him, her big brown eyes softening seductively, and he knew she wasn't a girl, but a young woman in full bloom, just waiting for the right man.

"It matters when I tell you I already have someone, Lily," he said.

"Is that where you're going?"

"That's where I've been."

"You left her?"

"It's a long story, one you wouldn't want to hear."

She frowned. "Do you love her?" she asked.

"Very much."

"Will you ever see her again?"

"I don't know. I don't think about it. At least I try not to think about it."

"Was there some reason you couldn't marry her, like her parents or something?" she asked.

"Something like that."

Her frown deepened. "You don't have to be lonely, Duke," she whispered softly. "You could stay here with us. Pa says that someday there'll probably be more people coming out, and we'll have a regular town. You could be a part of it, if you wanted."

"And what would I do here?"

She blushed. "To start with, you could maybe build yourself a cabin, and then once you were settled, who knows . . ."

He sighed. "Don't dream so much, Lily," he said thoughtfully. "They have a way of not coming true."

She stared at him, wishing that just once he'd quit treating her like nothing more than a friend. "You're afraid of me, aren't you, Duke?" she suddenly said.

He laughed, low and throaty, not at her, but at himself. She was right. He was afraid of her. Afraid to let his body give in to some of the thoughts that had bounced around in his head, watching her when he didn't think she was aware he was watching. Lily wasn't thin by any stretch of the imagination; in fact, except that she was shorter, she was built a little like Lizette. And more and more as he had watched her, he remembered Liz telling him that he'd never even look at a fat girl. At the moment, it seemed incongruous, because not only was he looking at a girl most men would consider quite plump, but for some reason, she was so sensually attractive that he had been wary of her right from the start.

He saw tears in her eyes and suddenly sensed that his laughter had hurt her. "Lily!" he said as she looked away, trying to avoid his eyes. "Don't feel bad!"

"You're . . . you're laughing at me," she murmured.

"No, not at you. At myself," he said quickly. "Because you're right, you know." He pulled his hands from the pockets of the buckskin he was wearing beneath the fur robe, and reached out, taking her face in his hands. Her cheeks were rosy and cold against his warm hands, and he looked down into her brown eyes. "I am afraid of you, Lily," he whispered huskily. "Because my body keeps egging me on, when common sense keeps telling me to let it be." His green eyes relaxed gently, and he suddenly had an urge to feel her lips, soft beneath his. "Like right now . . ."

Lily had been kissed before, but never with such wild abandon, and she welcomed it with her own surge of passion that had been held just beneath the surface from the first moment she had looked at him.

The kiss was long, dredging up familiar longings in Cole's loins, and without consciously realizing it, his fingers eased open the buttons on her heavy coat, finding their way beneath it, and he cupped one of her breasts tenderly.

An ecstatic moan emitted from deep in her throat, and he suddenly realized what he was doing. He wrenched his lips from hers, and straightened reluctantly, his hands withdrawing from her breasts, and he began to close the buttons on her coat again.

"No!" she cried passionately. "Don't stop, Duke, please," she groaned, her eyes warm with desire. "I don't care if you want to make love to me . . . I want you to."

He was breathing heavily. "I know, that's just the trouble," he told her, hoping to make her understand. "If I made love to you, I'd feel obligated to stay because you're not the kind of woman a man can play games with, Lily," he said. "And I can't stay, no matter how long or hard you beg. I have to move on." He frowned. "It wouldn't be fair to you, can you understand?"

"I'm trying." Tears were in her eyes again and her lips quivered. "But it's hard. I need you, Duke," she whispered softly. "Can't you just hold me for a while? You don't have to do anything else."

He sighed. "I'm not a saint, Lily."

She smiled seductively. "I know, and neither am I. Sometimes I think I'll go crazy. Just to have somebody love me." Her eyes shone hauntingly and she blushed hotly. "I've heard Ma and Pa, Duke," she whispered hesitantly. "My room's up over theirs. There are times when Ma can't do anything and yet Pa finds his pleasure and she doesn't mind . . . and I wouldn't have to worry about any babies, Duke . . . please, I feel so strange inside, like I could explode."

He stared at her hard. Did she really know what she was suggesting? "Would that be enough, Lily?" he asked hesitantly.

He felt the heat of her embarrassment, as her hand found his, and fumbling awkwardly, she guided it back to the buttons on her coat. "Don't make me beg, Duke, please," she whispered softly. "I've never done anything like this before, but I know it must be better than nothing at all. Please . . ."

His hand touched her breast again, and once more the

flame was kindled, and he pulled her hard against him, his mouth on hers, and the bargain was sealed without any words spoken.

Afterward, Cole held her close, still no need for words, glad because the darkness had hidden her embarrassment, because for all she said she wasn't a saint, doing was harder than just knowing, and he knew she had never known a man's touch that could arouse and make her cry with need.

Cole leaned back against the side of the cave now, holding her in his arms, feeling a little guilty for giving in to his emotions. She gazed up at him, her body still throbbing from the magic his hands had performed on her, yet knowing when tonight ended, there'd be no more.

"I thought I knew," she said against his neck. "I heard Ma and Pa, and I thought I knew."

"But you didn't."

"No," she answered hesitantly. "If this is so wonderful, Duke, then the other must be grand," she went on breathlessly. "Oh, I wish you didn't have to go."

But he did. When they finally left the cave and returned to the cabin, the moon had moved behind a cloud and snow began to fall again, but a light snow that didn't even last until morning.

The next day, early, Cole mounted his piebald mare again and set out north, bidding his newfound friends good-bye, and hoping beyond hope that he hadn't spoiled Lily for the right man when he came along. As he nudged his horse, moving off among the trees, following the bank of the river for a while before veering to the northeast, he felt a sense of loss, as if he was once more leaving a family behind.

The next few weeks dragged on as winter set in with full force, and at times Cole felt he'd never get warm again. His father had been worried that he wouldn't find his way, and he probably wouldn't have if he hadn't had a small map Uncle Heath had stuffed into his hand when he'd given him the fur robe. He checked it now, figuring he still had almost a hundred miles to go before reaching Portsmouth on the Ohio River, and Franklinton was beyond that.

There had been a thaw a few days before, but now the weather was getting cold again, and he was moving slowly. Ice often clung to the ends of his whiskers that were now a beard that almost reached to his chest. Damn, it'd be good to feel the heat of the Carolinas just once more for about an hour.

He was some twenty feet from a riverbank, studying a

rock formation up ahead as he rode, and checking with the map in his hand, when he suddenly reined up. A sixth sense told him that the quiet scene before him wasn't as tranquil as it appeared. His eyes scanned the area. Heavy patches of snow clung here and there, with stretches of bare ground between, and naked trees stood stark against the gray afternoon sky.

He cocked his head, listening, ears tuned to every sound around him. Then he heard it, the faint cracking sound. He waited for more, but only the sharp wind creaking through the branches overhead could be heard. He shoved the map back in his pocket and reined his horse away from the riverbank toward where he was certain the sound had originated, moving cautiously, eyes studying every rock and tree ahead as he rode along. Occasionally he took time to glance at the muddy, half-frozen ground, hoping to catch a sign of what might lie ahead; then suddenly his head snapped up again as another cracking sound echoed on the cold wind. He frowned. He had thought perhaps it was a rifle at first, but no rifle sounded like that.

He reined up cautiously and listened again, this time hearing a voice following the strange sound, yet he couldn't make out what was being said. He was at the foot of a small rise and it sounded like whatever was going on was on the other side. How close, he had no idea.

The country was desolate. He hadn't seen a soul since leaving the Baldridges' settlement weeks ago. Frowning, he slid from the saddle, grabbing the rifle from his back on the way down. He ground-reined the piebald mare, then stood for a moment deciding whether to scale the small hill or go around it. He glanced up to the top, then moved in that direction toward some saplings that dotted it, his neck stretching with each slow step; then suddenly he dropped to the snowy ground and hugged it as his eyes took in the scene ahead.

There was a clearing just the other side of the rise, and the start of a woods the other end of the clearing. At the edge of the woods stood an Indian in worn buckskins and heavy furs; with him were what looked like two white men bundled up against the cold, and all three were staring at a bearded, bare-backed man who was tied to a small maple tree, the skin on his back already branded with sticky red welts.

One of the men walked over, grabbing the hair on the head of the man tied to the tree, and snarled something into his face. Cole squinted, swearing he saw the victim spit, and the other man shoved his head forward, letting it hit the bark as he snapped something curt to the Indian.

Then Cole saw it, the reason for the strange noise as the Indian backed off a few feet and swung a bullwhip, the tip cutting across the man's back, drawing blood again. Three against one. Cole's frown deepened as he saw the man flinch, yet not a sound left his lips.

He had to get closer to find out what the hell it was all about, but with the stark landscape, it wasn't going to be easy. He studied the area, spotting a small group of young pine trees not quite a hundred feet from the men. At least they afforded some cover, and a line of wild cedar bushes dotted the approach to the trees. Hugging the ground again, he made his way back to his little mare and led her partway around the side of the hill to where she was screened behind the scrubby cedars. He didn't want to take her too close for fear she'd spot the horses the men had been riding and nicker, giving him away.

Once more Cole dropped the mare's reins to the ground, then moved out, his feet hitting bare ground whenever possible, making his way in close enough so he could hear. He stopped, his head resting against pine needles, and listened as the Indian coiled the whip in his hand, turning to the two men beside him.

"He die before he tell us," the Indian said.

The taller of the two men, who was wearing a dirty gray scarf tied under his chin to keep the worn black hat on his head, snorted angrily. "He can't die. Not till he's told us where it is. I ain't gonna come outta this empty-handed. He's got furs and who knows what all stashed away somewhere in these parts, and by God, if he ain't gonna lead us to 'em, then he's gonna tell us where they be!"

"Christ, Legget," argued the other white man, "we followed him for nigh onto a week and he never went near no hidden fur cache. A man stubborn as that ain't gonna tell you nothin'."

"He will or he'll get the hide worn off his back," said Legget, and signaled the Indian, who uncoiled the whip again and set it to the victim's back once more, this time dragging a low moan out of the man.

Cole flinched as he saw blood splatter. The man taking punishment from the whip was evidently a trapper, and the others were bent on robbing him of his winter's work. It was the end of February already and the trapping season was almost over. That meant the man probably had a good stash of furs somehwere. Damn! Cole wanted to help him, but how?

There was only one way to even the odds. His decision made, he quickly left his spot against the pine and made his way cautiously back to where the piebald mare stood patiently waiting, and in minutes was back in the saddle, his rifle in one hand, reins in the other.

Slowly, deliberately, he rode his mare out from behind the small knoll, cautiously getting as close as he could; then, when he was certain to be in range, he raised his rifle.

"Hold it right there, gents!" he yelled, his voice carrying across the clearing, and all three whirled around, looking directly into the muzzle of Cole's double-barreled flintlock.

The Indian started to move. "You're dead!" Cole hollered. The Indian stiffened, straightening.

"And drop the whip!"

The Indian's face darkened, but he complied.

"Now," Cole said firmly. "You two," and he motioned toward the white men. "Move away from the Indian and step up to those trees yonder," and he motioned with his head to two trees next to the one the man was tied to.

The men shuffled reluctantly to the trees.

"Now, you each hug one, both arms around it, your backsides to me!"

The men did as he said.

Cole's eyes fastened again on the Indian. "Now, you." He nodded toward their victim. "Cut him down, put his coat back on him, and get him onto his horse."

The Indian glared at Cole, then slowly turned.

"Shoot him, Black Hawk!" yelled one of the men.

"Don't try it!" Cole called. "Whether you noticed or not, gents, this rifle has two barrels," he said quickly. "One false move, and you each get a bullet right in the back." His eyes settled on the Indian again. "Now, cut him down, but stay on this side of the tree. And only use your knife on the ropes, then throw it into the bushes."

Black Hawk did as he was told, throwing his knife far out of reach, then reached out to help the trapper to his feet.

"Get your stinkin' hands off me!" the trapper snarled as he straightened, the ropes that had held him falling to the ground; then he grabbed his coat from where the men had thrown it, slipping into it as he headed for his horse. His legs were a little unsettled and wobbly for a couple of seconds, and he winced as the coat pulled across his back, but he kept on going, reaching the saddle in a pained leap.

Cole was pleased to see that the flogging hadn't had too

much effect on him, and the man dug his horse in the ribs, heading toward where the other horses were tethered. Bending down, the trapper unfastened the reins of the three horses, then led all three away toward where Cole sat astride, his rifle still trained on the scowling trio.

"Thanks, stranger!" he called as he neared Cole, and Cole made the mistake of taking his eyes off the three men just long enough to glance at the man he had saved.

That fraction of a second was all the Indian needed. He dropped to the ground, ducking stealthily behind the tree the trapper had been tied to, a pistol suddenly appearing in his hand, and all hell broke loose as he aimed it at the man leading the horses away and a shot split the air. The trapper grabbed his upper arm, dropping the reins from the three horses as Cole's rifle barked back, answering the pistol, and the two white men, taking advantage of the confusion, slipped around, hiding behind the trees they'd been hugging, but not before a bullet from Cole's gun caught one in the leg.

Cole cursed, swinging his empty rifle in the air as he spun his little mare around. "Let's get out of here!" he yelled anxiously, and the trapper nodded, teeth gritting against the pain that was searing his arm.

"Follow me!" he yelled, and he rode past Cole.

Cole didn't even take time to look back, but shouldered his rifle and took off after the injured man, who was bent low in the saddle now, heading northeast, away from the clearing, while the three robbers rounded up their horses.

They had been riding for a little over an hour when the trapper turned around, slowing down to wait for Cole. "We can't outrun 'em, stranger," he said breathlessly. "They're still dogging our trail. We're gonna have to make a stand!"

Cole inhaled anxiously. "Where?"

The man nodded with his head toward a rocky area above them. "Up there." He reined his horse between scattered rocks and boulders, then dismounted when he reached the crest of the hill and led his horse behind some boulders, grabbing a rifle from the scabbard on his saddle.

Cole reloaded his rifle, then followed suit, and both men dropped to the ground behind some rocks, rifles trained on the trail below.

"Don't give them a chance," said the trapper nervously. "The minute they move into the open, pick a target. Once they know we've stopped up here, they're sure to lay low, and we'll be lucky if we get off a shot."

Cole nodded, staring down the trail they had used only

minutes before, waiting for a movement, anything, hoping the three men weren't too far behind them. He wanted to get a better look at this bearded man he'd saved, but didn't dare take his eyes off the trail. The last time he'd let his guard down had been lesson enough.

"How's your arm?" Cole asked as he squinted, keeping his voice low.

The man beside him shifted restlessly into a more comfortable position against the rocks. "The bullet went right through the fleshy part, but it hurts like hell," he answered, chewing his lip nervously. "Just let one of those bastards get in my sights."

"Looks like you get your wish," whispered Cole, and nodded toward a bend in the trail, and both men set their eyes to their gun sights.

"I'll get the one with the gray scarf," whispered the trapper.

"And I'll try for the other two," said Cole.

All three were still out of range, and both men waited; then: "Now!" whispered the trapper, and both rifles fired in unison.

Cole saw the white man on the left slide from the saddle, then tried to get a bead on the Indian, but the man was too quick. He was already diving into the underbrush at the side of the trail, and Cole cursed.

"Don't fret it," said the trapper from beside him. "We've more than evened the odds, and I don't think that Indian's going to be any too eager to take us on all by himself."

Cole's eyes sifted across the trail to where the other robber was lying sprawled on the ground. Both men's horses were prancing restlessly about, and Cole nodded toward them. "You want the horses?"

The man pondered the question. "Might be a good idea at that," he said slowly. "I could use a couple of good packhorses if you think you can get them."

Cole nodded. "Stay here," he said, and reloaded his rifle, then handed it to the man. "And hang on to this."

He was gone before the other man could protest. He moved down through the rocks, crouching, keeping behind boulders and small pines that dotted the hill, then moved off into the woods, moccasins quietly carrying him toward the spot where he had seen the Indian disappearing into the underbrush. When he was close, he slowed, eyes penetrating the area. There were few places for the man to hide, and Cole, who had slipped a pistol from the front of his buckskins, searched for them, finally letting his eyes settle on a mass of sticks caught over the base of a large fallen tree. His eyes narrowed. The line of the tree wasn't right, nor was the density of the mass of underbrush.

Cole dropped flat, crawling on his stomach on the cold, wet ground until he was close enough to the fallen tree to see the uneven line that told him he was right. Deftly he slipped behind a big oak, peering around it, eyes intent on the spot where he knew the Indian was hiding. Sooner or later he was going to make a break for his horse; Cole could wait.

Time passed, and Cole stayed motionless, watching, waiting. It seemed like the man was never going to move; then finally Cole saw the uneven line ripple, and his body tensed, hand tightening on the pistol as he pulled his head back so he wouldn't be seen.

Black Hawk felt the hair on his neck prickle. There hadn't been a sound from the rock-strewn hill, but he still wasn't sure. Had they left? Anger filled him. Legget and Stone were dead. Ha! The fools! He had told them the man wouldn't give in, yet the two white men had insisted. Now, he had to try to get out of here alive.

His head moved up so he could see over the top of the log. Nothing was moving, the silence heavy. Slowly he shifted into a crouch, then straightened the rest of the way. His eyes studied the area. His horse was some twenty feet away, standing restlessly at the side of the trail they'd been following, and the other horses were just wandering around aimlessly, avoiding the two sprawled bodies on the frozen ground. Black Hawk slipped a leg over the fallen tree and began to climb gingerly out from his hiding place, eyes alert.

Cole, who had been pressed hard against the huge oak, pricked up his ears at the scraping sound as the Indian started to move out, and he leaned over, peering out again from behind the tree trunk just as Black Hawk's eyes fell on it.

Black Hawk cursed, grumbling low in this throat, his pistol barking instantly, but Cole, anticipating it, dropped quickly to the frozen ground, his own pistol answering. In the flurry, both men missed their targets. Black Hawk, hoping to keep Cole from reloading, reached to where his whip usually hung at his waist, then cursed again, remembering it was still back at the clearing, along with his knife. However, he still had his tomahawk, and grabbing it hard in his hand, he made a lunge for Cole, who was quickly regaining his feet after the near-miss of his shot.

Cole's useless pistol fell from his hand as the Indian rushed him, and he slipped a knife from the sheath at his waist. By the time Black Hawk reached him, he was ready for him. He ducked the tomahawk, sidestepping agilely, and ripped the Indian's side open, hitting a spot where the heavy furs the man wore slipped aside, leaving him vulnerable.

Blood gushed from Back Hawk's side, splattering onto the skins, and he was crazed now with pain and anger. He swung the tomahawk blindly, and whirled toward Cole again, rage contorting his snarling features. But again Cole leaped aside, the knife snaking out deftly this time, finding its target in the Indian's breastbone, and with a startled cry Black Hawk flung his arms skyward for a second, then crashed to the ground in a shuddering heap.

Cole breathed heavily, catching the cold air into his lungs. He'd come close so many times, and gooseflesh rose on his skin as he watched the last few twitches of muscle playing out on the Indian's face.

Cole exhaled heavily, then knelt down, grasping the hilt of his knife, pulling it from the Indian's chest, wiping it on the dead man's buckskins before sheathing it. He studied the man's features, so still in death. It was hard to tell what tribe he might be from, because he had a mixture of sign. His hair was worn like the Cherokee, but his tomahawk had Shawnee markings on it, and the beading on his moccasins and buckskins was Iroquois. He was probably a renegade who didn't care where his heritage lay anymore.

Cole stood up, then turned, walking toward the horses, cupping his hand over his mouth as he reached them, calling to the man who was still up in the rocks waiting. "Ho, friend! It's all right, you can come down now," he called. By the time he got the horses in tow, the trapper had made his way down the hillside, leading his roan and Cole's piebald mare. His face was a little pale and he looked like he could use a long rest.

Cole motioned with his head toward the dead men as the trapper reached him. "What do you want to do with them?" he asked.

The man glanced about at the bodies on the trail, then off toward the woods where the Indian lay, and he shrugged. "Let the buzzards get 'em, I guess," he answered grimly. "I hate to waste good time and energy on the likes of them. Besides, I couldn't help you with 'em if I wanted to, not with this shoulder and my back kickin' up the way they are."

For the first time since the start of their brief encounter,

Cole got a good look at the man he had rescued. He was rough in appearance, maybe somewhere in his late forties, sandy hair streaked generously with gray, and inquisitive eyes that could take a man in with one quick stabbing look. A bushy beard, grayer than the hair on his head, sprouted from his face and practically hid his wide mouth.

Cole frowned. "I don't know what to say. I know you're going to need help with that arm and your back, but I've already lost more time than I'd planned. Are you going to be able to make it to wherever you're going on your own? I mean . . . do you have far?"

The trapper stared at Cole, his face vacant of any other emotion except the pain he was feeling. "I'll be all right, young fella," he said, then sighed. "You headin' somewhere in particular?"

"North. I'm supposed to meet a man up by the Scioto, and I've already lost time with this bad weather. I sure as hell didn't want to lose more sticking around here, not knowing what I might be getting into, but I never could walk away from a good fight."

The man reached up with his good hand and slipped Cole's rifle off his shoulder, handing it to him, then offered his hand. Cole took it, clasping it firmly.

"Eli Crawford, at your service," the man said gruffly. "And I thank you, lad, for your help."

The trapper felt the hesitation in Cole's hand as it clasped his, and saw the strange look of disbelief in Cole's face. "I say something wrong, lad?" he asked cautiously.

Cole shook his head. "Hell, no," he said, staring at the man in disbelief. "Are you really Eli Crawford?"

Now it was Eli's turn to stare. "You sound as if you should know me," he said hesitantly.

Cole's face reddened. "I was told I could find you up at the Scioto."

"You were told? By who?"

"My Uncle Heath. He said you'd help me," Cole said quickly. "I've come up from the Carolinas."

Eli grabbed a fur hat out of his coat pocket and shoved it on his head as he studied the lad. He was in his early twenties—part Indian, that was for sure. "Your Uncle Heath?" he questioned.

"You really Eli Crawford?" Cole asked again, unable to believe his good fortune.

"Yep!"

"Well, damn! And if I'd kept on going . . . What are you doing this far south?"

Eli's eyes narrowed, but he answered. "Too many settlers movin' in up near Franklinton. I need room to breathe." He straightened, staring hard at Cole. "You mentioned Heath?"

Cole nodded. "Heath Chapman's my uncle. I'm Cole Dante—at least I was when I left home. I've been using another name since then."

"What name you usin' now?"

"Duke Avery."

Eli looked Cole's fur robe over closely, remembering when Heath caught and skinned the critter that furnished it. "Guess you wouldn't have Heath's furs if you weren't who you say you are," he said. "Again, I gotta thank you, lad, for helpin' me out," he went on, then sighed. "But, come on . . ." He motioned with his head back down the trail. "Since you seem to have been lookin' for me, you might's well stick around awhile," and he climbed into the saddle of his roan gelding and waited for Cole to mount his mare; then the two of them, leading the extra horses, headed off southeast, back toward the river.

"This here's home," Eli finally said about an hour and a half later as he gestured toward a cave in some rocks up ahead, and Cole winced as they dismounted and walked their horses inside. The cave was huge, and Eli had everything set up comfortably for his long winter stay, but it was crude to say the least. He'd been hoping the man would have a cabin.

"You don't like it, you don't have to stay," Eli offered curtly as he caught the expression on Cole's face. "The roof fell in on the only cabin around here a few years back, and nobody bothered to fix it, and I ain't about to." He eyed Cole curiously. "But before we decide either way, I think you'd better let me know what this is all about and why Heath sent you," he said. "And it better be the truth."

"It is," said Cole, and while Cole tended to Eli's wounds, then fixed supper over a smoldering fire, just close enough to the mouth of the cave for the smoke to pour out, yet not close enough to be spotted by strangers, Cole told him everything that had happened back home. When he finished, Eli shook his head.

"Seems you and your uncle got a penchant for gettin' in trouble, don't it, lad?" he said. "Now, your uncle, there's a man. 'Course you already know'd that. Surprisin' to find out he's got a daughter and all. Last time I seen him he was headin' for Washington on the trail of that Warbonnet fella let's see, that was back in the spring of fourteen, before the war ended. Lost track of him after that. Glad to hear he finally found that gal he was moonin' over, though. Lord, sometimes he drove me near to distraction, talkin' about her."

Cole spooned up some of the stew he'd cooked, setting the bowl in Eli's lap so he could feed himself with his good hand. Eli was resting his back on a bundle of furs, and it felt somewhat better since Cole had cleaned and bandaged it with strips made from one of the white shirts he'd brought along.

Cole stared at Eli for a long time, then frowned. "Eli, were you with Jackson down New Orleans way?" he suddenly asked.

Eli picked the small bowl up and tried the stew. "I was," he said, then blew across the top of the bowl to cool it. "I was the one who led Jackson's men out to the Horseshoe Bend back in March of 1814, when we went after the Creeks. That was right after your uncle and I parted company," he offered.

Cole nodded. "I thought so," he said. "The men down there called you Sandy, though, didn't they?"

"You were there?" Eli asked, surprised.

"I was a shavetail lieutenant," Cole answered. "I thought you looked familiar, only you didn't have a beard then."

Eli wriggled his bushy beard with his chin. "Never grow a bush when I move that far south," he said. "Gets too hot. And as for the name Sandy, the general never could remember my first name, so I never bothered to correct him." He surveyed Cole closely. "I met a lot of youngsters down there, Cole," he said. "I imagine if you had that brush off your face, you'd be a mite more familiar too. As it is, those eyes of yours look like I might've seen 'em before. They're somthin' a man don't soon forget."

"I don't suppose so," Cole said.

"You ain't sensitive about it, are you?" asked Eli.

Cole shrugged. "I guess not, it's just that most folks think I'm a half-breed. My mother's English, my father French and Tuscarora."

"Aha! Your father was the privateer Heath sailed with years ago, right?"

"Right."

Eli grinned. "He used to tell me about some of the adventures they had." He finished the last of his stew. "But that's all over the hill. What I want to know is, if I let you stay, can you keep up with me?"

"Where to?"

"Well, as soon as I have enough furs, I'm headin' for the nearest tradin' company, then I'm headin' southwest. I might even go down the big river a ways, or I might decide to go see what's beyond it, and that ain't gonna be no picnic."

Cole stared at him hard. "I know I can keep pace with you, Eli," he said hesitantly. "I think I proved that when we met up. It's just that . . ."

"I know what's botherin' you, young fella," Eli said, saving Cole the trouble. "But you gotta remember, there's a price on your head, and it's going to be a long time before you can show your face in that part of the country again, if ever."

"But what about Heather? And I have a child back in Port Royal."

"Someday, son! But for a while, you'd best just forget they're even there, or you'll make yourself miserable."

"How do I forget, Eli?" he asked.

"The same way I forgot about my wife and children when they were killed. You remember the good times—nothin' wrong with that—but keep your mind doin' things, learn all you can, 'cause a man who's busy don't have time to feel sorry for hisself." He straightened. "You with me?" he asked again.

"I'm with you," said Cole, and the pact was made. By the time spring began to make its appearance, the snows melting in the warm breezes from the south, Eli's wounds were healed, and the two men headed out of the wilderness, moving north toward the Ohio River and civilization again.

19

The leaves on the trees were green again, flowers were blooming in every garden, and today was Saturday, March 1, the opening of the races at Palmerston Grove. Lizette sat on the edge of her bed and let her thoughts wander back over the past few months.

Cole had made good his escape and the wanted posters that were hung up all over the state had already become worn and tattered, the writing on them hard to read after being washed by the rain and wind. She thought of him so often, wondering where he was and if he was all right.

She glanced toward the window, at the sun streaming in. It was going to be a beautiful day for the races, and she began to wonder about Heather. It had been such a long time since she had been able to really talk to her. There were a few times when she had run into her in town, but either Carl or Everett was always with her. Lizette was still banned from the house at Palmerston Grove, as were her parents, although her father was planning to attend the races.

So far, the only one who had been able to visit Heather since she had recovered from the trauma of losing her husband and baby was her mother. Everyone else, including Loedicia, was always stopped at the door, where the elderly butler had been replaced by a powerfully built black man towering well over six feet. But even Darcy was turned away at times and was never allowed to see Heather alone; Carl or Everett was always present.

Heath had even appealed to the courts, with Rand Kolter's help, trying to force Everett Palmer to relinquish his hold on Heather, but the man's influence was effectual. She was his son's widow, and as such, he was responsible for her care. The court upheld him, even when he refused to let Heather appear herself, using the excuse that she still wasn't well enough to talk about the whole affair. That was shortly before Christmas. Now, a little over two months later, she was still living at Palmerston Grove, and the only consolation any of them had was that Tildie was still with her.

Lizette rose from the bed, pulling the sash of her wrapper tight about her, then walked over and stood staring at herself in the mirror. What a difference. She had lost almost forty pounds over the past two months. Not because she'd been trying all that hard, because she hadn't. It was just that she couldn't keep anything on her stomach anymore, and had lost her appetite on top of it.

Her eyes moved up her figure, hesitating for a moment at her waistline, then up to her face, where they stared back at her intently. Well, at least no one seemed to be suspicious. Her parents merely assumed she had been trying harder to lose weight and that worrying over Cole didn't help. If her father had even the slightest suspicion she was pregnant, she hated to think what he might do.

She sighed. Well, she had known it was a possibility. You couldn't make love with a man without taking the risk. She turned abruptly and walked over to the desk at the far side of the room. The fancy contraption Cole had given her was gone, and in its place was a beautiful gold velvet chaise lounge. She took a letter off the desk and dropped gently onto the chaise, leaned back, and opened the envelope, reading the letter over once more.

It was from Felicia, inviting her to dinner with her parents on March 9 because it had been so long since she'd seen her. That was a week from tomorrow. Time was running short. She had already made up her mind that if Stuart wasn't home by the first part of April, she was going to try to find some reason to get away from Tonnerre and head for Washington. She had to know what Stuart wanted her to do.

At first she had thought of trying to find a way to get rid of it, but each time she made up her mind that it would be the wisest thing to do, she'd remember how wonderfully the child had been conceived, and she just couldn't. She had given Stuart her love. At least she thought she had, although there were still moments when he reminded her so much of Bain. She closed her eyes, letting her thoughts go back to that day on the bank at the old swimming hole. She was no longer the same young girl she had been then. So much had happened, and she no longer felt the restless urge to see what she could get away with, to shock people with her antics. Although sometimes the urge did still nibble at her, especially on days like today. She'd give anything to go to the races with her father.

Her eyes flew open, and she straightened. That's it. Why not? Wouldn't that turn Everett Palmer purple with rage? She smiled. She'd worry about the baby in due time; for today she'd watch the eyebrows rise and have a little fun. It had been months since she had done anything wild and reckless.

She stood up, tossing the letter onto her desk, and rang the bell pull for Pretty.

"I want bathwater set up, Pretty," she ordered quickly as she shuffled through her armoire, looking for something to wear. It had to be something extra special. Let's see, she thought as Pretty left, the brown velvet was too big now, and so were most of the others. She reached in, pulling out her red velvet, wondering if it would still be too tight. She untied the sash on her wrapper, slipped it off, then pulled the riding habit down over her head. It wouldn't fasten. About half an inch more. She exhaled, disgusted, and took it off again, wearing only her nightgown as she continued shoving clothes aside. Then suddenly she straightened, pulling a deep violet riding habit from the armoire. It would be a little big, but if she had Pretty bring needle and thread, it should take only a few minutes to take it in on the sides. She walked over, laying it across the bed as Pretty came back in, followed by a long line of servants with her tub and the water. Now all she had to do was convince her father that it was a good idea.

At first Beau was stubbornly against it, but the more Lizette talked, the more he listened, and when she told him it would be a good chance to try to see Heather, he finally gave in. He turned to his wife. "You might as well come too, Reb," he said, shrugging. "If I'm going to get thrown off of Palmerston Grove, I might as well do it in style, my wife and my daughter at my side." So Rebel joined them.

Beau wore his usual black frock coat and today Rebel wore black too, a color that contrasted vividly with her pale hair. They were a striking couple, and Lizette was proud of them as they all rode up the lane toward the crowd already assembled at the racetrack. Heads turned and eyebrows rose as they made their way toward the grandstands and dismounted, tying up at the hitching rail.

Beau helped Rebel and Lizette down, and whispered in Lizette's ear as he did, "All right, young lady, you see what you can do about sneaking a visit with Heather, and the day will be worth it."

She smiled at him conspiratorially and glanced over toward the platform where Everett and Carl were both sitting watching the races. They hadn't turned to look their way yet, and as her feet touched the ground, Lizette slipped quickly away from her parents, letting them move off among the others without her.

She was making her way through the crowd, trying to keep close to the line of trees where the horses were tethered, backing up partway, trying to get as far away from her parents as possible, when suddenly a pair of hands spanned her waist, halting her backward progress, and a low masculine voice spoke close to her ear.

"It is Lizette Dante, am I right?" he asked. She knew the voice so well. It was deep and vibrant, and she suddenly felt her knees weaken.

His hands forced her to turn, and she found herself looking directly into Bain Kolter's warm gray eyes. He was still wearing the short clipped beard he'd been wearing the last time she'd seen him, and the past two years had changed him very little. Lizette stared, transfixed. She couldn't believe it. She had had no warning. Felicia had mentioned nothing.

"You don't look pleased to see me," he said curiously.

She shook her head. "I don't believe it," she exclaimed, astounded. "I just don't believe it!"

"Pinch me," he said. "I'm real."

"Pinch? I ought to *kick* you," she said, suddenly flushing, remembering the way he had left with no good-byes, no warning. "Why didn't you let me know you were leaving?"

His eyes darkened. "I'm not exactly used to tearful farewells from adolescent girls."

She laughed cynically. "Why would I have cried? You didn't mean anything to me."

"Didn't I?" He laughed, the sound low and throaty. "You've grown into a lovely young woman, Lizette," he said, and his eyes devoured her.

Lizette's flush deepened. "Do you really care?"

"What do you think?"

"I think I hate you, Bain Kolter," she whispered softly.

The light in his eyes deepened. "I think you're a liar," he murmured, then reached out, taking her hand, pulling her with him.

"Where are we going?" she asked breathlessly as she tried to keep up with him without falling.

"Where we can talk."

"About what?"

"About you!" He found a quiet spot away from the crowd and pulled her up abruptly, so she was standing in front of him.

"What do you think you're doing?" she asked.

"Taking up where I left off."

"You can't," she said stubbornly. "You can't just pop back into my life as if nothing's happened. I'm not fifteen anymore, Bain."

"I know, you're almost eighteen."

She shook her head. "Why did you leave?" she asked miserably. "Why couldn't you have stayed?"

"And end up tarred and feathered because I couldn't keep my hands off you? Be sensible, Lizette," he said. "When a man can't win a battle, he retreats until the tide of the battle turns in his favor."

"Or until the battle's lost."

He frowned. "What do you mean?"

"Never mind," she murmured softly, and suddenly she wanted to cry. She forced the tears back. "It's too late, Bain," she said unhappily. "Too much has happened since you left."

"You mean Cole?" he asked.

"That . . . and other things."

"Tell me about Cole," he said. "Father tried, but you're closer to it. What happened, Liz?" he asked.

She told him as best she could without telling him about her argument with Cole or about Stuart, but the color was high in her face until she had finished.

"Hasn't Heather told the authorities the truth?" he asked.

"How can she?" she exclaimed. "They might as well put iron bars around her, for all anyone gets to see her."

Bain glanced toward the platform where both Palmer men were seated, their eyes glued to the racetrack. "Would you like to see her?" he suddenly asked.

"Now?"

"Now," he said. "While they're both occupied. Remember, I knew Witt for a long time. I think I can possibly get us into the house without being seen, but we'll have to ride out of here together."

She looked at him curiously.

"When Witt was younger, he had a way of getting in and out of the house so his father didn't even know he was gone."

She frowned. "What if we're caught?"

He smiled. "Trust me."

She nodded. "All right."

He began ushering her back to where their horses were, and helped her into the saddle. "Too bad you didn't wear pants today," he said, remembering the last time he'd helped her onto Diablo.

She remembered it too. "I don't race anymore," she said curtly, but he only smiled as he led her palomino over to where Amigo was tethered, and in minutes they were trotting their horses slowly down the lane, trying not to look too conspicuous.

When they reached the main road, they headed toward town, but about a quarter of a mile past the house at Palmerston Grove, Bain rode off the road into a dense wood that opened up a few hundred feet off the road into a rock-strewn meadow. He reined his horse up among the trees at the edge of the meadow and jumped down, tethering the small Morgan horse on a nearby bush. Then he walked over and lifted Lizette from the saddle.

She felt solid in his hands, and he realized she was a little heavier than she had been two years ago. But it looked well on her, and was in all the right places. His hands flexed on her waistline for a moment, and he drew her close in his arms.

"We were going to see Heather?" she questioned softly.

He took a deep breath. "I've waited a long time," he said, and without warning his head bent, and as he kissed her, Lizette felt a rush of fire shoot through her. The kiss deepened, and suddenly her arms moved up to caress his neck. He drew back and stared at her flushed face. "Now tell me you don't care!" he whispered gently.

She swallowed hard. "Heather . . ." she gasped breathlessly.

"Heather," he confirmed, his own breathing labored. "There'll be time for this later," and he took her hand, leading her through a line of trees that ended about two hundred feet from the east wing of the house. There was a hill some fifty feet from the line of trees, and in the middle of the hill were a couple of bushes. Almost hidden by the bushes was an old wooden door.

"It's the root cellar," he offered, as he saw the frown on her face. "It's cold and damp, but a door at the back leads into the cellar of the main house."

They kept as low to the ground as possible, and Lizette was shaking with fear as they heaved the door open and ducked inside, dropping down the two steps that led into the place. "It's dark in here," she gasped, trying to keep her voice down.

"Shhh," Bain cautioned. "Hold my hand and don't let go." He led her across the dirt floor, then felt along the back wall with one hand until he reached another door. He slowly pushed it open and stepped into the damp cellar, motioning for her to be quiet.

"Look," he explained, his voice hushed in the dank cellar, "these old houses were built funny. Everett Palmer had a few ideas on how to amuse himself when he was a younger man and his wife was still alive, and he had to sneak behind her back. There's a staircase over at the side that winds up inside the walls and opens into one of the upstairs bedrooms. The bedroom was always used as a guest room, so I imagine it still is."

They were careful making their way across the cellar, stepping gingerly over dark objects scattered about the floor, moving past the steps that led upstairs, then on into the wine cellar. Bain felt along the wall, then slowly began to open a door that was barely visible. It creaked as it began to open, and he winced, opening it slowly. Finally he sighed, and Lizette glanced into a dark passageway. Bain reached in and felt about. The steps were still there. He grabbed Lizette's hand and stepped into the narrow passageway and began making his way slowly up the stairs, with her close by his side.

It was stuffy in the narrow space between the walls, and Lizette held tight to Bain's hand, tiptoeing as quietly as she could with her riding boots on. After what seemed like an interminable time, Bain finally quit climbing and Lizette pressed close against him on a small landing.

"Are we there?" she whispered, barely breathing.

He nodded. "Shhh." The wooden door before him slid sideways, and he grabbed the edges, moving it only enough so he could look out through a slim slit. When he was certain the room was empty, he opened it the rest of the way, then helped Lizette step out into the sunlit room.

There were cobwebs hanging on her clothes, and she brushed them off, shuddering.

Bain tiptoed stealthily to the door and leaned against it, listening. The hallway sounded quiet, and he opened the door slightly, peeking through the crack.

"Do you see anything?" asked Lizette close to his ear, and he shut the door quickly, startled to find her standing so close behind him.

"Do you have to breathe down my neck?" he asked.

She bristled. "I only thought I could help."

"You can," he whispered. "Here, get in front of me and see if you can guess which room might be hers."

He opened the door again and they peeked out just as a head popped up at the top of the stairs. Bain started to shut the door.

"Wait, that's Tildie!" said Lizette eagerly, and Bain frowned. "She's on our side." She motioned quickly for him to trust her, made sure Tildie was alone, then opened the door farther, gesturing for the startled young woman to join them.

Tildie's eyes were puzzled as she entered the room.

"Lordy—" she began, but Lizette covered her mouth, warning her to keep quiet. "What you all doin' here?" Tildie asked anxiously when Lizette freed her mouth.

Lizette grabbed the girl's shoulders and hugged her, much to Tildie's surprise. "How's Heather, Tildie?" she asked eagerly.

Tildie frowned. "She's all right . . . at least she is now," she said nervously. "But she don't like it here."

"I didn't think so," said Lizette.

"We want to talk to her," said Bain quickly. "Can you bring her here?"

The girl looked troubled. "I think so. She's downstairs in the parlor."

"Then go get her," said Lizette quickly. "But whatever you do, Tildie, don't let anyone know." She saw the hesitancy in the girl's eyes. Something was wrong. "They haven't hurt you, have they, Tildie?" she asked.

Tildie bit her lip. "No, ma'am, please," she said. "I'm all right."

Lizette held her arm, her fingers tightening on it. "Tildie, what have they done?" she asked.

Tears welled up in the young girl's eyes. "I . . . I can't tell you."

Lizette's eyes hardened. "Tildie, you don't belong to them,

you still belong to Grandpa Roth," she said. "If they've done anything to you, Grandpa can bring them to task. What have they done?"

Tildie's lips were quivering.

"Can't you see she's scared?" said Bain quickly. "Let it go for now, Liz. It's more important we talk to Heather."

Lizette stared at Tildie, then conceded. "All right, but you will bring her, Tildie?" she asked.

Tildie nodded. "I'll bring her," she said, sniffing in, wiping a hand across her eyes. "I promise."

Bain moved to the door and opened it again, peeking out to make sure no one was coming, then let Tildie out.

When she had disappeared back down the stairs, he shut the door and turned to Lizette. "I'm glad you didn't press her for the answer," he said. "I don't think you'd have liked it."

She eyed him curiously. "You know, don't you?" she said.

He frowned. "I think so. At least I can make a good guess." His eyes darkened. "That's one reason I could never really call Witt a close friend. He and his father and brother had strange ideas about their privileges with the female slaves. From the look in her eyes, I'd say they either raped Tildie or let one of their blacks do it. How old is she, anyway?"

"Somewhere around fourteen."

"Damn them!" he said, then his eyes searched hers thoughtfully. He reached out slowly and took her hands, gradually pulling her against him.

"This isn't the time, Bain," she whispered.

"This is the best time," he said. "There's no one to interrupt us for a few minutes, and no one to see."

"Bain!"

"What's wrong," he asked, frowning. "You know you still care. I can see it in your eyes."

"I told you before, Bain. Too much has happened."

"Like what?"

Her jaw clenched. She couldn't tell him. "Bain, you don't seem to understand. I haven't heard anything from you for two years. You didn't even think enough of me to say good-bye, and now you . . . you just think you can come back here and act like nothing's happened. Life doesn't work like that. Life goes on, and things change, and nothing is ever as it used to be."

"You're right there," he said. "You're even lovelier now than you were then." His fingers stroked her neck, and he leaned forward to kiss the flesh beneath her ear, but she stopped him.

"Don't please," she begged helplessly, pushing him away.

He straightened and looked down at her, the warmth suddenly gone from his eyes. "You're serious, aren't you?" he said.

She sighed. "Very serious."

He was about to say something more when the doorknob began to turn.

"Heather!" gasped Lizette, and hurried to her cousin and hugged her ecstatically.

Bain stepped over quickly and shut the door behind Heather and Tildie, then cautioned them to keep their voices down.

"How on earth did you get up here?" Heather asked Lizette, looking her over. "It's so good to see you!"

"You can thank Bain," Lizette said. "If it hadn't been for him, I'd never have gotten close to you."

"But how?" she asked again.

Lizette led her over to the door in the wall, and Heather stuck her head into the dark passage, looking down the stairway. "Good heavens," she said. "I had no idea."

"Neither did I," said Lizette. "It was Bain's doing."

Heather drew her head back in and looked at Bain. "Thank you," she said, then looked over again to Lizette. "I can't get over it," she said. "You look so good, Liz."

"But you don't," Lizette said unhappily. "You look tired, Heather."

"I'm all right," she said, but Lizette didn't believe her.

"What's going on here, Heather?" she asked. "Why haven't you gone back to the Chateau?"

"I can't," she said miserably. "I just can't, Liz."

"But why?"

Heather pursed her lips, staring at them nervously. She was wearing a pale yellow dress trimmed with white embroidery and white ribbons that only emphasized how pale she had become. "Liz, there are reasons why I can't leave here," she said. "But if I tell you, I want you to promise not to tell a soul, either one of you," and she looked at Bain too.

He frowned but didn't answer.

"Please, Bain," she said, "please promise you won't breathe a word. If you do, it could ruin everything."

"I won't say anything, Heather, you know that," said Liz; then she too looked at Bain. "Promise her, Bain," she said.

He hesitated, then nodded. "All right, what's the big secret?"

Heather glanced at Tildie, then back to the two of them. "I'm quite certain the baby isn't dead," she said uneasily.

Lizette stared at her, her eyes narrowing in disbelief.

"I know what you're thinking, but I'm sure I'm right," Heather said. "Ask Tildie."

Lizette turned to the young maid, who was still fidgeting from fright. "She's right, ma'am," Tildie answered.

"Let me explain," said Heather quickly. "You see, the night Witt died, I was so upset myself, what with having been beaten and all. At first I thought I remembered hearing a baby cry, but everything was so hazy. Oleander told me I'd only imagined it, but now that I think back, I'm not so sure." She saw the uncertain look in both their eyes. "I never saw the baby again, Liz," she explained hurriedly, keeping her voice low. "Not except for those first few moments when Oleander held it up right after it was born, when it was quiet and wasn't crying or moving. I didn't see it in the coffin—they only told me it was there." She clasped her hands together nervously, then continued. "Shortly after Tildie came to stay, Everett Palmer warned her to stay away from the other slaves, but one day she saw something strange and followed one of the other servants down to the slave quarters. Unfortunately she was caught, and he punished her . . . I won't go into that now," and she looked at Tildie with concern. "But the point is, I think my son's alive and that Everett Palmer is planning to raise him as one of his slaves."

Lizette stared at her dumbfounded. "He wouldn't dare!"

"Wouldn't he?" she asked. "He knew Cole was the father. If the poor little thing had Cole's eyes, there's no one who would believe Witt had been the father, and they'd know why Cole had been here that night. Everett couldn't stand that. He has too much pride."

"Well, if he has the baby, then why hasn't he just let you go?" Bain asked. "It would only be your word against his that Witt was the real culprit and not Cole."

"I know, but he's afraid someone will start checking, I guess, or maybe believe me." She sighed. "Don't you see," she said. "He doesn't want me to leave, and I know I'm playing right into his hands, but I can't leave Palmerston Grove until I learn the truth. I have to see the baby for myself. Tildie says there's a little boy, a little over three months old, with deep red hair and dark green eyes. I'm going to stay here until I find him."

Lizette stared at Heather. "Oh, Heather," she pleaded. "Why don't you just come home and tell your parents? They could get to the bottom of it."

She shook her head. "No! The minute I left Palmerston Grove he'd sell that baby to someone else, I know he would," she said. "And who's there to stop him? No," she insisted. "I'm staying here until I have proof and until I can take him with me."

Bain glanced over at Lizette. "So now you know," he said.

"But it doesn't help."

"Please, Liz," said Heather, her violet eyes unyielding. "I know what you're thinking. I'm all right, really I am. Carl sort of gives me the jitters sometimes, but I think he's harmless, and I realize everyone's worried, but look at it my way. I'm not going to leave here if there's the slightest chance I may be right."

Lizette sighed. "I don't blame you," she said. "But what do I tell everyone? They know you're not happy here."

"Tell them I wouldn't tell you why I wasn't coming home, but that they shouldn't worry."

"You sure you're all right otherwise?" Bain asked.

"I'm fine, Bain," she said. "Just a little unsettled at times, that's all." Then she frowned. "I never thought," she suddenly said. "When did you get home? I saw Felicia in town the other day, but she didn't mention you were home."

"I wasn't," he said. "I just rode in the day before yesterday. Thought I'd been away long enough."

Heather looked over to Lizette remembering their conversation those long-ago months on the banks of the river up by Tonnerre when Lizette confessed that he'd made love to her. "I'm glad you're back," she said quickly. "And I'm sure Liz is too." Then she glanced toward the door. "I think we'd better be going back down," she said unexpectedly. "I'd hate for anyone to find you here. That would mean we'd never get to meet again. You will come back, won't you?" she asked.

Lizette looked at Bain.

"We'll sure as hell try," he said, then straightened, tiptoeing to the window, keeping behind the curtain as he looked down into the yard below. "Oh, oh, company coming," he said. "Carl's on his way across the lawn."

Heather reached out and grabbed Lizette's hands. "Oh, please," she said quickly. "Go, please, go. If he finds you here . . ."

Bain was already beside Lizette. The two girls hugged while Tildie wrung her hands nervously; then Lizette and

Bain stepped back onto the small landing, slid the door shut behind them, and began slowly descending the stairs that wound their way down through the middle of the house. It wasn't until they felt the warmth of the afternoon breeze on their face and were ducking in among the trees, heading for their horses, that they both began to relax.

Bain stopped for a minute, leaning against a tree, the bushes near it screening him from the house, and he grabbed Lizette's hand, pulling her up close beside him. His arm went about her and he held her tight. "What are you going to do?" he asked a little breathlessly.

"I've been thinking about it," she said. "I don't think I'm going to do anything. At least not just now. I'm afraid if I tell my parents or anyone else what she told me they'll try to do something about it, and like Heather says, Everett won't keep the evidence around long. No"—she took a deep breath—"that baby is Cole's son, and if I did anything to separate him from Heather, where she'd never see him again, he'd never forgive me as long as he lives."

"You have no idea where Cole is now?" he asked.

"No. Uncle Heath told him how to get to a friend of his somewhere, but we have no idea whether he made it or not."

His arm eased about her and he walked her to her horse. "Are you heading for Tonnerre?" he asked.

She thought for a minute, avoiding his eyes again because they seemed to have such a powerful effect on her. "I think I'd better go back to the races," she said. "Mother and Father should still be there unless Everett Palmer has had them escorted off the premises. If not, they'll be worried, wondering where I am. But I'm not even going to tell them I saw Heather. If I do, they'll want to know what she said, and I'd have to have an answer for them." She finally looked up at him again. "So don't tell them, please," she said.

Bain gazed down at her. "On one condition. Let me ride out to Tonnerre with you."

"Determined, aren't you?" she asked.

He smiled. "I don't give up easily."

She sighed. "All right. Perhaps you'd better stay for dinner too, or my parents might think it's rather strange."

"I'd love to," he accepted quickly, and helped her into the saddle.

When they returned to the racetrack her parents were along the side rail talking to Bain's father. "Did you get to see her?" asked Beau after the preliminary greetings were exchanged.

Lizette glanced quickly at Bain, then answered her father negatively.

He swore. "I wish I knew what the hell was going on there, Rand," he told Bain's father. "If I can ever get to the bottom of this whole thing with any proof, I'm going to see that Everett Palmer gets what's coming to him, that's for certain."

Lizette felt guilty at first, lying to her father, but when she remembered Heather's look when she begged her not to tell anyone, she knew her decision had been for the best.

Later that evening, back at Tonnerre, with dinner over, Lizette sat at the piano in the music room playing for Bain. She finished her song, then sat for a moment with her hands on the keys just staring straight ahead.

"What's the matter?" he asked, stepping up behind her.

Her lips trembled and she closed her eyes to fight back the tears. All evening Bain had been so attentive, and from the moment she had looked into his gray eyes at the racetrack she had known her feelings for him were unchanged. Her affair with Stuart had only served to keep it alive. And yet, she was so mixed up. She knew now she was still in love with Bain, and yet she cared for Stuart too. There was a bond between them. Not just because of the baby she was carrying, but because Stuart had been here when she needed someone. And yet . . .

She pushed the piano bench back and stood up, walking over to the window. It was open and the breeze coming in was warm with the scent of the river in it. She knew Bain had followed her, and she could feel the warmth from his nearness through the sheer pink muslin dress she had changed into when they had arrived home.

Bain stared at Lizette's hair. How dark and silky it was. He sniffed it. She smelled like cape jasmine. A thrill swept through him, bringing back so many memories. How strangely this young woman had fired his blood, even as a girl. Now, full grown, it was even stronger. He had purposely stayed away from Tonnerre for the past two days since he'd come home, because he was afraid Lizette had changed. She had, but he liked the change.

He reached out and put his arms around her, pulling her back against him and he felt her tense. "I'm sorry, Liz," he said softly agianst her hair. "I wish I could have stayed. I'd have loved to watch you grow up."

"No you wouldn't," she said. "I was fat and ugly."

"Never ugly," he whispered.

"You don't know." Her voice broke. "I hated you for leaving, and now I hate you even more for coming back."

He turned her to face him. "Your words are hollow, Lizette," he said. "Your eyes give you away."

She stared at his cravat, her fingers toying with the front of his shirt. "Why *did* you come back, Bain?"

"I wanted to see you," he answered. "Is that so bad?" He reached out and tilted her chin up so her eyes locked with his; then he leaned down to kiss her, but she turned so his lips touched her cheek. He drew back, startled by her rebuff.

"It's too late, Bain," she said. Her voice was brittle with emotion as she thought of the life growing inside her. "I tried to tell you earlier . . ."

He frowned. "I don't understand. I know you still care . . ."

"But it's no good." Tears welled up in her eyes. "You weren't here when I needed you. Can't you understand that! You made me love you, then took that love away and left me empty inside. You can't just come back here and expect me to fall into your arms."

"I don't expect—"

"Don't you? What do you call it!" she yelled at him, trying to keep her voice down so her parents wouldn't come running. "I'm not a child anymore, Bain. And I have a right to be angry. I loved you and you let me down. I wanted you then and couldn't have you. Well, no way in hell are you going to have me now! You're two years too late, Bain," she said bitterly. "I don't need you anymore."

He frowned. "Why?" he suddenly asked.

She stared at him. "Why what?"

"Why don't you need me anymore?"

She swallowed, trying to think of an answer. There was none without telling him about Stuart. "Please, Bain, let it rest," she begged. "Don't press me for an answer to anything."

He hesitated, staring at her, wanting her so badly he felt sick inside. Something had happened, but what?

He reached up and touched her face, feeling her tremble. "Kiss me, Liz," he demanded roughly. "At least welcome me home," and this time she couldn't refuse as his mouth found hers and she let herself go.

This was Bain, her beloved Bain. The man who had taught her what love was all about. She moaned against his mouth, feeling the fire burning inside as his tongue parted her lips and he took the sweetness from her, blending it with his own passion.

Finally he drew his mouth from hers and gazed into her eyes. "I won't wait forever, Liz," he said fervently.

She nodded, unable to find her voice for a brief moment. "I won't ask you to," she said, then frowned, her thoughts suddenly returning to earlier in the afternoon and a thought that had occurred to her. "Bain," she said, her face flushed from his kiss, lips still quivering. "I hate to change the subject because you seem to be enjoying it so much, but I've been thinking about Heather all day."

"And?" he asked, watching her intently, yet refusing to let her out of his arms.

"What if Tildie's story isn't true? What if they coerced her into telling Heather a story like that just to get her to stay without having to use force?"

"I hadn't thought of that."

"I did."

"So what can we do?"

She bit her lip. "You'll probably say no."

"To what?"

"It could be gruesome."

He stared down at her, his eyes suddenly wary. "What do you have in mind, Liz?"

She gazed up at him hesitantly, hoping he'd help her. "I know you'll probably think it's stupid," she said reluctantly, "but if there's no baby buried in the grave at Palmerston Grove, that would prove something, wouldn't it?"

"You want to dig up the grave?" he asked incredulously.

"Let's face it," she explained hurriedly, trying to make her point, "Everett Palmer would never consent to letting the authorities examine the casket, but the private cemetery at Palmerston Grove is at the far end of the property from the house." She grabbed his arms, her hands tightening. "If we could prove they never buried any baby . . . Oh, Bain, that would mean Tildie was telling the truth. It would ease Heather's mind, too. At least we could erase her doubts."

"We?" he questioned.

She smiled up at him, the tears that had been in her eyes earlier completely gone, replaced by a devilish look he had been afraid he might never see again.

"You will help me, won't you?" she pleaded.

His eyebrows raised. "You and I?" he asked skeptically.

"Yes."

"I don't know." He ran the idea around in his head for a few seconds, wondering why he was even considering such a crazy stunt. Then knew why. He wanted to please Lizette

"All right." He reached up, brushing a stray hair from her forehead. "When?" he asked.

"I don't know, but it should be soon." She looked into his eyes again. "Could we maybe do it tonight?" she asked.

"Tonight?" He shook his head. "I don't know . . ."

"I won't sleep a wink if we don't," she said.

"But your parents . . ."

"I still know how to sneak out of the house," she said furtively. "You pretend you're leaving for home. I'll go up and put on some other clothes and meet you out by the road with a shovel."

"What about your horse?"

"We'll have to ride double if that's all right with you," she said. "I wouldn't dare go near the stables to get Diablo. Aaron's always up puttering around at all hours."

"That means I'll have to ride back again too."

She nodded.

He sighed. "I thought you said you were through getting in trouble," he said. "But I see you haven't really changed that much."

Her heart went out to him. "Thank you, Bain," she said, wishing with all her heart she could give him more of herself. "Thank you."

They left the music room and wandered into the parlor, where Beau and Rebel were reading, and Bain stayed only a short time longer, excusing himself and promising to be back again soon. Lizette walked him to the door, and Rebel was surprised when she came back and announced that it had been a long day and she was going to bed.

"It's barely eight-thirty," Rebel said as she stared at her daughter curiously.

Lizette stretched, yawning. "I know, but with the races, and Bain coming home and all . . . I'll see you in the morning. Good night, Mother." She kissed Rebel. "Good night, Father." She kissed Beau's cheek and headed for the stairs to go up to her room.

Half an hour later, dressed in some of her brother's old clothes and carrying a shovel she had taken from the barn, Lizette was seated in front of Bain, riding astride Amigo, and they were headed toward Palmerston Grove.

20

Bain was glad the moon was out, because they couldn't use a lantern. The small private cemetery, where Everett's parents and his wife, along with his son and supposed grandson, were buried sat out in the open, back some two hundred feet from the road. A wrought-iron fence surrounded the gravestones.

Lizette was wearing black pants and black shirt, but Bain still had on his ruffled white shirt, and the moonlight reflected off it like a beacon as he sank the shovel into the ground, lifting it and setting the dirt aside. He had done a lot of foolish things in his lifetime, but this was the limit. And what would they do if they didn't find a body in the small casket? Moreover, what would they do if they did?

He yanked the handkerchief from his pocket and wiped the perspiration from his forehead, then rubbed it along his clipped beard. This was hot work. He hoped they hadn't buried the infant too deep. As it was, he had already dug a hole waist-deep. He caught his breath and glanced over at Lizette, who was on her knees peering into the hole. She was also keeping an eye on the road, and three times in the past half-hour they had flattened themselves to the ground while riders went by.

"What are you looking for?" he asked.

"Can't you see it yet?" she countered. "Good Lord, it seems like you've been digging for hours."

He sighed, shoving the handkerchief back in his pocket. "The things you get me into," he admonished her, half-amused. "Hold on, it'll be just a bit farther."

He was tossing the dirt up beside her, and suddenly the shovel hit something solid, echoing in the quiet night.

"Is that it?" she asked anxiously.

He cautioned her. "Shhh . . . let me check." He dug a little more around it, then sighed. "That's it." he said. He reached up, and she took his hand so he could help her into the hole, and together they worked the coffin lose from its surrounding dirt, then lifted it out of the depression in the ground.

"We've got to get it up out of here so we can see," she said eagerly.

He agreed, and together they hefted the small casket up, setting it on the ground beside the hole; then they crawled out, kneeling beside it.

"Ready?" Bain asked.

She nodded. "Ready!"

To her surprise, he grabbed the shovel and used the sharp metal edge to pry around the lid that was sealed with heavy wax. When it was loose all around, he put pressure on the handle of the shovel and pried up easily, brushing the soft dirt aside as the lid moved up; then he flipped the lid all the way so the inside of the tiny silk-lined casket was revealed in the moonlight.

"Rocks!" gasped Lizette in disbelief. "Heather was right. They buried rocks. That means her baby's still alive. Oh, Bain!"

He grabbed her hand, squeezing it. "Shhh! Voices carry in the night!"

Her eyes were shining as she rested back on her heels. "Now all we have to do is get a good look at that baby in the slave quarters," she said.

"Liz, be reasonable," he cautioned. "We've done enough already. When Everett gets wind of this, he's going to be furious."

"What can he do without admitting he buried rocks instead of a baby?" she asked.

"He can say we stole the baby's body and put the rocks in ourselves." He put the lid back down. "Come on, let's put it back now and get out of here before we get caught."

She stared at him, knowing he was right, but reluctant to move.

"Liz?"

"All right," she said. "But at least now we know."

"Now we know," he agreed. "Now help me."

They slid the coffin over, then climbed down into the hole again and lifted the small casket down, putting it back where it had been. He helped Lizette back out, then climbed out himself and began filling the hole back in. Before he had started to dig, Bain had carefully lifted the sod off the top of the grave, and now, as he patted the last of the loose dirt down, he set the shovel aside and lifted the pieces of sod, setting them down over the loose dirt, so that from a distance it was hard to tell the grave had been disturbed. Lizette helped him, and they patted them down into place; then he brushed his hands off and slipped his frock coat back on.

He grabbed the shovel. "Come on," he said. "Let's go," and he took her hand, pulling her with him to where the horse was tethered in a grove of trees to their left.

He leaped into the saddle, then held his hand down for her and helped her up in front of him, handing her the shovel to hold.

They rode along in silence for a long time. Lizette was enjoying the ride. Bain's left arm was around her waist, and she was leaning back against him, savoring the feel of his chest muscles against her back. It was a sensuous feeling. She gazed overhead at the moon as he reined the horse to the right at the cutoff and headed upriver toward Tonnerre.

Lizette's hair kept brushing against Bain's face, touching his lips and tickling his nose, but he wouldn't have had her change positions for the world. She fit so neatly against him. He began to hum, his voice deep and rich, and she listened closely, wishing the moment didn't have to end, but knowing the wish could never be fulfilled.

He stopped humming as they neared the drive to Tonnerre, then rode past it and reined up at the edge of the road. He sat for a moment, still holding her against him; then his lips moved close to her ear. "I'll walk you to the house," he offered.

She trembled, his warm breath sending chills down her spine. "I know the way," she said.

"I know you do, but I'll feel better knowing you're safe." He slid from the horse, then helped her down. She slipped into his arms easily, and he sighed. "What if you're caught going in the house?" he asked.

She smiled. "I won't be. Cole and I have a way of sneaking in and out. We've done it dozens of times."

He smiled back at her. "And I thought you had changed." His eyes focused to a spot on her face. "You've got dirt on your cheek," he said.

She reached up, rubbing it away, but her hands were dirty too, and it didn't do much good. She looked so irresistible, like a reckless young girl again. The laughter left his eyes and they grew hungry with desire.

"It's late," she said, sensing the change in him. "If you're going to escort me, we'd better be going."

He realized the brief interlude was gone, and sighed, letting his arms ease from around her, then took her hand and they set off through the woods.

Bain had to help her a few times when she tripped on roots and fallen branches in the dark. The moon couldn't shine down through the thick leaves on the trees, and it made a difference. They left the small woods near the north wing of the house, and Lizette cautioned him to be quiet, as they worked their way around to the barn and set the shovel against it, near the door.

"Someone will find it in the morning and just think it was left out by mistake," Lizette whispered to him furtively. "If we try to get it inside, everyone will hear. The door creaks like mad. As it is, the only reason the dogs aren't barking is because they know my scent. If you were alone they'd be going crazy."

"How did you manage to get the shovel out?" he asked.

"The door was open when I left."

He nodded, then hunched down again as she began moving toward the house, and he followed her. Just to the left of the front door, she hugged the house, searching down near the foundation. "It's still here," she whispered, relieved. "That means nobody saw me."

"The front door, no less?" he asked.

She looked over at him. "Cole and I have always had a key to the front door," she explained quickly. "What we'd do is sneak out any way we could, hang the key on a hook Cole put down here, then take it back in with us when we got back." She started toward the steps, but he took her hand, stopping her.

"Lizette," he asked, "may I see you tomorrow?"

She stared at him, watching the moonlight on his face casting flickering shadows from the trees that surrounded the house. How good it was to be able to look at him again, to know he cared. "We could go riding?" she asked.

He sighed and pulled her into his arms, kissing her thoroughly, then took the key from her hand, helping her up the steps. He unlocked the door, then handed her the key, wrapping her dirty hands about it. "Until tomorrow," he whispered huskily, then bounded lightly down the steps and disappeared across the front lawn and into the night.

She gazed after him, wondering if she was doing the right thing. She should just tell him to stay out of her life once and for all, but for some reason she couldn't. She was in tears again as she turned, opened the door, and slipped into the house.

On Sunday they went horseback riding. Monday afternoon he took her for a buggy ride, Wednesday he had dinner at Tonnerre and afterward they took a long walk down to the river's edge. The moon was waning and the air was cooler tonight than it had been the last few evenings.

Lizette had a white cashmere shawl covering her shoulders, the red embroidery on the border matching her silk dress with puff sleeves and lace-trimmed bodice. She pulled the shawl tighter around her as they walked along, and she watched the moonlight rippling across the river, turning it to a ribbon of silver. She stopped and glanced surreptitiously at Bain. He looked quite elegant tonight in a deep russet frock coat with satin lapels and gold buttons, his highly polished top boots shining in the moonlight below buff trousers.

Bain sighed, stopping beside her. "I have to leave for a few days," he said.

"So soon?" she asked.

"It's only for a few days," he explained. "I have to go to Charleston on business. I should be back early next week."

"At least you have the decency to tell me this time," she said.

His jaw tightened. "You're never going to forgive me for that, are you?"

"Should I?"

"Damn it, Liz, I've told you—"

"I know, but for some reason it doesn't seem to be much comfort."

He reached out and took her in his arms. "What do you want me to do, Liz, get down on my hands and knees?" he said angrily. "Because I don't intend to. I came back because I wanted to see you, but I'm not going to crawl."

"Nobody asked you to."

"But you'd like it, wouldn't you?"

"No!"

He pulled her hard against him. "Then just what do you want?" he asked huskily.

She stared at him. "I don't know," she whispered breathlessly. "I know I can't forget the past two years that easily. I can't just say they didn't happen just because you decided to come home."

"Then let me make them up to you."

"You don't understand," she groaned agonizingly. "It's too late. There's nothing you can do to change what's already happened."

He reached up, cupping her head, burying his fingers in her hair. "Let me try," he murmured softly, bending down, his lips caressing her throat. "Let me try, Liz, please," and with his lips begging her, she gave in to him for the moment, letting his words try to soothe her and help her forget that she was carrying his brother's child.

For the rest of the week Lizette argued with herself constantly, insisting one moment that she was going to tell Bain the truth when he returned, then turning coward the next, afraid to tell him, knowing that if she did, she'd probably never see him again. And on top of everything else was the knowledge that Heather had been right, and her baby was still alive. She would have loved to go see Heather again, but she was afraid to go by herself, especially so soon. Maybe when Bain returned she could talk him into it, but for now she decided to just bide her time.

Sunday evening was the dinner at the Kolters' and Lizette spent the afternoon looking for something to wear. She wanted to look extra nice, in case Bain might have returned from Charleston. She picked out a dress of bright green silk with puffed sleeves and green velvet ribbon. It had a matching pelisse in case it was cool after sundown.

It was almost six o'clock when they arrived at the Kolters' in an open carriage. Beau was dressed in his usual black velvet frock coat with satin lapels and buff trousers strapped beneath his Wellington boots. Beside him Rebel looked lovely in a dress of pink gauze over pink satin, lace trimming the sleeves and neckline, her matching satin regency hat decorated with soft, feathery ostrich plumes. She wore a pelisse of pink satin over it.

There were a number of other carriages pulled to one side when they drove up, and Rebel glanced over at Beau when she saw them. "When Madeline asked us to join them for dinner, I didn't think she was planning a big dinner party," she said.

Beau frowned. "Maybe she was afraid we wouldn't come. Let's face it, Reb, there are still some people who believe all this nonsense about Cole, and we haven't been attending too many social functions lately because of it."

Their carriage stopped and the driver got down to help them out; then, a few minutes later, with Madeline escorting them, they stood at the threshold of the drawing room, where some thirty or forty people were gathered, all of them staring at the newcomers.

"I thought you said a small dinner party," said Rebel apprehensively.

Madeline smiled. "I hope you don't mind, Rebel," she said with a twinkle in her eyes. "Some of your friends wanted to show you they really care. I know your birthday isn't until the thirteenth, but we thought you wouldn't mind celebrating it ahead of time."

Rebel stared, dumbfounded, as everyone in the room suddenly began to converge on her, wishing her a happy birthday.

Lizette watched the astounded look on her mother's face, then moved to one side and looked for Felicia. Suddenly she felt her heart drop to her stomach. At first she thought it was Bain, but as he moved out of the shadows in the back of the room, with Julia beside him, she knew it was Stuart. She had no idea he'd come home, and she began to tremble as Felicia's voice brought her up short.

"I think your mother's in a state of shock," Felicia said anxiously as she grabbed Lizette's hand from behind, pulling her with her into the drawing room. "And look who's here," she went on, dragging Lizette over toward Stuart and Julia. "He got home yesterday."

Lizette tried to avoid Stuart's eyes but could feel the flush beginning to replace the pallor that had hit her at the sight of him. "Senator, Mrs. Kolter," she said unsteadily.

Stuart reached out politely and took her hand, his eyes studying her curiously. Two months ago he had left a plump young woman behind; now he was suddenly confronted by a strikingly gorgeous slim woman. "Lizette Dante?" he asked. At first she thought he was pretending surprise.

It wasn't until she realized Julia was staring at her too that she was aware the shocked surprise in Stuart's eyes was real too.

"Miss Dante? Lizette?" Julia said with some trepidation.

"What a surprise. You look so . . . so . . . different. I hardly recognized you."

"Doesn't she look luscious?" said Felicia, smiling triumphantly.

Lizette's flush deepened until her cheeks were crimson.

Stuart tried not to show any emotion other than friendly warmth. "Felicia's been all atwitter waiting for you to get here, Lizette," he said. "I suppose your mother was thoroughly surprised."

His remark was a good reason to look away, and they all glanced over to where Rebel was enjoying the attention of her friends.

"I'm sure she was," she said, trying to keep her voice steady. "She wasn't planning to celebrate her birthday this year."

Julia glanced at Lizette. "You mean because of your brother?" she asked.

"I'm afraid things haven't been the same at Tonnerre since all this happened," Lizette answered, watching her mother's face. It was the first time in ages she'd seen her smile so freely.

Julia stared at Lizette. She couldn't get over the change in the young woman. She had been pretty enough before; now she was absolutely lovely. Then Julia noticed the intense light in Stuart's eyes as he too watched Lizette. Strange, she had never seen him look at anyone in quite that way before. Oh, well, it was probably just that he too was struck by the difference. She reached out and took his arm, suggesting that they too should wish Mrs. Dante a happy birthday, and Lizette was thankful for the reprieve as Julia and Stuart excused themselves and walked away.

The evening was going well. Lizette and Felicia had had a long talk, catching up on all the things young women talk about, and there were a number of young gentlemen at the party, sons of some of her parents' friends, who discovered that Lizette had miraculously, in just the past few months, become one of the loveliest young women in Port Royal and Beaufort. They tried to make up for their earlier neglect of her by fawning over her, but it did little good. Lizette was cool toward them, treating them with a haughty indifference, and she enjoyed every minute of their embarrassment at her rebuffs.

However, it was taxing to act as if she didn't have any cares in the world, when all the time she knew what lay ahead of her. Bain hadn't returned yet, thank God, but she knew he was expected within the next few days. That meant she had to tell Stuart about the baby as soon as she could. Tonight if possible, only it seemed like he was never alone.

She was standing near one of the rear windows that overlooked the garden. Dinner had been over for almost an hour and everyone was milling about, talking. Her eyes began to scan the room, then suddenly she froze as Stuart spoke from close beside her, his voice low, hushed.

"I have to see you alone," he said.

She flushed, then glanced about quickly to see if they were being watched. No one seemed to be noticing them. "When?" she asked.

His eyes darkened. "Now. You know where the library is?"

She nodded.

"I'll meet you there as soon as I can slip away."

"You think that's wise?"

"To hell with what's wise. The library," he whispered, then suddenly began talking about something completely unrelated as someone came up to ask him a question about some bill that the Senate had been voting on.

Lizette excused herself quickly and melted back into the crowd, making her way toward the drawing-room door. She hurried down the hall, stopping in front of the library, then opened the huge carved door and ducked inside. Only the lamp on the desk in the far corner was lit, and it was turned as low as it would go, making the room intimate and shadowed.

She straightened, taking a deep breath, her hands trembling. She had to tell Stuart not only about the baby but also about Bain. What a mess she had made of everything. If she had only waited. But how was she to know Bain would come home? And even if she had waited, she'd still be fat and ugly; it was only the pregnancy that was taking the weight off her. If she had stayed fat, Bain would have turned and run at the sight of her, just like the other men. All except Stuart, that is.

She didn't have to wait long. She was standing by one of the windows a few minutes later, staring out, when she heard the doorknob turn.

Stuart had made sure Julia was busy talking to friends before leaving the drawing room, but even then he had had a hard time getting away. There was always someone who wanted to talk politics. The hall had been brightly lit, and now he stood leaning against the library door, adjusting his eyes in the dimly lit room. He straightened, every nerve in his body tingling as his eyes fell on Lizette. She was standing in front of the window, the lamplight brushing her like a painter's brush, so that she almost looked unreal.

"I knew you were beautiful," he whispered softly, "but I guess I never realized just how lovely you really were."

She swallowed hard, remembering the last time they were together and the way he'd made love to her, but then in the next instant she remembered Bain kissing her good-bye before he left for Charleston. She was so terribly unsure.

He walked toward her and took her hands in his, his eyes poring over her newly slimmed figure. "What a shock," he sighed appreciatively.

She flushed uncomfortably, looking up into his dark blue eyes. "I have another shock for you, too," she began, but he stopped her.

"Later. First things first," and he pulled her into his arms, his lips covering hers with a trembling hunger that had been waiting for too long for appeasement. The kiss was long and slow as he savored every moment, and she kissed him back, responding once more to the familiar feel of him. "I missed you terribly," he said against her mouth. "You're so lovely . . ."

"And so pregnant," she whispered back, and felt his body tense.

He drew back, his eyes locking with hers. There was no teasing sparkle to her eyes, only a sad acceptance. "You're sure?" he asked tonelessly.

She nodded. "It happened when you were home over the Christmas holidays."

He took a deep breath, his arms still about her, his eyes unreadable. "Damn, I was hoping it wouldn't happen, since we rarely get to see each other."

"It only takes once, Stuart."

"I know, I know." He was frowning, his jaw tense as he tried to think. "Maybe I could find someone . . . you couldn't have it done here in Beaufort or Port Royal either," he said slowly, thoughtfully. "Someone would surely find out. Maybe you could go to Charleston or—"

"No!" she said emphatically, not letting him finish. "That's not why I told you. I'm not getting rid of it. I thought of that already. I can't, Stuart, not that."

"You can't? Then what do you plan to do?" he asked. "My God, Liz, I can't father a child out of wedlock!"

"You already have."

"You don't understand." He took her by the shoulders, looking down into her face, his heart twisting inside him. "I can't acknowledge the child, Lizette," he murmured agonizingly. "My family, my career, everything I have . . . and you seem to forget, there's a law—they can hang a man for bastardy."

"I don't have to tell anyone. It can be our secret," she offered. "There's no way they can make me tell if I don't want to."

"You think I'd do that to you? No, we have no alternative, darling," he whispered softly. "You'll have to get rid of it."

"No!"

He drew her closer and leaned down, kissing her neck, begging her softly, his lips torturing her with their soft caresses, and she kept whispering no, over and over again, until he was suddenly kissing her mouth.

Neither of them heard the library door open until it suddenly clicked shut again and Rand Kolter cleared his throat. "Stuart! What the devil is going on here?" he demanded harshly, and Stuart's lips stopped on hers.

He jerked his head back, straightening as his father strode angrily across the room.

"I asked you, what the hell are you doing?"

"What does it look like I'm doing?" Stuart replied curtly.

Rand's eyes narrowed. "I can see what you're doing," he stated furiously. "What I want to know is why?"

Stuart's arm went about Lizette, and he felt her shudder. "I'm sorry, Father," he said, and his own knees felt a trifle shaky; still he braced himself stubbornly. "Lizette and I have been seeing each other for almost a year now . . ."

Rand was stunned.

"I know what you're going to say," Stuart told his father. "But there's no need, I've told myself the same things a thousand times already, and it hasn't helped."

"But Lizette . . . ?"

"Does it really matter who, Father?" he asked. "I didn't ask for it to happen. We met and . . . No one sets out to have an affair."

"Then, dammit, why didn't you stop it!"

"Because I couldn't! And now . . ."

"Now what?"

Stuart took a deep breath, then faced his father squarely, his face crimson. "She's pregnant," he answered softly.

Lizette saw Rand's eyes ignite as his face paled, the veins in his neck tightening. "You damn fool, you!" he yelled, trying to keep his voice down. "Don't you know what you've done?"

"For God's sake, Father, I'm a grown man, not a little boy!" Stuart yelled back.

"Then why didn't you remember that? Why didn't you remember who and what you were before you let something like this happen! You're a United States senator, for Christ's sake. What are people going to say!"

"They won't say anything," he answered. "She's going to get rid of it."

"I am not!" cried Lizette, finally interrupting them. "I told you I wouldn't."

"You have to. If anyone finds out, I'll lose everything."

She shook her head, tears in her eyes. "I won't, and you can't make me, Stuart," she murmured softly. "It's my baby and I'm going to keep it."

"Be sensible, Lizette," said Rand, embarrassed by this whole thing. "If anyone found out . . . Stuart's career's at stake, his whole life."

"What about my life?" she asked bitterly. "Women have died trying to do what you're suggesting."

Rand stared at her; she was right. In the first place, how could they locate someone who would be discreet? People like that couldn't be trusted, and if anyone got wind of what was going on, Stuart would be leaving himself wide open for blackmail. In the second place, she was the daughter of his best friends, and if the operation was botched, he'd never forgive himself. But most of all, there was no way they were going to talk her into it. There had to be some solution somewhere.

He watched Stuart trying to persuade her, touching Lizette's face tenderly, trying to wipe away her tears. Dammit anyway, Stuart cared, and that made matters worse. Rand watched her green eyes plead with his son, and suddenly he saw in her face what Stuart had seen months ago; Lizette wasn't a little girl anymore; her eyes were filled with a deep passion, their youthful innocence replaced by a seductive yearning. Suddenly he remembered why he'd come looking for Stuart, and the answer came to him loud and clear.

"That's it," he said, his eyes focusing on his son's face as Stuart turned toward him. "I think I've found the answer. It's so simple I should have thought of it before. My God, it's the only thing we can do!"

Stuart frowned, puzzled.

"Bain!" Rand Kolter exclaimed carefully, and Stuart was startled.

"Bain? What does he have to do with this?" he asked, bewildered.

"He's our way out," his father said, determined. "I was trying to find you to tell you that Bain just got back from Charleston. Don't you see? There's our answer—Bain will marry Lizette and no one will be the wiser. He's been up at Tonnerre visiting her every chance he's had since he got home as it is, so no one will suspect a thing."

Stuart let his father's last statement sink in, then turned slowly and stared at Lizette. "You . . . and Bain?" he asked, his voice breaking.

She withdrew from him, her eyes faltering. "I . . . he . . . we . . ."

He grabbed her wrist, anger flashing in his eyes. "You . . . and Bain?" he asked again, the anger rising in his voice.

Rand stepped forward and took Stuart's arm, trying to cut through the rage that was making his son tremble. "For heaven's sake, Stuart, let it be," he said bitterly. "Haven't you done enough damage? What right have you to be jealous of what she does, when you leave her arms to go home to your wife? Good Lord, don't ruin the only chance you have to salvage the mess you're in!"

Stuart's eyes darkened, his face like granite as he stared at her. His father was right, but that didn't mean it didn't hurt. He let go of her arm, his jaw tightening. "Where is Bain?" he asked through clenched teeth.

Rand sighed. "That's better. He's up in his room. I'll go get him. You two wait here. And for heaven's sake, control your temper!"

Stuart nodded, and his father left, leaving them alone in the room. It was so quiet you could hear the faint creaking of the old house. Lizette stared at him, waiting for the condemnation.

"It's always been Bain, hasn't it?" he said huskily.

She wanted to cry. "I don't know."

"He's made love to you since he returned?"

"No!"

"You're lying!"

"Why would I lie?"

"Because you're still in love with him."

"Oh, Stuart!" she cried unhappily. "I don't know what I feel anymore." She walked over into the shadows and sat on the sofa, slumping dejectedly. "I know I'm sick most of the time, I'm alone most of the time, and I hate having to share you with Julia when you are home. It just isn't enough anymore, and when Bain came home unexpectedly, I didn't know what to do. I never realized how much the two of you are alike." She glanced over at him and felt a pang of hurt sweep through her. This was the end, and she knew it. Bain wasn't about to marry her—that was wishful thinking on his father's part—and her brief interlude with Stuart was over too. Even if Stuart hadn't learned about Bain, now that his father knew about them, he'd never let it go on. No, there was nothing left for her but to leave Port Royal and try to make a life for herself somewhere else where no one knew her, and that meant giving up both of them. When Bain learned about her affair with Stuart, he was going to hate her. She was going to be left with nothing, only the baby. Well, that they'd never take from her.

"Stuart," she said unsteadily, "don't hate me, please. You weren't here, and I had to have something."

"So you let Bain make love to you!"

"I let him kiss me, that's all." Her eyes filled with tears. "Stuart, I'm scared," she cried helplessly. "He won't marry me, I know he won't, not when he finds out what I've done, and I can't have you! Please, everything's gone wrong. I didn't want this to happen. I only wanted someone to love me."

Stuart stared at her hesitantly, then walked over and looked down into her eyes. He reached out and wiped a tear from her cheek. "Someone does love you, Liz," he whispered softly, and he bent down, his lips touching hers for what she knew was probably the last time, and her mouth clung to his desperately.

Bain was still in his room. He had washed quickly and freshened up since arriving home, changing his dusty boots along with the rumpled clothes. Now he was elegant in a midnight-blue velvet frock coat, Wellington boots beneath his buff trousers, a ruffled shirt, and a pale blue silk cravat at his throat. He was taking one last look in the mirror when there was a knock on the door. "Come in!" Rand's head appeared in the mirror behind him. "Did you find Stuart?"

His father's face was troubled, and Bain frowned. "What is it? What's happened?"

"I found him . . . but I'm going to need your help."

"Don't tell me the good senator's drunk!"

"I wish it were that simple, Bain."

Bain studied his father's face. "All right, Father, what is it?" he asked.

"I'm afraid Stuart's gotten himself into a rather delicate situation, Bain," he said, hoping to break it to him gently. "To put it bluntly, he's been having an affair, and now the young lady's with child, and dammit all to hell, I don't know how we're going to handle it."

Bain whistled softly in disbelief and shook his head. "Not Stuart," he said. "Not the big brother who's always walked the straight and narrow?"

"I'm afraid so."

"Where is he?"

"They're both downstairs in the library waiting for us to join them." Rand Kolter bit his lip. "I was hoping maybe you'd come down . . . we'd like to talk to you. I'm hoping maybe you'll help."

"I don't know what I can do," he said. "But let's go down. I imagine by now he's in quite a state."

Bain studied his father as they headed downstairs. There had been something about the look in his eyes when he'd told him about Stuart, a suspicious reluctance, and he wondered just what was running through his head. And that was another thing. If Stuart had gotten himself in trouble, with his influence, why didn't he just pay the lady off and have her disappear from sight? Unless maybe she was blackmailing him. Was that why they were asking for his help? His father suddenly looked tired, the crow's-feet deepening about his eyes, and—it was probably just Bain's imagination—for some reason tonight the gray at his father's temples seemed to have spread up into his hair more, making him look so much older. Maybe he just hadn't taken time to notice before, he'd been so wrapped up in his pursuit of Lizette since arriving back in Beaufort.

The thought of her stirred the blood in his veins. She was supposed to be here tonight, and he was restless, anxious to see her. That's why he had hurried home. They reached the library door. "Whatever happens, I hope this won't take too long," Bain said as his father began opening the door. "I'm all for helping Stuart out of this mess, but I've been waiting all evening to see a certain young lady, and I'd like to be able to spend as much time with her as I can."

Rand stared at him for a long hard minute, suddenly wishing now more than ever he didn't have to do what he was about to do, yet knowing he had no choice. He opened the door quickly and gestured for Bain to go in, then followed close at his son's heels, shutting the door firmly behind them.

The library was still deep in shadows, the lamp barely burning as Bain stepped into the room. His eyes adjusted slowly as he stepped forward, and he saw Stuart standing near one of the sofas, his back to them, talking to someone.

Stuart glanced at his father. "Did you tell him?" he asked.

Rand nodded. "I told him," his voice broke—"all but her name."

The woman Stuart had been talking to looked directly toward him as Stuart moved aside, and the flickering light fell across her, throwing the features into sharp relief.

Bain stood stock-still, the color draining from his face. "Lizette . . . ?" he whispered in disbelief.

Stuart turned back to her and helped her to her feet.

"You . . . ?" Bain asked again.

"I tried to tell you," she said softly. "I told you it was too late."

"This is what you meant?" he asked, anger beginning to replace the shock. "This is why you said too much had happened?"

"Bain, you have to understand—" she began.

"Understand?" he shouted. "Understand? Oh, I understand only too well." His eyes were hard. "Goddammit, did you have to pick on Stuart? You could have had your pick!"

"Could I?" she yelled back. "How would you know? You weren't here. You ran out on me, and now you think you have the right to condemn!"

"Quiet!" shouted Rand, trying to make some sense out of the whole mess. He looked at Bain. "What the hell's going on here?" he asked. "What does she mean, you ran out on her?"

"Never mind!" Bain snapped.

"I don't blame you, Bain," said Stuart deliberately. "I wouldn't want him to know either!"

"Know what?" demanded Rand.

"That she was a virgin until Bain got hold of her."

Rand's eyes widened. "You and Lizette?" he asked incredulously, looking at Bain. "You lay with her? My God, she was barely fifteen when you left!"

"Why do you think he left?" exclaimed Stuart.

Rand's jaw clenched. "Is he telling the truth, Bain?" he asked.

Bain straightened, broad shoulders flexing as he stared at his older brother. "Yes, it's true," he said, eyes smoldering. "But I'd like to know how the hell he knew," and his eyes moved to Lizette, settling uncomfortably on her face.

Lizette cringed. There was hatred in his eyes, and she felt sick. "He guessed, Bain," she said reluctantly. "I didn't want to tell him."

"It didn't seem to change things, though, did it?" he said, looking at Stuart.

Stuart's chin tilted stubbornly. "Was it supposed to?"

Bain sneered. "I should think you wouldn't want my left-overs!"

Stuart's eyes narrowed savagely and he grabbed for Bain. Both of Bain's arms came up as he tried to ward him off, and they scuffled furiously for a few breathless moments until Rand managed to break it up, stepping between them.

"For God's sake!" Rand yelled, trying to keep his voice from carrying as he hung on to them, holding them apart. "This is no time to argue over who was first and why." He eased off with his hands, watching each of them closely to make certain they weren't going to continue their altercation when he released them. "We've got things to settle here, and I don't need you two at each other's throats."

Bain was breathing heavily and so was Stuart, their eyes locked in silent combat. Lizette was staring at them, tears streaming down her face. "Please, I don't need any of this!" she cried miserably. "I don't need any of you. I'll have this baby by myself. I'm sorry I even told you!"

Rand stared at her, suddenly realizing what she must be going through. He looked at his sons, first one, then the other. "The both of you ought to be horsewhipped," he growled viciously. "Now, stop the nonsense and let's get this settled." His eyes were hard, unyielding, as he walked over and took Lizette's arm, handing her a handkerchief, then making her sit back down on the sofa. He looked at Bain and Stuart again, and his mouth twitched nervously. "We can argue all night," he said, "and it's not going to help Lizette." He took a deep breath and looked back at Bain. "That's why I asked you here to help, Bain," he said. "There's no way in hell I'm going to let Stuart lose everything over this."

Bain took a deep breath. "So what are you going to do?"

"You're going to marry her!" he said without changing expression.

Bain's eyes narrowed and he stared at his father, the room suddenly growing as silent as a tomb. "You're joking," he said, his voice vibrating with emotion.

"Not in the least," said Rand sternly. "Stuart has not only Julia and the children to think of but also his career. I don't intend for him to lose either."

"So instead you'll sacrifice me!"

"If that's the way you want to put it."

"And if I say no?"

"Then I'll have to get rough."

"What do you mean?"

Rand walked over to his desk, unlocked one of the drawers and opened it, pulling out a sheaf of papers, handing them to Bain. "Do you know what these are?"

Bain looked at the papers, then stared at his father. "The notes on my loans," he answered.

"That's right," said Rand. "You asked me to back you, I did. Now I'm asking you to back me."

"And if I don't, you'll call the loans in!"

"You'll lose everything."

Lizette saw Bain's jaw tighten angrily. "You can't do that. There's two more years standing on them!"

"Not if I sell them. Remember, I drew up the papers. If the notes are sold to another party, the loans automatically come due on transfer."

Bain threw the papers down on his father's desk and glanced over to Lizette, his mouth trembling with rage. "You win," he snarled bitterly, then looked back at his father. "You know damn well I can't let you call in those notes."

"I thought you'd see reason," said Rand, picking the papers up and putting them back in the drawer. "I was hoping you'd help your brother because you care, but I can see this whole mess isn't quite that simple."

Bain shoved his hands in the pocket of his frock coat and walked over to one of the windows, staring out, his back to them.

Stuart stared at him. They had never been close, but they had always gotten along until now. "Bain, I'm sorry," he said, his deep voice vibrating emotionally. "I never dreamed anything like this would happen."

Bain snorted a half-laugh and whirled around, his mouth twisting cynically. "What did you think was going to happen?" he asked bitterly. "You make love to a woman, she gets pregnant. It's as simple as that."

Stuart's eyes grew distant for a moment; then he turned to Lizette and they softened. He walked over, sitting down beside her, and took her hand and was about to say something, when he was suddenly interrupted by Bain who had stridden purposefully across the room and was standing next to Lizette.

"Since Lizette is now the future Mrs. Kolter, Stuart," he said through clenched teeth, "I want you now, and in the future, to keep your distance. Is that understood?"

Stuart looked up at his brother, frowning deeply. "I only wanted to try to make her feel better," he tried to explain.

Bain's eyes were like steel. "I think you've done quite enough."

Stuart stood up. Bain's face was like granite, his eyes boring into Stuart's as if waiting for a challenge. "You're right, of course," Stuart said diplomatically, then glanced back down to where Lizette sat staring up at them.

Stuart trembled. It was ending too quickly, all the warmth and passion, all the soft intimate moments that had filled his life. She was the loveliest woman he had ever known, and he felt a tug at his heart. If only . . . A sadness veiled his eyes, and Lizette felt his withdrawal.

"Stuart . . . ?" she whispered breathlessly.

"You heard Bain," he said. "It's over, Lizette. I'm sorry it's ending like this, but he's right. The farther I stay from you, the better, for both our sakes."

She bit her lip nervously. "Thank you for being there when I needed you," she said softly; then added, "Forgive me."

He took a deep breath and looked at Bain again. "Take good care of her, brother," he said, his voice breaking. "Because if you don't, you'll answer to me."

"I answer to no one, Senator," Bain said angrily. "Least of all you. She'll be my wife and I'll treat her as I see fit."

Stuart grimaced, ready to defy him, when Rand interrupted.

"Don't start again," he said furiously. "I won't put up with it. We have plans to make. There's a date to decide on, and when we're going to announce the betrothal."

"Do her parents know?" asked Bain.

They all looked at Lizette.

"I didn't tell anyone except Stuart," she answered timidly.

Rand sighed, relieved. "Thank God!"

Bain was still staring down at Lizette. "How far along are you?" he asked.

She swallowed hard. "A little over two months."

She saw the bitterness in his eyes. He tried to mask it as he addressed his father. "Then I think it would be wise if you announced to your guests before they left this evening that your son and the Dantes' daughter have eloped," he said quite calmly.

Rand stared at him dumbfounded. "Eloped?"

"It's the only thing we can do," said Bain, watching his father's face. "By the time we announce a betrothal and wait for a wedding, she'll be almost four months. I don't intend to look like that big a fool."

"But to elope . . . ?"

"Why not?" Bain looked down at Lizette. "You don't mind, do you?" he asked. "It's to your advantage too, you know."

Lizette wanted to cry, but fought back the tears. "I don't know," she answered apprehensively. "Where would we go? And my parents . . ."

"That'll be my problem," he said quickly. "Will you go with me tonight? It'll save a lot of embarrassment."

He was right. If they left now, she wouldn't have to face any of them again as Lizette Dante. She'd be Bain's wife, something she'd always dreamed of becoming, although not like this. Oh, God, not like this!

"Lizette?" he asked again.

"I'll go," she said, half-whispering. "If that's what you want."

"It's what I want," he said, and took her hand, pulling her to her feet again.

"You can't just walk out!" said Rand as he stared at them.

Bain put an arm around Lizette's shoulder. "Don't tell me what I can or can't do, Father," he said acidly. "I'm marrying Lizette, and your precious senator is safe, but I'm doing it my way." His hand dropped from about her shoulder, and he walked to the desk, uncapping a bottle of ink and taking a pen and paper from one of the drawers. He wrote something on the paper, blotted it, then handed it to his father. "Here," he said. "Show the Dantes this—it should be enough." He walked back over to Lizette. "Are you ready?"

She was still fighting back the tears. "Yes," she said softly, her voice almost lost in the big room.

Bain stood tall and firm, his head high as he started ushering her toward the door.

"Where will you go, Bain?" asked his father, distress filling his eyes.

Bain stopped for a minute and looked back. "Do you really care?" he asked sarcastically, and opened the door, leading her out.

No one was in the hall. "Did you wear a wrap?" he asked.

"I had my pelisse."

He ordered one of the maids to bring it to him, then helped her on with it, hoping they could get out before anyone saw them.

"Aren't you going to take anything with you?" she asked when the maid had left.

He looked into her eyes. "I'm taking you."

She flushed, and the tears finally came.

"Come on," he said quickly, hurrying her toward the front door. When they were finally outside, he sighed. "You'll have to share my horse," he said. "But it won't be for long."

When they reached the stables she watched him saddle the horse, her mind racing over the past hour, trying to remember everything that had been said and done, but it had all happened so quickly. And now she was going away with Bain. But where? What lay ahead, and why did it have to be like this? They had nothing with them. No clothes, no money . . .

He interrupted her thoughts. "Amigo's ready," he said quickly.

She glanced up. He was on the horse already, and she shook the cobwebs from her mind.

"Give me your hand," he said roughly.

She gave a slight jump and he pulled her onto the horse, settling her in front of him, the skirt of her green silk dress bunched up around her legs.

"Are you all right?" he asked.

She nodded. "Yes." But she wasn't. As they rode out into the cool night air, Lizette could feel the anger that drove Bain, and her tears began anew as she wondered what was in store for them.

21

The trees along the side of the dusty road whispered in the night breeze that had kicked up since they had left Beaufort, and Lizette huddled closer to Bain, hoping to ward off the chill that was beginning to make her shiver.

"We're almost there," he said as he saw houses up ahead.

She knew they were heading toward Port Royal, but had no idea why. Bain had said little to her on the long ride, except to ask occasionally if she was comfortable.

They had forgotten to get her bonnet when they'd left the house, and she reached up, pushing a strand of stray hair back out of her eyes. They began riding by houses, and unable to contain her curiosity any longer, she finally asked, "Why did we come to Port Royal?"

She felt him take a deep breath, but his answer was unenlightening. "You'll find out."

She pursed her lips tightly, deciding she wasn't going to say another word to him until he spoke to her first. After a few minutes, she realized they were heading for the wharf.

It was close to midnight by now, and the place was deserted as Bain reined Amigo down a short street that ended at the wharf. He pulled back on the reins and sat for a minute gazing at a ship resting all by itself, bobbing gently on the water, the rigging gaunt and bleak against the deep purple of the night sky.

She felt him stir against her, and he slipped from the saddle; then he reached up, pulling her down with him. "Come on," he said, taking her hand, leading both her and his horse out onto the pier. She frowned as he let go of her hand, then watched him raise a hand to his mouth, calling. "Ho, there! Captain Holley!"

He waited a few minutes, then called again, and suddenly a light shone aboard ship and a body appeared in its glow, a husky figure of a man dressed in a captain's uniform. "Who's there?"

"It's Bain!"

"Mr. Kolter?"

"Yes!"

They watched the man turn, saying something to someone behind him, and then there was a scuffling and confusion on the deck of the ship and a gangplank came sliding out, clanking against the wharf. Down the gangplank came two sailors, one carrying a lantern. Bain didn't explain anything to her, or even try; all he did was hand the reins of his horse over to one of the sailors, instructing him to take Amigo aboard, then he took Lizette's hand, pulling her toward the gangplank.

"Hang on to the guideline," he ordered as he ushered her onto it ahead of him. "And watch your footing."

She glanced at him, unable to see his face clearly in the light from the flickering lantern the sailor was holding; then she sighed, starting up the gangplank. Moments later she was being helped onto the ship by a ruddy-faced man who looked to be in his mid-forties. He wasn't tall, but he was broad and brawny, with dark whiskers starting where his hairline ended and dipping down to the bend in his jaw, where they stopped. He had dark eyes that studied Lizette curiously as he let go of her hand, then greeted Bain. "You going back with us, Mr. Kolter?" the captain asked rather hesitantly.

"I'll explain later," said Bain, then glanced about. "Think there's enough wind to get her under way tonight?" he asked.

Captain Holley gazed at him in surprise. "Now?" he asked.

"Now," Bain repeated.

The captain straightened. "No problem at all," he assured him.

Bain nodded. "Good! I'll take her down to my cabin"—he motioned toward Lizette—"then I want to talk to you once we get under way." The captain nodded to him firmly, and Bain turned to Lizette. "Come on, I'll take you belowdecks."

He took her arm again, and she let him guide her, while she tried to take a closer look at the ship they were on. It was larger than her grandfather's ship, the *Interlude,* and sleeker than her father's ship, the *Duchess*. It was a three-master with trim lines, long and narrow, similar to the packet ships she'd read about in the newspapers that had run the British blockades during the war.

As Bain opened the door for her to go below, she wondered where he was taking her and why he seemed to be so at home aboard the ship. A few minutes later he ushered her into a small cabin at the end of the passageway. It was so dark she couldn't see anything, the only light coming from a dimly lit whale-oil lamp overhead.

"Make yourself at home," he said, walking past her and turning up the lamp so the soft glow fell on the furniture.

She had expected to see a crude cabin with only the bare necessities; instead she stared at a compact room with a double bed fastened securely to the floor, a built-in desk at the far end beneath windows set in the bow of the ship, and a small table with chairs anchored in the middle of the room. An armoire was secured to the inside wall next to the bed, and the covers on the bed were neatly done up, a red brocade bedspread covering it.

She looked at Bain, her eyes bewildered. "Whose ship is this?" she finally asked.

His smile was twisted. "Mine," he answered. "Welcome to the *Dragonfly*."

She stared at him in surprise. "I had no idea you owned a ship."

"I own three. This one, the *Sparrow*, and the *Raven*. We ran the British blockades during the war."

"I didn't know," she said softly.

He straightened, his eyes studying her intensely. "I think there's a lot about me you don't know," he offered, then started for the door. "For now, just sit and rest a bit. I'll be back in a short while, as soon as we've cleared the sound."

He left the cabin, and she stood in the middle of the room staring after him. The ship heaved beneath her feet as the sails unfurled, and little by little the ship began to inch away from the pier. The rolling glide of the ship caught her off balance for a second, and she took a step toward the bed, falling across it.

She gasped audibly, then stood up again, trying to get her

sea legs. Once the ship was on its way, the pitching stopped and there was only a gentle rolling. She eased with it, and began walking around the room, inspecting everything. The cabin was neat. Papers were kept in the drawers, and she was surprised to find the armoire full of clothes. Men's clothes.

With a sigh she walked to the window and opened it. The night breeze hit her in the face, and suddenly she began to realize Bain was right. She knew so little about him. She stared out into the darkness for a long time, then sat on one of the chairs at the table, her hands folded in front of her.

She thought back over the past few years. Hardly anyone knew anything about Bain. He always came and went without warning. No one ever seemed to know where he came from or where he went. She remembered the notes his father had held over his head and wondered why he had borrowed money. What did he need money for? She tried to recall if anyone had ever dropped even a hint as to how he made his living, and she could remember nothing. Not even a tiny clue, yet he always seemed affluent.

She was still sitting at the table wondering, staring at her hands, almost an hour later when Bain walked in with the captain at his heels.

"We've cleared the sound now, Lizette," he said, his voice impersonal. "Did you want to freshen up any, or have the ceremony just as you are?"

"What ceremony?" she asked.

He looked surprised. "Why, we decided to get married on board ship, love, remember?"

Suddenly she understood. "I . . . I forgot for a minute, I guess," she said. Then shook her head. "I'm all right." She stood up. "I'm just tired."

He took her arm. "It won't take long. The men are all waiting, and Captain Holley said he'd be pleased to officiate."

"Are you sure she's not too tired tonight, Bain?" he asked. "We could always wait until morning."

"Nonsense," said Bain. "I told her we were going to be married tonight, and by God, we're going to!" He took her arm, leading her to the door of the cabin. The captain followed.

It was cool on deck, the sea breeze lifting the sails as the ship cut the water, and Lizette breathed deeply of the salt spray. It hung in the air as they stood in the bow while some two dozen or so sailors crowded around watching.

Lizette was nervous. She had always hoped to be married in a church with all her family and friends around. She'd wear a white satin dress with a long train and filmy veil and walk down the aisle on her father's arm. Instead, she was standing on the rough planks of a ship with a lot of rugged sailors gawking inquisitively, and on top of it, ever since the ship had started moving down the waters of the sound, her stomach had been doing occasional flip-flops. She didn't know whether it was from nerves or from being pregnant. She held on to Bain's arm not only for moral support but also to steady her knees. She was tired, close to tears, and could hardly find her voice when it was her turn to repeat after the captain:

"I, Lizette Dante, take thee, Bain Hadley Kolter . . ." The ceremony droned on. She heard Bain as if in a dream: "I, Bain Hadley Kolter, take thee, Lizette Dante . . ."

"I now pronounce you man and wife," said the captain firmly. "You may kiss the bride."

Lizette stared at Captain Holley, then turned to Bain, her eyes searching his face. Was he going to kiss her?

Bain saw her confused look, and for a brief moment he forgot why he was marrying her and remembered only what it was like to feel his lips on hers. He bent down, planning to do nothing more than touch her lips lightly with his own, so the men didn't think there was something wrong.

But as their lips met, the vague scent of cape jasmine drifted up to him, and the soft flesh of her full lips, slightly moist from the salt spray, was just enough to ignite the fire that had been smoldering inside him. With a groan escaping from deep inside him, his lips almost devoured her and he pulled her roughly against him.

The men let out a whoop, calling and cheering, and Lizette could feel herself beginning to grow hot all over. She tried to remain passive in his arms, but it was no use. She loved him too much, and with a surge of passion she was unable to suppress, she gave her lips to him eagerly, her body melting into his arms.

Bain was on fire, his body trembling as he drew his mouth from hers and looked deep into her eyes. The light on deck was dim, but he could see they were glazed with passion, her lips quivering. He took a deep breath and held it for a brief second, his body crying with need of her; then he reached down, sweeping her up, cradling her against him, and headed belowdecks.

The overhead lamp was still lit in the cabin as he stepped in, shutting the door behind him with his foot, and he walked over, standing next to the bed with her still cradled in his arms. He stopped motionless and stared down at her, and suddenly something happened inside him.

He began to remember that she was pregnant, that the baby was his brother's, and all the raging hunger to possess her was instantly replaced by a bitter torment that broke like a storm, bringing with it a violent anger he was helpless to control.

He inhaled sharply as he stared at her, then quite abruptly threw her on the bed. "You'd like that, wouldn't you?" he said viciously, his emotions in a turmoil. "You'd like me to make love to you!" He sat down on the bed beside her and leaned over her, holding her arms, pinning her to the bed. "Oh, how you'd like that, but it's not going to happen, Lizette, do you hear me! It's not going to happen! I'm not going to touch you. Not tonight, not tomorrow night. Not ever! You'll be my wife and you can have your damn baby, but by God, you'll never have me!"

The blood drained from Lizette's face as she stared up at him, frightened at the force he was using to pin her down and at the fury that blazed in his eyes.

"Bain, don't, please," she begged helplessly. "You're hurting me!"

He stared at her hard for about half a minute, then released her wrists. "I could kill you," he snarled. "Why didn't you tell me? Why did you let me go on believing?"

"Because I didn't know how to tell you. Because I wanted you to believe, even if only for a little while."

He saw the tears in her eyes, but hardened his heart to them. He stood and walked to the armoire, opening one of the doors, reaching in, pulling open a drawer in the bottom. He took out a rumpled shirt and threw it at her. "You can wear that," he said angrily. "I'm afraid I never carried any ladies' nightgowns on board!"

She reached down, laying her hands on his white silk shirt, her eyes on him warily.

"Don't worry, I won't hurt you," he said, his breathing heavy, body rigid. "I have things to do. Go ahead and get some sleep," and without saying another word, he turned and walked out.

Lizette stared apprehensively at the closed door, then slowly stirred, moving to the side of the bed, sitting up with her feet on the floor. The silk shirt was slippery in her hands, and she clenched her fists, looking down at it, the hurt inside causing an ache in her chest.

She sat for a long time just gathering her thoughts, trying

to get the strength to accept the sentence he had imposed on her. Never touch her? Never hold her and make love to her? Tears welled up in her eyes and her jaw tightened stubbornly. All right, if that's the way he wanted it, that's the way it would be. She didn't care. Why should she care! She had already done without him for two years.

When she had changed into the shirt, her clothes tossed onto a chair in the corner, she turned the whale-oil lamp down as low as she could get it, then went to the bed, pulled back the covers, and climbed in. She buried her head into the pillow and pulled the covers up, snuggling down, forcing herself to think of everything and everyone but Bain.

She had no idea when she had finally dozed off, but now, slowly, she began to awaken, aware that someone had just climbed into the bed beside her. The cabin was pitch dark now. "Bain?" she asked hesitantly.

"Who else!"

She relaxed. "Just wanted to make sure," she mumbled sleepily, and turned her back to him, settling down again.

He glanced over toward her vague form beside him. "What would you do if it wasn't me?" he asked softly.

"I'd scream," she answered nonchalantly, then yawned. "Good night, Bain."

He took a deep breath. "Good night, Liz."

He stared into the darkness, heart pounding, every nerve in his body tense. He could feel the warmth from her body even though they weren't touching, and the faint scent of cape jasmine filled his nostrils, bringing an ache to his loins. She was beside him, and yet he had vowed he wouldn't make love to her. He wouldn't . . . oh, God, but he wanted her so badly. Maybe he could just touch her, maybe that would help.

He turned toward her and reached out gingerly at first, not knowing what to expect, not knowing where his hand would touch, and suddenly his fingers slipped on the silk shirt. His hand pressed on her back, and he felt her tense, yet she didn't move. Slowly, deliberately, he moved his hand from her back to her arm and traced it with his fingers, stopping at her elbow. The tips of his fingers lay poised at her elbow as if waiting; then, while Lizette held her breath, she felt him move closer until he was snuggled against her, the silk shirt she had on rubbing against the curling hairs on his bare chest.

She almost gasped as his arm trailed across her waistline, pulling her hard against him. "Shhh," he whispered softly. "Just let me hold you." His lips were against her neck, and she quivered, feeling the tingling down her spine where they touched her flesh.

He kissed the nape of her neck and the pulse beneath her ear, his lips trailing down her neck as his hand began to trail down her body, lifting the shirt until he touched the flesh beneath it, his hands stroking sensuously down the side of her hip.

She moaned without thinking, and felt his sharp intake of breath; then slowly, deliberately, his head reeling with the feel of her, his hand moved back up her body, staying beneath the material of the shirt until he cupped her breast, fitting it comfortably in his hand. The nipple hardened and he called her name softly.

"Liz! Liz!" he whispered, groaning helplessly, and then she felt it between her legs, searching from behind, hot and moist, its hardness probing smooth and slippery between her thighs, touching, twisting, and as his hand left her breast, reaching down across her, pulling her back hard against him, she felt him enter, and a wild shock went through her, carrying her with it to a wonderful, throbbing delight.

He held her against him for a moment, thrusting deep, then slowly began to ease in and out, loving her with every fiber of his being. Wanting her, needing her, forgetting his vow, forgetting everything but his craving to possess her. Then slowly he withdrew and turned her to face him, opening the shirt, exposing her body, reaching out, touching, fondling, his lips finding hers in the dark, and when he moved over her, entering her from above this time, she arched to meet him wantonly, her need for him as strong as his need for her, and they floated together in a world of rapture apart from all the anger and hurt, to a peak of pleasure that left them both breathless.

Bain lay above her, his breathing labored, body satiated, his hunger for her appeased, then slowly slipped from her. Lizette sighed, expecting him to come to his senses and turn away, but he didn't. Instead he reached out, pulled her close in his arms, and kissed her lingeringly. "Good night, Liz," he whispered huskily.

His arms were still about her, and she closed her eyes. "Good night, Bain," she said, and this time when she dropped off to sleep, the aching in her chest was gone, replaced by a gently throbbing pulse that filled her body, lulling her to sleep.

The next morning Lizette awoke with the sun streaming in the window, but the bed beside her was empty. She turned over, stretching in the luxury of its softness, and stared thoughtfully at the dent in the pillow where his head had lain. He had made love to her! Bain had made love to her, and the thought brought a smile to her lips. He loved her, he still cared, he had to; but then, seconds later, her dream was shattered again as Bain strode into the cabin, snapping at her irritably and acting like nothing had happened.

He helped fasten her dress when she slipped it on, and saw that she had her breakfast, but there was no mention of the night before. No tender remarks, no words of love, only a brisk impersonal politeness he might have afforded to any female in his company.

For the next few weeks the *Dragonfly* plied the coastal waters, stopping in ports here and there, where Lizette began to build herself a small wardrobe of new clothes, and she learned a great deal about the man she had fallen in love with as a girl and now found herself married to.

She discovered that he owned a tobacco-processing plant in Virginia although he didn't even smoke so much as a pipe himself, was part-owner in an iron works near a town in Pennsylvania. Owned two copper mines in Mexico and a freighting business in the frontier town of St. Louis, plus a few other small enterprises here and there. They were all run by other people and he'd just show up occasionally to see that everything was going smoothly. His favorite pastime seemed to be roaming the countryside looking for new and different opportunities to come along. Lizette had never dreamed he was anything except a wanderer and no one had ever said anything about him to make her change her mind. Now, she discovered he was a shrewd businessman with diversified interests scattered across the country.

She also learned that he owned a small house in Beaufort, and it was to this house he brought her when they returned the first week in April. She had stood at the rail of the *Dragonfly* and watched the familiar skyline of the town of Port Royal emerging on the horizon, and now she watched attentively as the ship eased up to the pier, readying the gangplank. She leaned far out from the rail, trying to see if there was anyone at the docks she knew.

Bain would have had the ship set in at Tonnerre or the Chateau, but he wasn't certain how her parents and grandparents would greet them after what they'd done, so instead he'd leave the ship in Port Royal. He rented a rig from a liveryman near the waterfront, tied Amigo to the back, and set out for Beaufort with Lizette beside him in the buggy.

Lizette glanced over as they rode along. He hadn't touched her since the night of their wedding. Night after night she lay beside him in the big bed in his cabin waiting, but never again had he made love to her, although she knew he wanted to. There were times he looked at her with such hunger in his eyes that it was frightening, and he was like a coiled spring ready to explode.

When they reached Beaufort and he pulled up in front of the empty stone house, she stared at it in surprise. "You own this?" she asked.

"I bought it just before we left," he explained. "That's what I was doing in Charleston, making arrangements. The former owner moved to Charleston, and there were some things that had to be taken care of concerning the deed and some liens."

Lizette liked the house right away. He let her furnish it whatever way she wanted, his only stipulation being that she show him the costs before making her final decision, and Lizette threw herself into the task with vigor, even hiring a housekeeper and buying two young black girls to help with the work, along with three sturdy slaves to care for the horses and lawns and drive the carriage for her. She bought all of them with the same promise her father and grandfather gave their slaves, that someday they'd be free men and women.

She acquired Pretty quite by accident, her first visit back to Tonnerre, and it was a visit she'd never forget.

They had arrived home on Friday, the fourth of April, and on Saturday morning, after spending the night in the empty house, except for the bed they were sleeping on that Bain managed to acquire between the time they arrived and darkness settled in, they headed for Tonnerre to let her parents know they were back.

Rebel and Beau were so enthusiastic to see them and so happy that she was all right that they didn't even question the fact that they had married so quickly. Bain was quite attentive to her in front of her parents, leading them to believe that the marriage was a happy one. Since they hadn't been able to give her a big wedding or a wedding present, Beau presented her with Pretty's papers, letting the young black woman come with them, with the stipulation that she'd be freed someday, just as he had planned.

And what a help she was. Between Lizette and Pretty the old stone house with its frame portico out front and small flower garden in back soon took on a lived-in look, and Mr.

and Mrs. Bain Kolter slowly became a part of Beaufort society.

Bain had wanted to avoid his parents on their return, but he knew if he did, questions would be asked that neither he nor Lizette wanted to give the answers to, so they were obliged at times to call on them, but tried to keep their visits at a minimum. It was a complete shock, however, when they discovered Julia was planning an elaborate party for them to celebrate their return.

"I won't go to Stuart's house," insisted Bain the afternoon he heard of it, but Lizette reminded him that it would look suspicious if they didn't go. So two weeks after their arrival home, the newlyweds were guests of honor at a party given by Senator and Mrs. Kolter.

Lizette was nervous as she dressed that evening. She still hadn't put on any weight, and Bain had bought her a beautiful dress when they stopped in Charleston, where they visited some of his friends. The dress was white gauze with tiny crystal beads sewn on the skirt and decorating the bodice, making it sparkle like diamonds. The sleeves were the new rage, large and bouffant above the elbows, then hugging the arms until they reached the wrists, where they ended in a deep point on the back of the hand, where crystal beading formed a flowery design. The neckline was low, and she wore a single diamond lavaliere that rested low on her bosom, with matching teardrops in her ears.

The house wasn't complete yet, and she stood in the sparsely furnished bedroom studying herself in the mirror, wondering how she was going to make it through the evening with the knowledge that the man whose child she was carrying was to be treated like a casual acquaintance and that the man she should rightfully be able to call her own was more the stranger.

When she joined Bain in the small foyer at the front of the house, she was pleased at least to see that he was dressed in the height of fashion, with Wellington boots, buff trousers, a deep indigo velvet frock coat with satin lapels, and the white silk shirt she had worn her first night aboard ship, only now it sported a pale blue silk cravat at the throat.

She stared at the shirt for a moment, a flush spreading over her, suddenly wondering if he had worn it on purpose to remind her to whom she belonged. He needn't have gone to such lengths, she thought as he set the white cashmere shawl about her shoulders, then took her arm and ushered her out to the waiting carriage. All he had to do was tell her he loved her, and everything would be all right.

The evening was a disaster for Lizette. From the moment they arrived until it was time to go home, she felt she was on display. Questions were asked that she couldn't answer, about the suddenness of their elopement, since Bain had been home such a short time, and more than one woman made her uncomfortable by insinuating that she was lucky to have caught a man like Bain, because he was the kind of man who could never be content with just one woman, telling her that was why he roamed so much.

Then there were her moments with Julia, trying to be polite and feeling guilty because of the baby inside her. And then there was Stuart, whose deep blue eyes haunted her every moment, even though she avoided him as much as possible. And on top of everything else, Heather's absence from the party. Everett Palmer was there, as was Carl, but again they made their excuses for Heather, her reason being that she was still in mourning and therefore shunned all social events.

Lizette had thought a great deal of Heather those long days on board ship with nothing to do but stare at the rolling sea. On the way home from the party, she pulled the shawl tight about her shoulders and glanced over at Bain. "I want to go see Heather again," she said suddenly.

"Now?" he asked.

"Well, not tonight," she said. "But soon. We should have gone back long ago. She probably thinks we've forgotten all about her."

He studied her for a minute, then shook his head. "You can't go now, Liz. We'd have to use horses. There's no way we could get that close with a carriage, and you shouldn't be riding now."

"Don't be ridiculous," she insisted. "I don't even show yet. We have Diablo down at our place now, and I'm used to riding him. He'll be gentle."

"And take a chance on a miscarriage?"

"Would that be so bad?"

His eyes narrowed. "We'll talk about it when I get back," he said.

She frowned. "Back from where?"

"I thought I had everything settled with the house," he explained. "But I have to go back to Charleston to clear up a couple of matters. "I'll probably be gone almost two weeks, because I'll have to ride Amigo. The *Dragonfly* left for New

Orleans two days ago and won't be back for at least a month."

She sighed, and he saw the studious look on her face. "And don't you go trying it without me, either, Liz," he ordered harshly. "Because if you do, and you lose that baby, you can kiss this marriage good-bye. I'll have it annulled so quickly you won't even have time to catch your breath."

Her eyes narrowed. "You'd do that to me?"

"Is it any worse than what you've done to me?"

Tears sprang to her eyes and she looked away, her mouth trembling, and the rest of the way home she never spoke a word, nor did he.

Bain left early Monday morning and Lizette spent the rest of the day rearranging the furniture in the house, then took Pretty with her and rode into town and bought a new hat. That had always seemed to perk up her spirits before, but for some reason she just couldn't get Heather off her mind.

Finally she made her decision as she stood in the backyard watching the sun go down.

"Are you going to sit outside on the bench, Miss Lizzie?" Pretty asked from behind her. "If you are, I can bring you a shawl. The air's cooler tonight than it has been."

Lizette shook her head. "Pretty," she said thoughtfully, "you've been with me a long time, haven't you?"

Pretty nodded. "Yes, ma'am."

"Can I trust you?" she asked a bit breathlessly.

The young black woman stared at her, her dark eyes intense. "With what?"

"You have to promise on pain of death, to help me, no questions asked," Lizette said seriously. "Just like when we were younger. Promise?"

Pretty frowned. "Is it something bad?" she asked.

"Not really," said Lizette. "But it's something no one knows about, and I need your help. Please, Pretty."

Pretty had seen that look in Lizette's eyes a hundred times over and knew she was up to no good. But she belonged to Lizette now, and if Lizette needed help . . . "I promise," she said.

"Good," said Lizette. "Because I want you to do something for me tonight, but you mustn't tell anyone, not even Bain."

Lizette had had to do a great deal of maneuvering to get out of the house by herself, but now she was on Diablo's back, heading down the back alleys of Beaufort toward the main road that led out of town.

Pretty had helped her by distracting the housekeeper while Lizette sneaked out the back door, then helped her again by keeping the groom busy while she quietly took Diablo from the small pasture beyond the stables. As soon as Lizette had cleared the gate and moved far enough away from the house, she had leaped onto Diablo, thankful she was used to riding him bareback, and headed for Palmerston Grove.

She was wearing a dark shirt and pants of Bain's and had braided and pinned up her hair, and with one of the groom's hats on her head, she looked like a boy. The air was cool, but it felt good on her face. She almost felt free again. Strange she should think of it that way. Maybe if things were different between her and Bain . . . She brushed thoughts of him aside. Tonight all she'd think of was Heather.

A short while later, as she rode past the open area at Palmerston Grove and saw the wrought-iron fence silhouetted around the small graveyard, anger began to smolder inside her. A few yards down the road, she reined off into the woods and tethered Diablo in the meadow where Bain had taken her the day of the races. She followed the line of trees to the house. She stopped, listening, then heard a carriage rumbling by out front. When it was past, she moved on slowly, heading for the door of the root cellar.

By the time she reached the upstairs bedroom in the house, she was shaking from fear and her knees felt like they were going to give out any minute. The cellars had been pitch dark, and she had almost upset a storage rack when she was feeling her way through the wine cellar. Then she tripped halfway up the stairs and thought for certain she had given herself away. She had stayed motionless for the longest time before starting out again.

Now she breathed a sigh as she tiptoed across the floor and checked the bed to make sure no one was in it. This done, she moved to the door and broke it a crack, peeking out. The hallway was dimly lit, and empty. Now what?

She stood for a long time staring into the hallway, wondering what her next move would be. Suddenly a door across the hall opened and Oleander came out. She walked over and knocked on the door Heather had pointed out as hers, then waited. Lizette saw the door open.

"Are you coming downstairs anymore this evening, Missus Palmer?" Oleander asked.

"Who wants to know?" asked Heather.

Oleander smiled. "Don't worry, I haven't been downstairs in the past hour. I don't think Mr. Everett or Mr. Carl arrived home yet. I just wanted to know if you were going to come down for your usual cup of tea."

"I don't think so tonight," Heather answered. "When are they due home?"

"They said they'd be late."

Lizette breathed a sigh. She couldn't have asked for anything better. Everett and Carl were out for the evening. Heather said something else Lizette couldn't hear, then shut the door, and Oleander headed for the stairs.

As soon as she was out of sight, Lizette slipped from the room and hurried to Heather's door, tapping on it lightly.

"I told you, Oleander . . ." Heather began as she opened the door, then let out a squeal when she saw Lizette.

"Shhh!" cautioned Lizette. "She'll hear you." She grabbed Heather's hand. "I can't talk to you in there. Come to the other room," she suggested, and Heather nodded.

When they were in the other room, in the dark, with the door shut, they practically fell into each other's arms.

"At first I thought you'd forgotten all about me," Heather gasped breathlessly as she hugged Lizette. "Then Carl came home with the news about you and Bain eloping. Oh, Liz, I was so happy for you," she exclaimed.

Lizette clung to Heather, then held herself away some so she could look at her. The room was too dark and she couldn't see Heather's face, but she knew what would be in her eyes. "It isn't what you think, Heather," she whispered softly.

Heather stared at her. "What do you mean? You were always in love with Bain."

"I know, but . . . Heather, if I tell you something—and I can't even tell you all of it—but if I tell you, will you promise not to tell anyone else?"

"Haven't we always shared secrets, Liz?"

Lizette squeezed her hands. "Heather, I was pregnant with someone else's baby when I married Bain."

Heather stared at her, frowning. "Oh, Liz, you didn't . . . ?"

"No, I didn't. Bain knows all about the baby—that's why he married me."

Heather stared at her hard. "But you aren't going to tell me whose it is, are you?"

Lizette shook her head. "I wish I could, but I promised. As it is, if Bain knew I told you this much, he'd be furious."

"Where is Bain?"

"Out of town—he won't be back for a couple of weeks, maybe longer."

"You mean you came all by yourself?"

"I had to," Lizette replied. "I had to tell you that you were right about your baby, Heather," she said. "Bain and I dug up the grave. There was no baby buried in that casket, it was full of rocks!"

Heather sighed. "I just knew Tildie was right," she said. "Oh, Liz, I don't know what I'm going to do!"

"Don't do anything, Heather," cautioned Liz. "At least not until we can think of something."

"But you don't understand," said Heather. "Carl has decided that when my year of mourning's up, he's going to marry me."

"He can't—he's already married."

"Everett's been working on getting an annulment. They expect to have it by the end of the year."

"Oh, my God." She looked quickly at Heather. "He hasn't touched you, has he?"

Heather shook her head. "Everett caught him trying to kiss me once and warned him if he touched me again he'd never let him marry me. I don't intend to marry him, Liz," she said emphatically, and Lizette agreed.

They talked for a while longer, and Lizette promised to get back to see her soon. It was almost an hour later when Lizette finally started back down the steep steps, feeling her way in the darkness between the walls of the house. When she reached the cellar without mishap, she sighed, relieved. But the worst wasn't over yet. She left the stairs, crept noiselessly across the cellar floor, then suddenly, as she reached the door that opened into the root cellar, she accidentally kicked over something. She didn't know what it was, but tried to stop it, only to hear it crash and clatter resoundingly.

She pulled her hands back and grabbed for the door as she heard a scuffling on the floor above her and realized someone had heard. Her heart was pounding, when she finally found the door handle and pushed it open stumbling into the root cellar.

"Straight ahead," she kept mumbling to herself. "Straight ahead to the steps!"

She was running in the dark now, bumping into things, tripping. Jars crashed to the floor, crocks smashed against unseen obstacles, and with a lunge she careened into the steps, scraping her shins as she fell, hitting her stomach hard.

She could hear shouting behind her as she struggled to her

feet and crawled up the rickety steps, flinging open the door to the root cellar, the fresh night air hitting her in the face.

Leaving the door open behind her, she began running in the direction where she'd tethered her horse. Her breath was coming in short gasps now, and as she glanced back over her shoulder, it was just in time to see someone coming from the back of the house, running after her.

Dogs were barking furiously amid shouting and cursing, and heavy footsteps fell behind her, getting closer with each second. Then suddenly, just as she saw her horse, a hand grabbed her from behind and whirled her around. She struggled, kicking and scratching, feeling as helpless as a small child, realizing the man was far stronger than she was.

Then she remembered something Cole had told her a long time ago, and as the man started to pick her up off the ground in an attempt to carry her back to the house, she drew back her foot and let it fly, hitting him square in the groin. A bloodcurdling shriek filled the night air, and his arms loosened from about her.

She hit the ground with a thud as the man doubled up in pain; then she bit her lip to ease her own hurt and scrambled to her feet, scurrying the rest of the way to Diablo, half-stumbling as she grabbed the reins. With a quick leap, brought on by fear and anger, she reached Diablo's back, slapped the reins against his neck, and dug him in the ribs, heading recklessly through the woods toward the road.

Behind her she could hear shouting and horses' hooves on the drive at the other side of the house. My God, Everett and Carl must have just been arriving home, and now they were chasing after her on horseback. But Diablo could outrun anything on the road, except Bain's Morgan horse. She spurred him on daringly, then peered back over her shoulder and saw the two horses pursuing her get smaller and smaller in the distance. She had gotten away.

22

Lizette's breathing was steadier now as she slipped the halter from Diablo and turned him loose again in the small pasture, but her insides were still trembling. She had almost gotten caught, but it had been dark and she was certain that dressed like she was the man who had run after her wouldn't be able to identify her. She hung the halter on the fencepost where she had instructed Pretty to put it earlier in the day, and reminded herself to have Pretty put it back in the harness room tomorrow, then started for the house.

Pretty had done just as she asked. She was sitting outside on the bench in the yard, pretending to be enjoying the evening. "Are you all right?" asked Pretty when she saw Lizette limping slightly.

Lizette nodded. "I'm fine. Now, make sure the coast is clear and let me get upstairs. I banged my shins and fell down."

Pretty went on ahead of her, distracting the housekeeper and the two young servant girls who were in the kitchen helping get things ready for morning, while Lizette climbed up the back stairs, much more slowly than she had descended them earlier. She reached her room, ducked quickly inside, then shut the door and grabbed the bell pull summoning Pretty before falling exhausted on the bed.

It wasn't just the exhaustion, though; there was something else the matter, and suddenly Lizette was scared. She felt the pain, like a dull ache at first spiraling out from her loins, then pushing into her belly with a fierce shove until it took her breath away.

By the time Pretty stepped into the room, Lizette was perspiring profusely, her face contorted in agony. Pretty started to back out of the room to go for help, but Lizette stopped her.

"No!" she cried breathlessly. "Come here . . . you're going to have to help me!" She grabbed Pretty's hand. "Pretty, what happens in this room tonight is between you and me, and only you and me, do you understand?" she gasped.

Pretty nodded, eyes wide and frightened.

"There's something you didn't know," Lizette went on, her breathing still labored. "I'm pregnant, Pretty, and I'm just far enough along that I think we're going to have a mess. Something happened tonight and I got hurt, and I think I'm losing the baby. You've got to help me, Pretty. Promise me!" she begged.

"I promise, Miss Lizzie," said Pretty, her voice unsteady. Lordy! She hadn't expected this!

Lizette tightened her jaw as another pain tore through her, and she suddenly felt a gush of blood.

It was late evening and Lizette stirred, staring up at the ceiling, stretching lazily in the bed as she glanced toward the window, watching the stars come out in the sky. It had been two and a half weeks since she had lost the baby, and Bain still wasn't home yet. She had been trying to forget that night, but it wasn't easy. Rumors had circulated that the Palmers had scared a prowler, but other than that the incident was forgotten quickly, by everyone but Lizette.

She had sworn Pretty to secrecy, and although it had been a tremendous thing to ask, Pretty had managed. She had tended Lizette all by herself, disposed of the bloody bedclothes and remains of what would have been the baby, then nursed Lizette back to health, telling everyone that she had caught a fever that had laid her low for a few days.

Lizette sighed. She had stopped bleeding a week ago, and everything seemed back to normal again, including her appetite, and she'd swear she had put on a few pounds. She reached down and felt her stomach. It was still flat, and she worried, wondering if Bain would notice that she wasn't showing yet. Probably not, since he didn't make love to her anymore. A tear reached her eye as she remembered his warning about what would happen if she lost the baby. Well, she sure as hell wasn't going to volunteer the information, and she turned over in bed with her back to the door and settled down for another lonely night.

Lizette had no idea what time it was, and no idea what had awakened her, but she was suddenly wide-awake and it was still the middle of the night. She exhaled, turning over, then froze as she saw a figure silhouetted against the window at the other side of the room. "Bain?" she questioned softly.

He grunted. "I didn't mean to wake you."

She raised a little, shoving the loose hair back from her face. "What time is it?"

"Three in the morning."

She yawned. "No wonder I'm so tired." She rolled onto her back and sighed. "Are you just getting home now?"

"Something wrong with it?" he asked.

Her heart sank and a stab of pain shot through her. "I'm surprised you even came home at all," she said sarcastically. "It's obvious you have no reason to."

He stopped undressing and stared toward the bed for a long time, then began undressing again.

She breathed deeply, fighting back the tears. Oh, how she had hoped he'd be changed when he came back, but he hated her, and that one night, the night of their wedding, was simply a mistake, the natural way a man satisfies his hunger for a woman. It had nothing to do with love. She pulled the covers up to her chin and closed her eyes as she felt his weight on the bed as he crawled in beside her.

Bain lay for a long time on his own side of the bed, listening to her breathing. He had wakened the housekeeper when he'd come in, and she had told him Lizette had been sick while he was gone. He tried not to worry about her, but couldn't help himself. In fact, there were so many things about Lizette that he couldn't help feeling. Like now.

He could hear her breathing and feel the warmth of her body so near, yet so far from him. How many times he had lain beside her and forced himself to think of other things, to take his mind from the remembrance of what it was like to make love to her.

He closed his eyes, but it didn't help. He hadn't seen her for almost three weeks. She turned over, her back to him, the scent of cape jasmine once more mesmerizing his senses, and without thinking, he reached out, drawing her long dark tresses from the back of her neck. He snuggled close until hi lips found her warm flesh. The kiss was long and sweet on the nape of her neck. "Come to me!" he whispered softly, then with deft hands turned her to face him. Moonlight was coming in the window, falling across her face and he looked deep into her eyes for one brief moment, then lowered his head, his lips claiming hers in a fiery kiss that he was soon unable to control. His mouth played on hers sensuously, opening, drawing her lips into his, his tongue caressing hers until he felt the scorching flame of desire fill every nerve in his body. He moaned, his hand touching her breast, wanting her, needing her, and once more he made love to her as he had on their wedding night, leaving her body satiated, as was his own, and when it was over, their moment of ecstasy reached, they fell asleep in each other's arms again.

The next morning, as before, the bed beside Lizette was empty when she opened her eyes. She lay passively, staring at it, then looked toward the open window, listening to the chirping of the birds outside. He was home. Bain had come home again. She lay for a long time remembering last night, wondering if it was to be like before. Would this be the last time? She had her answer two days later, when, after they retired for the evening and all the lights were out, Bain once more slowly drew her to him and made love to her, and again her heart sang for joy.

However, things were still unsettled between them. There were nights when he ignored her, and the days were even more puzzling. He never once mentioned their lovemaking, nor was he intimate in any way, treating her with a crispness and nonchalance that was maddening.

Occasionally she'd catch him staring at her curiously, and she wished she knew what he was thinking. Had he realized that her stomach wasn't getting any larger? She was wearing flowing dresses, hoping he wouldn't notice, but she knew that eventually she would have to tell him. Not just because he was going to wonder why she wasn't getting any bigger, but because it would be her time of the month again soon and he'd have to know so he wouldn't climb in bed some night and start making love to her.

However, before she had a chance to tell him, he had to go away again for a few days to Columbia, so she put off telling him until he got back. Only, to her surprise, her time of the month never came. At first she thought something was wrong because of the miscarriage, but when she started getting sick again in the mornings, she knew what it had to be: Bain's lovemaking had borne fruit, and she was pregnant again.

Fortunately, or unfortunately, however she wanted to look at it, her morning sickness didn't last long, nor did her loss of appetite, and so she didn't lose weight as she had with her first pregnancy. In fact, by the time Bain had returned again she had actually gained a couple of pounds due to her nervous eating. It didn't seem to cool Bain's ardor, however, and life took up for Lizette again as it had before, with nights of tender lovemaking and days of frustration.

As the cool days of spring retreated before the onslaught of the summer's heat, Lizette made two more visits to Heather. Both of them were when Bain was out of town, and neither visit was detected by anyone.

Lizette had decided on a plan to help Heather. Her first priority was to get the charges against Cole dismissed, and in order to do that, somebody had to learn the truth, so on her first visit she told Heather to write out and sign a statement of what really happened; on her second visit Lizette had the statement in her pocket when she rode away from Palmerston Grove on Diablo. Once home, the paper was tucked away in the bottom of a drawer for future use, when the time was right.

Lizette's eighteenth birthday came and went quietly, with a family dinner at Tonnerre. She received a beautiful cameo brooch from her parents, a jewelry box from Grandma Dicia and Grandpa Roth, a ceramic statue of a horse that looked just like Diablo from Felicia, a silver music box from her in-laws, an emerald ring from Bain, and a tortoiseshell brush-and-comb set from Julia and Stuart. The senator couldn't be present, since he was in Columbia working on some new legislation they were preparing for the fall session, so it was at her birthday dinner that Bain took the opportunity to announce to everyone that Lizette was expecting a child, telling everyone the child was due in late November or early December, expecting it to show up earlier than that and never dreaming it was really due a month later than his prediction.

Stuart came home for the Fourth of July, arriving a few days before the actual holiday, and fortunately for Lizette, Bain had sailed to Savannah on the *Dragonfly* just that morning without the knowledge that his brother was home. Lizette had learned of it when her housekeeper returned from marketing and said she had seen him in town. It was time to put her plan into action, and that meant it was imperative she see Stuart.

Time was running short. They had only four months before Heather's year of mourning was up, and so much to do in that time, and there was no telling when she'd have another chance like this to see Stuart. However, it had to be done in secret, and that was the problem. There was only one place she could meet him where no one would know, and she hated to go there.

Although she should have been showing more, Lizette was only about three months along and could still ride sidesaddle on Diablo. So, swearing Pretty to secrecy, explaining to the girl that she was helping Heather, she sent her with a note to Stuart, telling Pretty to put it in no one's hands but the senator's, and if anyone asked who it was from, she was to say it was from his brother.

On the second of July, Lizette rode Diablo down the overgrown path through the woods and reined up in front of the old stone building where she and Stuart had met so many times before. That now seemed so long ago, like another life, another time. So much had happened since they had parted here last year, and she flushed as he came from the stone building to meet her, reaching up to help her off her horse. The carefree twinkle was gone from his eyes, and there was a hardness about his mouth that hadn't been there before. "The note said you wanted to see me," he said without even a greeting first.

She nodded. "Yes. And this was the only place I knew where we wouldn't be disturbed."

"I see."

She reached inside her riding habit and drew out an envelope, handing it to him. "Read this," she said softly, then watched his face as he took out Heather's clearly written statement and read it. She had explained everything in it, except the suspicion that her baby was still alive.

"Why doesn't she just come forth and tell the authorities this?" Stuart asked Lizette when he had read it.

She shook her head. "She can't. They keep her virtually a prisoner, yet there's no way to prove it. Even her parents have never been alone with her since all this happened."

"How did you get this?" he asked.

"I know a way into the house at Palmerston Grove they don't know I know," she answered. "Bain showed me a long time ago."

He studied her thoughtfully. "So what do you want me to do?"

"I want you to get the charges on Cole dismissed," she answered.

His frown deepened. "Why don't you just take this to the magistrate in Beaufort?"

"Because Everett Palmer owns him," she said unhesitatingly. "But he doesn't own the governor. Please, Stuart," she begged. "Take this to the governor for me. If anyone can do anything, he can. If he had the charges against Cole dismissed, Everett Palmer wouldn't dare defy him. He'd have to admit the truth; then there'd be no reason for them to keep Heather isolated from everyone the way they do. She could go back to the Chateau and be a part of the family again. I can't leave her there at Palmerston Grove like that. I just can't!"

Stuart stared at the paper, then looked hard at Lizette.

"What is it?" she asked as she saw the puzzled look on his face.

He rubbed his jawline, his fingers running over the rough stubble of his clipped beard. "Why did you lie, Lizette?" he asked suddenly.

She stared at him. "I didn't lie," she said, gesturing toward the paper he held in his hands. "Heather wrote it herself."

"I'm not talking about Heather's statement. I'm talking about your pregnancy. Why did you tell me you were pregnant back in March, when it's obvious you're no more pregnant than I am."

She blushed, and her mouth twitched nervously. "But I am pregnant, Stuart," she said softly. "I'm probably at least three months along by now. Didn't Julia tell you?"

"Yes, Julia told me," he said. "But I thought she was telling me . . . Well, you know what I thought she meant." He gazed at her with disdain. "What did you have in mind, pulling a stunt like that?" he asked.

She half-laughed, her mouth twisting cynically. "You too?" she asked.

"What do you mean, me too?"

"Are you going to hate me too, Stuart?" she asked.

"It all depends. Why did you lie?" he asked again.

"I didn't lie," she said desperately. "I was pregnant, Stuart. I lost the baby on the twenty-first of April, right after the party you and Julia gave for us. Only Bain never knew. You see, he had left that morning for Charleston, and by the time he got back, everything was over. I swore Pretty to secrecy. I never told him because he said if I ever lost the baby he was going to have the marriage annulled, and I couldn't stand that."

"You do love him, don't you?"

She nodded. "Yes. And now I'm pregnant with his baby, only he doesn't know it. I got pregnant right away after the miscarriage, as soon as he got home, so I never let him think any differently, and I've put on a couple of pounds, so he hasn't guessed yet." She straightened and faced him squarely. "But we were talking about Heather and Cole," she said, changing the subject when she saw the pained look in his eyes. "Will you do this for me, Stuart, please?" she asked.

He stared at her hard. "For you?"

"For me," she whispered.

He wrenched his eyes from hers and looked down at the paper in his hands. "I'll always love you, you know that, don't you?" he said.

She shook her head. "Please, don't!"

"Don't worry," he said huskily. "From here on in I'll behave myself. I just want you to know that I'll do this because of what we once had and what we once meant to each other. At least I'll try."

"That's all I can ask," she said, then smiled. "Thank you, Stuart," she whispered.

He smiled back, a sadness in his smile. "I only wish . . ." he said softly.

She reached out and squeezed his hands, then stood on tiptoe, kissing him on the cheek. "I know," she said softly, then brushed away a tear. "Good-bye, Stuart," and she turned to her horse as he stepped forward quickly and helped her into the saddle, then watched her ride off alone.

Bain arrived home the night before the Fourth, and except for the annual picnic and political rally that marked the celebration in Port Royal and Beaufort, Lizette's life once more became a waiting game. She was waiting for Bain to confront her with the suspicions she was certain he had by now, waiting for her new pregnancy to start showing, and waiting to find out if Stuart was successful on Cole's behalf.

It was the first part of August when Bain finally broke his silence. She had noticed him staring at her more and more whenever they were together, but she was certain it was at his parents' home, where they had all assembled to have dinner in honor of Felicia's eighteenth birthday, that his suspicions finally became more than just suspicions. And Lizette could thank Julia for it, because it was Julia who made the offhand remark that she had no idea where Lizette was carrying the baby. "Why, by the time I was six months, I was huge," she said when the ladies were all together after dinner, and

Lizette had looked up just in time to notice that Bain was walking by and heard her.

On the way home, Bain stared at Lizette hard as they rode through the streets of Beaufort. Julia's remark had disturbed him, because what Julia didn't know was that instead of six months, Lizette should really be closer to full term. And now that he thought of it, when he made love to her, her protruding stomach had never been an obstacle. But then, he had purposely avoided contact with it, refusing to admit to himself that it was there, and that his brother's child was inside it. Whenever the thought occurred to him, he had unconsciously avoided the fact, but now, suddenly, he couldn't ignore it any longer. The fact was that Julia had been right. Lizette hardly showed at all. How could he broach the subject tactfully? He couldn't; all he could so was try to get her to talk about it.

"Did you have a nice time tonight?" he asked.

She nodded. "Yes, although I was surprised Alex Benedict wasn't there seeing as how Felicia said she'd be announcing her betrothal to him shortly."

"You don't seem to like Alex."

She made a face. "I honestly don't know what she sees in him," Lizette said. "The man's a snobbish boor."

"Then it's probably best he wasn't there. I thought perhaps you might not have felt much like going, since it's so close to your time," he said.

She shrugged. "I guess I'm not like some women," she said. "I can't see hiding away in the house. Anyway, I'm not really all that big like Julia was," she explained, hoping it would suffice. "Father said his mother surprised his father when he was born because no one suspected she was that far along. I guess maybe it's because she wasn't real thin like Julia either." She turned to him, trying to look naively innocent. "Do you suppose that's why I don't look too big?" she asked. "Julia even commented about it tonight."

His eyes narrowed for a moment. Was she too quick with an explanation? He wondered, and that night when he made love to her, for the first time since their marriage he let his hand rest on her stomach, feeling the firm hard ball there. Damn, she was pregnant, there was no mistaking it, it was evidently just going to be a very small baby, and God, how he wished it was his.

It was nearly two weeks later that Lizette had the shock of her life. Bain was busy somewhere on business. He had been negotiating some sort of business deal for the past few weeks, so she had ridden up to Tonnerre in the buggy, with Pretty to keep her company and their black slave Lucifer driving. However, when she arrived at Tonnerre, her parents weren't home. They had ridden into Port Royal earlier in the day, and she had missed them by a few hours.

It had been a long time since she had been back for a visit, so instead of turning around and going on home, it was such a beautiful day that she left Pretty at the house talking to some of her friends, and took a walk to the old swimming hole. As she neared the place, she felt a strange tingling that made her tremble. There were so many memories.

She stepped into the clearing and slowly strolled forward, her eyes on the brier bushes across the pool of water where Bain had cut her hair to free her, and tears suddenly sprang to her eyes. That seemed like centuries ago, and yet at times it seemed like yesterday.

She sank to the ground and plucked a small wildflower from beside her, holding it reverently between her fingers, staring at the delicate bloom. If only he loved her instead of just using her to satisfy his needs. And every time he went away, she wondered whose arms he ran to, whose lips surrendered to him, and the hurt was almost more than she could bear.

She was musing over the state of her marriage, when she suddenly heard a hissing sound, as if someone was trying to get her attention. She sat motionless, listening intently, then heard it again. Straightening, she looked around, then focused on some bushes below the dam, which was beginning to wash away from time and neglect. Something moved. She stood up quickly, then frowned as two figures stepped from behind the bushes and came toward her.

One of them was older, his sandy hair beginning to show streaks of white, his gray eyes hard like flint as his muscles stretched cautiously beneath the buckskins he had on. He was clean-shaven, his jaw square and determined as he walked beside the younger man, who was every bit as tall as he was, but leaner, with a clipped beard and green sloe eyes that clung to Lizette's hopefully.

"My God, Cole!" Lizette gasped breathlessly as she watched him walk toward her, moving with the grace of a cat, his muscular frame poured into soft worn buckskins.

He stopped for a moment and stared at her in disbelief, then swept her into his arms, hugging her for all he was worth as he fought the tears in his eyes. "Oh, Liz," he said, burying his face in her shoulder. "I never thought I'd ever see you again."

They laughed and cried together for a few minutes, hugging each other, then finally Cole raised his head and turned to Eli. "Liz, this is Eli Crawford," he introduced her. "Eli, my sister, Liz."

"It's Liz Kolter, Mr. Crawford," she said quickly, and saw the puzzled expression on Cole's face. "I'm married to Bain now, Cole," she explained.

"Bain . . . but—"

"Not now, please, Cole," she said interrupting him. "First of all, tell me what you're doing here."

"I couldn't stay away," he said unhappily. "I had to know about Heather and the baby."

"He near drove me crazy worryin'," cut in Eli. "Danged bad as his Uncle Heath was when he was always moonin' about that redhead."

Cole glanced over at Eli. "I told you, you didn't have to come."

"And let you sneak in on your own." He shook his head. "Land sakes, lad, we been through too much together already for me to desert you now."

"Did you come on foot?" asked Lizette.

"I came across the river by boat, but Eli brought our horses over on the ferry. Nobody knows him around here. Our horses are over beyond those bushes," and he pointed to where they had been hiding.

"Then you just got here?"

Cole nodded. "We haven't been to the house yet."

"Maybe you'd better not go," she said quickly. "The slaves will recognize you, and one of them might talk."

"Well, Hizzie won't," he replied. "Nor will Liza, Job, or Aaron. So if I can sneak into the house and stay in my room, nobody'll know the difference."

Lizette thought over his suggestion. "I don't like it," she said. "All it would take is one person to spot you." She thought for a minute. "I've got got a better idea," she said, and suggested Eli and Cole hole up at the old abandoned stone building down the other side of the Chateau. Cole knew which one she meant.

He thought it over. Maybe she was right. Nobody ever went there anymore, and it would be dry. He looked at Eli. "What do you think, friend?" he asked. "The place is isolated, Nobody will even know we're around."

Eli nodded. "I think you have a smart sister."

"What about Heather, Liz?" Cole asked.

She stared into his eyes, wondering how much to tell him, then decided he deserved to know it all. So for the next half-hour they sat on the bank at the old swimming hole and Lizette brought Cole up-to-date on the happenings at Port Royal and Beaufort, but when he learned about the baby being held in the slave quarters at Palmerston Grove, he became livid and in the next breath began making plans to get both Heather and the baby away. Lizette explained that Heather had made her promise not to tell anyone else about the child, so Cole agreed to do nothing until they could think of a plan.

When Rebel and Beau finally returned to Tonnerre from Port Royal, they found Lizette still there to break the news to them about Cole's return, but Cole and Eli had gone to the old stone building.

All that evening Lizette was terribly on edge. She wanted to tell Bain about Cole, and yet because of his attitude lately, she was hesitant. Unfortunately, she knew there was no way she could show Eli where the secret entrance was to Palmerston Grove, yet she knew in order to make any kind of plans, he had to know. That meant she had to tell Bain whether she wanted to or not, so that evening while they were getting ready for bed, she asked tentatively, "Bain, what would you say if I told you Cole was back in Port Royal?"

He tossed his shirt aside and stared at her. "When?"

"I told you about taking a ride to Tonnerre this afternoon. He showed up there."

She had her nightgown on already, and he watched her climb into bed, noticing that she was moving a little more clumsily now. "Doesn't he realize the chance he's taking?" he asked.

"When you love someone as much as he loves Heather, you really don't mind the risk, I guess."

"I guess not," he said. Then he stripped his pants off, threw them on the chair with his shirt, walked over, blew out the lamp, and climbed in beside her. "How is Cole?" he asked as he settled his head into his pillow.

"That's what I wanted to talk to you about," she said. "He brought a man named Eli Crawford with him, and they plan to take Heather and the baby away with them when they leave."

"And how do they intend to accomplish something so drastic, since there's a price on Cole's head?"

"That's where you come in," she answered softly. "You're

going to have to show Eli how to get into the house and tell him the layout of the slave quarters."

Bain raised up on one elbow, staring down at her. "Do you realize what you're asking?"

She gazed up at him and suddenly reached up, running her hand along his beard, then dropping it to his bare shoulder, flushing self-consciously. It was the first such overture she had made since they were married. Her fingers caressed his shoulder, and she watched them, avoiding his eyes, knowing what they'd do to her if she looked into them. "Yes, I know what I'm asking," she said. "I love my brother, and I love Heather, and I want them to be happy."

"What if I'm caught taking him in?"

"You won't be. Besides, no one knows who Eli is, so there'd be no connection to Cole."

"How would I explain what I was doing there?"

"You'd think of something. But you won't get caught. Please, Bain?" she begged, and this time she looked directly into his eyes. A shiver went through her. Lord, how much she loved him!

His mouth twisted cynically. "I have a strange feeling that if I don't go, you'd be just fool enough to try it yourself, wouldn't you?"

She sighed. "I have to help him somehow, Bain."

"All right," he half-whispered. "I'll help, but you're to stay out of it, understand?"

She nodded. "Thank you, Bain," she said softly.

"Don't thank me yet, Liz," he whispered huskily. "Because you're going to pay for it," and before she could respond, he bent down, his mouth covering hers, and made love to her so tenderly there were tears in her eyes as she nestled into his arms afterward.

In the days that followed, plans were made and changed a half-dozen times. Lizette had told Bain where he could find Cole and Eli, and Bain helped them plan what they were going to do, although he declined to be a part of the actual escapade. However, he did promise to arrange to keep Everett and Carl Palmer away from Palmerston Grove on the night they picked, and he did it by making certain they were invited to a political dinner that was being held in Beaufort.

The final plan had been decided on. Cole was to lead Tildie and Heather from the house while Eli went after the baby; then they'd all meet in the woods near the root cellar at a specific time, with the horses waiting. Cole had told his parents and grandparents about Heather and the baby, so it was decided that the *Interlude* would be waiting at the pier at the Chateau to carry them away from Port Royal to safety. It was a dangerous plan, but it could work if carried out efficiently.

When Bain took Eli to see Heather for the first time, she was ecstatic to learn that Cole was back, but frightened for him. However, she agreed that the only way they were going to get the baby off Palmerston Grove was just to take it. Because of her promise to Lizette, Heather said nothing to Bain and Eli about Lizette's earlier visits and the statement she had signed for her, so the plans were confirmed with Tildie's help. She had learned which shack the baby was in and gave Eli the routine on where the slaves were at certain times in the evenings.

The second time Eli went to see Heather was to tell her the date they had chosen, and when he returned to the old stone building, he and Cole stayed hidden, waiting impatiently for the day to arrive.

They were scheduled to put the plan into effect on Friday evening, September 5. Bain made sure the Palmers planned to attend the political dinner at a friend's home, and now, earlier in the day, he was on his way home, riding through town, when he ran into Julia. She had just left one of the shops and hailed him.

"My goodness, Bain," she said as he rode over to her on his little black stallion. "We see hardly anything of you anymore. You ought to bring Lizette over for dinner some evening. The children would love to see the two of you, and it gets so lonesome sometimes with Stuart gone."

"I imagine it does," he said, dismounting so she wouldn't have to look up at him. "But I'm afraid we don't go too much of anyplace anymore, what with Lizette's condition."

"I remember what it was like," she replied knowingly, then suddenly stared at him curiously. "By the way, I meant to ask you at Felicia's party last month, did you and Stuart get everything settled when he was home over the Fourth?"

"Settled?" he asked, frowning. "What are you talking about?"

"About the urgent message you sent," she answered. "I told Pretty where to find Stuart that day, but he seemed rather vague about the matter when he arrived home that evening, and then I discovered you had left to go out of town for a few days. I hoped I hadn't messed up any business deal or anything."

Bain was staring at her peculiarly.

"Are you all right, Bain?" she asked with concern.

Bain nodded absentmindedly while he tried to run back through what he had just heard. "I . . . You say Pretty came with a message for Stuart?" he asked.

"For heaven't sake, Bain, you surely remember," she said. "You insisted it had to be given directly to Stuart. I remember the young woman insisting that she could only give it to the senator, because it was too important."

"And this was just before the Fourth?"

"Now I'm sorry I mentioned it," she said. "But at the time I thought it was important and I was a little worried that the servant girl might not have found Stuart in time."

Bain shook his head. "No, that's all right, it's just that I'd forgotten, Julia," he said, his jaw suddenly clenching as he began to unravel the mystery with answers he didn't like.

They talked for a while longer, then he excused himself and headed for home.

Lizette was taking a nap when Bain arrived home, so he was able to confront Pretty alone in the parlor. He ordered her to his study off the downstairs hall and shut the door. "Pretty," he began, trying not to show too much of the anger that was seething inside him, "you took a message to Senator Kolter last month, a few days before the Fourth of July. Who gave you the message?"

She stared at him dumbfounded. She didn't know what to answer. Miss Lizzie had been so insistent that not even Mr. Bain was to know.

"I know about the note, Pretty," he insisted, the timbre of his voice dropping low. "All I want to know is, did my wife send it?"

"She said I wasn't supposed to tell you, Mr. Bain," she answered finally. "That it was something to help Miss Heather, and I belong to Miss Lizzie, I have to do like she says."

"Tell me, Pretty," he asked, still holding his temper in check. "Did Miss Lizzie go out that evening?"

"No, sir," she answered.

"The next day?"

"Why, I think she did, sir, yes," she said in surprise. "But how did you know?"

"Just a guess," he said, then excused Pretty and fortified himself with a glass of brandy. As soon as the glass was empty, Bain turned and headed for the stairs, the anger inside him finally boiling over.

Lizette hadn't been sleeping, only resting; she was thinking about tonight, hoping Cole and Heather would be successful, and wondering what the consequences would be if they failed. But she wouldn't think of that. She couldn't. They had to succeed.

Suddenly the door opened and Bain came in. He stood on the threshold for a brief moment staring at her, then stepped in and shut the door. He leaned back against it, still staring at her, and Lizette swung her feet to the edge of the bed and sat up.

"Is something wrong?" she asked anxiously. "It's not Cole?"

"No, it's not Cole," he said, walking farther into the room. "I wish I could understand you," he said bitterly as he stood looking down at her. "You have everything you need, don't you, and still you go back to him, Liz. Why?" he asked.

She frowned. "What are you talking about?"

"Stuart! That's what I'm talking about! Why, Liz?" he demanded angrily. "Haven't I given you enough? Why do you have to go to him?"

"I . . . I didn't!" She shook her head. "I don't understand."

"Don't tell me you didn't! I know all about your romantic tryst during the Fourth of July holidays when he was home!" he shouted, trying to keep his voice down. "Dammit, I don't like being cuckolded by my own brother! It's bad enough I have to acknowledge his bastard as mine, I don't intend to keep sharing you with him!"

"You're crazy!" she yelled back. "I haven't been seeing him!"

"Don't lie!"

"Not the way you mean." She tried to explain. "I saw him, yes, but only to try to persuade him to see if the governor would drop the murder charges against Cole!"

"You expect me to believe that?"

"It's the truth!"

"Then why didn't you just go to the house and ask him?" he countered. "Why did you make such a secret out of it?"

"Because you told me I was never to see him again."

"That's ridiculous. I'd have gone with you if you'd asked."

"It wasn't that simple." She held her breath, staring at him. If she told him about the statement from Heather, she'd have to tell him she had been to see her, and that would only make matters worse; he might find out about the miscarriage and how she had tricked him. "I couldn't tell you, Bain," she pleaded. "But it isn't what you think."

His eyes narrowed. "You lying bitch! I'm giving your baby a name. I've given you a home, and you do this to me!"

"I didn't do anything to you! Please, Bain," she pleaded. "Stuart hasn't touched me!"

"Oh, how you must have been laughing at me," he said acidly. "Letting me make love to you, letting me make a complete ass of myself, while all the time you were probably pretending it was him, using me to feed your ego until he showed up in town again." He straightened, his eyes blazing and stared down at her, his face livid. "Well, no more, Mrs. Kolter," he spit through clenched teeth. "I'm through playing the fool. I swore once before that I wouldn't touch you, then let my body overrule my head, but no more!" He turned, walking over to the dresser, and opened one of the drawers, pulling out rows of shirts, throwing them on the chair beside the dresser, then grabbed one to take with him. Then he walked over to the armoire and took out the clothes he was planning to wear that evening. "I'm going out tonight," he informed her furiously. "While I'm gone, I want you to have Pretty put my things in the guest room. I'll be sleeping there from now on, I can't stand the sight of you!"

"No, Bain, please!" she begged, but he ignored her pleas, slamming the door as he went out.

Lizette had been sitting on the bed for a long time, and hadn't even gone downstairs for dinner. She was just staring out the window, an empty feeling inside. It was dark out already, had been for almost an hour, but she had paid little attention to the fact and hadn't even bothered to light the lamp. Pretty had come and gone, but she hadn't bothered to talk to her either.

She stood up now and walked to the window, staring out, then looked up at the waning moon. Tonight was the night Cole was going to rescue Heather and the baby. At least someone was going to be happy. She certainly wasn't.

Why couldn't he have loved her? In all the months they'd been married, never once had he said, "I love you." Not even when he took her in his arms and made love to her. Her eyes filled with tears again. She thought she had cried herself out earlier in the day, but for some reason the tears just seemed to be there again. Damn him!

Suddenly her fist clenched over her stomach as a thought struck her. Never touch her again, that's what he had said. She wouldn't be his wife anymore, not really. She'd have his name and his baby, but that's all she'd have. She'd never have him!

Well, by God, he'd never have her either, not again. The faraway look left her eyes, to be replaced by a look of determination. A light—she needed a light. Hurrying to the door, she yelled for Pretty, then lit the lamp.

By the time Pretty came upstairs, Lizette was trying to find a way to hold a pair of Bain's pants up over her stomach. As it was, they didn't want to fasten in the front and she had the front panels tied with hair ribbons.

"What on earth are you doin', Miss Lizzie?" Pretty exclaimed as she stared at her in wonder.

Lizette straightened stubbornly. "I'm doing what I should have done a long time ago, Pretty," she said. "But I'm going to need your help."

"Not again," said Pretty unhappily. "Miss Lizzie, you're only going to get yourself in more trouble."

"More trouble? Pretty, I couldn't be in any more trouble than I am right now," she said, then explained to Pretty that she wanted her to distract the housekeeper again so she could sneak out, but first she'd have to go out and make sure Diablo was saddled. "I'm afraid I can't ride bareback anymore, Pretty, but I can still get up into the side saddle."

Pretty shook her head.

"Don't do that, Pretty," Lizette complained. "Just do as I say." She walked over to the dresser, opened one of the drawers and brought out a small metal box. When it was open, she took papers out and showed them to Pretty. "Do this for me, Pretty," she said, "and I'll sign these, making you a free woman. Do you understand? That's how important this is for me. After tonight I won't need you anymore, and you'll be free. Do you understand, Pretty?"

The young black woman stared at her mistress, then nodded. "I'll go, but you be careful, Miss Lizzie," she cautioned. "Remember about the little one."

Lizette glanced down at her stomach. "How could I forget? Now, go quickly, then come and let me know when Diablo's ready."

When Pretty was gone, Lizette signed the papers, then finished getting ready. She knew she looked ridiculous in her own riding boots, Bain's pants and shirt, her hair pulled back again and braided and stuffed under the same cap she had used before, but it didn't matter. All she wanted to do now was get as far away from Bain as possible.

A quarter of an hour after handing Pretty the papers to

free her and hugging her good-bye, Lizette was riding toward Palmerston Grove.

Bain had been in a turmoil all the way to his friend's house. He hated politics, not just because Stuart had chosen politics for his profession, but because he disliked having to try to be nice to people he didn't like. But tonight he had promised to show up at the dinner if the Palmers were invited.

Now, as he stepped into the dining room and gazed about, spotting the Palmers across the room, he thought of Cole, wondering if everything was going all right. Reaching in his pocket, he checked his watch. He had left the house just at dark. Lizette was still in her room, refusing to come down, and he wasn't about to go up and order her to. So he'd left without even so much as a good-bye. Damn her anyway! And damn Stuart for what he'd done to her!

He slipped the watch back in his pocket and glanced up again, then whirled, startled, as he heard a voice behind him greeting their host. Stuart? He stood motionless, body rigid, breathing heavily. Then, realizing where he was, and not wanting to cause a scene, he walked over. "Stuart?" he asked in surprise. "When did you get home?"

"This afternoon, and I ran into our host here on the way in. Sorry I didn't get a chance to warn you I was coming, but since the ladies aren't present tonight, you shouldn't be too upset, my surprising you like this."

"I wish I had known you were home, Stu," he said, trying to steady his voice. "There's a matter of utmost importance I have to talk to you about, and if I'd known it, it could have been settled by now." He turned to his host. "Do you mind if we use your library?" he asked.

Their host shook his head. "Not at all, go ahead," he said. "But remember, dinner will be served within the hour."

Bain nodded, and he and Stuart headed for the library. Bain shut the door behind them and turned angrily on Stuart. "I should call you out right here and now," he snarled. "Why, Stuart?" he asked. "Why couldn't you keep your hands off her!"

Stuart stared at him dumbfounded. "Why couldn't . . . ? What the hell are you talking about?"

"I know all about your secret meetings whenever you showed up in Beaufort and I was out of town," Bain yelled. "Father's not here to protect your precious career tonight, Stuart, so don't try to lie your way out of it!" He reached out, grabbing the front of his brother's shirt, tightening his grip savagely. "I know all about you and Liz!"

Stuart reached up, grabbing Bain's wrists to keep his hands from choking him. "You're insane!" he gasped. "I haven't been seeing Liz!"

"You deny you saw her during the July holidays?" he asked, and saw recognition in Stuart's eyes.

"For God's sake, Bain, let me explain," he cried. "Don't do something you'll regret for the rest of your life!" Bain's eyes locked with Stuart's, a wild storm raging in them, and Stuart pleaded with him, "Please, Bain!"

Bain's hand eased on the front of his brother's shirt, then dropped. "Don't lie, Stuart," he said through clenched teeth.

Stuart shook his head, a hand going to his throat, straightening his rumpled cravat. "I have no reason for lying," he said, swallowing to make sure he could still talk. "Lizette came to me to ask me to try to get the governor to drop the murder charge against Cole," he said. "She had a paper, a statement Heather had given her, telling the true story of what happened that night."

Bain stared at him in disbelief. "Now I know you're lying!" he said halfheartedly.

Stuart shook his head. "Why would I lie?"

"To cover yourself."

"There's nothing to cover for, Bain," he said, and reached in his pocket. "In fact, that's why I came back this weekend." He drew a paper out of his inside pocket and handed it to Bain. "Here, you don't believe me, read this."

Bain hesitantly took the paper, unfolding it, then read it. When he was finished, a flush spread across the upper part of his cheeks, and his gray eyes were troubled.

"I brought that tonight because I wanted you to give it to her," Stuart said. "It's a pardon for Cole, declaring that he acted in self-defense, and the murder charge is dropped. Now do you believe me?" he asked.

"But why? How? How did she get a statement from Heather? She hasn't been to see her, not since before we were married."

"That's where you're wrong, Bain," Stuart said. "She's been to see her a number of times—that's how she lost the baby."

Bain's mouth fell. "She what?"

"You didn't know that, did you, Bain?" he said. "She's not expecting my baby, not anymore, she's expecting yours. She lost mine back in April. That's why she doesn't really show all that much."

Bain shook his head as if to clear it, not certain he was hearing right. "She lost your baby?" he asked incredulously, then looked uncertain. He shook his head. "No, I would have known."

"You were in Charleston for almost three weeks on business."

"Then why didn't she tell me when I got back?"

"Because you told her if she lost the baby you were going to have the marriage annulled. She loves you, Bain," he stated flatly. "She always has. Why do you think she turned to me in the first place? Because of the family resemblance. My God, Bain, how could you have been with her all this time and not realized that?"

Bain's head was reeling. It couldn't be, yet he had the paper in his hand. "You're really not lying?" he asked Stuart apprehensively. "I won't play the fool again!"

"Bain, what more can I say to you?" Stuart asked, his eyes filled with remorse. "When I moved back to Beaufort, Lizette was a beautiful young woman who had just turned seventeen, and she called herself fat and ugly. She had gained considerable weight, and the young men around here were treating her badly because of it. I didn't see her that way, and I don't think you do either. But you weren't here, and she was starved for someone to love her, starved for what you'd once given her, then taken away. She saw you in me, and unfortunately I fell under her spell. She's always loved you, Bain, I knew that long ago."

Bain stared at his brother. "Oh, my God, what have I done?" he cried helplessly.

Stuart frowned. "Bain . . . ?"

"I told her I couldn't stand the sight of her," he said bitterly. "I turned on her like . . . Stuart, what am I going to do?"

Stuart sighed. "I guess you forget about the dinner tonight and go home and do some crawling, Bain," he suggested. "She's worth it, believe me. I know you're in love with her—I knew that the night you promised to marry her. Now go home and make it right for her, tell her you love her. You should have done it a long time ago, and you'd have saved yourself all this."

Bain stared at his brother for a brief second, then shoved the governor's pardon in his pocket and headed for the door. Suddenly he stopped, turning back. "Oh, one thing, Stuart, will you make sure the Palmers don't leave the dinner party until late tonight? I promised someone, and I'd hate to go back on my promise."

"Go on," said Stuart. "I'll take care of it."

"Thanks," Bain called back. "I'll explain later," and he left the library, hurrying to the door, where he made a quick excuse to his host. Then he called for his horse, mounted, and headed toward home at a gallop.

Cole put his hand on Eli's arm, whispering close to his ear, "Listen!"

Both men were standing between their horses deep in the middle of heavy brush in the woods next to the rambling house at Palmerston Grove.

"There it is again," Cole whispered anxiously.

Eli nodded, cautioning him. "Shhh!"

The soft nicker of a horse and rustle of leaves along with the definite crushing of ground matter underfoot could be heard mixed in with the usual night sounds around them. Someone else was sneaking through the woods.

Lizette was scared half to death. She knew Cole and Eli had to be close by, but how close? She had ridden Diablo hard, and he was lathered heavily. Reaching up, she wiped her hand down the side of his neck, trying to keep him from pawing the ground restlessly or neighing, giving her away. Bad enough he had let loose a soft nicker seconds ago. Suddenly she stopped, sensing that she wasn't alone anymore. Maybe it wouldn't hurt to call softly. Otherwise she'd never find them. "Cole?" she called, so low the whisper was almost lost amid the rustling leaves overhead.

This time Cole squeezed Eli's arm. "Who the devil . . . ?"

"Cole?"

The soft call came again; then as he glanced over the top of his piebald mare's back, he saw a vague movement in the dark shadows not ten feet away.

"Cole?" Lizette called again, and this time he recognized her voice. He handed his horse's reins to Eli, and stepped out, moving toward the figure that was only a hazy blur in the darkness.

"What the hell are you doing here?" he asked as he reached Lizette.

Tears welled up in Lizette's eyes. She didn't know whether they were from relief at finding him or left over from the hurt Bain had inflicted on her. She wiped them away, then grabbed his hand. "Cole, I'm coming with you," she said quickly.

"You're . . ." He inhaled sharply. "Don't be a damn fool, Liz," he said roughly. "You can't come with us."

"I can, and I am," she argued. "I'm leaving Bain."

"Why?"

"Never mind why," she said. "Just don't argue, please, Cole," she went on. "I can't stay anymore. Too much has happened. Please . . . I have to come with you. I'll tell you about it later. Just don't tell me no."

"You're crazy," he said. "What if we get caught?"

"We won't. Now, where's Eli?" and she began looking about.

Cole shrugged and moved off toward Eli, Lizette close at his heels. "It's Lizette, Eli," he informed him. "Says she's going with us."

Eli sighed. "What about your husband?" he asked.

"Please, Eli," she said. "I won't change my mind, and I can help."

"How?"

"You've told Cole how to get in, but he's never done it. I have. I can lead him in while you go after the baby."

Eli glanced at Cole. "She's got a point there, lad," he offered.

Cole hadn't relished trying it on his own, and with Lizette leading the way, the risk would be cut in half. He pondered the idea. "All right," he finally agreed. "But if we're going to get out of here tonight, we'd better get started. Heather passed a light across the upstairs window a few minutes ago. That means she's ready."

They tethered the horses, including those for Tildie and Heather, to nearby bushes, then set off on foot, crouching low when they reached the edge of the meadow. The moon wasn't due to rise until a little after midnight, and that was one of the reasons for getting started early.

Eli took a quick inventory, making sure everything was still quiet, then motioned for them to follow. At the door to the root cellar he wished them luck, then headed off up a small grade that took him to the far side of the barn.

Cole and Lizette watched till he was out of sight; then Cole swung the door to the root cellar open and they entered, Lizette first. "Take my hand," she whispered hurriedly in the dark, and hand in hand they made their way through the maze of jars, crocks, and barrels to the door in back. Once in the main cellar, Lizette cautioned him to be exceptionally careful, since they were directly under the house, and told him to make sure he stayed directly behind her.

Lizette knew her way, going slowly around unseen obstacles in the dark, until they reached the back of the wine cellar, and soon they were making their way up the narrow stairs built into the walls of the old house. When they reached the top, she held her breath for a few seconds, then slid the panel back. They were greeted by more darkness.

"Cole?" asked a soft voice from just inside the room.

Lizette sighed. "Heather?"

"Liz?"

"Cole's right behind me," Lizette said quickly, and stepped carefully into the room, moving aside for Cole to follow.

Cole hesitated, staring into the room, unable to see Heather at first in the darkness; then Heather stepped toward him. She let out a small cry and was in his arms in seconds, pressing close, savoring the moment. Cole held her tightly, hardly able to believe that they were really, finally together. Then after a few precious moments he drew back and reached up, cupping her head between his hands, and as his lips found hers in the dark, a muffled groan broke from deep inside him.

Lizette turned away, giving them a few moments together while she talked to Tildie.

The kiss was long and hard; then Cole drew his mouth from hers, his fingers caressing the side of her face before dropping to her shoulders, and he pulled her closer against him, his arms enfolding her. "You've lost weight," he said roughly, realizing she felt smaller against him.

"Nothing to worry about," she whispered back. "I'll put it on again. The food here isn't very good, that's all."

He looked into her eyes. "God how I missed you."

She sighed softly. "And I you."

"And we're all going to miss Eli," said Lizette as she turned back to them, "unless you two are finally through saying hello."

Cole grinned, then suddenly froze as he glanced across the room and saw the first faint streaks of a light beginning to show from the crack beneath the bedroom door. Someone was in the upstairs hall. He looked quickly at Heather.

"Oleander?" she guessed nervously, seeing it too.

Cole let go of her and moved stealthily across the room, flattening himself up against the wall next to the door. The light seeping in beneath the door was quite faint yet, but they could hear a soft rapping sound.

Heather moved close to Lizette. "She's knocking on my bedroom door," she whispered hoarsely.

Lizette put her hand over Heather's mouth. "Shhh!"

They all held their breaths as they heard Oleander's muffled voice calling Heather's name from the hall, then heard the sound of a door opening. The light faded completely for a few moments, then grew brighter again, and the silence in the room was frightening.

Heather grabbed Lizette's arm, Tildie began to tremble, and Cole took a deep breath as the crack of light suddenly became even brighter and they knew Oleander had to be standing right on the other side of the door. Then the doorknob began to turn.

"Missus Palmer?" said Oleander warily as she pushed the door open, and Lizette could feel Heather's fingers digging into her arm.

Oleander stood on the threshold, then took a step inside, holding out the whale-oil lamp so she could see into the room, and abruptly her eyes widened, shocked, as they fell on the three women standing motionless near the opening in the wall.

"What the . . . ?" Her eyes narrowed, hardening viciously as she stared at them, her turbaned head stiffening arrogantly. "What are you—?" But she didn't get any further; Cole slipped quietly away from the wall behind her, and his hand covered her mouth.

Taken by surprise, Oleander tried to pull the hand away, but Cole grabbed her wrist, twisting the free hand downward, pressing it against her body, and her only defense was to swing the whale-oil lamp, trying to hit him with it. But Liz was too quick. Realizing what Oleander was doing, she shook off Heather's clawing fingers and lunged across the room, knocking the lamp from Oleander's hand before it reached Cole, and as it hit the carpeted floor, Liz quickly snatched the spread from the bed and smothered the flames that were already beginning to lick at the oil that had spilled.

While Liz snuffed out the flames, Cole managed to imprison both of Oleander's arms, holding her captive, and although she tried to put up a fight, she was no match for him. He held her in a viselike grip, one hand still clamped over her mouth. "What the hell do I do with her now?" he asked.

Liz glanced up. "We can't let her go," she said quickly.

"Well, we can't take her with us, either!"

Liz stood up and hurriedly shut the door behind Cole before someone else came upstairs. "Is there anything in the room we can tie her with?"

Heather was still shaking so badly she could hardly keep her voice steady. "There are the curtain ties, Liz," she offered timidly.

Lizette glanced at her, then nodded. "Come on, help me get them off," she said, then turned to Tildie. "Find something we can use as a gag," she ordered.

Tildie shook her head. "I'm afraid to move!"

"Don't be a stupid goose," said Lizette, keeping her voice at a whisper. "If anyone downstairs had heard, they'd be up here by now. We're going to be all right. Now grab a scarf from the dresser, anything we can use to stuff in her mouth that won't choke her to death." Then Lizette joined Heather at the window, where they hurriedly stripped the ties from the curtains.

Tying Oleander wasn't that simple, however. She fought the whole time, losing the turban off her head and biting Cole's hand once. But with all of them to contend with, she didn't have a chance, and when they finally managed to subdue her completely, tying her onto the feather bed so she couldn't kick the floor to get anyone's attention from downstairs, they were all panting and out of breath.

"Let's get out of here," said Cole huskily as he tightened the last knot on the sash that held Oleander to the headboard. "Before something else happens."

Liz nodded and pushed Heather toward Cole, then grabbed Tildie's hand and headed toward the hidden stairs.

Cole took one last look across the dark room toward where Oleander was thrashing about on the feather mattress atop the bed; then he helped Heather onto the landing, sliding the door panel shut behind them, and they started down the steps.

Meanwhile, outside, Eli was having problems of his own. He had managed to make his way around the barn, moving toward the slaves quarters, then crouched in some thorn bushes and found himself staring into the frenetic eyes of three vicious dogs, their chains pulled taut as they barked and snapped. All he needed was for someone to come investigating.

Quickly he reached into his pocket and pulled out a piece of cloth, resting it on his knee as he opened it. Then he stood up, cradling the contents in his hand, and began talking, moving closer toward the snarling animals. "Here, boy, nice boy," he whispered warily, keeping his voice low. "I've got something for you, something real nice."

The dogs were lunging toward him, pulling against the chains until their necks twisted, yet their barking had turned to raspy growls and snarls at the scent of the food in Eli's hand. Good. Eli waved it about a bit, making sure they got a strong whiff, then threw the contents of the rag onto the ground and watched as the dogs whirled from him, instinctively drawn to the fresh meat, and within seconds they had gulped down every piece. He could only hope all three ate enough to be affected, and hurried back to his spot in the thorn bushes, watching and waiting.

It didn't take long, and he watched fascinated as the laudanum he had laced the meat with began to take effect. The dogs had started to kick up a fuss again, barking and snarling; then gradually their heads began to wobble and the barking became half-strangled growls, and within minutes the once-vicious dogs had curled up on the ground asleep.

Eli grinned, straightening into a low crouch, then glanced over to where the slaves' tumbledown shacks were nestled beneath the trees. Tildie had said the shack where the baby was being held was at the very back, farthest toward where the race grounds were, and that the fence that separated the slave quarters from the racetrack ended at the back of the shack.

He made his way into the field beyond the weather-beaten huts and strode stealthily toward a line of sycamore trees he knew were just the other side of the fence. The place he was looking for was easy to spot, and luckily the evening had cooled a little, keeping the slaves inside, except for the few who made their way to and from the outhouses. Eli moved in closer toward the hut, using the fence as cover so he could reach the window of the hut and look inside.

He rose up, peering in. The only light in the room was from the flames of a small fire in the crumbling fireplace, and two candles in candlesticks, one on the rustic table, the other on top of an old chest of drawers on the far wall. A plump woman sat rocking slowly in a squeaky rocking chair in front of the fire, staring into the flames as she hummed absentmindedly to the small bundle cuddling close in her arms. There was no glass on the window, and he could hear everything that was going on in the room.

"Toby? You could stoke the fire up a mite," the woman called back over her shoulder. "It's gettin' cold in here," and Eli saw a man pull himself off a cornhusk mattress in the corner, grumbling as he shuffled past the rocking chair. He grabbed a poker and stirred up the embers, then reached over and picked up a chunk of wood, tossing it onto the low flames.

"That do ya, woman?" he asked.

She grunted. "Have to, I guess," she said, then sighed. "I swear this child should be with its real mama," she said, hefting the baby into a different position over her shoulder. "The mastuh knows this little fella aint's gonna fit in, what with his red hair and them eyes. Besides, you cain't raise no white child as a slave. There ain't nobody gonna believe it. It'd be different if he was part black." The baby rose up off her shoulder, wide-awake, and reached out, touching the woman's mouth, pushing his fingers into it. "Look at him," she went on, circling his little body with her strong firm hands. "There ain't nobody gonna believe he's mine."

The man straightened, staring at the child his wife had standing on her lap. Every night she had to rock him to quiet him. It was as if he knew he didn't really belong. The man shook his head, then stretched. "I'm goin' to the outhouse," he announced matter-of-factly, and she nodded, trying to get the baby to settle down again and close his eyes.

The man headed for the door, and Eli glanced about quickly. He moved to the front of the building and watched the man leave, then took off into the bushes lining the path to the outhouses and waited. Everything had to be done just right, and the best place to catch the man off guard was the most obvious. No one else was about as Eli watched the man called Toby go into the outhouse; then Eli waited just long enough to hear the splashing noise that told him Toby had started to relieve himself, and he sidled up to the door. He had a pistol in his hand, and as he swung the door open, catching the vague outline of the man just finishing, he hit the back of the man's head with the butt of his pistol, then caught him as his knees buckled, pulling him out of the building and into the bushes, where he proceeded to tie him hurriedly with a rope he'd had hanging at his waist, and gagged him with the rag he'd carried the meat in; then he pulled him farther back toward the line of trees.

This done, he glanced up at the sky, wondering how late it was getting. He guessed he'd been almost an hour already. He had to hurry. With purposeful strides he headed back toward the shack, pistol ready just in case.

The woman had managed to quiet the baby at last, and was humming softly as she heard the door open behind her. "It took you long enough, Toby," she said softly as she rocked. "I wants you to get his mattress fluffed up so's I can set him down," she went on. No one answered her. "You hear me, Toby?" she asked. There was still no answer, and no other sound from behind her, since Eli's moccasins made no noise on the dirt floor. She stopped rocking and sat for a second, her face suddenly creasing into a frown. "Toby? You all right?" she asked suddenly, but this time Eli answered her, his pistol pointing at her head.

"Stand up, lady, and put the baby down," he said quickly as he moved his face into her vision, and without thinking, scared to death, instead of doing what she was told, the woman jumped straight into the air, startling him, almost knocking him over, and opened her mouth to scream. Eli didn't want to hurt her, but he couldn't let the cry leave her lips, and before the air left her lungs, his hand shot out, covering her mouth, and he forced her to the ground, his weight on top of her.

She was wriggling and squirming, and her teeth were clashing against the palm of his hand as she held on to the baby as hard as she could and still tried to twist away from him.

Eli took a deep breath. There was only one way he was going to quiet her down. With one big effort he raised his pistol high and brought the butt down on the side of her head just as she managed to free her mouth. A funny gurgle escaped her throat; then she went limp. Eli straightened into a sitting position and stared at the baby, who had begun to cry, frightened by all the commotion, even though the woman's body had cushioned his fall.

He was about ten months old, hair gleaming deep auburn in the firelight, his slightly sloed eyes filled with big tears as he stared at Eli. The frontiersman felt guilty enough at having to hit the woman so hard, without the baby looking at him so pathetically. Eli glanced about. He had to quiet the baby while he tied up the woman, but how? Standing up, he moved to the table and found a crust of bread left over from their evening meal, and snatched it up, giving it to the lad. The baby stared at the bread for a moment, then sat back on his rear end, eyes puffy from sleep and from crying, stuffed the bread in his mouth, and watched curiously as Eli rolled the woman away from him, bound her hands and feet, then tied a gag around her mouth. Then Eli picked the baby up off the floor, took a small blanket from one of the mattresses, and carried the nightgown-clad child out of the house.

Cole, Lizette, Heather, and Tildie had made it to the door of the root cellar without further mishap, and now they waited by the horses for Eli. Cole had his arms around Heather and glanced over in the dark toward Lizette, wondering why she had suddenly decided to leave Bain. He hadn't wanted to agree to her coming along, but at the time it seemed expedient, and besides, he felt it better to humor her, at least until they reached the Chateau; then maybe Grandma and the others could talk some sense into her.

Now they waited, eyes and ears alert, watching the faint lights flickering inside the big old house. It still looked quiet; that meant no one had discovered yet that Oleander was missing.

Lizette glanced toward the barn. Her heart was pounding. Eli should be here any minute. They heard a dog give a half-hearted bark, then quiet down, and Lizette's heart skipped a beat. God, this was awful!

Then they heard it, the slight trampling of feet breaking twigs. What if it wasn't him? What if he'd been caught? But he hadn't, and she sighed as Eli emerged from behind some bushes. They heard a baby laugh, and Lizette felt the goose-flesh rise on her arms.

"Let me have him," said Heather anxiously, but Cole shook his head.

"Not now, love, there's no time," he cautioned her. "And don't talk. We've got to get out of here as soon as possible."

Cole helped Heather and Tildie onto their horses, then came over to help Lizette, but she was already mounted.

He searched for his horse's reins, then made sure Eli was in the saddle, the baby in his arms, and they all started moving slowly toward the road. Cole rode ahead to check the way, then gave them a nod and they reined their horses onto the dusty road, heading toward the Chateau. After they were past the main house of Palmerston Grove, they spurred their horses into a gallop, and the last thing Lizette heard before the pounding hoofbeats drowned it out was the baby's laughter echoing on the night air. He was actually enjoying himself.

Bain had been restless all the way home. Stuart's words had been ringing through his head over and over again, and yet it still seemed so preposterous. He had to know, had to hear it from her lips, and then maybe it would seem real.

He had left his horse at the hitch rail out back, brushed by the housekeeper without saying a word, and had taken the stairs two at a time. Now he stood outside the bedroom door trying to think of the right words. He had gone over them in his mind a half-dozen times and still wasn't sure they could make up for what he'd done, but he swallowed hard, turning the knob. It was now or never!

He flung open the door, then stared, startled by the sight of the empty room. The closet was open and the dress she'd been wearing was lying on the bed, but Lizette was nowhere in sight.

"Pretty!" he yelled down the hall.

There was a scuffling toward where the servants' stairs were, and Pretty's head peered up. "Yes, sir?" she asked.

He was sharp with her. "Where's Lizette?"

"Miss Lizzie?"

"She's the only Lizette I know!"

"I don't know," she answered.

"What do you mean, you don't know? Come up here, Pretty," he ordered.

She shook her head. "No, sir, Mr. Bain. You're mad, and I ain't gonna take a chance on getting hit," she said. "Besides, I don't belong to Miss Lizzie anymore. She freed me tonight."

"She what?"

"She freed me. I got her horse saddled and helped her, and she signed the papers giving me my freedom."

He stared at her in consternation, the impact of her words sinking in. "You got her horse ready for her?" he asked.

"Yes, sir." He was coming at her slowly, and she stared at him apprehensively. "She said I could leave if I wanted, that she wouldn't need me anymore after tonight, so I've been packing."

He cursed. "Pretty, tell me, did you know that Miss Lizzie lost a baby in the spring?"

"Yes, sir, I knew it," she confessed. "She made me promise not to say nothin' to nobody. I helped her and took care of everything. She was real sick, she was."

He was on the stairs next to Pretty now, and he grabbed her by her shoulders. "Where is she, Pretty?" he asked desperately.

She shrugged. "I don't know. She dressed herself up like a boy in some of your old clothes, said her grandma did the same thing once years ago when she ran away, then she took off on that horse of hers, and I don't think she's ever comin' back!"

Bain's eyes were like steel as he stared at the young black woman; then suddenly it hit him. Where else would she go? Whom else would she turn to? His hands dropped from Pretty's shoulders as he ran down the stairs and out the servants' entrance, paying little attention to propriety, and within minutes he was on his way out of Beaufort on the road to the Chateau.

Lizette stood on the back terrace at the Chateau looking out over the river, listening to Eli describing to all the others how he'd fed the dogs meat with laudanum to put them to sleep so they wouldn't bark, then tied up the slaves who had charge of the baby so they wouldn't be able to spread the alarm.

"I told you Eli could help," said Heath.

They were all assembled: Heath and Darcy, who were so glad to see Heather that they were both in tears; Rebel and Beau, who insisted on being here to see Cole and Heather leave; Aunt Nell, who was still grumbling and complaining between her tears and recriminations; and Grandma Dicia and Grandpa Roth.

Lizette had been sipping a glass of cool cider. The warm night air and long ride had upset her stomach somewhat, and she was trying to calm it.

Grandma Dicia stepped up beside her, putting a hand on her arm. "Are you sure you want to do this, dear?" she asked as she gazed at her granddaughter.

Lizette nodded. "I'm sure, Grandma. I can't stay any longer with a man who doesn't love me."

"How can you say that, child?" she asked, trying to console her. "He wouldn't have married you if he hadn't loved you, and the baby . . . I'm sure if you stay, it'll work out."

She shook her head. "You don't understand, Grandma Dicia," Lizette tried to explain. "There are things you know nothing about. Things between Bain and me, things no one else knows. Don't ask me to explain, please. I can't." She took a long drink of the cider, then turned as she heard Cole say they should be shoving off. The alarm could be sounded at any time, and the Chateau was the first place anyone would look.

"If they dared," said Loedicia angrily. "If Everett tries to do anything about this, I'll tell the whole world how he kept my great-grandson a prisoner, trying to make him a slave, and he'll never be able to hold his head up in Beaufort or Port Royal again."

The baby was sound asleep, his sloe eyes, so like Cole's, closed peacefully, his dark red hair ruffled, his pudgy hand curled into a fist where it lay on Rebel's arm.

Loedicia stared at the baby, and her heart went out to him.

If she had only known sooner. A great-grandchild. God, could she be that old? And yet, she was so proud. She reached out and touched the baby's hand, then looked at Rebel holding her first grandchild and remembered when Rebel had come home those long years ago with Cole asleep on Hizzie's shoulder, just as Cole's baby was sleeping now.

They all stood up and started moving toward the pier. "I want to clear the sound as soon as we can," said Cole anxiously. "Once out to sea, I'll feel safer."

Rebel handed the baby over to Cole, and they all left the terrace, moving down the walk in unison, Cole and Heather eager to be on their way, to be free, and everyone else wishing they could prolong the good-byes for just a little longer.

They were almost to the ship when Beau stopped, cocking his head to the wind. "Listen!" he cried, alarmed.

Everyone stopped; then Lizette heard it too, the drumming of a horse's hooves on the road out front.

"They're turning in at the drive," Beau exclaimed. "Hurry, Cole, it may be Everett or Carl. Get to the ship, quickly!"

It was pandemonium as Cole broke into a run, the baby jouncing in his arms. Eli grabbed Heather's hand, and Lizette tried to run along behind, helping Tildie, whom Roth and Loedicia insisted Heather take along.

Cole, Eli, and Heather were up the gangplank, already on deck, and Lizette was halfway up, pushing Tildie ahead of her, when Bain saw the sails beginning to unfurl on the ship and gave a yell, stopping all of them in their tracks.

"Lizette!" he shouted at the top of his lungs, his voice carrying on the night air as he rode his horse across the lawn, leaving the saddle on the run. "Lizette!"

She whirled around, staring dumfounded as he ran right by her parents and grandparents, onto the gangplank, and didn't stop until he was directly in front of her, staring down, his gray eyes worried. He was breathing heavily.

Captain Casey had been all set to cast off; now he held back as everyone stared at the two figures on the gangplank, silhouetted in the moonlight.

"Lizette, for God's sake, what the hell do you think you're doing?" Bain asked breathlessly, trying to retain some of his dignity.

She stared up at him, tears flooding her eyes, her lips trembling. "What does it look like I'm doing?" she said. "I'm going away"

"Why?"

"Oh, Bain, how can you ask that?" she said helplessly. "You know why. You don't love me, you never have!"

"Who said so?"

"You!"

"Did I ever say I didn't love you?"

Her forehead creased into a frown.

"Well, did I?" he asked. "I've been mad at you a few times, and I might have said a few things to hurt you, but I never said I didn't love you." His voice lowered vibrantly. "Liz, I do love you," he said softly, his voice vibrating passionately. "Why else do you think I married you!"

"Your father made you."

"You believed that?" he said. "If you did, then you're the fool instead of me." His voice was warm, vibrant. "I could have paid those notes off with money to spare," he said gently. "They didn't mean a thing. I wanted to marry you. Father didn't know that, but there are a lot of things he doesn't know. I've always loved you, Liz, ever since that day I pulled you off the ladder at the cockfights and saw what a beautiful young woman you'd grown into."

"You called me a child."

"In age you were, in love you weren't. I had to protect myself somehow, so I went away."

"But I'm fat and ugly."

"No, you're not, you're pregnant, and even if you weren't having my baby, I'd love you if you were as round as a barrel. I didn't fall in love with a body, I fell in love with you!"

"Oh, Bain, you really mean it?" she gasped. "And you know about the baby?"

"I know everything, love," he said softly. "So why don't you come home with me and we'll start all over again and do things right this time. Are you willing to forgive me?"

"Yes, for God's sake, Liz," Cole urged from behind her. "Will you two get off the gangplank and let us get out of here? I don't like the thought of a rope around my neck."

Bain glanced behind Lizette to where Cole was standing, nervously waiting for Lizette to come to some kind of a decision. "Oh, I almost forgot," Bain said anxiously as he reached into his inside pocket. "Here, Cole, here's a wedding present for you," and he handed him the paper Stuart had given him, then grabbed Lizette's hand, leading her off the gangplank.

Captain Casey started to cast off, the gangplank went up, and suddenly Cole shouted from the rail, waving the paper in the air, unable to read it in the dark. "Hey, what the hell is this anyway, Bain?"

Bain smiled. "It's your pardon, Cole," he yelled back. "The governor's dismissed the charges against you. You're not going to hang after all."

Cole stared at the paper, then glanced beside him to where Heather stood holding the baby. "Did you hear that, Heather?" he said quickly. "We can go back. Bain says they've dropped the charges. This paper says I'm free again," and he tightened his fist on it as he put an arm around her.

She stared at him, her violet eyes moist with tears, then put her hand on the baby's head, holding it close against her shoulder. "I don't want to go back, Cole," she said softly. "I hope you don't mind, but I don't ever want to go back again. I want to go away with you where no one will know we're related, and marry you, and to hell with the rest of the world!"

He bent down and kissed her on the lips, trembling with happiness. "Amen!" he said firmly, then turned toward Captain Casey, nodding for him to finish casting off, and as the sails continued to unfurl and the *Interlude* slipped her moorings, heading downriver, Lizette stood on the pier with Bain's arms close around her.

Loedicia watched them as they cuddled lovingly, glad in her heart that everything had turned out all right. How tragic it would have been if Bain had arrived too late, and now even Cole and Heather had a new lease on life. Everything was going to be all right after all. She sighed and glanced out again toward the water, watching the silvery sails of the ship disappear in the warm, moonlit September night, then turned toward the rest of her family and they all started moving slowly away from the edge of the pier, leaving Lizette and Bain to themselves.

Lizette and Bain stood for a long time after the ship was out of sight. His arms were still around her and he held her close against him, then leaned down, whispering in her ear. "Don't ever scare me like that again, love," he said, his voice low and hushed. "And don't ever leave me, Lizette, please. I couldn't stand that."

She turned in his arms and looked up at him. The cap was off her hair, dark curls escaping from the unruly braid she had twisted it into earlier, and her eyes were filled with love. "I'll never leave you," she murmured breathlessly. "For as long as you want me, Bain, I'm yours," and with a sigh he pulled her closer in his arms, his mouth covering hers in a long, hard kiss.

Lizette kissed Bain back like she had never kissed him before. She was loved, and she was going home, and it felt so good to be alive that her heart was full to overflowing.

About the Author

The granddaughter of an old-time vaudevillian, Mrs. Shiplett was born and raised in Ohio. She is married and lives in the city of Mentor-on-the-Lake. She has four daughters and several grandchildren and enjoys living an active outdoor life.